THE BEST
PRIVATE EYE
STORIES
OF THE YEAR
2025

THE BEST
PRIVATE EYE
STORIES
OF THE YEAR
2025

EDITED WITH AN INTRODUCTION BY

MATT COYLE

SERIES EDITOR MICHAEL BRACKEN

Contents

Foreword

My second published short story ("City Desk," *Gentleman's Companion,* January 1983) featured a newspaper reporter, which meets the Private Eye Writers of America's definition of a private eye, but my first story featuring a traditional hardboiled gumshoe didn't appear until a few years later ("Partners," *Hardboiled,* Winter/Spring 1988), and I've since written several stories about that story's protagonist, St. Louis's Nathaniel Rose. I've also written several more about Waco's Morris Ronald Boyette, as well as scads of one-off private-eye stories. One even earned a Shamus Award nomination ("Disposable Women," *Tough,* July 19, 2021). Additionally, one of my few novels (*All White Girls,* Wildside Press, 2001) featured Chicago's Big Dick Rickenbacher, I've edited several anthologies of private eye stories, and I've been an active member of the Private Eye Writers of America since 1990, which includes one term as vice president.

So, yeah, private eye stories have played an important role in my writing and editing career. That's why I'm pleased to serve as series editor for the inaugural edition of *The Best Private Eye Stories of the Year,* a celebration of the many wonderful PI stories first published last year. Reading the stories—and I know I missed a few—provided me with a sense that the genre is in good hands, and winnowing the long list of great stories to only thirty, which I then shared with guest editor Matt Coyle to select the final twenty, was a difficult task—difficult because there were so many good stories to choose from, and the differences between stories that made the cut and stories that didn't were often barely perceptible.

I owe a special thanks to Matt, bestselling author of the Rick Cahill series and recipient of Anthony, Shamus, and Lefty awards, for serving as guest editor. I first encountered Matt in 2016 when my wife, Temple, won a copy of his novel *Night Tremors* following a panel at Bouchercon New Orleans, but I didn't get to know him until I joined the late-night poker games at subsequent Bouchercons.

Thanks also to Kevin Burton Smith, creator and driving force behind *The Thrilling Detective* website, for providing "The Private Eye Year in Review," and to mystery writer and voracious reader Robert Lopresti for directing my attention to PI stories I might otherwise have missed.

Now it's your turn to walk the mean streets. So, turn the page and begin.

—Michael Bracken

Introduction

Private Detectives. Private Investigators. PIs. Someone you need when the police won't help you and you have nowhere else to go. They've been stalking the pages of crime fiction for over a hundred and forty years.

Some toil in the dark alleys between civilized society and lawlessness, where the law of the street is the same as that of the jungle. Others tightrope between corporate boardrooms and big city penthouses where the jungle is dressed up in pearl necklaces and tailored Italian suits, but where a misstep is just as deadly. All work to find the truth, no matter who gets hurt, to right wrongs and, sometimes, bring justice to an unjust world.

The crime solving is diverse as their backgrounds. Some use superior intellect, others rely on specialized skills, and many use bulldog determination to unravel the truth. But the truth will always be found, and the guilty will always be unmasked.

Some PIs help the police, others interfere with police investigations.

The motivations vary even if the ultimate goals are the same.

Some are upright citizens, some live outside the law. Some solve crimes for fun of the chase. Some do to try to redeem themselves from earlier catastrophic mistakes.

The paychecks, wire transfers, or overstuffed white envelopes are important. Everyone has to eat. But the best PIs work cases because someone has committed a horrible crime and gotten away with it, and the PI, walking in that dark alley between civilization and barbarism, cannot let that stand.

The guilty must be brought to justice. Even if that justice is outside the law.

The private eye stories you'll read in the following pages are some of the finest written in 2024 or any year. They honor the tradition of private detective storytelling and expound on it in each's own unique way.

Fictional PIs are in good hands. Enjoy the new horizons.

—Matt Coyle

The Private Eye Year in Review

Dear Denizens of the Shamus Game,

The state of the union is strong.

No matter how you date it—whether you start counting from Edgar Allan Poe or Sherlock Holmes, or even Daly and Hammett in *The Black Mask*, the private eye genre is well over a hundred years old. It's been bent, folded, and mutilated, and has certainly come a long, long way from three-pipe problems, snooty gray cells, and hard-boiled dicks, but the essence, the very soul of the genre, continues: that one person, that eternal outsider not beholding to government or to the strictest rules of what passes for "society"; that stranger who will seek out and find the truth; their only loyalty to their client (mostly) and to their own personal code of honor (always).

So, it's particularly gratifying to see the continuing explosion of short stories featuring private eyes over the last few years. They're everywhere—in the usual places of course, both print and electronic: *Ellery Queen, Alfred Hitchcock, Mystery, Pulphouse, Black Cat,* and their brethren, but also in far stranger and unexpected places, such as *Yellow Mama* and *Jerry Jazz Musician,* and in countless assorted anthologies, both expected and unexpected, themed and unthemed (*Private Dicks and Disco Balls,* anyone?).

Short stories, of course, are the original form of the genre, the stomping ground where the private detective was born. The short stories and novellas predated *The Hound of the Baskervilles, The Maltese Falcon, The Big Sleep,* and all those classic PI novels, and even today continue to play a vital and exciting role in its development.

Much of the evidence of that lies in your hands; a sure indicator of the form's continued muscularity, but of course short fiction isn't the only game in town.

Last year saw a glut of novels in the genre, from both new kids on the block and long-time favorites.

Standouts include Kate Atkinson's *Death at the Sign of the Rook*, which brought back fan fave Jackson Brodie, and Kwei Quartey's powerful *The Whitewashed Tombs*, which saw Emma Djan tackling Ghana's virulent homophobia when she investigates the murder of a young activist. Ken Bruen's *Galway Confidential* saw Jack Taylor awaking from a coma (the aftermath of a beating, of course) to discover he's completely missed a global pandemic, but not the violence that continues to plague his beloved Galway. Meanwhile, *Holy City* by Henry Wise, introduced intriguing loose cannon PI Bennico Watts, who teamed up with an outcast sheriff's deputy to investigate the death of an old friend.

Also drawing plenty of attention was *Rough Trade* by Katrina Carrasco, which followed the continuing adventures of former Pinkerton Op turned opium smuggler Alma Rosales, played out against the rough-and-tumble background of the late-1880s Pacific Northwest. Other outstanding historicals included Gary Phillips's *Ash Dark As Night,* which brought back 1960s crime photographer and sometime-eye for another go, once again drawing the ire of the LAPD, this time against the backdrop of the Watts riots, while Jacqueline Winspear wrapped up her much-cherished Maisie Dobbs series with the haunting *The Comfort of Ghosts*, as World War II finally draws to a close.

Of course, plenty of vets checked in with strong additions to beloved series, like Walter Mosley's Easy Rawlins in *Amethystine,* Joe R. Lansdale's Hap and Leonard in *Sugar on the Bones,* and Mike Lawson's DC fixer Joe DeMarco punching way above his weight in the conspiracy-ridden *Kingpin.* Marcia Muller served up *Circle in the Water,* with Sharon McCone investigating a string of increasingly dangerous "pranks" in a posh San Francisco community; and Sara Paretsky delivered a new V.I. Warshawski, *Pay Dirt,* with the force-of-nature Chicago dick digging up all sorts of unwanted dirt in small-town Kansas.

Also clocking in were Janet Evanovich with *Now or Never* (Stephanie

Plum), John Connolly with *The Instruments of Darkness* (Charlie Parker), and David Housewright with *Man in the Water* (Mac McKenzie), while James Lee Burke graced us with *Clete*, which finally gave New Iberia deputy Dave Robicheaux's troubled PI best friend some much-deserved and long-anticipated time in the spotlight.

Other strong contenders were Will Thomas's *Death and Glory*, with London's Barker & Llewelyn, Cara Black's *Murder at La Villette*, with Paris's Aimée Leduc, and Alexander McCall Smith's *The Great Hippopotamus Hotel* with Botswana's Precious Ramotswe and her No. 1 Ladies' Detective Agency, while closer to home, Alex Kenna's moving *Burn This Night* found ex-cop and former addict Kate Myles still trying to rebuild her life. Also into serious life-rebuilding was forty-something ex-vice cop turned PI Whitlock from Charleston, South Carolina, who makes his debut in Richard Helms's *Holy City*.

Other promising debuts include Delia Pitts's *Trouble in Queenstown* (starring pissed-off Jersey cop turned PI Vandy Myrick), and *The Thursday Murder Club*'s Richard Osman gave us *We Solve Murders*, introducing the intriguing odd couple of British Security specialist Amy Wheeler and her ex-cop father-in-law Steve Wheeler. Another promising debut was Rob Osler's *The Case of the Missing Maid*, which saw turn-of-the-century Harriet Morrow seeking to carve a place for herself in an all-male detective agency. That she's a bicycle-riding lesbian helps kick up a little historical dust (and spice) to the proceedings.

The James Patterson Industrial Complex also offered up some PI goods. Teaming up with the bestselling author in the world was Brian Sitts for *Holmes, Marple & Poe*, featuring a modern-day Big Apple detective agency whose chief operatives boast some major (and convenient) name recognition. Also on the PI front, Patterson (with Adam Hamdy this time) delivered *Missing Persons*, the twentieth (and counting) entry in the long-running *Private* series, which features operatives from the global Private Agency from all around the world. This time, though, it's agency founder Jack Morgan who's on the case.

And finally, although it isn't a private eye novel *per se*, true fans will dig

Corey Lynn Fayman's *The Esmerelda Goodbye*, which features aging writer Raymond Chandler on the outskirts of a major investigation into police corruption and murder in La Jolla. Alcohol may be involved.

COMICS/GRAPHIC NOVELS

Despite the competition from the spandex-clad bozos who continue to dominate the form, along the edges the private eye continues to appear regularly in comic books and graphic novels, in many a splendored (and occasionally bat-shit crazy) form. Among the highlights were:

Jeff Lemire's oddly captivating, long-running Eisner-winning superhero fairy tale noir *Black Hammer* returned in *Spiral City*, an eight-part mini-series, this time featuring perennially upbeat private eye Inspector Insector, a giant bug in a trench coat and fedora, wondering where it all went wrong.

Only slightly less weird was *Calvera*, a four-parter following a 1930s Hispanic private eye working a kidnapping case. Only problem? This dick been dead for five years.

Too much? Try *Profane* by writer Peter Milligan and art by Raül Fernandez, but make sure your head's screwed on tight. Will Profane is your classic, meat-and-potatoes no-nonsense LA private eye, until he begins to suspect he's only a fictional character in some other guy's detective books. Very po-mo, but fun.

Slightly more down to earth, writer and artist Cynthia von Buhler's raunchy *The Girl Called Cthulhu*, brings back gumshoe Minky Woodcock in a new four-issue mini-series. With World War II raging, she encounters sea monsters, satanists, the US Navy, and assorted sexual partners, as well as legendary horror writer H.P. Lovecraft, occultist, writer, and certified weirdo Aleister Crowley, and a surprise visit from Ian Fleming. Minky, uh, gets around.

And last but not least, sneaking in at the very beginning of 2024 was *Where The Body Was*, a totally captivating standalone graphic novel from *Criminal*'s Ed Brubaker and artist Sean Phillips. It's a murder in a "quiet" suburban American neighborhood in the eighties, told through the overlapping (and

xii

sometimes contradictory) perspectives of all involved. Among the cast of characters? Jack Foster, a private eye who follows the trail of a runaway into the 'hood, not realizing what he's about to step into.

FILM & TELEVISION

Last year was a peculiar year for PI drama on any screen, big or small. Certainly there were no instant classics, and it remains to be seen how some of these controversial offerings will age. Still…

The gorilla in 2024's room has to be *Monsieur Spade*, AMC's divisive six-parter that gave us Clive Owen as Dashiell Hammett's iconic San Francisco hard-boiled dick Sam Spade, now older (if not wiser), retired and living in France's wine country. "Nobody cares about that Sam Spade anymore," says Owens in the trailer—and many felt that included everyone involved in the production of this "travesty," while others were drawn into the imaginative take on the afterlife of the *The Maltese Falcon* detective, which earned writers Scott Frank and Tom Fontana an Edgar earlier this year. Either way, though, there was plenty of meat here for PI fans to chew on.

Equally divisive was the stylish *Sugar* from Apple TV+, starring Colin Farrell as a film-obsessed but impeccably dressed LA private eye with a cool car and a shitload of personal problems and dark secrets (naturally), hired to find a powerful Hollywood producer's beloved granddaughter. The show offered jagged flashbacks of classic noir flicks as commentary, as Sugar followed the trail into the cesspool of celebrity, drawing sometimes ominous parallels, building up, episode by episode, into what was feeling like a new classic of the genre. Sounds good, right? But not everyone was as appreciative of the rug that was pulled out from under their feet at the butt end of episode six.

Far less controversial was the unexpectedly touching and sharply written Netflix mini-series *Man on the Inside*, a surprisingly enjoyable soft-boiled treat, featuring *Cheers*'s Ted Danson as a quiet, retired engineering professor who goes undercover at an old folks home to capture a jewel thief. You'll laugh, you'll cry.

Star power helped sell Apple TV+'s feature-length *Wolfs*, following two rival New York City fixers who discover, much to their dismay, that they were both hired to do the same job, and are forced to team up in this goofy but enjoyable action thriller. It certainly helps that the two fixers are played by George Clooney and Brad Pitt. Things blowed up here. Blowed up real good.

Star power also helped put *Fall Guy* over the top on the big screen, with Ryan Gosling as a much-battered stunt man roped into investigating the disappearance of the lead actor in a multi-million dollar production. (Very) loosely based on the 1980's TV cheesefest starring Lee Majors, this big budget rom-com/action flick also starred Emily Blunt (possessor of more than a little star power herself) and about a million explosions, this may have been the smartest (and most fun) dumb movie about movies I've seen in years. Things blowed up here, too. Blowed up even real gooder.

Last year also saw the second season of Amazon Prime's *Troppo*, the gritty, sweaty, swampy and totally awesome Aussie crime drama, heavy on the noir, featuring the uneasy partnership of Queensland private eyes ex-con Amanda Pharrell and ex-cop Ted Conkaffey and about a million ways to die (mostly nasty, some involving crocodiles) is back. Based on the acclaimed Crimson Lake series by Candice Fox.

The eight-part *Dead Boy Detectives*, based on Neil Gaiman and Matt Wagner's DC Comics characters, long-time cult favorites, finally made it to the tube in 2024. Initially an HBO production, where it had languished for years, it saw the light after it was scooped up by Netflix, which promised "a fresh take on a ghost story that explores loss, grief, and death through the lens of Edwin Payne and Charles Rowland…and their very alive friend, Crystal Palace. It's a lot like a vintage detective series—only darker and on acid." Which sounds about right.

And on the straight-to-video front, writer/director Max Allan Collins's *Blue Christmas*, based on his own short story, also offered some supernatural doings, as he has a little seasonal fun with this low-key mash-up of Hammett's *The Maltese Falcon* and Dickens's *A Christmas Carol*. It's Christmas Eve and Chicago private dick (and he really is a dick) Richard

Stone is about to have a few unwanted visitors.

* * *

In many ways it's been the best of times for the genre. As private eyes trudge into their second century of existence, always evolving and yet never abandoning their essence, it should be noted that in 2024 the genre also saw a major loss. There's a Randisi-shaped hole we can't overlook.

October 6 saw the passing of Robert J. Randisi, a giant of the genre who did more to promote the Shamus Game than any other single figure I can think of in the last forty or fifty years.

Sure, Bob wrote private eye stuff. Good stuff. By the tons. His fictional eyes included Miles Jacoby, Henry Po, Nick Delvecchio, Tru Lewis, and a host of others, appearing in novels and short fiction. All worth tracking down, all worth reading. A self-proclaimed "pulp writer," Bob claimed to have written more than 700 novels, but amazingly, the bulk of his vast output isn't even private eye fiction—almost all his books, under a slew of pseudonyms, were westerns.

But Bob simply loved the private eye genre.

As good as his private eye fiction was, he also penned numerous non-fiction articles for assorted mystery magazines, invariably and tirelessly championing the cause—including in *Mystery Scene*, which (oh, yeah) he co-founded with Ed Gorman.

It was that enthusiasm for the Shamus Game that finally prompted him to found The Private Eye Writers of America in 1981, and to serve as its first president (he subsequently became its executive director). He was also instrumental in establishing their annual Shamus Awards in 1982, which continue to celebrate the very best in the genre to this day.

That alone would have been enough, but you hold in your hands a prime example of Bob's ongoing legacy: a collection of private eye stories.

Under the auspices of the PWA, Bob collected and edited 1984's *The Eyes Have It*, history's first-ever anthology of all-original short stories featuring private eyes. It featured original stories by Lawrence Block,

Michael Collins, John Lutz, Bill Pronzini, Marcia Muller, Sara Paretsky, Rob Kantner, Stephen Greenleaf, and Loren D. Estleman, among others. When others refer to the eighties as the Second Golden Age of Private Eye Fiction, this may be where it started.

That one volume marked the first of an amazing string that would go on to include *Mean Streets* (1986), *An Eye For Justice* (1988), *Justice For Hire* (1990), *Deadly Allies* (1992; co-edited with Marilyn Wallace), and *Deadly Allies II* (1994; co-edited with Susan Dunlap)—all original stories, all essential reading for any devotee of the genre.

Bob went on the edit further PI collections and anthologies, rounding up not just more original stories that pointed to the genre's future, but also reprints that leaned on and celebrated its past, daring the genre to keep on; to challenge and defy, to go down those mean streets and other places, to not surrender.

And now, with this book, Michael Bracken has taken up that challenge.

We didn't always see eye to eye, but somewhere, I think Bob is smiling.

—Kevin Burton Smith

Deadhead

Tom Andes

My first client was an Uptown lawyer named Donaldson whose daughter had run off with a Deadhead. As anyone will tell you, back then New Orleans was a different city. Less attractive to the credentialled and more welcoming to those of us who couldn't make it anywhere else. I'd come from New England, a town called Waterford, and I was never going back.

"A Deadhead?" I repeated.

"He's one of those people who follow that band on tour." Donaldson shifted in his chair, crossing the opposite leg. New Orleans being a port city, his firm specialized in maritime law. He looked like he'd come from work. He was in a blue, custom-tailored suit I'd bet dollars to donuts came from Perlis, a shop at the swanky end of Magazine where his kind outfitted themselves for their weddings, parties, and funerals. He was forty-five, six-four, maybe two-twenty, with thinning brown hair and that pudge middle-aged guys carry in their jowls.

I told him I was familiar with the term.

"I don't mind their music," he said. "I just don't see why people need to make a lifestyle out of it. And let me tell you, it's a bunch of thugs, losers, and nobodies out there on Tour."

I told him I was not impartial to their music, either. Just the other day, I'd been listening to a cassette bootleg of Jerry Garcia and John Kahn at

Oregon State Prison, March 5, 1982. It had what was to my mind the definitive version of "Dire Wolf."

"Doesn't anyone listen to Barry Manilow anymore?" he said. "Neil Diamond?"

"Any idea," I said, "why your daughter would run off with this guy?"

To get my PI's license, I'd put in three years working for a firm across the river in Gretna. If that experience told me anything, his kid hadn't run away for kicks.

Donaldson looked baffled. Like there wasn't any reason his seventeen-year-old would've pulled up stakes and bailed except for the inherent wickedness of man- or womankind or the world. I gave him credit: it was a good performance. "We run a tight ship. My wife keeps a clean house, dinner on the table every night at six o'clock. Mass Sunday at St. Patrick's. My daughter has never wanted for anything."

"Where did she meet this guy? What's his name?"

"Erick," he said, the color rising in his face. "I don't know his last name. He's a dishwasher and a pantry chef. As for where she met him, I don't know that, either. Maybe he was trolling for jailbait, picking up schoolgirls at the streetcar stop. The nuns at Sacred Heart are usually better than this at keeping undesirable elements away."

"Nothing gets by those nuns," I said.

"Not usually." He huffed.

"What's the name of the restaurant?" I said, and he told me. I wrote that down, too.

Donaldson fidgeted, a pudgy man, picking his manicured nails.

"I don't like you, Donaldson," I said, and the guy started to sputter. Likely no one had told him that, not to his face. Not for a long time.

"I don't—"

I cut him off. Maybe my old colleagues were right, and I didn't have any business sense, saying that to the first guy who walked through my door, but I'd gone independent because I didn't want to kiss anyone's rear end. And teenaged girls didn't leave home because they fell in love with line cooks. No, they ran away from something.

I said, "There's something you're not telling me."

"Do you have children," he said, "Mister Genest? Have you raised a teenager?"

I'd played hockey in high school, and I still had that build. I'd had acne, too. That had mellowed with age but left scars. I'd had my nose broken a few times, too.

What did that guy see when he saw me, dressed up in the eighty-dollar suit I'd bought off the rack at Steinmart?

"No children," I said. "Not that I know of."

Sitting sideways in his chair, he waved, as if he were dismissing me. "I rest my case."

I might not have liked him, but I needed the money.

I slapped a contract on my desk. Donaldson gave me a nasty look. He didn't like me, either. But he signed.

"Boy howdy," I said, "we're off to a great start."

* * *

A couple hours after Saint Lucia opened, I walked in. Bistro tables crowded a tiny dining room with white tiled floors, paintings cramming the ochre walls like a Parisian salon. French doors opened onto a patio, a narrow, overgrown space out of *Gray Gardens*. A woman in server's black and whites came around the bar. Her smile didn't make it to her eyes.

"Help you?" she said.

"Erick around?" I said, and those eyes got a little wider as she shot a look at the kitchen door. Behind the porthole, guys in chefs' whites were working the line.

"He's busy," she said. Around us at those tables, the quality of Uptown New Orleans tried not to look up from their goat cheese and Belgian endive salads. But they were hanging on every word, all but drooling, fangs out. "Who are you?"

"I'm a detective." I wasn't yelling, but I made sure those fancy folks could hear what I said. "I'd like to talk to him about a young woman he's involved with. There's a question of the girl's age."

Had the woman sitting at the table by the bar gasped? Chewing, she set her fork down with a *chink* that was loud in the now silent room.

"I'm afraid," the woman behind the bar said, "I'm going to have to ask you to leave."

"Any idea where I could reach Erick?" I said. "A number, an address?"

"We don't give out employees' personal information." She walked out from behind the bar and backed me toward the door.

Outside, a guy with braided hair, a beard, and a ratty Morning 40 Federation T-shirt was sitting behind the kitchen, smoking a hand-rolled cigarette. He was wearing a rubber dishwasher's apron.

"You Erick?" I said.

"Who wants to know?"

"I waited half an hour for my crème brûlée. They told me that was your department."

He blinked, his eyes unfocused, then coughed, cleared his sinuses, and blew snot on the sidewalk. "I shot a bunch of Demerol last night. I told them desserts were going to take a while." He shrugged, dragged on his cigarette, flicked the butt into the street.

Sure enough, I had my man. Now, I wanted to give him a chance to lead me to the kid.

"See you around," I said.

"Better hope not." He went back inside.

* * *

A while later, the same guy came out the kitchen door, looked up and down the sidewalk, fists clenched. I parked across the street in my Jeep, Jerry playing "Deep Elem Blues" on the tape deck.

A Tacoma pickup rolled up. Erick climbed in. Four of them were sitting across the seat, two guys and two girls. They drove to Riverbend, stopped at Cooter Brown's long enough for the driver to grab a couple to-go boxes, then headed out Carrollton Avenue. They crossed Claiborne, made a U-turn, parked next to a duplex, and went in the bottom apartment.

I called Donaldson from a payphone in front of the Burger King down the street. A woman answered, said he was sleeping.

"He told me to call anytime," I said. "Day or night."

"I'll get him," she said. This must be the wife, the one who kept the house shipshape. It was a quarter of eleven, but she was wide awake.

"Yes?" Donaldson's voice was thick with sleep. I told him I'd tracked the kid down.

"What do you want me to do?" I said.

"Do?"

"Yes, do."

"Get her out of there."

"How?" I said. "I can't kidnap her."

"I don't care," he said. "Just don't make a scene like the one you made at the restaurant. We've heard about that."

"Good news travels fast," I said.

He hung up.

* * *

Next afternoon, I pounded on the door of the duplex. Donaldson had given me a yearbook photo of the kid, Liza. She answered. Still in their uniforms, she and a friend were lazing around the living room on an orange thrift store couch watching *The Jerry Springer Show* on a crappy set with rabbit ears.

"Pack your gear," I said, "you and your friend. Let's go."

"What the hell?" The driver, a guy with blond dreadlocks, was slurping noodles from a takeout container.

"I don't know how much weed you've got in this house," I said. I'd dealt with deadbeat kids like these across the river, and they were all the same. "But I'm sure the cops would be interested, just like they'd be interested in checking the IDs of the honors students hanging out in your living room."

The door to the back bedroom opened, and the guy who'd been sitting behind the restaurant came out. He was in the same T-shirt, cargo shorts, thick through the shoulders.

"Erick," I said.

"You got me in hot water at work," he said. "They almost sacked me."

For a junkie, he had a good right hook. It took two of them—his buddy with the dreadlocks and his girlfriend—to pull him off me. When I came to, I was slumped in the corner, and I could smell that sweet, skunky odor of good sinsemilla. A lighter flicked, water bubbling in a bong. Someone coughed. My jaw felt like it had been run over with a pickup truck.

I opened my eyes. They were sitting on that couch and in a busted La-Z-Boy that was missing half its stuffing, listening to that same Jerry Garcia and John Kahn bootleg, the show ending with "Dire Wolf," Jerry singing "Don't murder me."

"Want a hit?" The kid with the deadlocks offered me the bong. The stuff would've helped my head. But I was clinging to what was left of my self-respect after getting coldcocked by a hippie.

"This my bootleg?" I said. With my face swollen, the words came out funny. I swallowed blood.

The driver dipped his chopsticks into that container of noodles. "It's a nice jeep."

"I'm two payments in arrears," I said.

"We'll take it off your hands," the guy said, "you want to get rid of it."

"Dad sent you?" Liza was sprawled across Erick's lap, his hand on her thigh.

"Your folks want you home." Leaning against the wall, I struggled to my feet. I checked myself for dizziness, faintness, wondering would I puke.

"Show him," Erick said.

The kid unbuttoned her shirt. Inside her arm were ridges of scar tissue in half-moon shapes, eight, ten, more than I could count.

"What," I said, "did you do to yourself?"

"From her curling iron," she said.

I didn't want to twig what I was looking at. I'd known Donaldson was hiding something, but not this.

"Your mom?" I said, the kid biting her lip. Scars were on top of scars, burns that must've gone back sixteen, seventeen years.

"She gets so angry. She yells, throws things. I'm bad. I make her do it." The words choked off. Her eyes were shining, and she twisted away from me, wiped her cheek.

"Your dad knows?" I said.

She shrugged.

"You're seventeen," I told the kid, "so your boyfriend won't go to prison, but you're a runaway, and if the cops come here, they'll take you home."

"I'm going to school," she said. "Why can't I stay?"

The place was a dump, her boyfriend a junkie. Given her options, was it worse than home?

Dinner on the table every evening at six o'clock, Donaldson had said.

Mass every Sunday.

Well, hell.

"Your mom needs help," I said.

"And you're going to help her?" Liza said.

"If I report her to CPS, they'll get you out of there."

Liza looked stricken. "Please don't do that. I couldn't stand it." She cocked her head, too worldly for seventeen. "Just don't tell them where I am."

"I need a day." I left, then came back. "And give me my bootleg."

* * *

Opposite my desk, Donaldson was sitting with his knee crossed over his ankle. Embroidered streetcars were on his socks, which were likely from Perlis, too. Next to him, his wife was giving me the stink-eye. A short, plump woman, she clutched an overstuffed purse.

"I've seen the marks," I said, "the burns."

Donaldson opened his mouth, but I held up a finger, silencing him. His wife scratched the stitching, and if it was possible to pour more hatred into that look, she did. The Department of Defense should've recruited those eyes for their missile defense program.

"I know," I said, "it's embarrassing. You don't want your fancy friends to find out your daughter's shacked up with a junkie who's pushing thirty, and you don't want them to find out your wife is a child abuser out of *Mommie Dearest*, either."

Donaldson pounded my desk. "I don't have to stand for this."

"Sit down," I said. He looked like I'd slapped him. "We're not in court."

"I was King of Rex," he said.

"And your wife is certifiable," I said. "You want that to be the talk of the town?"

He was shaking. Hell, so was I.

I'd found the apartment that morning in the classifieds in the *Times-Picayune*. It wasn't much, a studio on Prytania near Zara's grocery, but it was the best chance the kid had.

"You're going to send her a check every month," I told Donaldson, "and you're going to keep paying her tuition. If you miss a payment, if you hold the money over her head, I'll find out. If your wife goes near her, I'll find that out, too."

Could I do that? I didn't know. I only needed him to believe it.

And I was angry enough to sell it.

Donaldson's wife was rocking in her chair.

"She's bad," Elaine Donaldson said. "She's rotten through and through."

She started crying. Donaldson put an arm over her shoulder.

On the landing, he shook my hand. His wife was at the bottom of the stairs, her purse hanging from her elbow. Dust motes swam in the sunlight coming in the window. The carpet was ratty, the stairwell smelling of mildew. Maybe I'd had it better across the river, when I was doing a job, and I didn't have to answer to these people, who were evil.

"Thank you," Donaldson said in a low voice. "I had an operation, years ago, so we wouldn't have another. She doesn't know."

"She needs help," I said.

He nodded, pudgy chin trembling. "I know."

* * *

Later, I picked the kid up at the duplex and dropped her at her new place, a pink stucco building a couple blocks below Napoleon.

"You don't have to date people like Erick to get back at your parents."

"He's not so bad, once you get to know him."

I told her I'd take her word for it.

She went inside, and I put that bootleg in my tape deck.

When Donaldson's check came a few days later, I caught up on my jeep payments. The check wasn't much. But back then, it was enough to scrape by a couple weeks.

Mexican Radio

Pete Barnstrom

The big man introduced himself as Herb Campuss. Then he added, "But that's not the name I use on the air."

"The air?"

He smiled. "I'm Wild Man Whittaker."

He said it like Marteens was supposed to know the name, so when he got no reaction, he tried another.

"Moondoggie McGilicuddy?"

Marteens shook his head.

"Jumpin' Jackie Joy, Your Boogie-Woogie Boy? You know, on the radio!"

Marteens pointed at the man's wide window, frost on the outside. "I don't think we get the Minnesota radio signals out in LA," he said.

The man who was only sometimes Herb Campuss showed teeth more fit for TV than radio. "That's where you're wrong, baby," he said, just like a Hollywood executive probably would have to Rock or Doris. "Southern California is one of my biggest markets. The kiddos go koo-koo for my late night platter parties."

Marteens didn't have anything to say to that. He wasn't a kiddo.

He'd gotten the call, a resonant male voice, deep and warm like a wade though butterscotch sundae topping. It asked if he was the private investigator who spoke Spanish. It asked if he was available. It asked could he fly up to Minnesota for a day?

Marteens had never seen the Great Lakes. He agreed.

Nobody told him it was going to be freezing. Maybe he should've known, it being February, but it had been cool and sunny when he left Los Angeles. He decided a trip out to the shore was no longer on the agenda and told the cabbie to drive him to the address he'd been given.

Turned out the man's office had a pretty good view of a lake. Marteens didn't ask which one.

The man matched his voice. Quite tall, not quite as wide, hair swept back at a length that might've fit a kid twenty years younger, but he pulled it off. He ran an advertising agency, and a prosperous one by the look of things.

"If you don't know those names, then you probably won't know XLR." Marteens agreed that he did not. "A radio station across the Texas border, over a hundred thousand watts."

Marteens said that sounded like a lot of watts.

"About double what's allowed stateside. Which means the audience is big down there. Seventy-five share in the last quarter of fiscal '56, and we're expecting it to go up as high as ninety this year."

"That's a lot of numbers too."

"And with the range of that signal, we sell our clientele not to just Mexico, but the whole spread of the Southwest." He grinned back in his office chair. "When the weather's right, you can hear us all the way up in Canada."

So it was money. Marteens had begun to wonder which way this was going to go, money or love. It was always one or the other.

"I have a partner there, more of an employee, really. Figurehead, so that the Mexican government won't get exercised. Those people don't want us gringos owning business in their country, you dig?"

Those people. Marteens allowed no expression onto his face. He'd been without a paying client for a month.

"I hardly ever even go down there, believe it or not." He nodded at the door Marteens had come through, some room on the other side of it. "Got a recording studio just down the hall. State of the art, bubelah!"

Marteens said, "And?"

The big man looked at him. "And?"

"You didn't fly me to the Great White North to sell me on your business prospectus." Marteens lifted his chin. "So give me the And."

"Ah," Herb Campuss nodded. "Get down to the skinny, as the hepcats say."

Marteens doubted anyone said that, but if it would make this man stop talking and start saying something, he would take it.

"You see," the big man started, and then his eyes got soft and watery and damned if he wasn't crying when he stammered out, "there's this young lady…"

* * *

And so Marteens found himself driving Interstate 10 from LA to El Paso, then taking the furtive right turn across the Rio Grande. Top down on his almost-new 1955 Cadillac, empty road so arrow-straight that he could afford to look away from it and up at a sky with stars that were a frozen fireworks display.

Marteens thought that what this night could use was a bit of smooth and cool on the radio. Soft sax, flutes, muted trumpet. Some Brubeck, Chet Baker. Maybe Coltrane, if he had a girl along.

What he got instead was grating piano and banging drums and a tight-pants castrati hollering a-wop-bop-a-lu-bop. But that was the only station he could get out here.

And when the music cut, in came Moondoggie Whatzit. His voice was just enough different from the one that greeted him in Minneapolis that he could tell it was a character, howling and vamping, a show for the "kiddos."

There was a thick envelope on the seat next to him. His client had given it to him to deliver.

He'd been so sure this job was money. Herb Campuss did not figure for a lover. Especially not with some dewy-eyed Señorita half his age, with the unlikely name of Angelita Azucar. But clichés are clichés for a reason.

Look for the antenna, he'd said. You'll see it when you get close.

Turns out, Marteens saw it even when he wasn't close. It was tall as a skyscraper, and lit up like Bing Crosby's fondest dreams of Christmas.

He was well past the border towns and deep into the countryside before he got to the fence that surrounded the place. There was a gate. And a guardhouse occupied by an old guy with a mustache that made up half his body weight. He let Marteens through without question.

His headlights showed a grassy farm trail, two ruts just wide enough for his tires. No trees of note, maybe a couple of scrubby mesquites. He saw some cactus.

He didn't see anything like a radio station.

What he did finally see was a wooden shack. It was under the huge legs of the antenna. It would be more stable than it looked, the shack. It had to. But it wasn't a sound-proof studio, that was clear.

Marteens walked to the door and pushed it open. There was a kid inside, and a yellow three-legged dog. They looked around at him. A few electronic devices, not big, and an arm-thick cable that ran up and through the roof.

"I don't guess you're Señorita Azucar?" Marteens asked in Spanish.

The kid grinned big. "You mean *Señor* Azucar."

Marteens didn't, but he wanted to hear what the kid had to say.

"He doesn't work here." The boy pointed at the window, barely translucent. "He's at his office in the city."

"The city?" Marteens held his hands wide, then pulled them together small. "You mean pueblo?"

"No, no," the kid shook his head. "He's in El Paso!"

The old guy with the mustache waved merrily as he drove out.

* * *

"How can I serve you, sir?"

He'd found Adan Azucar's office the next morning, after a night in the overpriced hotel his client recommended. For what he'd call a pueblo, the town sure cost like a *ciudad grande*.

The man's English was unaccented, his tones quiet and gentle. He was smaller and less garrulous than Herb Campuss, but he might've been as prosperous. The hair on the sides of his head was gray and well-barbered, and the furniture was expensive.

Marteens had been wondering how he was going to handle this on his way over, and he still wasn't sure. He hadn't come to this part of the world looking for Adan, but Angelita. And he had the feeling it would be a mistake to drop that name to this man.

"Herb Campuss sent me," he tried.

"All the way from Minnesota?" His smile wasn't as white as the big man's, but just as genuine, for all that was worth.

"I'm from Los Angeles," Marteens said. "He wanted someone close enough to be hands-on."

Señor Azucar raised his bristly eyebrows. "That sounds ominous."

"Just checking on his investments," Marteens assured.

The older man smiled. "Investments?"

"Sure," Marteens said. "His radio station."

Adan Azucar chuckled without mirth. He waved his hands at the rich-smelling cedar-paneled walls, the broad and glossy desk. "We Mexicans are a poor, uneducated people who require the guidance of the white man, as I'm sure you're aware."

There was nothing in his tone suggesting sarcasm, and Marteens couldn't be sure if the man was making fun of him or trying to fool him. Maybe both. "Sir, I don't—"

"However, your Mr. Campuss," Señor Azucar went on, "may have left you with some misconceptions."

The older man leaned at him. "He owns nothing here," he said. "And less across the border." There was a little iron in his tone now, the genial host veneer just barely cracking. "I merely play a few of his amusing radio shows. For which I remunerate him handsomely."

Señor Azucar smiled thin. "I believe in treating my employees like family."

Employee. Herb Campuss had used that descriptor too. Just possible there was some competition going on between these two, Marteens thought. Which gave him an uncomfortable idea about why he'd been sent here.

"Of course you do, sir," he said. "But you have your own family, of course?"

Azucar moved his lips into something like a smile. "My late wife gave me two strong sons," he said.

"Just sons?" Marteens asked. "No daughters?" He hoped he was coming across as conversational, polite, but if he was going to find Angelita, it would be here. Couldn't be too many Azucars in this town.

But the old man shook his head. "Sadly, no." And that steely set to his lips softened ever so slightly when he said, "However, I am hopeful that my young, new wife will bless me with many daughters, someday soon."

"New wife?" Marteens felt it in his gut, but kept it out of his voice. "*Felicidades*, señor."

"Yes," Adan Azucar continued, and were he the sort, one might have called his tone dreamy. "My lovely Angelita."

* * *

"You didn't think to tell me she's married? To the man who pays the bills for your late night platter parties?"

"No legal bond may stand in the way of true love."

The rich and deep voice on the other end of the line was not as clear as it would have been over the phone in the room, but this was no conversation for a hotel switchboard. He pushed the door to the booth open, hoping to get a breeze in there. "I'm not in the business of breaking up marriages."

"No one's asking you to break it up," Herb Campuss replied. "Just deliver the envelope to her home. True love will do the rest."

Marteens would've pushed his head out of the opening into the air, but the cord on the phone wasn't long enough. He loosened his tie. How could it be this hot in February? Was this natural? "You're too old for true love."

The voice sounded injured. "A man can find love at any age."

"Sure, you can have all the wives and mistresses you want, what do I care?" Sweat tickled the hollow of Marteens's back. "But you're too old to be doing something this stupid."

"Have you forgotten who's paying you?"

"Have you?" A fan, this booth needed a fan. "This man can stew your golden goose, then where will you be?"

"He'll do what he's told."

"Talk to him about that," Marteens suggested. "There's some disagreement about who wears the pants in your corporate boardroom."

The static on the line was all Marteens heard for a moment, and he wondered if he'd lost the connection, and the client with it. Then Herb Campuss said, "Just give her the envelope. We'll see what happens after that."

Marteens let out a quiet sigh. What's the worst that could happen? Except this guy loses his job and can't pay?

"Sure," he said. "We'll see."

He kept the windows down as he steered the Cadillac away from the phone booth. If he drove fast enough, the breeze almost felt cool.

* * *

He found the address Herb Campuss gave him, up on a crag overlooking the city. A ranch-style hacienda, with white-wash and red tile and big, arching, churchy doors. It was wrapped in enough land that an actual ranch could've gone along with it.

Marteens rang the bell. It chimed some classical refrain he vaguely knew; Bach or Beethoven, he was no expert. Sounded like a baron must live there.

No one came, so he walked around the side, a path that led to the back. He thought a moment about Texans and their preoccupation with guns and property, and he did his best to look harmless.

An opening in a vine-choked fence, and he heard a radio as he stepped to it. Something Mexican, an old canción from across the border. Not the family station, he was pleased to note.

The sound brought him back to his childhood. His stepfather. *Guitarra* ringing out in the weekend afternoon. A cold *limonada* puddling the porch floor with condensation. He could smell the dust, feel the breeze. He hadn't thought of that since before the war.

Then he was through the fence and back in El Paso, and he saw the pool.

He spent a moment admiring the dappling green-blue of it. He'd seen them before, of course, but at hotels or in movie magazines, or at the Y, never at a private residence. Probably some of his clients had them, but he wasn't invited over for backyard barbecues.

A plump woman dipped long-handled tools in to clean it. She wore mannish shorts, legs sturdy and brown. Her hair was tied in a bandanna. She worked in rubber gloves.

He cleared his throat and she looked up, startled, but not afraid. Harmless, he was.

"Is Señora Azucar at home?" he asked in Spanish.

She nodded.

"Can you please tell her I'm here?"

She said, "Tell her yourself."

Marteens dealt with his clients' sassy servants often enough. He considered it a good sign. Meant he was going to get paid. People who put up with back-chat from a maid didn't usually balk at paying for his. "Where do I find her?"

The woman pulled the long brush from the water and put it on a short wall, dripping. She stripped the gloves inside-out and slapped them down across the handle. "I'm right here," she said.

"You're Señora Azucar?" He slid his sunglasses down his nose and looked again, as if they'd been what gave him the wrong impression. "Of course you are, *lo siento*."

Her eyes were less forgiving than sardonic, but she nodded him toward the covered porch. As she approached, Marteens saw that he'd been hasty in his initial assessment.

"Plump" wasn't the word. She was a solid woman, thick, almost rubbery with muscle. She gave the impression that she'd pose a challenge to him arm wrestling, and probably beat him across that pool.

She passed, telling him to wait, and she walked into the house.

Much as he hated to leave the shady porch, Marteens walked back out into the yard, along the edge of the pool. There was another shaded area at the far end, a little vine-covered cabaña with iron braces that held flowerpots. It was lovely, but that's not why he went to it.

It perched at the edge of the rock the house was built on, and the view from it showed him the town below. All of it.

Looking down over the Texas desert, Marteens realized he'd underestimated the town last night in the dark. There were buildings that would qualify as tall even in LA. Not many, but some. He saw a small airstrip.

Not many swimming pools though.

He wondered how much of it belonged to Señor Azucar. He could imagine the man looking down from up here, master of it all, like some medieval lord with his fiefdom, serfs working the land in his service. In a town like this, he could have anything, everything.

So why this woman? What was it about Angelita Azucar that inspired powerful men to act like children?

A screen door slapped, and Marteens turned from the view to see her coming out. She was still wearing the shorts and bandanna, and he realized he'd expected her to go in and change, pretty herself up.

But no. There was no coyness to her, none of the polite deference he might've expected from the wife of an important figure like Adan Azucar. Or that might bring Herb Campuss to buy into the lovesick singles he played on the radio. She was entirely her own person, not a half that needed a man to complete her.

Maybe that was the appeal. If so, he hadn't given either of the men enough credit.

She carried two sweating bottles, dripping onto her wide, bare feet. Her eyes were dark under heavy brows, but he could see her looking at him, through him. He resisted the urge to put his sunglasses back on.

The bottles held light-colored Mexican beer. She handed him one, then cracked the cap off the other with a chunky silver ring she wore on her right hand. It was her only jewelry, and he couldn't remember if Señor Azucar had been wearing a wedding ring.

She did not offer to open his bottle.

Marteens lipped his bottlecap over one of the cabaña's iron planters and slapped down. The cap arced off and down the cliff-face below them, bouncing off the rock as it fell and fell, the quiet, ticking music of metal on stone coming back up to them until it was lost in the brush and cactus below. A dollop of white foam hissed onto his shoe through the open top of the bottle.

"Salud," he told her, and poured some of the beer into his parched throat. He hadn't realized how much he needed one.

While she wasn't as young as he'd pictured, she was younger than she looked, he now saw. Her hands were thick and strong, but they hadn't yet turned rough. The flesh of her neck was smooth as she swallowed, and the hair that curled around the back of it was dark.

"You speak Spanish well," she told him.

"So do you," he said. She almost smiled.

The envelope in his pocket pressed against his chest. He said, "Do you like it here?"

She turned her head toward him and looked at him a moment. He didn't meet her eyes. She said nothing.

Marteens touched the mouth of the bottle to his own, and tried to imagine what her life with old man Azucar must be like. He didn't see how it could be any better with Herb Campuss.

She finished her beer and placed the empty bottle on one of the horizontal beams. "What are you selling?"

Marteens shook his head, but what he said was, "Do you know Herb Campuss?"

He half-hoped she'd say no, so he wouldn't have to deliver his parcel, so he could walk away from this. But she said she knew him. There was nothing for him to read in her tone or face, her expression as empty as her beer bottle. He wasn't sure if that was good or bad.

He pulled the thick envelope from his pocket, trying not to feel like a pimp, and held it out for her. "He wants you to have this."

She looked at it in his hand for a moment, then took it.

He placed his bottle, not quite finished, next to hers and stepped out of the shade. He told her, "I'm staying at the hotel—"

"I know where you're staying," she said. Not that many choices, he guessed.

"Call me if you need something. I'll stay until you tell me to go."

"I'll call you," she said. She gave no indication of what she'd be saying. He didn't ask.

* * *

Marteens forked a cross-section of enchilada into his mouth and closed his eyes. It had been too long since he had food like this.

He'd spent the rest of the afternoon at City Hall. He told them he represented the city planners of San Ysidro, a similarly developing border town, and that they wanted to replicate the booming success of El Paso in Baja California. They wouldn't mind him combing over property documents, would they? The flattered clerk most certainly did not mind, and showed him how to find everything.

Marteens had never been to San Ysidro.

What he'd discovered was that Señor Azucar hadn't lied. There was no deed in the files under the name "Herb Campuss," or any variation thereof. It didn't include land across the border, unsurprisingly, but he knew it would be no different.

He did find lots and businesses under the name "Azucar," plenty of them. Most belonged to Adan, although a few small ones were listed in other names. The sons, he guessed.

Nothing in Angelita's name.

But he wasn't thinking about that now.

Food. His first real Mexican meal since he was a boy. Back home, it was all pillowy flour tortillas full of a garden's worth of gooey vegetables, sour cream. Had its place, he supposed, but the authentic food, that was gone, gone since…

Since that day in La Placita, the men in the uniforms, the guns. Jobs were scarce, money was scarce, and they took people away, right out of downtown Los Angeles, and sent them back to Mexico. They called it "repatriation." They took his stepfather away.

Another thing he hadn't thought about in years. Marteens put his fork down.

"Thought I'd find you here. Best food in town!"

A meaty hand on his back, and Marteens looked around. "What are you doing here?"

"She called," Herb Campuss said. His eyes were lit up like a jukebox, he didn't take his hand off of Marteens as he sat. "I owe it all to you!"

How long had he been at City Hall? "Did you charter a plane?"

Herb Campuss still held onto Marteens's sleeve. "Just from Dallas. Direct flight there this afternoon." The big man sighed like a schoolgirl practicing her signature with the prom king's name. "She called!"

"Yeah." Marteens extricated his arm. "Yeah, good."

"Here." Herb Campuss pulled another envelope out of his jacket. He handed it to Marteens. "For you."

Marteens opened it. This one had cash, a nice stack, not a bill under twenty. He put it down. "You already paid me," he said. "A week in advance."

"Consider this a bonus," the big man beamed, nearly bouncing with excitement. "I'm seeing her tonight."

Marteens looked at the envelope on the table, bills peeking out. He felt a little ill. "And what about her husband?"

"She'll make the right choice." Herb Campuss winked at him, then jabbed a thumb into his own chest. "She'll be leaving with me, Daddio."

It was the "daddio" that made the decision for him. Marteens stood from the table and took the envelope.

He didn't finish his meal.

* * *

The phone woke him in the hotel room. She said, "I need you here."

* * *

The pool had a light in it. And a man.

He floated face down and unmoving, a dark business suit rendered darker from water and shadow. Hands extended forward and ahead, like the conductor for an underwater orchestra.

"Is that Adan?" Marteens asked. First names seemed more appropriate in such an intimate moment, respect for the dead notwithstanding.

Angelita stood inside the vine-lattice cabaña, right at the edge of the cliff. It was dark under there, he couldn't see her face.

"What happened, Angelita?" Marteens backed from the pool, then looked around. "Where's Herb Campuss?"

She remained silent.

Marteens moved toward her, silhouetted against the lights across the border. The radio tower was almost as tall as she was.

Then he saw. The railing beside her was gone.

He stepped into the structure, not too near to her. Not too near the newly accessible ledge.

"Angelita." Marteens looked to her. Her face showed no expression in the dark. "What did you do?"

"I didn't," she said. "You did."

Marteens didn't move.

She pulled up the envelope, the letter Herb Campuss paid him to deliver. "It says here he sent you to do whatever it took to get me away from my husband."

"I never said—"

"It says he paid you. To do what I say."

"Angelita."

"But because I wanted to be sure, I saved your beer."

Beer? The bottle he'd held here, earlier in the day. "What are you saying?"

He heard a siren. Not close, not yet. "The police will see the bottle, with blood on it. And your fingerprints. The bottle you used to hit my husband."

Marteens looked at her, then at the open space over the empty fall. "Where's Herb Campuss?"

"He left everything to me."

The siren noise grew closer.

Marteens saw the ends of the wood that had once spanned the opening. They were splintered, broken. Like a heavy man had fallen against it, through it.

He remembered his bottle cap, tumbling, bouncing, cracking against the stone and down into the brush below.

Herb Campuss had been wrong. She didn't have to make a choice. She took both of them.

"Was his letter right?" she asked, her voice calm and even. "Will you do what I say?"

The siren noise stopped, but he saw lights strobing around the edges of the house.

* * *

Marteens told the police what she told him to. That the two men had been quarreling over the radio station, over her, that they fought. Adan Azucar had gone into the pool, Herb Campuss stumbled away and tripped through the railing. He had to say it twice, once at the pool, and again at the police station.

Eventually, they let him go. He wasn't sure they'd ever even held Angelita, but it was clear she'd shown them the letter. They understood there was a romance angle, and that let him off.

One suspicious detective suggested to Marteens that since Angelita was going to inherit small fortunes from both men, she'd be a very wealthy woman. A woman might do a lot to get that kind of money, and anything she paid to Marteens would show up eventually. Did that change his testimony at all?

He knew there'd be nothing coming to him from Angelita, and he still didn't know what happened to the incriminating bottle. Marteens told him he was sticking with this story.

* * *

The next time he saw the town, it was from a plane.

It was a city now, El Paso. A *ciudad,* a real one, with a lot of houses and buildings and a college and highways, and a real airport. He saw swimming pools.

He was flying to Houston, tracking a runaway high schooler who'd holed up with an ex-con. He didn't yet know where the money came in, but he knew it would.

He'd long given up this theory that a case was about love or money. There was always an And.

He tried to pick out the Azucar house, but couldn't find it. Maybe it was torn down, maybe it had been absorbed into the other estates up on top of the crag.

He wondered if Angelita was still there.

As expected, he'd never heard from her again. Probably she went back to Mexico, where her varied inheritances would last longer. Or maybe she'd gone to Minnesota, what did he know? She had an advertising agency up there, he assumed.

Last time he'd heard anything about it, the radio station was sending out religious programming. Guess that's what you get when you no longer have a Moondoggie McGillicuddy to pass off to the kiddos.

The radio tower would've been on the other side of the plane, if it was still there, but he'd have had to unbuckle his seatbelt to check.

Restoration Software

Robert J. Binney

The lock didn't even require picking. Fact is, most locks are installed wrong to begin with. Then you add years of drunks and pros and johns and wife-beaters and beaten wives slamming the door, plus a nonexistent maintenance staff, and even a moron with a pocketknife could jimmy his way in.

And make no mistake, the two rain-soaked thugs breaking in were morons.

Traffic raced past, headlights barely glancing off the intruders. Used to be that Aurora Avenue, the too-narrow three-lane escape route from downtown Seattle, was littered with places like this—"no-tell" motels rented by either the hour or the month. It wasn't always random indiscretions behind these mostly hollow doors; cops, teachers, and newly divorced department store managers were all just as likely to need a temporary bed as some runaway. In the weeks before Alaska king crab season, and crews steaming out the Ballard Locks, you couldn't get a room at any price.

But these days, the Stay-Rite, broadcasting its Free HBO and Microwave Oven in neon, was the last of a dying breed. First Microsoft money and now Amazon money crept through downtown and then Belltown, razing local history for fancy reclaimed-materials towers in retro colors that robbed this once-rugged logging town of its soul.

"You gonna bitch? Or you gonna work?"

Jonah, the older of the two, stepped inside and lit his arm-length Maglite, weighed down by D cells; his partner used the flashlight app on his iPhone. A goddamn app! Good luck swinging that in a fight.

"Just saying, I kinda miss the old days. You could earn decent and get a place near the water."

"Whaddaya mean, 'the old days'? I got flannel shirts older than you."

"So do I. Buy 'em at Pioneer Thrift."

It didn't take much effort for the two of them to toss the place. A one-room "efficiency," the bedroom was the living room was the kitchen. Everything had the slightly mildewy smell of fleece that had been worn and put away damp, over and over again.

A mostly-empty growler—its remnants hazy, hints of mango fighting the hops—attracted fruit flies on the counter. The bed, unmade, showed signs of a single sleeper. No hanky-panky. The older thug opened and closed dresser drawers while his companion rifled through the closet, the rings of the anti-theft hangers like the brake pads on his brother-in-law's El Camino.

"Get the feeling we're being watched?"

"That's just nerves."

This was Jonah's favorite part of the job, rooting through strange women's things. Particularly their privates. When his partner—he thought his name was Grant, or Gus, he never bothered learning with the new kids but there was something tattooed on his neck—wasn't looking, he'd take a sniff. They were under strict "Leave No Trace" orders, so he couldn't take any souvenirs. But one pink pair of hip-huggers caught his eye. They looked like they might fit, and his pulse raced, just thinking about how the silky polyester would feel.

"Whoa… Shit! Gnarly!"

Gus—or Grant—came out of the bathroom, a palmful of hair dripping on the chipped tile. The long strands, a bushy, tangled mess, spilled in all directions. "It's…sticky. Like pine tar or something."

Jonah grunted and wondered why he even picked it up. "Not hers. You saw the pictures. Short, straight hair. Blond. Not…what is that? Looks like the carpet in my basement."

"She coulda cut it and dyed it. And that's why it's here."

Kid had a point.

"Weird it was just on the floor, like not in the drain or anything." He flicked it back where he found it, the gloppy pile smacking against the floor. "Find anything?"

Jonah shook his head and closed the drawers, carefully smoothing the nightgowns into place while his partner slid the closet shut, his phone's flashlight bouncing off the mirrored door.

In the mirror, thin, beady red eyes danced behind him.

"Shit! *Oh shit! Shit! Shitshitshit!*"

He fumbled his phone, dropped it, firing its beam on the ceiling.

"Hell you on about?" Jonah spun his beam right into his partner's eyes.

"I saw something. It…was looking at me."

"The woman's here?"

"It was an 'it.' And it moved."

Jonah painted the room with his Maglite. He didn't see anything. The curtain fluttering in the open door's draft was the only movement. He walked to where Gus had been standing and slid the closet door back and forth. He thought he saw a shadow, but more likely it was the light ricocheting off the folding mirrors, like the cover of that Pink Floyd CD.

"Its eyes were on fire."

"Look, it's the goddamned Exit sign." Sure enough, the light from outside blinked on and off, right at eye level, in the mirror. "Now go put the bathroom back together. Make sure her powders and makeup and shit looks right."

Jonah kneeled to pick up the kid's phone. He heard a slapping sound behind him—reminded him of his swim coach sneaking up on him after practice—and he spun his light. Nothing.

The two thugs took one last look around and made for the door. On the white tiles the Maglite caught a muddy footprint. Not a shoe print, but a bare foot. And not the dainty arch of the woman they were pursuing, this stretched across several tiles. At least one-and-a-half times bigger than Jonah's size fourteen boot.

"Do you…think that's…"

Jonah snapped off his light and lightly slapped the back of his partner's head. "That's just your imagination, kid. There ain't no such thing as—"

***

"You Sasquatch?"

"What it says on the door."

In fact, it didn't. The WeWork rules strictly prohibit tenants from installing any personal signage. Some nonsense about aesthetics. That didn't stop them from charging fifty bucks a month for a shingle behind the receptionist. He just liked saying that; he heard it on a detective show once and thought it sounded cool.

The line had one of two effects on dames. It either slaps what little self-confidence they have left right out of their mugs, and they wobble on their heels into the chair opposite the bigfooted detective's desk, hands nervously clutching their pocketbook on their laps…or this. This one oh-so-subtly raised her freshly tweezed eyebrows, pursed her lips, tucked back her long raven hair and took command of her strut across the office.

She crossed her yoga-toned legs. It took all his effort not to check if she was Sharon Stone-ing him. She used her pinky nail to pick an imaginary speck off the corner of those lips. Trying to unnerve him. Wouldn't work.

Sasquatch, Private Investigator, had been leaning back in his chair. He wanted to look like he was thinking deeply about a case, but he was having more fun seeing just how far he could tilt. If he balanced just right, it made his tummy feel funny and he pretended he was flying.

But now that he had a client, Sasquatch had to look serious. He came forward, too fast, and the wheels skidded out from under him. His arms spun at his sides as he fumbled to steady himself. He grabbed the desk and hoped it looked natural. Furniture was still a strange concept, and he wasn't really that good at chairs. He'd much prefer to pop a squat on a rotten log, but the others in his suite complained about the grubs.

He shuffled some papers on his desk. He didn't know what any of them were—he couldn't read—but he'd seen the move on a different show and thought it looked professional.

"You are…?"

"Marilyn Kegel. I have an appointment."

"We finally meet in person."

She wrinkled her nose.

"Do you have a dog?"

"What? No. Look, I did what you asked on the telephone. I went to your motel room—"

"Did anyone see you?"

"Why are you so nervous, Miss Kegel?"

She smoothed her pencil-thin skirt.

"I…I'm not nervous."

Sasquatch shook his head. "You can cover it up with perfume, but I can smell it."

"Did you find the documents?"

"Why did you lie to me about whose room it was?"

She came around to his side of the desk, picked a burr off his chest. Played with the gold chain around his neck. He might be an eight-foot-tall mythological savage covered in mottled, tangled fur, but he was no dummy.

"Why won't you answer my questions?"

"Not until you answer mine." He swatted her hand away. "Whose room?"

Marilyn bit her lip flirtatiously. "What makes you think it wasn't mine? That I invited you up for a little tête-à-tête?"

"A couple of reasons. Chief being, the clothing in there was all size twelve or fourte. And you are…not." Also, he didn't know what a tête-à-tête even was. "So whose room?"

He could hear her lipstick crinkle.

"It was my sister's room. But you knew that."

"Of course." He had had no idea.

"I guess you have to be smart, to make up for…" She waved her hand, dismissively.

He shrugged. *What?*

"I mean, don't detectives have to be sneaky? To skulk about and lurk?"

"What makes you think I can't be stealthy?"

"You're so…big."

He chuckled. It came out husky, like a cougar's growl.

"I'm pretty good at being elusive."

His guest looked skeptical.

"Go ahead, try to take my picture."

She started to protest but leaned back on the desk. In the time it took her to pick up her phone and open the camera, he was gone. Marilyn gasped and looked around the room.

Sasquatch stepped out from the room's corner, where he'd disappeared in the shadows.

"Now why don't you tell me what this is really about. You told me there'd be folders of documents in that room. I thoroughly searched, and there was no paperwork of any kind."

She took a deep breath and made her eyes grow big, he supposed in an attempt to look frightened. "Her ex-husband had been threatening her, so she stole those documents—"

He held up his hand to stop her. "And you need them, why?"

"She's missing, don't you see? And now this! Please help me!" Again, she threw herself at him, burying her fake tears in his shaggy chest.

He couldn't deny that it felt nice. But he wasn't going to fall for another client, not after last time. He pushed her away and loped back toward his desk.

Dejected, she fumbled through her purse for a cigarette and flicked her lighter. His paw snapped out and stopped her.

She rolled her eyes in frustration and muttered something about the nanny state.

He held tight. "What about secondhand smoke? Cancer? Forest fires?"

"*Forest fires?* I thought that was the other guy's thing. With the hat."

"Forest fires are bad for everyone." He sniffed the air and nodded behind her. "Seems like cities aren't much safer. The two goons that rolled your sister's motel room are paying a visit."

They heard a commotion in the kombucha lounge outside his door, and through the frosted-glass walls he made out the shadows of panicked suitemates running away. So many goddamn glass walls at WeWork. He opened his desk drawer and pulled out his .357 just as Jonah and Gus kicked his door in.

The smart play would be to breach in a two-man hatch-and-flank, one low and the other high; these were not smart men. After fighting with the weight of the door, they bumped against each other and fired blindly into the office.

Sasquatch realized he was never going to get his furniture deposit back.

He grabbed Marilyn's wrist and pulled him behind her.

"Put your arms around my neck," he barked.

She did as told.

Taking one step backward, he kicked at the glass panel. It gave way and shattered into the architect's office next door. A man in floodwater slacks and a bowtie yelped.

"Sorry, Mitch," Sasquatch said. "Kicked the wrong one."

He used his other foot to press on a neighboring pane. It popped out and crashed to the ground, four stories below. "Hold on," he told Marilyn, and he leaned out of the breach and grabbed the gutter pipe, hoping it would hold their weight.

* * *

They huddled between dumpsters in the alley. If this was one of those days when SPD swept Third Avenue clean, every nook and cranny back here would be filled with addicts smoking out of tin foil, or toothless schizophrenics shitting through the flaps of makeshift tents.

Sasquatch tried to have empathy for them; he knew what it was like to be ridden roughshod out of your home and trapped away from your element, even as he was disgusted by the litter and animal-like suffering on the streets. He didn't know what the answer was, but he knew it wasn't this.

Luckily, today wasn't one of those days. The prolonged rain had hosed things down, so only the faint smell of piss lingered among Wild Ginger's trash bags. He pulled Marilyn close, deeper into the shadows, as Gus and Jonah splashed by, oblivious. Seattleites loved bitching about mid-afternoon twilight, but it had its advantages.

He could tell Marilyn was terrified. Whatever she thought she was getting into, she hadn't bargained for gunshots and jumping out of windows. He felt her heart racing while she tried to catch her breath. He stroked her hair to calm her.

Her hands snaked up around his neck. Her breathing slowed, falling into sync with his. She looked up at him. In his eyes. Beauty to beast.

Ever the coquette, she pulled up onto her tiptoes and whispered, "You saved my life."

Sasquatch took her hand. "Your brother-in-law's men?"

"Hm?"

He nodded up the alley. "Your sister's husband. The woman we're saving."

"Right."

"So who is this guy?"

"I thought you knew."

"Of course I know," he lied. "But I want to hear it from you."

She nuzzled his neck. "Cameron Blacksmith."

Sasquatch was both impressed and intimidated.

Cameron Blacksmith was one of the first dot-com millionaires in the '90s, and he'd only grown richer and more powerful. He and one or two others owned most of Seattle's real estate and its sports teams, and all of its industry. A guy with power like that left few places for Marilyn's sister to hide. Or Marilyn, for that matter.

Sasquatch took one look to his right at the disappearing goons, pulled her into the alley and ran to the left. She stopped, digging in like a stubborn puppy. "Don't you find me attractive?"

He did not. Too bony and lanky. He knew enough about women, though, to let her down easy. "Look, Ms. Kegel. It's not you. It's…it's not even mating season."

"There they are!"

Behind Sasquatch and Marilyn, Jonah yelled to his partner. They turned and ran back toward the fleeing detective and his distressed damsel.

Sasquatch grabbed her wrist and ran out onto the side street, stopping in front of his Buick Riviera. He pulled the passenger door open.

"Get in!"

"What the hell is this?" She looked more terrified of his car than of the gunmen. "There's no roof!"

"It's a T-top! I need the headroom!"

"It's pouring rain!"

An errant pistol shot ricocheted at their feet.

"It's about to rain bullets, sweetheart!"

One sniff of the coupe's mildewed interior and she shook free from his grip, running across the street toward two Lime scooters. A passerby yelled at her for jaywalking as more shots rang out. Sasquatch ran after her, and the passerby threatened to call the cops on both of them.

"I can't ride one of these," he said.

She had already swiped her phone over one scooter, causing it to light up and unlock, and she started to do the same on the other. "Don't worry, I'm paying."

"You don't understand. I *can't* !"

"Nonsense! It's so easy!" Marilyn stood and kicked away, racing down the sidewalk toward the waterfront and narrowly missing pedestrians.

Groaning, Sasquatch put one foot on his scooter and its deck collapsed under his weight.

He stepped backward, disappearing into the shadows, while Jonah and Gus ran past.

* * *

Sasquatch still had not heard from Marilyn by the next afternoon. He

33

supposed he should put some effort into finding her, but she wasn't his primary client, after all. Even if she didn't know that.

Besides, he was hungry.

He strolled along Pike Place Market, pushing past The Line. Even in the rain, there was always The Line. Idiots waiting an hour for a cup of coffee. He had given up yelling at people that it wasn't the "original shop"; the corporate website said it was, so that's that. *It's amazing, the crazy nonsense people believe on the internet*, Sasquatch thought.

His stomach growled. Most people went to Ivar's or Elliott's for takeout, but to his way of thinking, there was nothing better than catching a fresh salmon in his teeth.

As if on cue, the Market fishmonger yelled out, "Hey, Chewie!" and tossed a ten-pound Coho over the crowd.

Sasquatch laughed. "No autographs!" he shouted, and took a bite out of the fish, like an apple. If he'd known that would be the last pleasant moment of his day, he would have savored it.

Before he finished his lunch, his keen rainforest hearing detected a familiar sound—Marilyn Kegel, screaming. He ran to the top of the Hill Climb and scanned the area.

There! He saw the backs of the previous night's goons down at the Seattle Aquarium's otter exhibit.

His big feet took the steps three, four at a time, and he ran through the waterfront construction to save her. But he was too late.

* * *

Sasquatch leaned against the side of the Seattle Aquarium, more upset than he should have been, watching the medics fish Marilyn's floating body out of the tank.

Even with all the commotion—emergency workers, press, lookie-loos—no one gave the towering furball a second glance.

No one, that is, except for Inspector Ness, somehow always first on the scene. They made quite a pair to anyone paying attention—five-and-a-half feet in work boots and receding gray curls, he had to crane his neck to speak to Sasquatch. He grilled the private detective about another dead client, and confiscated his weapon.

Sasquatch tried to protest—Marilyn hadn't even been shot—and he'd almost convinced the inspector when he saw, across the pier, his chief suspect: Cameron Blacksmith. He excused himself and lumbered after him.

* * *

If Cameron Blacksmith thought he could shake a giant feral bipedal hominid who was also a licensed private investigator, he had another think coming, Sasquatch thought, laughing to himself.

Blacksmith slinked into the crowd queued up at the Great Wheel, but the Bigfoot caught up to him just as he paid his admission and boarded a private gondola.

Sasquatch strolled past the ticket taker and climbed in with the elusive entrepreneur. "Surprised?"

"Of course not. I knew you'd follow me here."

Blacksmith grabbed a handful of trail mix, popped it in his mouth, and offered the bag to his new companion.

Sasquatch shook his head. He'd eaten enough nuts and berries to last a lifetime. "You're less lumpy than you look in the paper."

Blacksmith threw back his bald head and cackled.

"After my divorce, I got buff. You don't land a smokeshow like Marilyn without burning a few calories. You know, I could hook you up. A little Paleo, some wax… You'd be something!"

Sasquatch looked out the window, fogging it, amazed at how quickly the streetscape recovered from a murder scene to a tourist thoroughfare.

"Not going to offer your condolences, detective? I have very recently become widowed."

"Marilyn was your second wife," Sasquatch muttered.

Blacksmith nodded.

"I knew that." He had not. "So what's your game, Mr. Blacksmith? What is everybody going crazy for?"

The Ferris wheel groaned under the unexpected bulk of its newest passenger as it started its rotation.

"Control, Mr. Sasquatch. Control."

"How do these documents give you control?"

"They're not just documents! I knew I shouldn't have expected a stupid ape to understand true genius!"

Sasquatch bristled, hoping Blacksmith didn't notice that the man was getting under his fur. "It's more like an app?"

That laugh again. An actual supervillain's cackle. "No, not an app! But complete control. Forget the One Seattle Plan—I'm talking about making the parks safe again, air and water clean, every day a sunny day…"

"That actually sounds great. How does your app do that?"

Blacksmith sighed. "Not an app. First, I take the parks—Myrtle Edwards, Discovery, Gas Works, even that shitty small one—and transfer their deeds to me."

"Privatize them."

"You do get it! Build luxury condos and get rid of the riffraff, the drugs, the filth, the protesters…"

"Get rid of them? Where will they go?"

"Tacoma?" he scoffed. "What? You think they'll notice the smell?"

This wasn't sounding as terrible as it should, Sasquatch felt. But, still. "Don't you see how guys like you are the reason…" He realized this was futile and changed tack. "How will you stop the rain? Clear the air?"

"You know the roof on the ballpark?"

"You're going to put a roof over the city?"

Blacksmith tapped his forefinger on Sasquatch's forehead and nodded. He sat back and shoved more trail mix into his smug kisser.

Maybe not a terrible idea, but certainly a crazy one. "What's in it for you?"

Blacksmith was already leaning forward; the carriage was tilted heavily toward Sasquatch's side. He pulled himself closer to his companion and held his gaze. "Think."

Sasquatch did. He thought hard. Finally it dawned on him. "You're going to sell advertising on the inside of the dome?"

The tech billionaire slapped his knee, barely containing his glee.

"You'll also control the air that people breathe. And the water that they can drink. Which means you can add—"

"Nutrients. Vitamins. People will be the healthiest they've ever been!"

"I was going to say 'poison,' but…" Sasquatch watched the city rising on his horizon and tried to picture anything good coming out of this plan. He couldn't. Then he noticed the gun Blacksmith was pointing at him. "I've seen this movie. I think I even streamed it on your service. You're no Orson Welles, sir."

Blacksmith smirked. "Why don't you just give me that chain that's around your neck."

"You know I can't do tha—" Sasquatch sniffed the air. "Have you been shooting pool?"

"What?"

He had suddenly picked up the smell of talcum powder. Even as the detective realized what was about to happen, he was too slow to stop it.

Glass erupted throughout the gondola. Sasquatch instinctively hugged himself, hoping to protect his vitals from the gunshot. He didn't feel a thing. Confused, he looked up and saw the red stain expanding across Blacksmith's chest.

The visionary slumped in his seat, spilling his gorp, and fell forward against the doors, fading fast.

Sasquatch mumbled, "All this death and suffering, over an app."

Blacksmith reached out to grab Sasquatch's hairy arm. It was as close a connection to humanity as either had had in a while. Blood bubbled up over his lips.

"It's…not…an…app" were the last words of the planet's sixth-wealthiest man.

* * *

The poor teenager working the ride had no idea what to do with a dead gunshot victim, and Sasquatch didn't care. He stepped his hairy legs over the body and onto the pier. He knew he had only minutes before Ness showed up, trying to pin the murder on him.

Joke's on the inspector, Sasquatch thought. *He already confiscated my weapon.*

He trudged to the parking deck, where the two thugs were leaning against his Buick. "Careful you don't scratch the finish, boys." As if another mark on its dented, rusty finish would even be noticed.

They didn't budge.

"Look, guys, your boss is dead. No need to keep hounding me."

"We had nothing to do with that," the older one, Jonah, said.

"I know." Sasquatch actually did know that. "If you get to the house before the cops do, you can have your own private estate sale, pick up a few nice things, if you know what I mean?" He nudged Jonah conspiratorially, causing the big thug to turn red.

His partner—the one with the neck tattoo—tried to look tough.

How does anyone forget to not get their neck tattooed, Sasquatch wondered.

"We just was wondering where all the paperwork was stashed in that motel room, and how's you sneaked it past us and all."

Sasquatch pushed them both aside and opened his car door.

"You never heard of DocuSign? C'mon, boys, it's all about the apps."

* * *

After a case, Sasquatch liked to clear his head by hitting the open road and blasting some tunes. Pulling out of the garage, he still didn't have closure on this one. He shook the water out of his Foghat eight-track tape and popped it in the dash and tried to peel out.

Traffic wasn't on his side today. Closed lanes, poorly timed lights, mostly empty buses crowding intersections. "Slow Ride," indeed. He squished in his rain-sopped seat and groaned.

He needed some time to himself, and yesterday's hijinks had earned him a permanent ban at WeWork. He made a U-turn across First —"Fuckin

Uber!" someone yelled at him—and pointed the Riviera toward Eastlake.

* * *

The climbing wall at the outfitter's flagship store essentially became a storage rack for returns during the pandemic and never reopened. That made it perfect for Sasquatch, since it meant no belayed eight-year-olds grinding their Amy's Organic crumbs into the handholds while he tried to think.

No one saw him as he scaled to the top. This was his favorite place in the city to reflect. Stretched out, in the glass-ceilinged atrium with fake plants and water sounds, Sasquatch started to empathize with Blacksmith's plan.

He wasn't sure how long he'd been there—it had been dark outside for a while—before he smelled her baby powder.

It took a few minutes of huffing and puffing, but eventually the first ex-Mrs. Cameron Blacksmith pulled herself to the top of the wall to join Sasquatch.

"Hello, Ms. Astor."

"Constance, please."

He lifted the gold chain from around his neck and handed her the tiny thumb drive that had been dangling from it.

"You were right, Constance, people lost their minds looking for this."

"Thank you for 'stealing' it from my motel room. I didn't know what they'd do to me if they found me. Or this. And the gall of that whore to hire you!"

"She told me you were sisters."

"Do we look anything alike?"

His eyes lingered over her body longer than professionally necessary. No, she was the opposite of Marilyn Kegel in many ways. *Niña pera*, the guys working the logging trucks would have called her. He would have liked spending time plucking that pear.

But one thing still nagged at him.

"Did you have to kill him?"

"He had to be stopped."

Sasquatch said he was confident that the city's crushing bureaucracy—the "Seattle Process"—would have moved with typically sluglike speeds and ground her ex-husband's plans to dust before the first permit was issued.

"But I couldn't take that chance. 'Money talks' and all that."

"So you stopped him." He nodded at the USB stick. "And now you have the app."

"It's more than an app! It's a revolution!"

Uh-oh, Sasquatch thought. Here we go again.

"You don't understand!" She turned and grabbed his paws. "With this I can roll everything back! Join me!"

"Roll what back?" He lay down, counting water spots in the acoustic tile.

"This is *control*! Don't you see that, you big lug? We can shut down the grid. Power. Internet. Sewers. Light rail."

"Losing all that will piss people off. They won't notice the light rail, but everything else."

"That's the point! They'll leave! Didn't you see the bunnies return when we locked everything down? Imagine that at scale. Everyone leaves, the buildings crumble, and nature returns! We will create a New Eden! Right here! Think about it!"

That was the second time today he'd been told to think. A New Eden did sound wonderful. But even as he entertained the idea of returning to the woods, he knew it was already too late. Too late for Seattle, too late for him, and definitely too late for Constance Astor.

Sasquatch leaned over the wall and extended his paw to Inspector Ness, tangled in his climbing harness, ears sticking out of a too-large helmet he grabbed off a mannequin.

Propping himself on one elbow, the inspector winked at Sasquatch. "You never make it easy for me, do you?" He shifted awkwardly and flashed his badge at Constance. "And you're under arrest."

Constance slapped Sasquatch. "I thought we had something!"

"I did too. But you murdered two people. And I got kicked out of my office." He grabbed the sexiest woman he'd ever met and threw her over his shoulder.

Her fists pounding against his back, Sasquatch scaled down the wall, taking her to the police car idling in the parking lot.

Genius in a Bottle

A Tom Boyle Mystery

Alec Cizak

I'd checked in with my personal pharmacist, Huey, to see if he'd front me a few days' worth. He said, "My man Willy Floyd's looking at time. He's collecting every day to make sure he's got money for a lawyer. You know how it is."

I said, "Let me call home, see if some work's come in." I used a cordless phone near a television on the floor of Huey's house, one side of a duplex on College Avenue. One of those Amityville Horror Dutch-Colonial joints with a chimney splitting a pair of mournful eyes. I dialed my office and entered the code to send the answering machine to Play mode. Some chump from a collection agency yip-yapped empty threats about a credit card debt I'd abandoned in 1985. A Puritan from the local Republican party wanted to take my pulse on the president. Did it bother me that he dodged Vietnam but had no qualms carpet bombing the Middle East? Did I have a problem with his pecker landing in every soft spot not named Hillary? About six messages in, a young woman's voice said she needed someone to look into something. Very vague. Could mean money. Could be a grift. I hung up and called her. "Is this Molly…" Took a moment to remember the last name. "Molly *Beckett*?"

"Who's this?"

"Tom Boyle."

"How soon can we talk in person?"

"Where's good for you?"

She told me to meet her at the German bakery on Pendelton Pike. A cramped building surrounded by lawn gnomes. Sold the best cake in the universe. Before the habit took over, I ate wurst and potato salad there once a week.

"Voilà," I said to Huey. "Now that I got work, how about some sympathy?"

"No can do."

"I should just quit."

"Not a bad idea." He lit an unfiltered Camel. "Let's see how sobriety looks on you. Then maybe I'll give it a go."

"How about you rot in hell?"

"The idea is to escape, isn't it?" He pointed his cigarette's cherry at a community of mustard-colored bruises splotched across his arm.

* * *

A mural depicting a Bavarian village in the Black Forest covered the side of the bakery. I chipped paint off it as I glided my '84 Buick into an angled parking spot. The brakes needed work. I'd have to rent a garage to fix them.

A host of vulgar German souvenirs greeted me inside as I wound through a constellation of wrought iron patio tables. Plastic gnomes coupled missionary style. Beer steins shaped like a woman's torso. Naked male and female salt and pepper shakers. Indicators of a culture drowning a guilt complex in kitschy perversion. Beer Garden oompah music pulsated speakers mounted in the ceiling. A tuba and accordion mating in a bounce house. Oddly comforting. I'd have to chat with a shrink to figure out why. A woman in a blue and white-checkered dirndl said hello. She'd contained her wild, scarlet hair in mini-lightning bolt pigtails. She told me she'd be with me as soon as she finished ringing out customers at the register. I said, "I'm good for now." Down a narrow corridor toward the bathrooms, I spotted a woman seated in the café's only private room. "Miss Beckett?"

She pointed to a picnic bench running alongside a wooden table. Glass covered the table's surface. Shielded a collage of photographs taken during the bakery's twenty years of existence. "Call me Molly." Faint eyeliner complimented by shaded lids matched her violet, form-fitting dress. The skirt stopped midthigh. She'd tied her long, auburn hair into a sloppy bun. Ignited a montage of Marian Librarian fantasies dormant since adolescence.

"What can I do for you?" I rested my elbows on the table. Folded my jittery hands together. How long since I'd felt the need to keep cool around a woman? Maybe Felicia, the last full-time affair I engaged in before letting the needle extinguish healthier appetites.

She leaned toward me. Her mango-scented perfume brightened the room's stale air. Clashed with the ambience created by antlers and other hunting trophies mounted on the walls. "My father, Melvin, Mel, most people called him, maybe you heard of him? Mel Beckett?"

Oh, how I wanted to lie and say I knew the man. "I apologize, Molly."

"It's okay." She wrapped her fingers around a glass of water in front of an empty plate. A slice of lemon floated amidst thin ice cubes. Flaking polish on her nails suggested she fussed over her looks every now and then. "My father invented Seraphim. Have we heard of it?"

An anti-depressant. One of several legal drugs designed to alleviate mortality's grim forecast. Daisy Chemical, a pharmaceutical company based in Indianapolis, led the charge in the late 1980s with Seraphim. A doctor from which I expected better advice once suggested I replace heroin with it—*Seraphim will alter your brain's chemistry so you no longer feel the need to escape reality*. What an idiot. Say what you want about dope, at least it didn't rewire the mind. "I've heard of it."

"Daisy owns the patent," she said. "I suspect my dad, who was a very stubborn man, decided to complain. Maybe he threatened legal action. Daisy's making all kinds of money off his work. Can we blame him?"

"So far," I said, "I can't see one good reason to think the man brought anything but good to this world."

Her eyelids dropped. The corners of her lips tightened. "Mr. Boyle…"

"Call me Tom."

"Mr. Boyle," she said, "I can't afford someone…*bigger* than you. Not at the moment."

I straightened my shoulders. "Please, continue."

"Official story, the one they printed in the back of the *Star*, is he was under the influence." She stared at the table. Traced a circle near her glass of water with her pinky. "Dad had a problem, it's true. And he was probably drinking that night. But he'd never get behind the wheel if he, you know, if he was so far gone…"

"Your father was probably a genius," I said. "Smart folks throughout time have needed something to quiet their thoughts."

"That's kind of you." She asked what I charged. Normally, I'd dodge a gig like this. Daisy Chemical *owned* Indianapolis. Sniffing around their porch could invite all species of trouble. But that wouldn't bode well for my wallet or my interest in a carnal conversation with Molly Beckett. I gave her the usual numbers. "Act fast," she said. "Find out what happened to my father. I'll pay you double when it's over." Her thick, glossy lips drifted into a smile.

* * *

By the time I returned to my office that night, the yearn had graduated to anxiety. Sweat. Chattering teeth. The entire body a whack-a-mole game starting fires a thousand mallets couldn't quell. Before the madness of withdrawal started, I'd have to solve Molly Beckett's case. I hopped into my Buick and drove north, for Broad Ripple. The woman told me her father fed his habit at The Outback, a restaurant/bar combo on the corner of Westfield and Winthrop.

The patrons, or the management, or both, must have considered darkness necessary for consumption of the nation's favorite dope. Neon lights behind the counter colored a fog of cigarette smoke so thick I copped a nicotine rush before I could sit down. Early 1980s Southern California punk rock battered a pair of speakers doubling as bookends for bottles on a glass shelf mounted in front of a wall-sized mirror. Odd hangout for a chemist of Mel Beckett's stature. Then again, what genius didn't have quirks? Molly had shown me a picture of her father taken at Christmas, the previous year. A bean-shaped man with an unruly mop of salt-and-pepper hair. Horn-rimmed glasses more appropriate for a 1960s NASA scientist. A frumpy short-sleeved button-down shirt, half of it tucked in baggy, beige dress pants. He seemed a tad too old for The Outback. Again, how could I judge the man? I didn't agree with his solution to the miseries of existence, but if he helped the bungled and botched get through the night, well, good for him.

The bartender shouted over the music. Asked what I needed. Alcohol never did a thing for junk sickness. I ordered a Jack and Coke anyway. Coming off as a customer might facilitate the interrogation. I didn't want to flash my license to snoop. Spook the guy into silence. He retreated to the ledge at the bottom of the mirror behind him. Popped the top off a prescription pill bottle. I pondered what poison fed his blood. Resisted my mind's prompt to ask whether the bottle contained a synthetic opiate. He took his medicine. Then he set to the burden of making my drink.

He placed a sweating, diamond-patterned rocks glass on a napkin and slid it to me. Faded tattoos covered his arms. He'd cut the sleeves off his jeans jacket. Patches advertising various bands—The Cramps, Big Black, The Damned, etc.—had been sewn to the jacket without mind paid to symmetry. The anti-aesthetic of punk, a trend I'd hoped would die when Nirvana commercialized it a few years earlier. He introduced himself as Glenn. He hadn't bothered to dye his Mohawk. His gray hair promised a rational, adult conversation. He said, "Starting a tab?"

I slid a Lincoln across the counter and told him to keep the change. "I wondered if I might ask you a few questions?" He held up the five-dollar bill. Looked at it as though he'd never seen anything so offensive. I fished a twenty from a wad of cash in my pocket. Some of the dough Molly'd given me as a retainer. Every instinct, every vessel of desire in my body insisted I forget the whole thing, ask Glenn what species of drug he'd just taken and, should it be Vicodin or Demoral or something equally benevolent, might he be willing to sell me half a dozen? My hand shook as I flopped the bill onto the counter.

The bartender scooped it up. His expression barely altered. "What's going on?"

"I wonder if you knew Melvin Beckett?"

Glenn leaned forward. "Who?"

I repeated the name.

Fast, confident nods. "Yes, yes," he said. "Mel. Used to come in here every night."

"Are you aware he drove his car into the canal a few weeks ago?"

"Yeah, dude," said Glenn. "Gnarly way to go. Nice car, too. Fifty-nine Chevy, I think. Cherry red. Sweet ride. I just nabbed a seventy-four Dodge Dart, myself. Cost a pretty penny. I can't begin to imagine what Mel's car is worth."

"Dodge Dart," I said. "Impressive. Let me ask you, did Mel drink here that night?"

The bartender grabbed a rag from a bucket near the cash register and wiped the counter on both sides of my Jack and Coke. "Already told the pigs he only had one, you know? Strange for him, I guess. He usually got blotto and walked home when I'd cut him off. He lives just over...*lived* just over on Broadway."

"Anybody else here tonight saw him that night?"

"Nah, dude. It was a Tuesday. Unless it's summer, when the Butler yuppies invade Broad Ripple with mommy and daddy's credit cards, we're slow on Tuesdays."

* * *

I didn't fall asleep until four in the morning. I curled up on the floor beneath my desk. Listened to classical music on the UIndy station. My usual diet of whale songs on the tape deck would only have reminded me of the absent medicine. My bones protested when I unfolded myself with the rising sun, used the edge of the desk to hoist myself to a standing position. Lack of sleep. Lack of dope. I felt a thousand years older. Dry mouth. Foggy brain. The elder gods of withdrawal, closing in.

When dealing with fresh worm cuisine, I usually checked in with my old girlfriend Felicia Hill. She studied the dead in the morgue on Market Street. The basement of the city-county building. A twenty-eight-story warehouse for bureaucrats, lawyers, and cops. Too many knew my name. I used to spill dirt on local dealers. Scored some scratch and confiscated dope in the process. The paperwork and courtroom dramatics required to remain copacetic interfered with my desire to stay wasted and stare into the abyss. Must have showed in my work. They gathered what few knickknacks I had on my desk—a framed picture of Felicia and I at Kings Island, a crayon drawing of my mother I made in kindergarten, and a ticket stub from a Lou Reed concert I saw in Merrillville in 1984—threw them in a box, and escorted me to the rotating front door. Can't say I blamed them for firing me. They wanted Huey and his supplier, Willy Floyd. I pretended I'd never met them. I fed the habit for six months off the unemployment checks. Snagged my license to snoop in my waking hours. Now, I had to sneak down a set of concrete steps in the back to avoid running into anybody with a score to settle.

The temperature dropped lower than the frigid October air outside. Camphor barely masked the unnerving stench of other chemicals used in the preservation of the recently expired. Felicia stood hunched over the corpse of a naked woman. The woman, while still alive, I assumed, had shaved her pubic hair. A bizarre new trend egged on by *Playboy* and porno flicks. Felicia peeled back the dead woman's scalp. Sawed off the top of her skull. Her eyes peered over a pair of work goggles positioned halfway down her nose. "Well, well," she said. "The invisible man."

"We're cool, right?"

"*Shit.*" She stepped away from the slab. Retrieved a clipboard from a hook on the wall. "What do you need?"

"You say that like I'm a leech or something."

"You are."

"You know anything about a guy named Mel Beckett?"

She returned to the slab. Refused to look at me.

"What's the story?"

"I didn't do the work on that one." She dug her gloved hands into the dead woman's skull and extracted the brain. Let the blood drip into a pan next to the dead woman's head. She plopped the organ onto a hanging scale.

"Who did?"

"Private party." She held up the dead woman's brain. Pointed to several gaping cavities in it. "That's from smoking crack," she said. "Daily use. I'd say three, four years in a row. Like Swiss cheese, don't you think?"

"Good thing that's not my kick."

"No." She made notes on the clipboard. "Your brain's just dull and gray."

"Kind of like my life…" I angled toward the slab. "Since we busted up."

"Whose fault was that?" She carried the brain to a metal cart with saws, drills, and a microscope resting on it.

"I'm going to eighty-six, if that makes a difference." I shoved my hands into my pockets. Shuffled my left foot back and forth like a windshield wiper. Felt stupid. A twelve-year-old asking a girl to the autumn dance.

As she set the brain on a tray and picked up a Gigli saw, she said, "To whom? Me?"

"What say you tell me what those private folks discovered when they did the autopsy on Melvin Beckett. This time, next week, we'll have dinner. I bet you we pick up right where we left off."

"What makes you think I haven't moved on?"

"I fully expect to have to win you all over again. Whether there's immediate competition or not."

She let out a *pfft* noise. "I'd have to break some rules." Her focus left the dead woman's brain. "I do an awful lot for you, Tom Boyle. When the hell are you going to do something for me?"

"I just told you…"

"I've heard this story before. You give sobriety a try, panic the first night, and wham bam, you're right back on the needle."

I couldn't tell her *she* had competition. "You could try to be encouraging."

"Once, maybe once," she said, "you could share some of the loot you make off these suckers. I'm the one who tells you how these chumps cashed in."

I studied the tiles on the floor. Caked blood stained the thin paths between them. "Okay," I said. "Thirty percent."

"Fifty."

"Thirty."

"Forty-five."

"Thirty."

"Forty, and that's as low as I go. For now."

"Thirty."

"Son of a…" A gust of air escaped her lungs. Her shoulders collapsed. A proud woman, defeated. "Meet me at the old spot, tonight. Seven."

* * *

If I returned to my office, the sickness would win. I'd double over, load the industrial trash can by my desk with vomit. Before my appointment with Felicia, I'd end up stopping off at Huey's. Plug my blood with junk. I'd risk losing Felicia's help, her trust. Again. I'd place myself back in the bubble preventing enjoyment of natural relationships with other human beings. Normality, according to those unafflicted. No, I decided, I'd fill those hours with productivity. I sounded like my angry old father, a working man who talked responsibility and discipline while scratching his bloated belly and dissolving his liver with beer and tequila. He'd worked at Klein Transmissions. Inhaled asbestos every day on the assembly line until it summoned cancer in his lungs and killed him.

Daisy Chemical's main offices sat on a fat strip of land between Market and Ohio, south of the city-county building. I ducked into Shapiro's, a deli nearly as old as the city itself. Nibbled on a pastrami sandwich. Eavesdropped on an argument between college students the next table over. They couldn't agree on whether *The Myth of Sisyphus* constituted blind optimism or cynical nihilism.

The sun set. I trekked east on foot. Used nervous energy storming my veins to climb a fence bordering a near-empty parking lot. Negotiated barbed wire looped across the top. As for the slim man in uniform in the booth at the gate, he must not have shared Daisy's concern for security. He slept with his hands folded across his stomach. Feet raised, poking from the sliding window I assumed he'd examine the identification of anyone driving up. I found a service entrance near the right. Generally, businesses in Indianapolis kept these doors unlocked. Not so with Daisy. I paced until it opened and a man in a gray jumper emerged. He pushed a rubber trash barrel on wheels. I crept inside the building before the door closed on its own. Fluorescents flickered and buzzed as I snuck down a corridor toward the main lobby. A directory board hung at the far end of an elevator bank. Management had yet to remove Melvin Beckett's information. Three-twenty-three. I pressed the Up button on the nearest elevator and waited.

Navy carpeting covered the floor of the hallways on the third story. Black and white photographs of scientists and business squares dotted the walls. I rounded a corner and found Mel Beckett's office. Lights out. Door unlocked. The office reflected Mel Beckett's dressing habits. Sloppy. Papers all over a teacher's desk in the corner next to a window with no shades or slats. The files spilled onto the floor, as though someone had knocked them off a pile as they exited. Or maybe someone had rifled through the man's documents to find something. Or hide something. I tried the drawers on a wooden filing cabinet. Someone had jimmied the lock on the top drawer. No surprise finding all the drawers empty.

I left the office. As I shut the door, the man who'd inadvertently let me into the building approached. He dragged a vacuum cleaner behind him. Stopped and said, "Could I help you?"

"Friend of Melvin Beckett," I said. "I was just seeing if he was still working tonight."

"Nobody else is here."

"You familiar with Mr. Beckett?" I pointed to the name stenciled on the door's smudged window.

The man let the vacuum cleaner stand upright. Ran his hand across his bald scalp. "I am new here." He picked at the ends of his handlebar mustache. "Diego," he said. "Diego cleaned the place before."

"Before what?"

"Before last Thursday. Before somebody put him in the hospital."

* * *

The days Felicia and I spent blue hours coiled at my old apartment in Broad Ripple, we'd meet up first at the Red Key Lounge. A small joint on College Avenue. Russ, the owner, prohibited foul language. Played Big Band music at a volume unable to compete with conversation. As the name promised, a scarlet glow animated the neon sign outside and continued inside, thanks to track lighting along the walls. The nuance, the quiet, all factors preventing babies in their early twenties from taking interest in the place and ruining it with drunken stupidity. When I arrived, Felicia waved from our booth. How many hours had we killed on those vinyl seats? We talked sex, religion, and politics. Never blushed at each other's opinions. The occasional gawker might give us static, Indianapolis still not used to seeing people with different skin tones getting down in the 1980s. Felicia, like all women, would insist I ignore it. Like all men untamed by offspring and a mortgage, I didn't listen. I'd invite the bigots to step outside. Like all bigots, they proved themselves cowards and attempted to laugh off the episode as a misunderstanding.

Felicia nursed an Irish coffee, steam rising off the rim of her cup and curling around her. She nodded at a checkered rocks glass filled with booze resting on a coaster. "If you're not shooting dope," she said, "I hope you're at least drinking." She sipped her coffee. The pleasant scent of Irish crème lingered between us. "You got to do something, right?"

I thanked her and took a swig. With my natural senses making a comeback, the Jack and Coke warmed the belly a bit better than the night before. "So," I said, "what do you know?"

Her lips curled inward. "No foreplay?"

"The clock is ticking."

52

"Yeah, it is," she said. "Melvin Beckett drifted off Westfield, into the canal three weeks ago. They planted him at Crown Hill two days later. Awful fast turnaround. He was driving his car, a nice one, apparently, one of those old models with fins, in the wrong lane. Police assume a car approached from the opposite direction. The man probably whipped the steering wheel to the right, thinking the guard rail would catch him. Thing is, they're repairing those rails right now, so it wasn't there. Car goes into the drink. Sinks. Beckett must have had his window up, must have had his seat belt on, something. He couldn't get out in time. Official cause of death? Drowning."

"And the contents of his system?" I said. "I mean, besides the crappy canal water and a goldfish or two."

"A smidge of booze."

"He wasn't drunk?"

"The man had Ativan in his blood." She sipped her coffee. "You mix Ativan with even a tiny bit of alcohol…"

"Yeah," I said, "Weeble-Wobble City. I've been there."

"Yeah," she said, "I drove you home that night. Watched you projectile vomit all the next morning."

"Memories." I tapped the table three times and stood.

"Where you going?" she said.

"I need to see someone in Methodist."

"You feeling sick?"

"Not quite," I said. "Not yet."

Russ chastised her for cussing at me as I walked out the door.

* * *

The lights in Methodist Hospital's windows lit up I-65 and the main roads surrounding it. Lazy clouds loitered overhead, illuminated by a golden half-moon. A sleepy eye guarding the night. I parked the Buick in the visitor's lot. Shuffled through the rotating front door. Clutched my belly. Cramps. Aches. Muscles tightening. I struggled to conduct myself like a civilized human being.

While inquiring as to the condition of Diego Sosa, Bonnie, according to the nametag pinned to the receptionist's mint green scrubs, asked if I needed to see a doctor. "Honey…" She spoke in a perfect Hoosier accent. Country, without the bullshit. "You look like someone dug you up from Crown Hill and flopped a ten-cent suit on your bones. Pale as a ghost, I tell you. I seen my Papaw stumble to his bedroom for the last time, Easter, 1981. Same ghastly Sammy Terry face you got." She handed me a clipboard, as though she'd settled the matter. "You fill in the vitals, we'll get you with a doctor in a jiff."

I gently pushed the clipboard back in her direction. "Long day is all." I asked again for information on Diego Sosa. She let some of that old Indiana bias leak from her lips:

"You mean the Mexican?"

"Naptown's got more than one," I said. "This guy's name is Sosa. Diego Sosa." I drummed my fingers on the top of a computer monitor to the right of Bonnie's thinning, curled hair. "Bet you two dimes you can type on that there keyboard and gather up everything I'm looking to learn." I couldn't help slipping into my own Hoosier habits. Talking like a poet who earned his bread harvesting wheat. Truth be told, yammering on like that distracted me from the urge to grind my teeth into nubs.

The woman probably dismissed me as one of these pesky progressives who believed in basic decency. She said, "He's recovering. Fifth floor." She gave me the room number. "You got thirty minutes before they give you the boot."

A ride up the elevator and a short walk to room five-ten. No less than three women in scrubs asking me my business. I showed them my license to snoop. Prayed my hand didn't shake every which way while I held out the laminated card. Diego Sosa rested in a bed hosting a tangle of IVs traveling from his arms to a forest of metal trees sprouting bags of fluid from their branches. A diminutive woman in a cobalt dress, dark hose, and large, clumsy work boots sat in a folding chair next to the bed. She held the man's right hand in both of hers. I explained why I'd come to see Diego.

"He barely speaks." She introduced herself: Marisol Martinez. Diego's wife. Wide, suspicious eyes framed by smudged eyeliner. "The police have all the information."

"I'm not the police."

Her head pivoted on her neck. A crane sensing danger in the water.

I couldn't waste minutes negotiating with her. I stepped around to the other side of the bed. Somebody had worked over Diego Sosa with brass knuckles or perhaps a lead pipe. His face must have resembled the Elephant Man when he arrived at Methodist. Purple welts zig-zagged up and down his skull. "Diego?"

"Please," said his wife.

"Diego," I said again. "You are familiar with Melvin Beckett? He worked at Daisy…"

The man's swollen eyelids separated. He groaned as he turned toward me. Studied me for a moment. "You are no police…."

"That's correct." I showed him my license. As though it would mean anything to anyone in his condition.

His chest rose. A wheeze worked its way through his lungs, his throat, and out his nostrils. "I can tell you one thing." He adjusted his curled fingers so a single digit extended beyond the others. He stared at the ceiling and said, so hushed I barely heard it, "*1959.*" The utterance apparently taxed him. He sank into the bed, shifted his gaze to his wife.

* * *

The UIndy station played two hours of music by Ligeti. The psychotic shrieks of violins enhanced the sensation of hooks attached to strings attached to my flesh controlled by unseen hands, threatening to tear off my skin. I fidgeted on my desk, humored myself into thinking I'd fall asleep. The night's pleasant shades of blue did nothing to quell the rage of withdrawal. At one point, I tried to wrap the desktop around me like a blanket and fell over the side. The pain of slapping my bones against the concrete floor felt wonderful. The senses alive and bickering. A brief victory in the war that takes place when the mind has accepted it's time to leave a destructive lover, but the body doesn't agree. I stayed on the floor. Watched reels of my life play out in the dark until the memories became dreams and my worn-out brain granted sleep.

I held my stomach as I woke up. Throat dry. The horrid stench of vomit and other fluids surrounded me. I'd thrown up. Lucky to be on my side. My body released other things. Stifled things that should have been ejected long ago. My belly rumbled. Begged for nutrition. My favorite suit, soiled and rank, required a date with the laundromat on 64th Street. I changed into an older black number I'd worn to court during the days I lied for the city.

I grabbed breakfast at Perkins near Castleton. Sunlight baked my booth while I ordered. I savored my stomach's renewed interest in tasty, destructive American cuisine. A stack of pancakes smothered in the blood of a maple. Eggs over easy. Buttered toast to sop up the eggs' yellow souls as they meandered across the plate. I used a payphone near the restroom to call Phil Hack, a technician at the city impound. Phil worshipped the same chemical god I did. Unlike me, he'd managed to keep his job with the police department. He told me to meet him at the Delaware Street entrance. I finished my breakfast. The best I'd had in years. Tried, with no success, to snag the waitress's phone number when she handed me the bill. Her strawberry blond hair bounced around as she explained all the ways her boyfriend would kill us both. "He used to be a skinhead," she said. "He's reformed, you know, from being a Nazi and all. But he still likes to hurt people. Says it makes him feel all tingly in the knuckles."

I thanked her for the detailed rejection and drove south. I'd had enough run-ins with neo-Nazis both current and rehabilitated. They never fought fair. Always required a mob of their own to take on a lone enemy. Most threw punches lighter than air. Every now and then, however, you'd run into a lunatic who worshipped violence.

The impound inhabited six blocks between Delaware and Penn. Rumor slated the land for development. A bigger venue for the Pacers. Because the city's youth getting dumber, the poor getting poorer, the corrupt getting richer, none of these things mattered in the face of entertainment. The basketball team had made the playoffs. This warranted shelling out millions of tax dollars to build a gaudier, more impressive arena befitting national heroes like Reggie Miller and Rik Smits. Even the vital work of containing cars confiscated by IPD played second fiddle to grown men chasing orange rubber balls across a hardwood floor. I told myself to calm down. Harsh cynicism always accompanied sobriety. Who the hell was I to judge how other people got their kicks? Felicia once lectured me about culture, how it donned multiple masks. People cheering on overpaid athletes, she'd said, qualified.

Phil Hack stood by a gate fashioned from tall white pickets. Dressed in an oil-stained diesel coverall. Dying cigarette drooping from the side of his mouth. He stared at the rocks covering the parking lot outside the fence. Barely hoisted his attention upward as I approached. "Hey…"

"What do you know?"

He spit his cigarette onto the ground. Crushed it underneath his combat boots. "Walk this way, brother." I followed him through the gate. We navigated a labyrinth of parked cars. Many species. Many conditions. An alarming number decorated with bullet holes. High grass sprouted through the interiors of vehicles long abandoned and deemed unworthy at police auction. He said, "I'm surprised the Beckett Chevy ain't been smooshed yet."

"Oh?"

"They stashed it in transition." He led me to an elongated building. Gray bricks. A dozen bays. Some open. Some closed. He rolled up a garage door near the middle. A cherry Chevy Impala with cream-colored trim stretching from the front to the fins glowed in the morning sun. Remnants of growth from the canal dangled along the bottom. Taupe strands of vegetation stretched across the hood and the roof. "Damn shame," said Phil. "That was one wicked whip."

"A little work," I said, "she'll roll again."

A slow, deliberate movement of his head from side to side. "Don't think so, brother. This honey's scheduled for block city. They just ain't got to it yet."

I strolled around the Chevy. Peeked into the windows. Mel Beckett treated his car better than his office. No trash on the seats. Nothing on the floor. An unpleasant mildew aroma surrounded it. Another souvenir from the canal. I tried the handle on the driver's side door. A slight squeal from the hinges. I reached into the folds between the seat cushions and backs. Impeccable. I leaned in and opened the glovebox. Mel Beckett had kept the original owner's manual. No webs on the spine. On top of the book, he'd placed the registration and what appeared to be a check stub. The man made good money. More in a week than I made in a month. Flipping it over, I found a note scribbled in blue ink:

They're nixing the 59. Gonna make it vanish for good. I were you? I'd let it go.
—Hank

Hank?

I couldn't figure out how the car, beyond diving into the canal and drowning Mel Beckett, represented any kind of threat. I shut the door and stepped away from it. Surveyed it once more, sought anything out of place. "What's so special about a 1959 Chevy, Phil?"

"Beats me." He seized a pack of Pall Mall cigarettes poking from his coverall's breast pocket. Knocked one out and lit it. "Don't see what any of that's got to do with this car." He pointed at the Chevy with the cigarette. "This here's a '61."

* * *

Molly Beckett worked in the reptile booth at the Children's Museum. They'd recently covered the square, red brick building with a giant yellow and green arch. Tried to make it look jollier than the other ten-thousand red-brick buildings in the city. Five floors of entertainment for kids, including a massive model train display on the top level, across from an old-time carousel. Like most museums in Naptown, no entry fee. Benevolence supported by donations and charity. A fleeting glimpse of the kinder iterations of human nature.

I found Molly Beckett on the first level. The Critter Corral, a miniature zoo of lizards and rodents in glass tanks. Kids fidgeted in an unorganized line to pet a boa constrictor coiled around Molly's waist. She explained to more than one anxious tyke they needed to calm down and gently stroke the beast. "If we anger him," she said, "he'll suffocate me. We don't want that, do we?" Some of the boys nodded and assured her they wanted *precisely* that. She acknowledged me and used her forehead to point at a clay bench outside the front doors. I waited a half hour under gray, autumn Indiana clouds. A thin chill lurked, announced itself in sporadic gusts. The cold needled me, taunted me. *Wouldn't a rocket full of heroin obliterate this frigid atmosphere?* Just a short drive north to Huey's place. Molly arrived in time to interrupt the debate. Her work uniform, apparently, a pair of khakis and a collared T-shirt with the museum's logo stitched over her left breast. Gorgeous, auburn hair in a ponytail. No makeup. None needed. She said, "God, I hate this job."

"I wonder if you know anything about the year 1959?"

"How old do I look?" She laughed before I made the mistake of taking her seriously. "I mean, no. I don't know anything about it."

"Your dad never mentioned anything about 1959?"

"If he did, I missed it."

"How about somebody named Hank? Your dad have a friend named Hank?"

"His boss's name is Henry Till, if that helps."

I spoke without thinking—"Want to go to dinner when things are all wrapped up? Maybe Steak n Shake. I'll pay for the skinny fries."

"I think we'd better get back to work." She swayed toward the Museum's entrance. Glanced back at me twice.

* * *

Despite the barbed wire atop the fence surrounding Daisy Chemical, they didn't seem too bothered by the idea of someone casually traipsing through the front gate during business hours. I parked at a strip club called The Magic Carpet Lounge. Neon silhouettes of dancers kicking their legs doused the asphalt with colorful lights. I greeted several ladies dressed in sweatpants and jeans jackets as they entered the club. The scent of Pink Lemonade sat on the air long after they disappeared. I dodged cars on Market Street. Strolled past the guard house in front of Daisy's lot without having to say hello to a thin, uniformed geezer seated in front of a black and white television set. I ducked my head to avoid making eye contact with cameras wedged in the ceiling over the main entrance. Checked the directory near the elevators for Henry Till's information. Third floor, same as Melvin Beckett. Employees, some in suits, some in white lab coats, scuttled about. Bosses at Daisy must have ruled with an iron beaker. Their wage slaves hustled like drones. Or maybe that's how workers behaved when they brought home paychecks like Mel Beckett's.

Henry Till's door stood half open. I nudged it with my foot until it creaked out of the way. A round man torturing a wobbly office chair tore his attention from a clump of dot-matrix printed files in his hands. "May I help you?" Ah, the old yuppie standard. Sounded polite. Blanketed an army of thorns intended to communicate how much the existence of another irritated him.

I produced Mel Beckett's pay stub from my pants pocket. Uncrumpled it and pointed at the note on the back. "You Hank?" My hand didn't shake as much as it had the previous two days.

The man placed the papers he'd been examining on his otherwise spotless desk. He took the stub from me. Elicited a concerto of tisk tisk tones. "Mel always was a slob." He gave it back to me. "He leave that on the street? In a public toilet?"

"What's the problem with 1959?"

Color evacuated the man's cheeks. His eyes, previously tiny behind his thick, rectangular glasses, doubled in size. "Are you crazy?" He jumped to his feet, pulled me into the office, checked the hallway for marauding ninjas or something equally upsetting, and shut the door. "Lord," he said. "That man is causing ulcers from beyond the grave."

"I'd think anybody working in a joint like this has ulcers." I stuffed the pay stub into my pocket.

"This is serious, ah, what'd you say your name was?" He stepped to a gray file cabinet five drawers high. He lifted a set of keys attached to a chain on his belt and inserted one into the lock on the top of the cabinet. He pulled out the fourth drawer. Scrunched a row of brown file folders toward him and grabbed a metal box with a combination lock on it. "Substance 1959, to be precise." He set it on his desk. "I have the only remaining sample." I looked away, gave him an opportunity to dial the combination. The lock clicked. Removing a clear, plastic container with a corked test tube inside it he said, "You're familiar with HIV?"

"Shouldn't we be wearing protective gear?"

"This isn't the virus." The man raised the clear container closer to the fluorescent light humming overhead. The dull glare illuminated an amber substance inside the test tube. "This is Substance 1959. One dose of this acts like a magnet. Like an ant trap, if you're familiar with the concept. The virus is induced to visit the injection site. Once there, Substance 1959 eradicates it and teaches the immune system to do the same to any future invasions."

"I haven't heard…"

"Nobody has." He placed the container back into the lockbox. "Nobody other than Mel, myself, and Leo Black, the man who makes executive decisions for Daisy." He locked the box and slid it behind the files in the drawer.

"People are dying," I said.

He secured the file cabinet. Let the zip line on his key chain return the flock to the side of his belt. "You ever wonder why there isn't a cure for cancer?"

"I was told we hadn't created one."

"There's multiple," said Hank. "But think of all the people put out of work if cancer is cured with a simple shot or pill."

I needed heroin. Right then, right there. Who did I think I'd fool, trying to tackle the wicked world without dope? A fresh ache twisted through my stomach. "This isn't available to the public because of…*profit*?"

"Welcome to capitalism, Mr., ah, what was your name?"

"Mr. Till," I said, "you have an ethical responsibility. People I know are in the graveyard because of AIDS." I stopped short of telling him what a nuisance bleaching needles had become. "Keeping this quiet is a crime against the entire species."

"You sound like Mel Beckett." The man assaulted his office chair once more. Ignored the crackling vinyl as he leaned backward. "You see where his optimism landed him?"

"Who did it? Leo Black?"

Hank Till peered over his glasses. "Why do you insist on pretending you're some kind of innocent, ah…what did you say your name was?"

"I didn't."

* * *

I hid my face a whole lot more on the way out. Ducked as I returned to the strip club. I'd forgotten how easy it is to feel no guilt if you've snuffed somebody without having to put your hands around his throat. Mel Beckett's killer, at least the one who did the deed, had enjoyed that luxury. Traffic up Meridian moved slow. The yearn for junk in my blood graduated from physical terror to a simple debate: If I plugged my veins one time, I'd collapse into the daily hunt all over again. It only took one time. The rational circuits in my head insisted such a backslide represented a lack of discipline. Hell, a lack of intelligence. The opposition, however, hinted at its defense. The same rationale that drove every rocket into my skin:

What's the fucking point?

I pulled into the lot at the McDonald's on the edge of Broad Ripple. Used their pay phone to call Molly Beckett. She suggested we rendezvous at the Steak n Shake on Keystone. Said she'd pay for the skinny fries.

After hanging up, I sat by a window in the McDonald's facing Winthrop. Watched the parking lot behind the Outback bar. A few beat up cars moseyed in over the next thirty minutes. Finally, a black Dodge Dart, gleaming in the red haze of the setting sun, rolled into a corner away from the other cars. The driver positioned it at an angle, communicating his disdain for anyone heartless enough to devalue the sight of the muscle machine by placing an inferior vehicle next to it. Glenn the bartender stepped out. Same drab, dated punk rock wardrobe he'd worn the night I spoke with him. The night I should have given in to the yearn and asked what pills his doctor had prescribed him.

I crossed the street and used the employee entrance to sneak into the Outback. Three cooks worked on prepping vegetables and meat for the evening. They noticed me, let their eyebrows communicate their concern— *Who the hell are you?*

Glenn stood behind the bar examining a row of booze bottles on the counter. He started to speak as I snaked around him and grabbed the pills on the ledge under the mirror. They belonged to him, according to the name on the label. Glenn, it appeared, suffered from anxiety. Hey, I could relate. He clearly didn't belong in Indianapolis. Neither did I. Indy catered to conformists. People content to grow a family and run the same cycle of life, over and over again. Oh, sure, the Phoenix Theater ran plays business types would call edgy, meaning, one or two gay characters and a live goat for shock value. The yuppies, the locals who'd landed jobs paying more than a nickel, they referred to this as culture, and assured each other it granted Indianapolis major metropolitan status. The truth being, however, the dominant forms of art in the entire state revolved around basket weaving and banjo music. Frankly, I had no problem with any of it as long as the yuppies and yipjacks left me alone.

Glenn asked what the hell I thought I was doing.

"Ativan?" I dumped the pills onto the counter. They made tiny white islands around a whiskey bottle at the end of the line.

The bartender knew I knew. He hesitated before offering a snotty, half-hearted, "So? I get panic attacks."

"I don't blame you," I said. "Life is rough." I grabbed a fifth of Jack Daniel's. Took a swig. "I gather you didn't come up with the idea to drop one in Mel Beckett's drink on your own."

If Glenn thought he'd mastered anxiety, he learned better in that moment.

I heard him swallow his fear as he stumbled backward. Caught himself on the lip of the bar. "I don't…"

"It's not me you have to worry about," I said. "Or even the cops." I helped him regain his balance. "My math says Leo Black, or someone associated with him, someone who looked like maybe they could crush your skull between their palms, slid you some cash. Enough to buy that sweet Dodge out there in the parking lot. Maybe they told you it was a gag? Let's see how Mel Beckett walks once he's committed one of the biggest no-no's in the wild world of inebriation. I mixed Ativan with tequila once. Suffered enough the next day to know I'd never make that mistake again."

"I…"

"I don't need an explanation, Glenn. If I were you, I'd use whatever money you got left from that gig to load up your belongings and drive as far away from Indianapolis as you can. If you think they're going to let you walk around with knowledge about what happened to Melvin Beckett, well, you haven't listened to enough Dead Kennedys or Circle Jerks, right? Power protects itself. Always."

"I don't know what I was thinking." He promised he'd do as I suggested. "I got family in…"

"Don't tell me," I said. "I don't want to know any more than I already do."

* * *

Molly Beckett stood near one of the large, plate glass windows in the Steak n Shake facing Keystone. A wonder she hadn't caused an accident. She'd squeezed herself into a turquoise one-piece tight enough to communicate her disdain for panties and a bra. I'd have to give her a mini lecture about not calling attention to herself at the moment. She might have to leave town, the same as Glenn, once she knew the truth. I parked and entered the side of the building. Molly beckoned me to join her in a booth in the corner. "You look terrible, Mr. Boyle."

"Call me Tom, please."

"I brought the rest of your salary, Mr. Boyle," she said. "I'm hoping we have a little more information today than we did yesterday."

"Your instincts are correct," I said. "Your father was killed."

Her lower lip curled inward. Her eyes followed her pinky, tracing a circle on the table between us. "Do we know why?"

"He developed something incredible, something that would prevent Daisy or any other pharmaceutical company from making lifelong customers out of HIV patients."

"I'm not sure…"

So, I told her. Pops found a cure for AIDS. In an upside-down world, this had been a problem. People in charge didn't consider it a lucrative discovery. She said, "You know this…for a fact?"

"I've seen the last remaining bit of it, in a glass tube in your father's boss's office."

"What's he holding on to it for?"

"Insurance, I suppose." I grabbed a menu wedged between a metal napkin dispenser and a bottle of ketchup. "If he didn't keep it, the same man who ordered the hit on your father would probably snuff him next."

A different gleam inhabited her eyes. I saw the vapid hunger before I heard it: "We could rake them," she said. "You tell them we know what they have, tell them we'll tell the world, or they pay us, monthly. I wouldn't have to work at the stupid Children's Museum anymore and…" Her thin, newly manicured fingernails nudged the sleeve of my sports jacket up my arm. Trailed across a mishmash of fading injection bruises. "And you, Tom Boyle, could feed your ugly habit for, well, as long as it takes before you do what all junkies eventually do…"

"Was this what you were actually looking for?" I don't know why I even asked.

"Are we scared?" She rested one hand over the other.

I demanded my salary. Double. And the skinny fries she'd promised.

* * *

The fantasy of living clean dissipated as the Steak n Shake's neon-soaked exterior diminished in the rearview mirror. Can't say conscious thought directed my hands to steer the Buick in the direction of College Avenue. Unconscious knowledge of myself, perhaps. An acceptance that the world didn't deserve the effort required to negotiate it sober. I parked down the street from Huey's and hiked through the alley behind his house to avoid any possible cop eyes lurking on the main road.

A peek in the kitchen window and I saw the glow of Huey's television casting strobing light in the living room. I knocked on the aluminum outer door. Knocked several times, assuming he'd fixed up already and required persistence, nagging, to get him to his feet. He wandered into the kitchen. Eyes barely open. Annoyance glued to his face. "Thought you were finished?"

"I'm not looking for charity, old friend." I turned so I could slide past him and ignore the horrid mess in his kitchen on the way to the living room. I removed a clump of twenty-dollar bills from the fold Molly Beckett handed me under the table at the Steak n Shake. She vowed to follow through with her blackmail plan. I'm not into necrophilia. Making love to the woman before Leo Black and Daisy Chemical cured her the way they cured her father would have been just as futile as anything else in this world. The only reliable lover rested snug inside a plastic baggie corner. Black tar. Cooked in a spoon. Or maybe a modified bottle cap. Absorbed into a fresh cotton ball. Drawn into a clean syringe and mixed with the blood of the faithful. "Let me get ten squares of the good stuff."

Huey prepared the order. He handed me a needle with the orange cap still attached. "Welcome back," he said. Junkies trusted each other in such circumstances, trusted the rocket hadn't been used, didn't require a round of bleach, and harbored no virus capable of turning the immune system inside out and laying waste to a human being for doing nothing more than seeking reprieve from the manmade bullshit spinning the world on a crooked axis.

Alibi in Ice

Libby Cudmore

Martin wasn't in when I got into the office. That wasn't too unusual; in another fifteen minutes or so he'd stroll in wearing one of his impeccable suits, the gray silk check, perhaps, or the dark blue pinstripes, his wool overcoat, Chelsea boots against the snow that had piled up overnight. I was a long way from my old alt-weekly in Memphis; no more skinny jeans and band shirts in the office. Martin didn't explicitly give me a dress code, but I wanted to make a good impression on my new boss, so I hit up Poshmark for a few vintage-look dresses and cardigans. Besides, I wanted to keep my tattoos covered up. I didn't need him asking questions as to why the garden scene on my left forearm had a long ugly scar running down it. I hadn't told anyone—not my Aunt Gina, not my brother Declan—about how that got there. That was between me and the girl who gave it to me. The last person I wanted asking questions about it was a private investigator like Martin Wade.

I checked my emails. Nothing important. No messages in voicemail. I made coffee in the kitchenette's French press. We were out of creamer. I sent Martin a text asking him to pick some up on his way in. If he didn't, I could always run to the store when he arrived. No real worry about missing an important call. The Wade Agency's caseload had been flagging lately; he told me that the month and a half between Thanksgiving and Christmas was always slow. It would pick up in January, when people started looking more closely at their bills to see gifts they didn't receive or business expenses they didn't authorize. Until then, we'd just have to make our meals out of background checks and leftovers.

It was ten fifteen and Martin still wasn't in. He hadn't responded to my text either. That wasn't like him. I called and he didn't pick up. This wasn't like him at all. I tried not to imagine the worst-case scenario. I failed hard. *He probably just overslept,* I told myself. I learned in the first few weeks as his assistant that Martin had a habit of staying up late working on cases; years of playing late-night shows as the frontman of the punk band The French Letters had hardwired him into a night owl. But he also had a long-dormant heroin addiction. I knew all too well that those kinds of habits had a nasty way of showing up when they were least welcomed.

At ten-thirty I tried calling again. He still didn't answer. To hell with waiting. I locked up the office and got in my car and drove over to Lido Avenue. His car was parked in the driveway. The walk hadn't been shoveled. I shuffled through the snow, anxiety gnawing at my gut like a dungeon monster in a D&D game. I rang the doorbell, trying not to imagine him at the bottom of the stairs with his neck broken, laid out on the kitchen floor from a heart attack, slumped on his couch with a needle in his arm and an empty bottle at his feet.

I heard movement. "Martin?" I called through the door. "Martin, it's Valerie, are you okay?"

He opened the door but not the screen. He was still in his pajamas, flannel pants and a Lemonheads T-shirt and a bathrobe tied loose around his waist. His face was flushed and unshaven and his silver hair, always perfectly combed into tight fins, was matted to his forehead. He coughed into his elbow when he tried to speak. "I'm sorry," he finally said when he finished. His voice was barely above a whisper. "I heard the phone ring, but I kept falling asleep before I could answer it. I've been up all night."

"Can I come in?" I asked. "It's freezing out here."

He nodded and unlocked the front door. I followed him inside and he slumped onto the couch. The wastebasket was filled with tissues; there was a mostly emptied mug of tea on the coffee table. "Let me get a shower," he said, reaching for a tissue to blow his nose. "And some coffee. I'll be in by noon."

"You can't come into the office like this."

"I'm fine," he insisted. "It's just some congestion."

I put my hand to his forehead. I couldn't help it; it was an automatic reflex, as though he was a child instead of a man twenty years older than me. "Martin, you have a fever," I insisted. "You need to stay here and rest."

He tried to answer, but started coughing instead. "I've got work to do," he choked out.

"Don't be stubborn," I said. "If you come into the office, ten bucks says you're asleep at your desk half an hour after you arrive, so you might as well be comfortable on your own couch. If you really insist on doing work, I can bring you your laptop. And some more tissues. Keep up at this pace and you'll be using paper towels."

"I don't want to make you take care of me," he said. "That's not your job."

I knew it wasn't my job. My job was boring. File reports. Type up the notes he took down in his lean scrawl. Mail invoices, pay bills, check the mail in the post office box twice a week. Call it compulsion. Call it addiction. Call it the first spark about caring for someone other than myself. If I got sick, I had Aunt Gina and Declan to baby me, stop by my apartment with homemade soup and cold juice and meds to bring my fever down. Martin had no one except for me, and I couldn't just abandon him.

"How's the snow?" he asked. "I'm sorry I haven't shoveled my walk."

"Roads are clear," I said. "And I'll shovel your walk. Don't worry about it."

He sighed. "Thank you," he said. "I'm not used to having someone take care of me like this."

"You just rest," I said. "I'll be back in a bit with some supplies."

* * *

I pulled into the Wegmans parking lot. Snow was piled high around the lampposts. I shoved my hands in my pockets and tried to make a mental list of what else I needed. Green tea, fresh ginger, honey, and lemons. Vicks and tissues. Everything Aunt Gina used to give me when I got sick as a kid. Everything I relied on in Memphis with no health insurance and no money. Creamer and extra coffee for the office. Martin refused my offer of cold medicine—it made him too jittery—but agreed to some nasal spray and vitamin C.

I parked at the far end of the lot. I was already dreading going back into office; the day would be slow and boring without Martin to talk to. I didn't yet know what to do other than follow his directive; send this invoice, type up these notes, close out this case and file it all away. I wondered if he would just let me take a snow day and go home.

The walk to the store felt like it was a hundred miles across a frozen wasteland. The wind that had brought the Christmas-card snow the night before had turned cruel, slicing into my cheeks. I passed a lamppost packed with the plowed remains like a ski slope in miniature. I heard a moan behind me. The wind, perhaps? I stopped when I heard it again. I turned back around and saw a brown shoe.

There was someone in the snowbank.

A young woman, skin pale and lips blue, dressed in a Raines College sweatshirt and black leggings and cheap boots. She had been there long enough that what had been powdery when she had fallen in had all but frozen hard around her. How many people had walked past her without noticing? "Call an ambulance!" I yelled at a woman pushing a cart full of groceries. "There's someone over here!"

I tried to shake her awake. I tried to find a pulse. I couldn't tell if the fluttering on her wrist was pumping blood or wishful thinking. "C'mon, open your eyes," I murmured. "Please wake up." I just wanted some tea and tissues. I didn't need to be responsible for a stranger's life.

Her eyes opened. She tried to focus on me. "It was an accident," she murmured. "It was an accident."

"It's okay," I said, gripping her hand. "You'll be okay. We're going to get you warmed up, I promise."

Her eyes rolled back in her head. She went limp. I held her against me, ignoring the snow seeping through my tights. I had to get her warm. I'd known people who had frozen to death; a customer from my aunt's bar who resisted her suggestion of a cab, the junkie father of a classmate who was found slumped on a park bench, wrapped in old coats and stinking of street life. The winters of Perrine demanded their sacrifice, but I wasn't about to let their ice queen take her tribute without a fight.

The ambulance screamed into the parking lot. EMTs got the girl onto the gurney and wrapped her up in blankets. "Second one this semester," he grumbled as he slammed the door. "What is it about deep freezes that makes these kids want to party their faces off?"

"Wait," I asked as he tried to get into the driver's seat. "Don't you need me to ride along with you, give a statement?"

"Only if she dies," he said. "Give your name to the cops if you want." He slammed the door in my face and hit the siren.

I stood there and watched him drive off. Was I simply supposed to go inside and get my groceries as though none of this had happened? The stock boys had scattered. I didn't even see the woman with the toddler.

I went inside and grabbed a basket. Every move I made felt deliberate and angry and sore. I got my damn groceries and paid with Martin's card. I went back to the parking lot where there was a girl-shaped hole in the snow. Her purse was still there. No sense in leaving it behind for someone to steal. She'd want it back when she woke up.

If she woke up.

* * *

Martin was asleep on the couch, wrapped up in a blanket, when I got back. He had showered and shaved and was now dressed in a sweater and jeans. He'd cleaned up the tissues and the empty mugs, made space on his coffee table for his laptop. I felt bad disturbing him. His eyes opened like bank vault doors, heavy and unwilling. He sat up, held his head for a minute, and coughed. "Valerie, you're soaking wet," he said. "What happened?"

I crumpled onto an armchair. I burst into tears. I didn't mean to, but all that fear and sadness came pouring out of me like wine at a wedding. I told him all of it between choking sounds and sniffles. I hadn't cried that hard in months, only this time, it was all over a girl I didn't know.

He passed me the box of tissues. "I'm sorry," he murmured. "I'm sorry you had to see that."

"Don't be," I said. "If I hadn't been there, who knows what might have happened to her?" That was the worst part. Someone left her there, and no one cared to find her. The casual cruelty of other people was too much to bear sometimes.

"You probably saved her life," he said.

"Yeah, well, I also stole her purse." I reached into my tote bag and retrieved the Coach clutch. "So don't give me the key to the city just yet."

He laughed a little. He got up and went into the back bedroom and returned with a sweatshirt and a pair of pajama pants. "You can get a shower, if you want to warm up," he offered. "Give me all your wet clothes; I'll throw them in the laundry."

"I'm all right," I insisted. "I can stop by my place and change before I go back to the office."

"Now who's being stubborn?"

He had me here. Because I wasn't fine. I was cold and I was angry and I was scared for whoever that girl was. I wanted her to be okay. I wanted to know who left her. Even in my cruelest hours, with sore feet and no more cash, I never left a friend behind. The Girl Code was the vow we upheld when we put on our wedges and our going-out tops. Someone had betrayed that vow.

And I wanted to know who.

I took the clothes he was offering. I went upstairs and turned on the shower. I didn't realize how frozen I was until the water hit my skin. I took long, slow hits of steam as though I was trying to melt myself from the inside out. Were the doctors able to get that girl warm under blankets and on top of heating pads? Would she lose extremities to frostbite? And how the hell did she get out there?

I cinched the pants as tight as the drawstring would go and rolled the cuffs so I wouldn't fall down the stairs. The University of Minnesota sweatshirt was soft and worn and smelled like Tide and sandalwood. It had been a long time since a man had let me borrow his hoodie.

When I got back downstairs there was a cup of tea waiting and a blanket draped over the armchair across the room from the couch. The contents of the girl's purse were spread out on the coffee table, next to a legal pad already filled with Martin's scrawl.

Martin returned with his own fresh mug and sat down on the couch. "Feel better?" he asked.

"A little," I replied. "What are you doing?"

"I had an idea," he said. "You should go by the hospital, take her some flowers, leave her my card with a note saying that we have her purse and her phone and can bring it when she's discharged. Don't want to run the risk it might get lost in the shuffle."

I didn't quite believe him. Something was turning in that suspicious brain of his, even if he was running on brief sleep and green tea. "Did you find anything in there?" I asked.

"Her Raines College ID and her driver's license identifies her as Amanda Harris, 20, East Beauty, New York," he said. "Also found a pink plastic lighter, forty dollars in ATM-fresh bills in her wallet, and a dead phone. No needles, no powder, not even a joint to spark with that lighter. I wanted to make sure she wasn't holding anything the cops could pin on her."

"Maybe she was in the parking lot to buy drugs?" I offered. "The EMT said that she was 'the second one this semester.'"

"Maybe," he said, packing everything back into the purse. He got one of his cards out of his wallet, sitting lonely on the end table, and handed it to me. "But she's the only one who can confirm that."

* * *

I picked up a bouquet of daisies at the hospital gift shop and saved the receipt. Martin paid me better than any other job I'd ever had, but I still had car payments and rent to make. Flowers for a stranger were not in my budgeted items.

"These are for Amanda Harris," I said, passing the flowers across the front desk. "The ambulance brought her in a few hours ago, from Wegmans. How is she?"

The nurse glanced quickly at her logs. "All I can confirm is that she's a patient here," she replied. "Are you family?"

A patient meant she was still alive. For a moment I considered pulling out Martin's card, introducing myself under his auspices, sitting down at her bedside to interview her about how and why she ended up in the snowbank. Because deep in my gut I knew she didn't get there by herself. There were no party houses around. No bars or clubs. Someone left her there, and I wanted to know who and why.

"I'm the one who found her," I finally said. "I just wanted to check in."

"She can't have visitors right now," the nurse said. "But I can let her know you came by."

I took out Martin's card. I borrowed a pen from the nurse, crossed out his number and wrote in my own before tucking it back into the flowers. "Have her call me when she wakes up," I said. "I found her purse and her phone, and she'll want those back, I'm sure."

* * *

Martin was set up with his laptop when I got back. He gratefully accepted the Tom Yung Goong I had picked up from Flower House, cracked open the lid, and took a spoonful. "That's really spicy," he gasped. "Exactly what I needed, thank you. How is she?"

"Stable," I replied. "That's all they would tell me."

"Good to hear, at least," he said, setting the soup aside. "I did a little digging into our frost queen while you were gone."

"You're supposed to be resting," I said.

He shrugged. "I got bored," he said.

Martin should have been back in bed. He should have been nested on the couch, watching old movies or game shows or reruns of *Law & Order*. He should have been napping, reading, or doing anything but trying to solve a puzzle that didn't come from the pages of the *New York Times*. But that just wasn't Martin. "What did you find?" I asked.

He flipped back a few pages on his legal pad. "She's a business major at Raines College. She was the salutatorian at East Beauty High School, but her graduating class was twenty-seven people, so that's not hard."

In the absence of clues, Martin once told me, background is the next best thing. Learn enough about your victim, and the assailant may reveal themselves. "Probably explains why she's studying business administration at Raines," I said. "Unless you're a musician, there's no reason to pay fifty-four thousand dollars a year to come here."

"Or your mother is an alumna," he said. "Charlene Black, Class of 1981. Has an endowed scholarship for vocal performance. I seem to remember she had some pop hit in the early nineties. Surprising Amanda didn't go someplace better, though. She's all over her high school yearbook."

Drama club, lacrosse, choir, softball. She had the lead in *Angel Street* that year. I guess all those banner ads I saw about looking into old yearbooks were legit. "What were your extracurriculars?" I asked, taking a generous helping of pad thai between cheap chopsticks.

"Jazz band, chess club, and cross-country in my freshman year," he said. "Played in the pit orchestra for the musical a few times too. Would have joined French club, but it met the same time as band."

"You speak French?"

"I'm pretty rusty these days," he admitted. "My grandfather was French-Canadian, so I heard it a lot growing up. At one time, I could carry a decent conversation. My bandmates would tell you that I had an obnoxious habit of switching to French when I got a few drinks in me. It drove them crazy, but it came in handy when we played Paris clubs."

I had abandoned the story I was writing about Martin for *High Wire*, but I still found myself wanting to know more about his time on the road. Not about the drugs or the sordid tales, but the little details about the clubs he played at, the people he knew, the backstage stories that made up the entire life before I even knew who he was. "The only thing I remember from high school French is *je suis un ananas*," I said. "I'm sure that will come in handy one day."

He let out a small laugh that turned into a cough. He took a drink when he was finished to clear his throat. "There's not much about Amanda at Raines," he continued. "She's not pledging a sorority, not a member of any campus organization as far as I can tell."

"Big fish, little pond?"

"Perhaps," he said. "You're the one who found her, what's your theory?"

I set down my take-out container. "I think someone left her," I said. "It may not have been intentional, but someone she knew was there with her."

"Elaborate."

"Last night was the first major snow of the season," I said. "Raines students have a tradition called the Apocalypse—first snowstorm means it's time to rage. No rules: booze, drugs, hookups with whoever you want. It's the end of the world, so none of it matters. My Aunt Gina used to dread the first snowfall; now she counters it by booking the most abrasive, loud band she can get on the phone. It's usually enough to keep the party crowds away."

Martin snickered. "Been to a few of those myself," he said. "We just called it the after-party. Sometimes we were the abrasive band. Go on."

I was on a roll. "The absence of a fake ID says more than if she had one," I continued. "They're practically standard issue when you arrive at Raines, and they're good. The bouncer at Topsy's has told me that as soon as he figures out how to spot a fake, they get better, but he still ends the night with a handful of them."

"Do you think someone has hers?" he said.

"Maybe," I replied. "That means she can't get into a bar, which means if she was drinking or using drugs, she was doing so at a house party. There's no party house within walking distance of Wegmans, so someone drove her there. Maybe the party is boring, they want food, they're on a beer run. She gets out of the car to take a phone call, hit her vape, or throw up, and passes out in the snowbank. Her friends are all drunk, so they don't notice she's missing. They still might not know. A drunk friend is always someone else's problem."

Martin was quiet for a minute. Had I upset him, cut too close to the bone, brought up something he couldn't or wasn't ready to remember? There were shadows of his past I had yet to shine a light on. There were fragments of who he was that I might never know.

He ate a little more of the soup and drank some seltzer to cool his tongue. "Look into your Apocalypse theory," he said. "Social media, chatter among bartenders. See if such a rager was held last night and figure out who might have been there."

"You're taking the case?" I asked.

"No," he said, sniffling. "You are. I'm taking a sick day."

I wasn't expecting that. "You can't be serious," I said.

"Why not?" he asked.

"Because I'm not a detective," I insisted. "I don't even know where to begin."

"You're a journalist," he said. "It's the same skill set. The story is that you found a girl abandoned in a snowbank, you think you know how she got there, and now it's just finding what you need to connect those dots."

"And if I'm wrong?"

"Then you're wrong," he said. "And life goes on. It's not like we can arrest anyone. You apologize and move on with your life. It happens sometimes."

Except the last time I was wrong about someone, I got my arm carved up. "Maybe we should hold off until you're recovered," I said.

He shook his head. "It'll be too late," he said. "It'll get harder and harder to track down witnesses, the memories become hazy. There's no reason to wait." He paused to reach for a tissue and sneeze. "You don't have to, of course. We can let this one go. I just figured since you're the one who brought it up, you might want to take a crack at it."

He knew I couldn't do that any more than he could get up and run a four-minute mile. "I'll see what I can come up with," I said. "And I'll check back in with you this afternoon."

* * *

The #ApocolypseParty hashtag turned up a trove of blurry nightclub selfies, Instagram reels of beer pong, and dance floors all documenting the evening's debauchery. If our victim had taken photos—and what girl doesn't these days—I wasn't going to see them. Her Instagram, @mandamanda, was private.

But she was tagged in a handful of photos. Her outfit was the same one I'd found her in, although in a handful of them, she'd ditched the sweatshirt. That small act—putting it back on before she went out in the cold—probably did more to save her life than I did. That thin blue crop top wasn't going to protect her tight, athletic abs from the elements.

She was tagged in a photo with @RyanOssing. Her arm was slung over his neck, a skinny red straw loose between her lips, gripping a clear cup filled with ice and lime and tonic and, guessing from the glaze in her eyes, cheap vodka. He was holding a beer and I somehow doubted it was his first. I made a note of his name and a screen grab of the photo, printed it out and tucked it into a new manila folder.

A cross-reference of his name turned up that he was also a Raines student, a soccer player on their D-III team, and also hailed from East Beauty. Her high school boyfriend, perhaps, but what kind of boyfriend doesn't notice when their girlfriend goes missing from a party or a car? I didn't like any answer I came up with.

The office felt lonely without Martin. I made a fresh pot of coffee and pulled a couple of his Elvis Costello records to get me through the afternoon. All my vinyl was back in Memphis, likely long pawned by my ex-roommate Katy, their proceeds smoked or snorted or put up for bail. I tried not to think about Katy. It made the scar on my arm hurt too damn much.

I kept coming back to the EMT's remark. *This semester*. Not overnight, which meant not from the party scene I was chasing. I scrolled back through the Perrine Courier archives to see if I could find any mention of the first person, hoping I didn't. You only make the papers if you die. Luckily, the only article on such a death was from last year, a man who froze to death outside the local warming station after he was asked to leave for threatening the staff. Grim, sure, but not quite the same thing.

When you wake up, I texted Martin. *Can you ask Chief Hollander about the other victims? Maybe they have something in common?* It was a stretch in all directions. If he had names, he wouldn't be able to give them to us. If he was able to give them to us, they might not show anything in common. This was my thirty-third winter in Perrine. I knew the dangers of the snow, that relentless, wet cold that got inside your bones. I just couldn't shake the frustration that someone had abandoned their friend—or girlfriend—to die.

It was just after one p.m. In another hour, Aunt Gina would be at Topsy's, accepting her deliveries and getting ready for another night's work. That gave me some time to check in on our party boy. I put my coat back on, tucked the folder into my tote bag, and stepped out once again into the cold.

* * *

Ryan's apartment smelled like Hot Pockets, unwashed sheets, and cheap beer. The cans were stacked in the window, as though he was an alcoholic conspiracy theorist trying to protect himself from government mind control. I should have taken some Vicks from Martin's bathroom cabinet and smeared it under my nose like a coroner tending to a dead body.

Ryan's hair was still wet from the shower. He was wearing sweatpants and a Raines hoodie, his feet bare. He offered me a beer. I declined. He took one anyway from a half-emptied case on the floor and flopped into an armchair with a tiny floral pattern from before he was born.

"We're following up on Amanda," I said. "When was the last time you spoke to her?"

His initial friendliness instantly changed to concern. "She okay?" he asked.

"She is now," I said. "But she was found in a snowbank by Wegmans, almost frozen to death. She's at the hospital."

He took a pull of his breakfast beer. "Shit," he murmured. "I knew I should have left the party with her. I didn't even think about the weather."

Maybe it was true. Maybe we all do things we regret, let accidents occur that we knew we could have prevented. But that wasn't the point. "We're just trying to figure out what happened," I said.

"You sure you don't want a beer?" he offered again. "I mean, it's the least I can do for someone who saved my girlfriend's life."

Just the thought of a room temperature beer made my stomach churn. "I'm good," I repeated. "When did you last see her?"

He sighed. He ran his hands across his face and through his wet hair. "How much of this stays between us?" he asked.

I knew what was going to come out of his mouth before he said another word. I knew the look in a man's eye, the slow motion of his jaw before he owns up to his own shitty behavior. "I was at the Apocalypse party," he said. "I was really hammered, and I was in the back bedroom with another girl. Shit, I don't even remember *who*, but Amanda caught me. By the time I got my pants on my buddy told me she had left. Next thing I knew, I woke up in my own bathroom, covered in puke. No idea how I got home."

So much for the end of the world. "Do you know who she left with?"

He finished the beer. He set the can on the heater, surely to join its aluminum brethren in the window soon. "I don't," he said. "I'm sorry. I really wish I could be more help. I feel like this is all my fault."

It might have been, in a way. I took out the printout of the two of them from his Instagram. I set it on the coffee table in front of him. He picked it up with one hand, wiped his wet eyes with the other. "How can I make it up to her?" he asked.

"You can help me find who left her in the cold," I said. "Think. Was there anyone else there you recognized? Didn't recognize? Who was the buddy who told you she left?"

He stood up without another word. He went into the bathroom and didn't close the door. I heard retching and plugged my ears and waited for it to stop, hoping I didn't react with the same sympathy. After living with Katy for two years, I thought I'd be used to it. Or maybe it was regurgitating memories I couldn't spit out right now. Either way, I clenched my jaw and held my breath until the apartment was silent again. He flushed the toilet, ran the tap, and returned.

"Do you have a card or something?" he asked. "I feel like shit, but maybe I'll think of something after I drink some Gatorade."

Unless I wanted to babysit him, I was out of options. I wrote my number down on the corner of some biology notes. I took down his phone number in case I had any other questions and left him alone in his garbage apartment to think about what he'd done.

* * *

In another six hours, the jukebox would be blasting R.E.M. above the chatter noise of Topsy's clientele, drink orders and work complaints and music trivia. But for the moment, it was as silent as a church, punctuated by the occasional rattle of glasses and bottles as Aunt Gina got ready for the night to start.

Topsy's was one of Perrine's oldest watering holes and best-kept secrets, a former speakeasy buried under what was now a sports bar. Our clientele was mostly locals, our jukebox filled with eighties alternative, high-top tables, and a good-sized stage. No Apocalypse revelers here.

"You're in early," Aunt Gina remarked. "Thought you were over at Martin's today."

After my parents died, Aunt Gina gave up her career as a drummer for the riot grrl band Icebox to raise my brother Declan and me. But the world of touring punk bands is a small one, and she recognized Martin from his days in The French Letters when she hired him to catch a bartender who was skimming from the till. She was the one who suggested I interview him for *High Wire*; without her intervention, I wouldn't be back here today with Amanda's photo in hand. "Actually, I could use some help on a case," I said, perching on one of the barstools. "Martin's out sick, so he asked me to do a little work for him."

"I heard there's a flu going around," she said. "Careful you don't get it."

Too late for that. If I did get sick, would Martin care enough to bring me soup and tea and tissues? Or would he be one of those bosses who made me work through it, just as he was? I would find out in a few days, maybe, as his germs became mine. Tonight would be vitamin C and sleep and plenty of water, a placebo to try and hold the line. I didn't have a choice. I couldn't miss work or I'd miss rent.

I showed Aunt Gina the photo of Amanda. I told her what I had found and what I was looking for. All she could say was, "That poor girl."

"Yeah," I replied. "Hospital said she's stable, but that's all I know right now. I figured since it snowed last night, it might be tied to those stupid Apocalypse parties. She didn't have her fake ID on her, so I thought maybe a bouncer confiscated it. Who would you suggest I talk to first?"

Aunt Gina thought for a minute. "The state liquor authority shut down Ultra about a month back," she said. "Place hadn't poured a legal shot since it opened, but Jack over at the Lion's Head said a lot of that teenage traffic came his way. Said there's been a few nights where his bouncer walked away from the door with a stack of fakes he could barely hold in his hand. And trust me, Elvis isn't a small guy. He's got hands like catchers' mitts."

I'd heard about Ultra. Of the 125 people in there, only six were over twenty-one, and four of them were bar staff. The place had gotten raided after a twenty-year-old girl was found in the dumpster; surveillance footage showed a still-unidentified woman carrying her unconscious body out the back door and shoving her in. Her assailant was never arrested, but the victim's age and inebriated state was enough to get a raid on the books. "Can you call over to Jack and let him know I'm coming?" I asked.

"Sure thing," she replied. "Anyone you think I should be keeping an eye out for?"

"If I identify anyone," I said as I hopped off my barstool. "I'll be sure to let you know."

***

I'd only been to the Lion's Head a few times. It had that friendly neighborhood dive feel, a place where you got a drink after work and kept conversation to a minimum. Outdated neon beer signs, cracked red vinyl barstools, chipped Formica booths lining the walls. There were only a few middle-aged men loitering around the back end of the bar, longnecks in hand. The dance floor had long been filled in with extra tables, the jukebox unplugged and collecting dust. Hard to imagine why a bunch of twenty-somethings would want to crash here. It wouldn't even look good on Instagram.

Jack had Amanda's fake ID waiting on the bar when I arrived. If she had handed that one to me at Topsy's, I wouldn't have been able to tell it was a fake. The weight, the lettering, even the holograph looked exactly like the one I had in my own wallet. "She was with her boyfriend," he said. "They all had fakes. Elvis kicked them out, one of them tried crying, *oh, but my friends are inside*, the whole spiel. I don't know where these kids got the idea that they could drink here. We're a townie bar. We've only ever *been* a townie bar, and the last thing I want is to become some pit stop for Raines power-drinkers."

I felt that same protective nature about Topsy's. "Do you know what time that was?"

"I could probably pull up the camera footage if you gave me a day or so." He sighed. "Now I kinda wish we had let her in. Maybe she wouldn't have gotten dumped like that. No one's there to keep an eye on these girls when they go to house parties, and bad shit happens."

The camera footage would help. "What do you know about the girl they found at Ultra?" I asked.

He snorted. "Only what I heard from the bartender," he said. "We hired one of their guys when the cops shut them down. Guess he was there that night and found her. To tell you the truth, it messed him up a little bit."

"What did he say?"

"Said they saw her arguing with a girl in the night," he said. "You know the way drunk girls argue; they storm away for a few minutes, then come back to pick up the fight. Guess she was doing that most of the night."

"You think someone knocked her unconscious?"

"No, I think she was really drunk," he said. "And I think when she passed out, her frenemy played a really shitty trick on her. She's lucky someone found her before the garbage truck came. Things could have gotten a lot worse. As it was, she got pretty cut up from all the broken glass."

Two girls found in two places they shouldn't have been left. I didn't have to be a licensed detective to recognize that the line between coincidence and pattern was a very, very narrow one.

* * *

I was halfway back to the office when my phone rang from the hospital. A knot formed in my gut like a hot egg. I answered tentatively, afraid of what the person on the other line might say. That Amanda was dead. That I was wanted for questioning about her stolen purse. That what happened in Memphis had finally caught up with me.

"I got your card," a girl's voice said on the other line. "And your flowers. Thank you."

Amanda. "You're welcome," I said. "Hope you've warmed up a bit."

"I have," she replied. "I'm so embarrassed. I literally owe you my life."

"I'm just glad you're okay," I said. "I can bring you your purse and your phone if you tell me where to meet you."

"I'm still at the hospital," she said. "Without my phone I can't call for an Uber, and without my wallet I can't even get the bus. I know you've already done so much for me, but is there any chance you could give me a ride home?"

* * *

Someone at the hospital had given Amanda a coat so she didn't have to go back out into the cold weather in just her sweatshirt. She carried a stack of discharge papers she rolled up in her hand. "The battery was dead, so I charged it up a little," I said as I handed her the phone.

"You're, like, my guardian angel," she said. "I don't even want to think about what would have happened if you hadn't come along. Can I Venmo you some gas money or anything?"

"Nah," I replied. "I just want to make sure you get home safe. Where am I driving you to?"

That must have stung a little where I didn't mean it to. "My apartment," she said after a minute. "I live at the Devon."

Of course she did. The Devon was a new build, apartments exclusively for Raines students who were too rich to be confined to the cinder-block dorms of their less-monied peers. It had taken me months to find an apartment that would rent to someone who wasn't a student; all I got was a converted third-floor walk-up studio on Fenton Boulevard with a pull-out couch and a kitchenette. No granite countertops and game rooms for the citizens of Perrine.

I was getting cynical where I needed to be gentle. Not her fault the housing stock was depleted. Not her fault predatory landlords locked us all out to take her parents' money instead. She was just a victim, a nice girl with bad habits and worse friends. And in fifteen minutes, this would all be a story I told Aunt Gina. Valerie Jacks, saver of frozen damsels.

"How are you feeling?" I asked.

She shrugged. "Okay, considering," she replied. "Docs gave me an IV, which probably helped with whatever hangover I was going to have. Things must have gotten *crazy*. I don't remember anything from last night."

I was worried about that. It meant she wasn't going to be any help in tracking down the people who left her to freeze. "Well, one of your fellow partygoers owes you an apology," I said. "Leaving you out in the cold like that."

She didn't say anything. I pushed forward. "I talked to Ryan this morning," I said. "He told me about why you left the party."

"Yeah?" she snapped. "Did he tell you why he decided to sleep with some sorority skank?"

So she did remember a few things. "He said he was drunk, but we both know that's no excuse," I said. "I would have stormed out too."

"She can have him, honestly," she said. "Whoever she is. I'm literally over it."

I thought about what Jack had said, about the mean-girl prank of dumping an unconscious rival in a dumpster full of broken bottles. In the summer it was cruel. In the winter it was a crime, the exact nature of which depended only on the observations of strangers. "Do you remember why you were at Wegmans?" I asked. "Someone must have driven you there, you were a long way from any party…"

"Just stay out of it!" she snapped. "It was a stupid mistake. I don't know what happened or who was there and I just want to move past it and get on with my life."

I understood that impulse. I had done it when I came here, Martin had done it when he left Los Angeles eighteen years ago. It was a trauma response, but not the healthiest one for any of us. The scar on my arm tingled. I wondered what was on that stack of papers. Finding her out in the snow was one bad thing. I hadn't even begun to consider what could have happened in the hours leading up to her getting dumped.

"I'm sorry," I murmured. "For everything that happened to you. I know how much it sucks when someone you care about hurts you like that."

She didn't respond. She nestled deeper into her coat, her fingers gliding over her phone screen. She was looking for clues the same way I was.

I pulled into the Devon parking lot. She muttered another thanks and stormed out of the car, slamming the door behind her. One of her discharge papers had fallen between the seat and the armrest. I grabbed it and rolled down the window, trying to yell out to her, but she was already inside the foyer. I turned it over and read what the doctor wrote.

Hypothermia, frostbite on hands.

No surprise there.

No signs of sexual assault.

That was a relief.

BAC, .09.

Lower than I expected.

Then those three little letters that make every woman's hair stand on end.

GHB detected.

I was back on the case.

* * *

Martin picked up just before the call went to voicemail. He coughed twice before he was able to speak. "Did I wake you?" I asked.

"It's okay," he replied, his voice so raw my throat hurt. "What did you find out?"

I relayed all the information I'd gathered, from Aunt Gina, from Jack, from Amanda. I told him about the doctor's instructions I found, Amanda's unwillingness to talk, Stephanie and Ryan, the raid on Ultra, the stacks of fake IDs. He listened; I imagined I could hear the faint scratch of his pen on the yellow legal tablet.

"Nice work," he said when I finished. "In between naps I reached out to Chief Hollander. He confirmed your EMT's outcry, that in the last month, three people were found outside in inclement weather. We've got Amanda, and this other girl from Ultra. There was a the third, an adult male, known to be unhoused and not affiliated with the school, found unconscious in the park pavilion. No names and he wouldn't go on the record, but he did mention the presence of GHB detected in the first girl. Liam said he'd fax over the files in the morning."

"Amanda also had signs of GHB," I said. "But no signs of sexual assault."

"That's a relief," he said.

"Is there any chance," I said cautiously. "That the two girls' cases are related?"

"It's always a possibility," he said. "What would the motive be?"

"Could be anything," I said. "A romantic rivalry, a prank for social media, or just your standard-issue creep who gets off on putting women in vulnerable positions. Whoever is behind it, they're lucky no one's died yet."

He was quiet for a minute. "It's almost five o'clock," he finally said. "Go home, get a good night's sleep, come back to it in the morning. You've done more than enough."

"Do you need me to bring you anything else?" I asked.

"I'm well-stocked and as comfortable as I am going to be while I recover," he said. "You need to get some rest if you're going to fight this off. The last thing I want is you getting sick."

He wasn't wrong. Except I didn't want to go home. I didn't want to be alone with all the pieces of this case shattered at my feet. I wanted to drive back over to Lido Avenue with more soup and ginger ale, pull an all-nighter trying to string this together. But Martin needed his rest, and he was right that I needed mine.

I went home, heated up my leftover Thai food, and tried to do anything but work. I read a little, flipped around on Netflix, took another hot shower to try and nuke the day's chill from my bones. I didn't even feel tired. I was wound up, my brain turning over every possible scenario for how two girls end up dumped outside in the freezing cold.

I ran the same search that Martin had. *Amanda Harris, East Beauty*. A few articles from a local paper about soccer tournaments and drama productions, a note about her acceptance into Raines. I ran Ryan's name and came up with the male version of the same. I went back to her yearbook.

One photo showed her with her arms around another girl, identified as Daphne LaChance. I checked back over the names. She was captain of the swimming and rowing teams, the choir and student newspaper too. Had I just found our first victim, the girl at Ultra? I ran a search for her name.

And found her obituary.

> *Daphne LaChance, 18, has joined those who went before her into the Kingdom of Heaven.*
>
> *A scholar-athlete, she was unstoppable on the open water and in the pool, but she also excelled at the arts, starring in both local and regional theater productions. She volunteered at the animal shelter, loved horses, and dreamed of becoming a journalist.*
>
> *She was predeceased by her grandmother, Josephine. She is survived by her parents, Sarah and David, her sister Molly, and several aunts, uncles and cousins. She will be remembered and missed by all of her friends at school.*

So much for that theory. I went back to the search results and pulled up the story from the *East Beauty Democrat*.

High Schooler Dies In Boating Accident
EAST BEAUTY—The body of high schooler Daphne LaChance, 18, was recovered this morning after she failed to return from a boating trip the previous evening.

According to Sheriff Lewis Ossing, LaChance went out in the boat on the Long Island Sound with two friends when the boat capsized. LaChance, who was not wearing a life preserver, failed to resurface, and the girls reported her missing when they returned to shore.

The two girls were not named. But I suspected I already knew one of them. I tried calling Martin. His phone went right to voicemail. Let him sleep. Let him gather his strength. Daphne wasn't going anywhere.

* * *

I didn't sleep well. I saw Amanda frozen in that snowbank; I kept dreaming of drowning, kept dreaming of Memphis, and woke up sweating and chilled. I hovered around the fringes of Netflix until the first peach-colored fissures of dawn peeked through my stuttering blinds. The rest of the world was finally waking up. There was more work to be done.

I stopped by Paul's Bagels and picked up breakfast; tall coffees and small bottles of orange juice and bagels for now and later. I didn't want to go into the office. It felt too sterile, too empty. If I got the flu, well, I could use a few days off from this case. But that gave me a ticking clock—figure out who was dumping these girls and why before the virus took me out.

Martin didn't look much better than he had yesterday, but he was at least showered and dressed for my arrival. "I can't seem to break this fever," he said, his voice still thick with mucus. "I haven't been this sick in years."

"Aunt Gina warned me there was a flu going around," I reported. "But if you're going to feed a fever, it might as well be with fresh bagels from

Paul's."

"I like the way you think," he said.

"Did you get some sleep, at least?"

He cleared the papers off the dining room table and got us place mats and plates and juice glasses. "Tossed and turned, as expected," he said. "Got up a few times. I kept having the strangest dreams, about holding an ice cube and it melting in my hands, flooding my hallway until I was up to my knees."

"Sounds about right for a fever dream," I said. I didn't want to tell him what I dreamed. Didn't want to share that I dreamed of the frozen girl again, only this time it was Katy, only this time, she was dead. Best to keep that to myself.

We sat down for breakfast. Between buttered bites I slid him the notes I had taken, the articles and obituary I had printed out. "Not sure if this has anything to do with any of it," I said. "But there were a lot of photos in that yearbook of Amanda and Daphne together. That just seems like there's a lot of drama coming out of a school with only twenty-five people in a graduating class."

Martin thought for a minute. He got up and went to the living room and retrieved his own notepad. "Of course," he said. "Of course I dreamed of water. I read her obit and that same article, in between bouts of sleeplessness." He took a bite of his bagel and chewed thoughtfully before speaking again. "You said you interviewed Amanda's boyfriend, right?"

"Yeah, Ryan Ossing."

He took a page out of his folder, a newspaper printout with a picture of the prom king and queen in the corner.

Ryan Ossing and Daphne LaChance.

I didn't like the thoughts that were beginning to form. "Do you think," I said slowly. "Do you think Amanda was in that boat with Daphne?"

"I don't know," he said. "But the real question is this—how does a swimming champion drown?"

* * *

Martin called in a request from the East Beauty sheriff's department for the files related to Daphne's drowning. They'd be faxed to the office sometime in the afternoon. I left a message for Amanda that I knew she wouldn't return. I needed some answers, real answers. She might be in more danger than she knew.

I could hear the fax machine screeching before I even got my keys out. By the time I got into the office, it was silent again. Just five pages, not much more than the newspaper write-up. Guess the cops didn't think there was a story to tell.

* * *

The coroner classified Daphne's death as accidental drowning, noting that she had alcohol and marijuana in her system at the time of her death. The police narrative read that she and two other girls, Amanda Harris and Kristin Burgher, all eighteen, had been at an after-prom party at Kristin's residence when they took the boat out. Drug-addled bravado and rough water capsized them, and although Amanda and Kristin made it back to shore, they delayed calling for help until their underage guests slipped out the back. But by the time the sheriff's deputies arrived, the storm that had been predicted earlier in the day had swept in. Dive teams weren't able to go out, and her body wasn't found until the next day, when the waves settled. Amanda and Kristin were both treated for shock and hypothermia. Both of them claimed Daphne was the one who insisted on getting in the boat and that they went with her for safety, even as they begged her not to go. Neither of them were charged in her death.

I'd never looked at a police report before. The narrative gave me chills. It was all so sparse and sober, the last moments of a girl's life summed up in a few paragraphs. I wonder what the police report said about Katy. I wonder if my name came up at all.

I recited the facts of Daphne's case to Martin over a video chat. "Amanda's and Kristin's parents must have done some heavy lifting to keep their names out of the papers," he said when I finished my presentation. "I'd be willing to bet there was money involved—a new cruiser, a couple of park benches. Small towns like that, it's much easier to bully an editor, especially when he's got advertisers to think about. A few bad weeks can fold a local newspaper."

I was relieved that Martin put to words what I was thinking. "Do you think," I began, "that whoever left Amanda in the snowbank was somehow connected to Daphne's death?"

"Would explain why she's reluctant to talk about it," he said. "What do we know about Kristin?"

A quick search and I had the answer. "She is also at Raines," I said. "Finance and art major. She was the salutatorian, but became valedictorian after Daphne's death."

"And what was she doing the other night?"

That was a very good question.

* * *

I found Kristin in the ceramics studio, working at the pottery wheel. The heat of the kiln in the corner warmed the room to the point where she had to roll up her sleeves; her arms were decorated with jagged, still-healing cuts. "Those look pretty rough," I said. "Have you seen a doctor?"

"It's fine," she said. "Just one of the occupational hazards of working in the glass studio. Can I help you?"

I believed her about the glass, just not the studio. We could get to that part later. I introduced myself. She didn't stop working the wheel, didn't seem that interested in talking to me. "Not sure if you heard what happened to your friend Amanda the other night," I tried. "But I was hoping you might be able to fill me in a bit."

"I don't even know what you're talking about," she said. "Amanda and I don't really hang out anymore."

I filled her in on the party and Ryan and her snowbank sleeping bag. She didn't look up once from the wheel, didn't grunt or gasp or give any indication that she even cared. "That sucks," she recited when I'd finished. "I'm sorry that happened to her, but like I said, we're not close."

92

"Sounds like you two went through a lot together, though," I said. "After what happened with Daphne."

The wheel sputtered. Her pot fell flat in her hands. She cursed under her breath. "Yeah, that was the worst night of both our lives," she spat. "And I don't think either of us are anxious to relive it."

"Somebody else might be, though," I said. "Amanda didn't get to the parking lot on her own. Someone dumped her there, and they might come for you next."

"Why the hell would anyone attack either of us?"

"Maybe they don't think Daphne's death was an accident."

She swiveled in her seat. Her glare was so hot I was surprised it didn't fire every piece of clay in the place. "You don't know a goddamn thing about what happened that night," she said.

"You're right, I don't," I said. "Care to fill me in?"

She turned back to her fallen pot. She started the wheel up again. "I'm done talking to you," she said. "Leave now or I'll call campus security."

The last thing I needed was to get hassled by a rent-a-cop. "You really should get those cuts checked out," I said as a parting shot. "They're starting to look infected."

* * *

Kristin's threat lingered in my ear. I wasn't sure how much longer I was going to be able to get away with passing for a Raines College student, but I had to milk it as long as I could. No one walking into or out of the dining hall gave me any notice; one girl even asked how I did on the midterm exam in the history class she thought we shared. I told her I got a grade that my parents wouldn't be pissed at. That seemed to satisfy her.

I waited for Ryan outside the dining hall. I could smell pizza and fryer oil and industrial-sized pans of onions sizzling. It took him a minute to place where he knew me from. He didn't smile. "I guess Amanda remembered more than I did," he lamented. "She broke up with me."

"Rough couple of years for you," I said. "First your girlfriend drowns on prom night, then the other one—her best friend—leaves you when you cheat on her. Might be time to take a year off and reconfigure your life."

I knew he wasn't going to hit me. Not in front of all his classmates. But the look in his eyes told me he wanted to. He resisted. "Just leave me alone," he said, trying to walk away.

"You know what I think?" I called after him. "I think Amanda knows something she isn't telling you. About the night Daphne drowned. I think Kristin knows it too. The question then remains, what do you know?"

That stopped him. He turned back. I motioned for him to follow me back inside to the rec lounge, two chairs in an alcove, facing the wide picture windows so we'd have the illusion of privacy from the other students. "You knew Daphne was a better swimmer than that," I said. "And you knew she wouldn't go out on a boat with a storm coming in no matter how hard she was partying. I think Amanda and Kristin lured her onto that boat. I think they let her drown. They might have even put her in the water, and I think someone here knows it. That person already went after Amanda, and Kristin has a bunch of cuts she declined to explain. They could go after you next, and they might not take a chance that their next victim will survive this time."

He wouldn't look at me. He just stared at the gray plank flooring as if he was hoping it might turn to seawater and wash us both away. "I always knew," he finally murmured. "As soon as I saw them leave, I knew something bad was going to happen."

I couldn't imagine killing my best friend over a man. Especially not one in high school, eighteen and reeking of AXE Body Spray and hormones and arrogance. Then again, my best friend had gotten high on meth and tried to kill me in my sleep, which was equally pathetic. Like Ryan, I was trying to stay a few steps ahead of the darkness in my own past. "Why didn't you tell anyone?"

"What was there to tell?" he said. "I was Wall Street high that night, and I was the one who brought the cocaine. Giving anyone else up would have ruined all of our futures."

I doubted that. Rich suburban kids always managed to glide down the waterslide of life without ever losing their shorts. "So you made a death pact?"

"A vow of silence," he said. "Saying anything to my dad or the deputies wasn't going to bring Daphne back."

"Someone broke that vow," I said. "And I think they're trying to get revenge for what happened. I think someone dumped Kristin in the alley behind Ultra. And I think that same person followed both of you to that party, spiked Amanda's drink, and gave her a ride. Only they didn't take her home. They left her in a snowbank. She's lucky she didn't die, but she might not be so lucky next time."

He snorted. "Is that really what you think this is about?" he said. "Look, I'm flattered, but I am not worth killing for. Especially with Amanda. I'm a pit stop on the way to whatever banker or lawyer or tech bro she mates herself with."

Men being bitter about their girlfriends wasn't new. But I hadn't heard one get bitter about the girlfriend he was caught cheating on when one of them was in the grave and the other got pretty damn close to it. "What does that mean?" I asked.

"It means small-town politics don't mean shit in the real world," he said, standing. "I've got class. I really hope I don't ever see you again."

"You might want to go home for a bit," I said. "You could be next, you know."

He shrugged. "I guess I don't care," he said. "I probably deserve it anyway."

* * *

The last place I wanted to be right now was Topsy's. Normally I liked my bartending gig, I enjoyed spending time with Aunt Gina, listening to all the bands that came through town. I had a few regulars who didn't bug me too much, and the music drowned out the ones who might want to. After sitting in the office all day, I didn't mind spending a few hours on my feet. Another round of beers for table four. Close out the tab for the couple in the corner. Banter, banter, repeat until 2:29 a.m.

But tonight, every customer felt like a suspect in a crime none of them knew had been committed. I was so close to putting all the pieces together, but pints and shots and cocktail orders stacked in a wall I couldn't see through. I kept checking my phone. Nothing new from Martin. Nothing new from anyone.

Around ten thirty Aunt Gina tapped me on the shoulder. I jumped so hard I dropped the glass I was drying. The shatter when it hit the floor startled me a second time. "I'm sorry," I gasped. For a second I forgot where I was. I was ready to grab a knife and fight back.

"Nope, I'm the one who's sorry," she said. "I should know better than to sneak up behind you. I'll get the broom. Just wanted to let you know that Jack is here. He wants to see you."

Jack was at the other end of the bar. He waved to me. I waved back, my heart still coming down from Aunt Gina's jump-scare. I still hadn't told her about what happened in Memphis. I planned on taking that secret to my grave.

"Can I get you anything?" I asked Jack.

"No time," he said. "I'm on a break; told the guys I'd go grab a pizza. But I wanted to bring you by a few things. I downloaded that footage you wanted."

"Well now I have to get you a beer," I said.

He laughed. "Next time," he said, turning his phone to me. "Besides, I owe Gina a solid. Consider us even."

He pressed play on his phone. The footage wasn't much to go on, especially silent and in black and white. Kristin arrived first with a group of four other girls, all shivering in tube dresses and platform heels and fake-fur shrugs. I could still see the cuts on her legs. "The girl from Ultra," he said. "Bartender confirmed that was her."

The bouncer took one look at their IDs and shook his head. They tried to protest, silently, but he wasn't having it, and they wandered off into the night. Two hours later, Amanda and Ryan tried the same, to a sequel effect. Amanda yelled at the bouncer, tried to hit him with her purse and missed. The same purse, I noticed, that I had retrieved from the snowbank.

"It's funny," Jack said, closing the window. "I actually pulled a third fake for you. Same town, East Beauty. I figured three girls, probably all in the same year. This girl came in about ten minutes behind—I can fast forward to there—and she wasn't passing at all for her photo. Think it might be an older sister's, even if she tried to tell me that she used to be a brunette."

He handed me the stack of IDs. Among them was Kristin's. Amanda's was in there too.

And so was Daphne's.

* * *

It was nearing three a.m. when I finally got to my apartment. I was more exhausted than I had ever been. I wanted to crash on my couch without even unfolding the bed. I wanted to fall asleep in my clothes. I was too tired to even take my shoes off. But I couldn't sleep. Not yet.

No wonder no one recognized Molly LaChance. Her yearbook photo, a year behind Daphne's, showed a girl with glasses and bad skin. But college is all about reinvention, some acne medication and contact lenses, her sister's old license, and some choice pieces from her wardrobe. The registrar at Raines had a first-year class of 437 people. He didn't have time to read headlines from downstate. If she said she was Daphne, she became Daphne.

Scrolling back through the #Apocolypse photos, I spotted Molly in the background of at least two, at the same party as Amanda and Ryan. I'm sure if I went back through the last days of Ultra, I'd find her there, too, right alongside Kristin.

Ryan's parting words haunted me. *I'm not worth it.* I didn't disagree; nothing worse than a sad-sack party boy, crushed under the weight of his own mediocrity. But it still didn't sit right. I didn't have a real motive, or any indication that anyone even loved Ryan enough to kill for him except for the personal knowledge that teenage girls have a bottomless capacity for viciousness.

I'm sure Amanda's parents had more money than I'd ever know, but there's wealthy and then there's rich, and she gave off the impression of being the second. The money in their family was new, it was on display, and it wouldn't last long. A couple of million in her daddy's bank accounts wasn't the kind of money that could cover up a murder. And what was Kristin's role in all of this? Something was missing and I couldn't stop until I found it.

I pretended I was back at my desk in Memphis. What would I need to know if I was writing this as a story? I had Amanda and Ryan, I had Daphne's obituary. I had to go deeper. I needed to know who they were in East Beauty, beyond the newspaper headlines and the fake IDs.

Martin had mentioned Amanda's mom was a singer. I looked back at his notes and typed her name. Her song "Diamond Life" had been a minor club hit in 1991, bigger in Europe than over here. Her album got middling reviews and she never had a follow-up single. Her wedding to real estate developer Alfred Harris was announced—but not the cover photo—in *People*, and I couldn't help but wonder if that was simply because they wanted to use "Six Carats for 'Diamond Life' Singer" as their headline. One gossip blog reported that she was making a play to join a *Real Housewives* franchise, complete with mocking commentary. A magazine photo showed her on a white couch, draped in beige and sunlight, announcing her lifestyle brand, Owl & Cork. I could almost hear the rattle of ice cubes in chardonnay.

And then there was the ground-breaking.

When I'd interned at the *Press & Sun Bulletin* in college, the reporter I learned under said that if I was ever short a story, there was always something sketchy in real estate. I pulled up the Real Property Tax website. I typed in Alfred Harris's name. He owned several properties, including a building in Midtown Manhattan, but there was only one parcel I was interested in.

Address: 119 Adcox Lane

Price: $4 million

Previous Owners: Josephine LaChance

* * *

My ringing phone woke me up. My laptop was dead, I was still dressed in my bartending hoodie and jeans, I had fallen asleep sitting up. Martin. I fumbled to slide my finger over the screen and mumbled a hello.

"You didn't sleep either, huh?" he said.

"What gave you that impression?" I said through a yawn.

"Credit my impeccable detective skills," he intoned. "That, and you sent me a text at about four a.m. What's on your mind?"

I had no recollection of any of that. Christ, I needed a good night's sleep. Hadn't gotten one since this case started. "What did I say?" I asked. I hope I didn't text anyone else in my sleep-starved state.

"You wrote 'found something. Call me when you wake up.' Only some of it is misspelled. Must be important."

"Yeah," I said. "Yeah, it is. Give me a few minutes and I'll be over. You sound better today."

"My fever broke around midnight," he said. "Still got the cough, though. Despite the lack of sleep, it's the best I've felt in days, which isn't saying much. But if you want to go back to bed, believe me, I understand."

"No," I said. It was all starting to come back to me. The property sale and the condos, the lifestyle brand and the police report. Maybe I'd look at my notes and they'd make no sense. Maybe I'd dreamed the whole thing. I wouldn't know until I plugged in my laptop. "I'll be over soon."

"I'll make us some coffee."

* * *

I didn't even stop to print it all out. We would have to work with tabs. Martin's coffee was hot and strong, exactly what we both needed. No bagels. There wasn't time to stop and get any.

"The one thing we've lacked this whole time is motive," I said as I set myself up on the couch. I didn't care about the blankets or the wastebasket. My heart was pumping too hard. "First I thought we just needed a motive for why someone would drug Amanda and leave her to freeze, but then I realized that person's motive was directly tied to Amanda's crime—and *her* motive."

"I figured it was all over the boyfriend," he said. "Ryan. His dad was the sheriff, after all, and that report was pretty damn sparse for a drowning."

"Maybe if it was just Amanda and Daphne," I said. "But having Kristin in there is what gave me pause. And that's a lot of effort to go to for one guy in a small town when you're on the verge of heading to college. If they had bludgeoned or stabbed Daphne to death, crime of passion sort of thing, maybe. But luring her out into open water always felt like something bigger. Because it was. A lot bigger."

I opened a new tab. I felt like I was giving the ugliest Ted Talk in the universe.

"The trail starts here," I said. "With Amanda's father. Mr. Alfred Harris, owner of Harris Brothers Construction. He buys a piece of property at 119 Adcox Lane, a properly formerly owned by Ms. Josephine LaChance, Daphne's grandmother, a property that's been in the family since the early nineteen hundreds. A demolition permit is first denied, with public comment from David LaChance, Daphne's father, who argues that the sale was contingent on Mr. Harris maintaining the home as a residential property. Then, six weeks later, the house, which Josephine had lived in up until just a few years previous, is suddenly condemned by the village. The permit gets approved and demolition begins. I'll let you decide whether it was money or the lovely Mrs. Charlene Black, Amanda's mother, who did all the persuading."

Martin let out a long sigh. "I'd say it's both," he said. "Go on."

I couldn't stop even if I wanted to. "In January, Mr. Harris unveils his plans for a row of three condos with a storefront for Charlene's lifestyle brand, Owl & Cork. Mrs. Sarah LaChance, Daphne's mother, leads the opposition. The main complaint is that it takes a beach formerly considered public and would completely privatize it, as well as block the view of the water from the road. Construction permit was denied. Then, two months later, Daphne drowns."

"Let me guess," Martin said. "Construction resumed after Daphne's death."

I opened the final tab. The groundbreaking photo, with the Harrises and the mayor, smiling in yellow hard hats and vests, holding golden shovels. "The buildings are slated to open next fall."

Martin leaned back. I held my breath and waited for his verdict. "What's Kristin's part in this?" he asked.

"Kristin's father is Mayor David Burgher," I said. "And he's been mayor for the last ten years. But he had a challenger in the last election who put up a pretty good fight. I'll let you guess who made the largest donation to his campaign."

"So what about Ryan?"

"Ryan brought cocaine to the party," I said. "It looks pretty bad if the sheriff's son has an eight-ball on him when his girlfriend drowns."

"Now to bring it all back to Perrine," he said. "Who left Amanda in that snowbank?"

I thought he'd never ask. I reached into my folder. "Meet Molly LaChance," I said, placing Molly's senior portrait and the fake ID on the coffee table. "Daphne's little sister."

* * *

I parked my car at the Century Estates apartments and waited. I'd done surveillance with Martin once before, a long night watching for someone who was sabotaging air-conditioning units during a heat wave. It was lonely work even with someone to talk to, but he was still too sick to leave the house. That meant I was on my own, blasting New Order through my earbuds to try and stay awake. At least he'd sent me with a thermos of coffee to keep me awake and warm. I'll sleep when I'm dead.

Half an hour crawled by before I saw Molly get off the East Line bus. She really did look like all her sister's photos. I took a final swig of coffee and followed her to her door. "Ms. LaChance," I said. "My name is Valerie. I work for the Wade Agency and I have some information on your sister's death. Do you have a moment to talk?"

It was the script Martin had given me and I just had to hope it worked. Everything we had was circumstantial, the nebulous netherworld between a conspiracy theory and a case. If she slammed the door in my face, if she called for a lawyer, we'd have nowhere else to go. She'd been so smart, so careful up until now. It was my job to trip her up. My heart was pounding from nerves and caffeine.

"Sure," she said. "Come on in."

Molly's apartment was considerably less opulent than Amanda's, a small studio in a mid-century complex. Formica countertops and fading carpets, elderly neighbors, and Hibachi grills on square cement patios. "I'm going to make some tea," she said. "Would you like some? I've got mint, rose hip, Oolong."

"No, thank you," I said.

She turned on the electric kettle and let it boil. She measured tea into a silicone manatee and placed it on the edge of her cup. Her deliberate calm made me squirm. "You sure I can't get you anything?" she offered. "A bottle of water?"

"The last time you offered a friend a drink, it was spiked with GHB," I said. "I can't take the risk that you'll dump me in a snowbank or a garbage dumpster."

She shrugged. "I have no reason to drug you," she said.

"Except that I'm about to have you arrested for attempted murder."

The kettle screamed. She made her tea and gestured for me to sit at the other end of her thrift shop couch. "Are you a cop?" she asked.

"No," I said. "I'm the one who found Amanda Harris in the parking lot of Wegmans. Where you left her."

"Did Amanda tell you that?"

"No," I said. "She didn't remember. It was quite a puzzle, but I figured it out."

Was she going to deny it? Attack me? Demand I leave before she called the cops, pitting us against each other with Perrine's Finest as our mediators? The last thing I needed was a couple of blues arresting me for trespassing and harassment. "Look," I tried. "I've got the evidence that puts you at the party and at Ultra the night of both attacks. I've got the ID you tried to use to follow them into the Lion's Head. You will get arrested, whether you tell me or not. The only question is whether you'll take them down with you—for what they did to Daphne."

She took a sip of tea that was too hot, wrinkled her face, and set the cup aside. "So you know," she said.

"I've got an idea," I said. "I know Amanda's father bought your grandmother's house, that he lied to your family about what he was going to do with it. I know about Ryan's dad and Kristin's mom. But I need you to fill in the plot holes."

She smirked. She let out a sad little laugh. "My family has been in East Beauty since the nineteen twenties," she said. "Back when it was all farms. My mother was raised in that house. My parents got married on that beachfront. East Beauty used to be a normal town, but it got absorbed by the Hamptons. People like the Harrises started treating it like a vacation property, then a second home, then a primary residence. It got too expensive for the rest of us to live there. My parents were barely able to pay the taxes on our home, let alone help out my grandmother with hers. When she got sick, we had to sell the house to pay for her nursing home. None of us wanted to, but we trusted Mr. Harris when he said he'd keep the property. That was our mistake, but we didn't have any other choice. And as soon as those papers were signed, he filed for demolition permits. We stalled them for a little while, but let's just say Ms. Harris got pretty persuasive with the Historic Review Board."

I couldn't believe I had been right. I'd half expected her to laugh in my face. But I wasn't over the finish line yet. "That still doesn't explain why Amanda and Kristin would kill your sister," I said. "The house was already sold and demolished. Their families had nothing to gain in her death."

"They had everything to lose while she was alive," she said. "Daphne wanted to be a journalist, and she put all that to work. She dug up the permits, she connected the dots, the money and the sex, the whole scheme. And she was going to expose it. Put it all on the Internet. All of it. Ryan's drugs, Amanda's slutty mother and scumbag father, Kristin's double-dealing dad. She had a lot more than just our house too. I've got the thumb drive, if you're interested."

I was interested. I had some of it, but I was sure there was more. How many other families had the Harrises—or their ilk—driven from their land with a lowball offer and cash on hand? That would have to come later. For now, I just needed her to talk. "Tell me what happened at the party," I said.

Her tea was finally cool enough for her to sip. "My best guess is that Daphne had a little too much to drink," she said. "And she went off on Kristin and Amanda. Told them she was going to spill all the gory details. They couldn't let that happen, so they got her in the boat and held her underwater. And of course, Ryan's dad didn't look too closely, or else he would have had to admit his son had enough powder to march an army. It was easier and safer for all of them to blame the victim and a couple of vodka tonics. But I knew from the minute the cops came to our door. She was training for the Olympics. She wouldn't have gone without a life jacket. She could have gotten back to shore."

Killers rarely seem like killers. That's the scariest part of all. We spend so much time afraid of a stranger with a machete that we don't notice the knife in our friend's hand. "So you went to Ultra," I said. "And you drugged Kristin. Why the garbage?"

"Trash goes out with the trash," she said.

I left myself wide open for that quip. "And Amanda?"

"That was almost by accident," she said. "I was actually following Ryan. But when I saw them fighting at the party, I knew I had an opening with Amanda. I offered her a ride home. I gave her a bottle of Coke spiked with GHB. She was already pretty drunk, so she took it without question. I was originally going to dump her in the park, but she said she was going to throw up. I pulled into the parking lot, shoved her in the snowbank, and drove off. I should have guessed someone would find her."

"It was lucky for you," I said. "Or you'd be facing a murder charge."

She shrugged. "At least now my story will be told," she said. "At least now they'll have to admit what they did to Daphne." She paused for another sip of tea. "Go on. You can call the cops."

I almost didn't want to. Sure she was guilty. Sure she'd methodically devised and executed a plan to kill two people and avenge her sister's murder. But neither of them had died. Hell, it might even become a party story in another year or so, *one time I got so drunk I woke up in a dumpster, in a snowbank.* Neither of them had to know. I could trade her story for an assurance she'd leave them alone.

The police came. She offered them tea as well. She calmly requested a lawyer, accepted the handcuffs, got in the car without bumping her head. But she wasn't going alone. I was going to see to that personally.

* * *

On Martin's recommendation, I called Amanda and Kristin and told them to meet me at the office. Told them I'd found who left them to freeze, that I needed them to come down and meet with the police to give their statements.

I paced the floors while I waited. The front buzzer nearly sent me to the floor. I let them in and offered them bottled water. I didn't take them into Martin's office. That seemed like sacred territory without him here. I got him on speaker phone, got them each an office chair, and got started.

"Molly LaChance," I said. "She's confessed to attacking both of you. She's agreed to turn herself in and face charges. You'll have to make statements to the police, but I thought I should tell you personally, give you a little time to prepare yourself."

"Daphne's little sister?" Kristin exclaimed. "Oh my God, why?"

I nodded.

"I just can't believe Molly would do this," Amanda said. "I always treated her like she was my own. What would make her do something this awful?"

I heard Martin cough on the other end of the line. I imagined he was standing behind me, giving me the words for what I was about to say. "Revenge," I said. "For the two of you killing her sister."

Silence.

Amanda finally spoke. "You were the one who saved me from freezing to death," she spat. "And now you come at me with accusations that I killed *my best friend?* Are you being serious right now?"

"Dead serious," I said. "Emphasis on *dead.* You two took Daphne out there. You both knew the storm was coming. You knew she was drunk. You convinced her to go out on the water, you threw out her life vest. You pushed her off the boat and held her underwater. Then you flipped the boat over and dragged it back to shore with your sob story ready to go. And for what? A parcel of real estate. A smutty story that everyone already knew."

Amanda started to cry. They were big fake tears, honed from years of practice—her mommy and daddy, the cops, Instagram stories with the hashtag #MentalBreakdown. I was not her intended audience. "It was an accident," she insisted. The same words she rehearsed a thousand times, the same outcry she'd made when I held her nearly frozen body. An alibi carved in ice, melting slowly to reveal the truth.

"It was all Amanda's idea!" Kristin blurted. "She said we had to. That Daphne was going to tell everything—about our parents, about Ryan, about cheating on the SATs, *everything.* She would have torn the whole town apart. None of us would have been spared. Our lives would have been ruined."

Drugs, sex, building permits. None of it was worth killing for. It never was, and yet it happened way too often. "So you took her life instead," I said.

"Don't listen to her!" Amanda cried. "She's just jealous."

"Jealous of *what?*" Kristin spat back. "Your drug-addict boyfriend? Your washed-up mom? She couldn't even get on *Real Housewives*, and you're as much of a joke as she is!"

I could watch these two tear each other apart all day. Honor among thieves was as mythical as Robin Hood, and when it came down to it, every broad was out for herself. I had the scar to prove that: an old friend I left behind in Memphis to fend for herself when the cops came to bust down her door.

"You ruined a family's whole life," I said. "They lost their property, their daughter and sister, and the two of you and Ryan all went on with your lives. Like nothing had happened. You just…moved on. I can't even understand that. How you can live with yourself, how you can cry for yourself? You two killed someone. How does that not haunt you?"

The tears stopped. Amanda let out a small puff of air, like she was exhaling from a hit off an imaginary joint. "I don't think about it," she said. "I try not to dwell on the past."

Money can buy a lot of things. But it can't buy empathy. That has to be earned, and it's hard to find that when you're buffered by servants and hedgerows and tinted windows.

"I should have known," Kristin lamented. "I should have known the second I woke up in that dumpster. I should have known this would all catch up to us in the end. And I should have never listened to you."

I was sick of listening to both of them. I picked up the receiver and spoke to Martin directly. "Do you want to call the cops?" I asked. "Or should I?"

* * *

I wanted to feel good about this case. I had rescued one damsel and put justice back in place for another. Instead, I went home and cried myself to into a long, dreamless sleep.

Molly was arrested on two felony assault charges and one misdemeanor for forging government documents that felt pale in comparison. The state police took Amanda and Kristin back to East Beauty to face their own juries. The papers had two good days of coverage before a referendum on building a new homeless shelter took over the front page. No journalists called me and I was fine with that. I didn't want my name appearing anywhere Katy might find it.

I woke up Friday morning with a fever and a sore throat. No good deed, as Aunt Gina would say, ever goes unpunished. In between coughing fits I managed to send Martin a text. *Your flu finally caught up with me.*

I was afraid of that, he wrote back. *You need anything?*

I needed a lot. But he could only bring me so much. *I'll be fine,* I wrote. *I just want to sleep.*

I should have known better than to lie to a detective. An hour later, Martin was standing in my doorway with coconut chicken soup from Flower House and a bag from Kinney Drugs. Tissues and tea, orange juice, and cold pills. He was wearing the three-piece with the dark blue pinstripes, a dark blue tie and pocket square, a pale-yellow shirt, polished Chelsea boots, and his gray wool overcoat. I had almost gotten used to seeing him in pajamas; now I was embarrassed to let him see me in mine.

"Just because I don't let myself have cold meds doesn't mean you have to suffer," he said, setting the bag on my coffee table. "Especially since I'm the one that got you sick."

"I'll have to file for worker's comp," I joked, cracking open a blister pack and washing down the two giant pills with the juice.

He laughed, a low rumble in his throat. "You did good work," he said. "That was a complicated case, a lot of factors, and you figured all of it out. I'm impressed."

"I wanted to walk away," I reminded him. "I only took it because you couldn't."

"That's not true and you know it," he scolded. "You took it because you knew it wasn't right, what someone did to Amanda. You didn't anticipate how big it would get, but you didn't turn away when it got hard and ugly. That's courage, Valerie, and I won't let you downplay it. That's what you need in this line of work. It's not for the faint of heart."

I wish I felt better about it. I saved a girl's life, sure, but I ruined three lives in the process. "Does it always feel so shitty?" I asked. "Solving a case?"

He leaned against my radiator. "Sometimes," he admitted. "You spend your days rooting around in human vice; you're seeing people at their worst. Sometimes you make a client's day a little better, but usually not without a little patina on it."

"Why do you do it?"

"Because someone needs to," he said. "There's not a lot of justice in this world, Valerie, so we do whatever we can to balance those scales. It doesn't always feel as good as it should, but you just have to trust that it's putting order back into the universe."

I came to work for the Wade Agency because I needed a job. But in the six months I'd been here, I'd seen Martin take on cases that threatened to pick his soul apart as though they were carrion birds. Cases he resisted, cases he dove into, each one a puzzle, each one with an outcome neither of us could have predicted from the outset. Even the cases that reminded him of the darkness in his own past, each one stretched beyond the simple act of order. He settled long-buried scores. He laid wandering ghosts to rest. Hell, one time, he told me, he tracked down a dog that belonged to a homeless woman. There was no money in it. No newspaper headlines. No glory. But each file he asked me to put away was a small justice restored. A wandering knight in a pinstriped suit of armor. I guess that made me his squire. There was nothing I wanted to be more.

I reached out my hand. For a handshake, a kiss, something just to feel connected to another human. He smiled. He laced his fingers through mine, his palms warm and soft. "Get some rest," he said. "Call if you need anything else."

"I will," I said, and I meant it.

My-O-My

O'Neil De Noux

Parents usually leave the bedroom of a deceased child unchanged but not the Vernets. The double bed lies stripped down to its sheet, pillows without pillow cases at the foot of the bed, the top of dresser and chest-of-drawers clear. The chifforobe stands open with only a few hangers in each. Nothing on the walls, the window curtains are closed to the bright sunlight outside. The room smells of lemon cleaner. I open the drawer of the small desk, find a Webster's dictionary, four pencils, a blank tablet, and a pencil sharpener. The other drawers are empty. So is the lone closet, more hangers but no clothes. I go back into the hall and down the mansion's spiral staircase.

The mother, Constance Vernet, turns to me from the living room's sofa. She's in a long dark gray dress with a high collar, her brown hair in a bun, no makeup. Looks to be in her mid-forties. She waves to her right as a man in his fifties steps into the living room.

"Mr. Caye, this is my husband, Zachary Vernet."

Zachary had been in his home office when I'd arrived a half hour earlier.

"So this is the private eye," says the balding man in the tailored dark brown suit as he sits in a stuffed chair. "I understand my wife gave you the pertinent details."

"Yes, she did."

When Mrs. Constance Vernet called me on the phone yesterday to hire me, she gave me the gist of the case—

Son Lloyd Vernet stabbed outside Club My-O-My four months ago, Sunday 2 a.m., April 4, 1948. Found in parking lot.

Mr. Vernet's voice rises, "What burns me up are two police agencies who won't even investigate the killing of my son. We've talked to New Orleans Police and the Jefferson Parish Sheriff and neither's working on the case. NOPD says the murder happened on the deck of the club, which is in Jefferson Parish. And the JP sheriff says the body was found in the parking lot in Orleans Parish, so it's an NOPD case. Meanwhile, we buried our son and no one's looking for his killer." Zachery Vernet slaps his knee. "We all know the reason. They don't give a damn about boys like my son."

Club My-O-My. Boys like my son. Haven't been to the club. The local radio ads say the club features America's most beautiful and talented female impersonators.

I take out my Moleskine notebook. "Where are Lloyd's personal effects?"

Mrs. V looks at her lap.

"What personal effects?" Mr. V asks.

"Everything that was in his bedroom."

Mrs. V says, "We gave his clothes to charity." She gives me a resigned look.

"Any notebooks? Diary? Journal? Address book?"

"What does that have to do with his murder?"

"He might have noted if someone had threatened him."

"Well, his stuff is gone."

I ask if they know of anyone who wanted to hurt Lloyd.

"Sons-a-bitches who hate boys like our son. Never figure why they get so hateful. They heckle the boys outside the club."

I nod and put that in my notes.

"Did Lloyd have any friends I can speak with?"

"No."

"Any siblings?"

"Brother at Notre Dame. Married sister in Pensacola."

Mr. V stands, pulls a white envelope from his inner coat pocket.

"Your retainer in cash. Five hundred dollars. I understand you charge twenty-five a day plus expenses."

"Yes, sir." I pull out my receipt book and he waves it away.

"Don't go over five hundred without checking with me."

"Do you have a photo of your son I can borrow?"

I wait in the foyer for Mrs. V to come down with a 4"x5" photo of her smiling son. He's leaning against a tree, arms folded. Good looking guy with curly blond hair. Mrs. V nods to me, turns away and I leave the house, stepping into the thick humidity of a typical New Orleans August. I take the seven steps down to the brick walkway, look back at the three-story Greek Revival on St. Charles Avenue. The mansion looks more like a bank than a home with four ionic columns supporting a second story balcony and wide gallery above. The bricks have been painted gray and two large magnolia trees in front cast long shadows across the façade.

* * *

I call the Detective Bureau, ask for my friend Frenchy Capdeville. He isn't in so I ask for Jimmy O'Malley who also isn't in, neither is Al Francona so I leave a message for Frenchy. Head over to the coroner's office, where it's all public record, to I pick up a copy of Lloyd Vernet's death certificate and autopsy report, take them back to my office.

The post mortem exam describes Lloyd Vernet as a well-nourished white male, 5'9" long (cadavers are measured in length, not height) and weighing one hundred fifty pounds with short blond hair and brown eyes. No scars, marks or tattoos listed. Toxicology report pending. The death certificate lists the cause of death as a stab wound of the heart. Manner of death—homicide. Lloyd was twenty-one years old.

The autopsy report lists six stab wounds—two in the left arm, one through the left hand, one through the right hand, one in the right shoulder and one in the chest, two inches from the sternum, which nipped the left ventricle of the heart. Wounds on the hands and arms are defensive wounds, the poor guy trying to block the knife. The pathologist lists the knife as a double-edged, nine-inch blade.

The coroner investigator's report lists the victim's personal items—clothes and an inexpensive Lancer wristwatch with broken crystal and a leather band.

* * *

Windblown rain bounces off my balcony's French doors and windows as I turn on the radio, find a blues station and listen to T-Bone Walker start up one of my favorites—*Call It Stormy Monday (But Tuesday Is Just as Bad)*. I turn my large, cushioned chair around to watch forked lightning dance over the nighttime rooftops across Barracks Street and Cabrini Park, thunder sending shivers through the old building. The French Quarter looks older in the rain. I take a sip of icy Falstaff and close my eyes, envisioning that boy coming out of the club at two a.m. and the knife impaling him, the painful, shuddering death. I see him stumble off the deck and into the parking lot to collapse, look up at the dark sky as the blackness takes him.

We know what happened. When it happened. Where it happened. But the elusive why and the more elusive who did it is out there getting drenched in the rain. The solution's always out there. I just have to find it.

The doorbell rings and I go over and hit the buzzer for the building's door, go out on the landing to look downstairs to see who I let in. Lt. Frenchy Capdeville takes off his raincoat, hangs it a hook outside my office door downstairs and looks up at me.

"You left a message?"

I wave him up and go back into my apartment for another beer.

My friend and mentor, this Zorro lookalike with curly black hair and pencil-thin moustache, raises his hand as he steps into my living room.

"Hit me."

I hand him a Falstaff and he moves to the sofa. He's in his well-worn brown suit, cigarette ashes dusting his lapel. I pull the easy chair back around to the sofa.

"So, what you need?"

"Four months ago, back in April, man killed outside the My-O-My."

He takes a drink of beer.

I go on. "Family tells me NOPD didn't handle it because they found blood on the deck of the club, which is in Jefferson, who won't handle it because the body ended up in the parking lot, which is in the city. I know the rule, wherever the body ends up works the case."

He takes another hit of beer.

"We worked that case. Came up blank."

"Worked? As in past tense."

Frenchy narrows an eye at me. "We got nothing. Midnight shift crew worked it. Det. Joe Chapman. I was busy with other cases."

"I need the reports."

He growls at me. "Victim's parents hired you?"

"Yeah."

"Okay. All right. We're up to our asses in cases. If you come up with anything, I'll move on it." He takes another hit. "Man, we drop the ball so many times. Not putting in the effort. I can't be sure but Chapman probably whiffed on this one because the victim was a transvestite."

"This is New Orleans, man. We don't do whiff on cases. No matter the victim."

"We? The parents know you're not really a detective. You're a private eye." He grins.

I take a hit of my Falstaff. How many murders do I have to solve before he stops with that joke?

He takes another deep draft of Falstaff, says, "I know. Anything goes here, but not everyone's on board with that."

"Have the managers at My-O-My complained about the lack of… anything?"

"Not to me or the captain."

We both drink our beer. Frenchy's only ten years older than my twenty-seven and the years in the Homicide Division have given his face lines I don't have.

He raises his hand, says, "Another smile."

In Frenchy lingo, a smile is a beer.

* * *

Park my pre-war DeSoto in the clam shell parking lot servicing all the restaurants, cafés, and nightclubs here at West End. My Bulova reads two p.m., a few hours before the first show at Club My-O-My. I put on my blue suit coat to cover my .357 magnum in its holster on my right hip, glance in the sideview mirror to straighten my silver and red tie, take out my Moleskine pocket notebook and a sharpened pencil before heading to the wooden steps leading up to the deck surrounding the club standing on wooden pilings covered with black creosote at the edge of Lake Pontchartrain.

A 6'5" bouncer with a crew cut, an appropriate scar on his chin, folds his arms to show me his muscles as I approach the front door My-O-My. He's in a black T-shirt and black slacks. I nod as I arrive, tell him who I am, hand him a business card.

"A private eye, huh? Like in the movies?"

"Exactly."

His upper lip curls.

"A wise guy, huh? We ain't open, yet. What you want?"

"I'm working the murder case."

"What mur…oh."

He takes in a deep breath, turns serious.

"I was here that night but I didn't see him leave."

"What did you hear about it?"

"Hell, we all talked about it but no one knows anything. It was foggy that night. He walked into the fog and ended up in the parking lot."

He makes a puff noise.

"Victim's folks hired me to look into the case. They're hurting."

He unfolds his arms, looks at my card again.

I ask for the manager, and he says, "He's inside. Lou Epstein. Office in back. Left side of the room."

"Hold on to my card. If you hear anything, give me a call."

I step into the main room and pause to take it in.

Long bars line both sides of the place, padded barstools for the customers. Tables fill the center area with a dance floor in back and wide stage facing the rows of tables, an orchestra pit on the right side. Bartenders wipe down the bars as I pass. Manager Lou Epstein sits behind a large black desk, a little guy with a cigarette dangling from his mouth. Epstein is bald on top, pushing sixty and wears a light green suit.

"What are you here for?"

"The murder. I'm a detective."

He sits back, waves me to a chair in his cramped office and I introduce myself, ask if he was here that night.

"Yeah. I was back here when one of my bouncers came and told me. You wanna question everyone, go ahead but don't get in the way."

"Do you remember Lloyd Vernet?"

"Barely. He was a dancer."

I ask if Lloyd had any friends at My-O-My.

"I wouldn't know."

"Y'all have problems with hecklers outside?"

"Hecklers? Yes. Bashers sometimes as well. They try to bash the performers but our bouncers run them off. Our guys who get beat up get beat up away from here."

"One more question. He left at two a.m. Is that when you close?"

"No. We close at five a.m. Different performers have different hours. He must have gotten off at two."

"He left alone?"

The manager shrugs.

I go back into the main room and watch them enter quietly—young, thin men moving to the dressing room. I follow the first ones in and they sit at a long counter in front of a wall of mirrors bathed in bright lights. I approach the first in line as he applies his make-up, introduce myself and spend the next hours talking to everyone who will talk with me in Club My-O-My—the performers—singers, dancers, musicians, bartenders, waiters, bus boys, and cooks. A few remember Lloyd but did not know him well, except for his only friend, Bobbie Pulline, who comes in after four, a good looking fellow with delicate features, standing a couple inches below my six feet.

I wait until he starts on his make-up and sit next to him along the counter, begin with, "I heard you were Lloyd Vernet's friend."

He blinks at me and I show him my credentials, tell him I'm working for Lloyd's folks.

"How well did you know Lloyd?"

"Only for the few months he worked here."

He turns back to the mirror and puts blush on his cheeks. "He was so young."

Pulline can't be more than twenty-five.

"He couldn't sing but was coming along as a dancer and looked great dressed up."

"He have any problems with anyone?"

"No."

"Any problems with bashers?"

"He got punched up once on Bourbon Street but two strip club bouncers ran them off."

"Any trouble from the bashers outside My-O-My?"

"Just taunts."

"Were you here the night it happened?"

"No. It was my night off." His sucks in a deep breath, shakes his head.

He tells me Lloyd was a reader. Read books. Novels. He reaches into a drawer under the make-up table and pulls out a book.

"He was reading this one."

Hemingway's *For Whom The Bell Tolls*.

"Kinda prophetic, wouldn't you say?"

Back in the main room I come across bartender Doug Jenson as he sets up a line of clean glasses. He doesn't remember Lloyd Vernet.

He tells me, "Only homo-hating basher I come across outside is a jackass I went to Fortier with. You know, high school. Dickie Barnett. Been a bully all his life. Our bouncers ran him off a couple times."

From everyone—the bashers don't mess with the customers, just the singers and dancers, the ones dressed up as women. A pretty brunette walks past me and I do a double take and Jenson snickers.

"Good lookin', huh?"

"Uh."

"Don't sweat yourself. That's a real girl. She's the head cashier. Works in the back." He nods beyond the orchestra pit.

The other bartenders know nothing about Lloyd and the killing.

I move to the office the head cashier had gone inside and she looks up at me from behind a small desk, her right hand on the handle of an adding machine.

"Sorry to interrupt." I hold up my credential pouch. "I'm a private detective. You have a minute to talk?"

She runs her free hand through her dark brown hair, blinks her large brown eyes and tells me no. She wears her hair in a long page boy, the only short haircut I like on a woman. Too bad the trend after the war has been with shorter hair on women.

"I take a break at the first intermission. At about six. I'll be at the bar on this side."

I leave a card on her desk, step out of the club, check the nearby restaurants, all within walking distance—Fitzgerald's, Kirsch's, and Brunings. Get nothing. Like My-O-My, they all stand suspended over the lake on creosote-covered pilings. Get back during the first show, watch a rollicking jazz number, dancers on stage in chiffon and sequins and feather boas and tight dresses, high heels. Three singers join them, one on each side of the stage, one in the center and they belt out Charlie Parker's "Billie's Bounce," followed by the lead singer with a melodic rendering of "Do You Know What It Means To Miss New Orleans."

A light haze begins to rise from the customer's cigarettes as they sit at the tables in front of the stage. Couples mostly, looking no different than customers at other nightclubs like The Blue Room at the Roosevelt Hotel and Starlight at the Jung Hotel. In their thirties and forties, laughing at the banter onstage, belting down cocktails. Having a good time.

The head cashier comes out of the back just as the stage show takes a brief intermission, the band switching to big band music. She moves to the bar just down from where I stand and signals the bartender who hands her a bottle of Coca-Cola. She climbs on the stool, leans her back against the bar, and takes a sip. She's in her mid-twenties, wears a fitted blue dress. She gives me a cocky look as I step up, the kind teenage girls used to give me when they knew they were good looking. I glance at the bartender, ask for a root beer.

"Barq's," I tell him.

"If you're investigating anyone here, you can get lost," says the head cashier.

"I'm here about the murder." My root beer arrives, and I take a sip of the root beer with bite, the one with extra caffeine. I ask her name, and she sips her Coke, sticks out her hand for me to shake.

"Claudia D'Amico."

D'Amico. That's Italian.

Her right eyebrow raises. "A private eye, huh?"

Her face loses the flippant look. She's not sure she remembers Lloyd Vernet, might have seen him but knows nothing about him. I show her the picture and she shakes her head.

"What have you heard about it?"

"Not much. He was stabbed outside. People think some homo-hating lunatic did it. Caught him alone in the fog." She shudders.

"Were you here that night?"

She nods, says, "Earlier. I leave at midnight most nights."

We sip our drinks and the band starts up again and couples move to the dance floor.

"Did you like the show?" Claudia asks.

"It's pretty damn good."

She raises her Coke to several of the performers talking with customers.

"A lot of our boys are heterosexual. Have wives. They just like to dress up like women."

She takes a sip of Coke, adds, "We've had Howard Hughes in here, Carmen Miranda, Alec Guinness." She presses a finger against her nose and bends it. "Mafiosi come in here on a lark, showing out-of-towners the ass-end of show business as we call it. But it is show business."

"Mafiosi?"

"Someone mentioned names like Cardone, Badalamente." She looks at the watch on her left wrist. "Have to go back before the second floor show."

Claudia climbs off the stool, shakes my hand again and says she'll ask around, maybe someone remembers something. I watch her walk away and the bartender steps close.

"That's the most she's said to anyone since she's been here."

I tell him. "Private eyes always get the girl. Don't you go to the movies?"

He gives me a sneer.

The second show is like a beauty contest runway with a parade of "the world's most beautiful boys in women's clothes" as the advertising says. The songs start up and the acts come on and I go outside to watch people enter and leave. There are no hecklers, and I leave before the rain comes.

* * *

The next evening, after a second night of getting nothing on the case, I open the French doors, as I usually do, and sit and drink a Miller High Life and look at the oaks and magnolias across the street in the park and the black sky above the rooftops of the old Quarter. Frenchy shows up with the police reports at eleven and I hit him with a Falstaff. He plops on my sofa, takes a drink of beer, puts the bottle on the coffee table, leans back and closes his eyes.

"What a damn day," he says. "Guy shot to death over a parking spot. Another guy tried to hang himself because his wife left him. Tried to use the second floor pipes outside his boarding house. Guy built like a rhino. Broke the pipes. Went next door with the rope still around his neck and borrowed his buddy's 1911."

My 1911 Colt 45 semi-automatic pistol sits in a desk drawer in my office downstairs.

"Took it to the ditch behind the houses and blew his brains out. Another guy robbed the Whitney on St. Charles. Ran outside like a bat outta hell only the mask he wore messed up his vision and he ran headlong into a telephone pole. Knocked himself out."

"Whitney on St. Charles? That's my bank."

"It was your money. He went in with a Colt .38 and told the teller, 'Gimme Lucien Caye's money.'"

Cops. All frustrated stand-up comics.

"Let me rest a minute. You read the reports. You won't believe how inept we can be."

Ten 8x10" black and white photos of the scene show the blood on the deck and steps, a picture of the club lit up in the background, a dog sniffing at the blood dotting the white clam shells of the parking area, the body of Lloyd Vernet lying on his back, arms curled in front of him, legs outstretched. There's a close-up of his face and the chest wound visible. I look again. Lloyd isn't wearing shoes.

The first officers on the scene checked Lloyd for vital signs, traced the blood trail to the steps and up the deck of My-O-My, talked to three people, all employees of My-O-My. Did not canvass. Didn't write down license plate numbers of the cars in the lot. Neither did the detectives when they arrived. Det. Joe Chapman who misspelled Lloyd's last name as Verget was the only detective to write a daily report on the murder.

In his follow-up report, Chapman spends most of his time describing how the stabbing occurred on the deck over the water, which means the crime occurred in Jefferson Parish. He spoke to employees—no names— and passersby outside the night after the murder. Again, no names. He says he canvassed the nearby restaurants, and no one saw anything. His final follow-ups were two phone calls to the manager of My-O-My a few days later to see if any new information had surfaced.

"Pitiful, huh?" Frenchy says.

"You let him close the case."

"I was out of town. Detective Sergeant Harvey Evers signed off closing it down. I told you, it slipped through my fingers. Notice how ole Chapman didn't mention the victim was in his stocking feet?"

"Yes, I did. The killer stole his shoes?"

"Unless someone came along and took them. Happens. Had a suicide once on the river batture."

Batture—the land between the levee and the water's edge.

"Man left a suicide note in car parked nearby, had gunshot wound to the temple, contact wound. No gun on the scene. We found the gun two days later. A teenager had picked it up and was showing it to his friends when his dad caught him and called us."

"Happens? Who found Lloyd's body? Cops didn't get the name of who found him, did they?"

"Anonymous phone call."

Frenchy lets out a long breath. "Never heard of a robbery a case where someone robbed someone for their shoes."

The photos show the wristwatch with the broken crystal on Lloyd's left wrist and the wounds on the hands.

I look at the reports again, drop them on the coffee table and Frenchy's eyes blink open.

"That's all the investigation a boy who dresses like a girl gets, huh?"

Frenchy curls his lip, takes a hit of beer.

What with the lip curling?

"Got Francona and Dickens working their asses off Back-a-town. Little colored boy got strangled to death two nights ago. See anything in the newspaper?"

I shake my head.

"Course not. Colored folk are killed, not murdered. But we're working it. Chief's already cautioned me about spending too much time on the case and I reminded him he has a seven year old boy, doesn't he?"

Frenchy holds up his hand. "I can still see the little boy's hands." He takes another hit of beer. "The face was lifeless, blued tongue protruding, body contorted and his little hands looked so delicate. I touched them at the postmortem, whispered to the little fella I'd catch who did it." Frenchy looks at me.

"Can only do so much, you know."

Later, after Frenchy leaves, I go through the pictures again, look at Lloyd Vernet's hands clenched in front of his chest and wonder, like the dead little boy's mother, how many times did Lloyd's mother kiss his hands when he was a baby.

* * *

The one-story wooden stationhouse of the Jefferson Parish Sheriff's Office stands a couple blocks from the end of Metairie Road near Causeway Boulevard with large letters JPSO printed in dark blue on the white wall facing the road. The desk sergeant asks what I want and I tell him about the case and he tells me a detective will see me.

"You're in luck," a short, thin, dark-complected man in a light blue suit says as he shakes my hand. "I'm Detective Frank Castellano. I'm the one who went out there. We turned it over to NOPD. The body was theirs."

Castellano is in his early twenties with eager brown eyes.

"I wanted to work the case, but our chief deputy nixed it." He raises his left hand to show me his wedding ring. "I was married right after the murder and…you married?"

"No."

"Well, it's a busy time, especially with an Italian wedding."

"Did you write a report on what you did?"

"Uh, no. But I should have my notes."

"Can I see them?"

"If I can find them. If I do, I'll call and tell you what I got. Probably just time of notification, arrival, and what I saw."

"What do you remember?"

"Lotta blood."

"Do you remember speaking to anyone?"

"Uh, I spoke to the NOPD guys."

"Any witnesses? Anyone at My-O-My?"

"Don't think so."

I thank him, rise to leave, pass him a business card and he gives me his.

"No offense but you look young to be a detective."

"Twenty-three. The Chief Deputy's my uncle. You gonna keep on the case?"

"Yep."

He shakes his head. "Wish I could. We don't get many whodunits out here. We get barroom killin's, husband and wife killin's, people killin' people they know." He stands and walks me out. "Chief Deputy says murders like the My-O-My ain't worth a lotta effort, like mooks killin' mooks."

Black folk.

"I think that's crap," Det. Frank Castellano says. "My uncle's full of it sometimes." He leans close. "The sheriff's worse." He sticks his hand out for me to shake. "Just let me know if I can help you."

* * *

Back at My-O-My, head cashier Claudia D'Amico tells me she's confirmed Lloyd Vernet had left alone the night of the murder. She's in a cranberry colored fitted dress with a high collar.

"How do you know?"

"Couple bartenders saw him leave. They told the police."

Probably the same bartenders who didn't remember anything to me.

"Was he wearing his shoes?"

"Shoes? Why wouldn't he?"

"Do you know who found the body? Called police?"

"No."

"How did he get to work?"

"That I do know. The West End bus. Most of us take it." She points her chin to the left. "Bus stop at entrance of the parking lot."

She looks down at the papers on her desk, reaches for the adding machine and I ease out of her office.

I find the costumer in the wardrobe room and he waves me over when I ask if he has a moment. He's a heavy-set man in a pink chiffon dress and I tell him who I am and ask if he could give me Lloyd's shoe size. He checks a list and tells me, "Vernet wore a size eight."

More canvassing inside My-O-My gets me nowhere, neither does more canvassing inside and outside of Fitzgerald's, Kirsch's, and Brunings, as well as two seafood places specializing in take-out orders and two small barrooms—Clearwater's and Sally's Long Tall Bar which isn't long or tall. Do learn there were a couple car burglaries in the parking lot the last few months and very little, if any, police presence in the area.

Three young guys stand at the bottom of the steps leading up to My-O-My. They separate, move out of the way as two couples go up the steps. The three reassemble and I step over to them. All three wear T-shirts and dungarees rolled up to show their high-top black tennis shoes.

"You got a cig?" the largest asks.

"Don't smoke."

I lean against a post at the bottom of the steps. The three collect at the other post, all three watching me. I watch them back, glance at my watch, have to turn my wrist to pick up the streetlight. It's ten p.m. Two more couples arrive, two come out, the men chuckling, the women chattering. The three eyeballing me take a few steps away. About fifteen minutes later, the biggest of the three—a few inches smaller than me but thicker around the middle with a crew cut—takes a step my way and calls out.

"You a cop or something?"

"Or something."

"What you waiting for?"

One of the other says, "Your boyfriend?"

The third one kisses the air.

"Any of you Dickie Barnett?"

The biggest glares at me, the other two taking a step back.

The one who blew me a kiss says, "Whaddya mean 'or somethin'?"

"I'm a private detective."

Two of the performers come out, both in dress shirts and trousers. Easy to spot as they still wear makeup. The three jerks start to follow, have to move past me and I step in their way. The biggest guy jumps back, opens his arms before balling his hands into fists.

"Don't even think about it, Dickie. I was an Army Ranger. I clean up all three of you before you can lay a hand on me. They teach you judo at Fortier?"

"We ain't doin' nothin'," the big guy says.

"We just tease them," says the smallest.

I pull out the picture of Lloyd Vernet, show it to the big guy. "Are you Dickie Barnett?"

"So what if I am?"

He doesn't look at the picture. I step closer, put it in his face. "This kid got murdered right here." I show the picture around so they can all see it. "Right here. Were you guys around that night, heckling people, bullying someone weaker than you? Did one of you jackasses stab him with a knife?"

If truth could not be easily concealed, if eye-opening looks are truthful, if the surprised looks on the faces are genuine, then these guys didn't kill Lloyd. *If.*

The shortest says, in a shaky voice, "Man, we don't know nothing about stabbing anyone."

The middle says, "We don't carry knives."

"We just tease them, man."

I pull out my small pouch of business cards and pass one to each.

"If one of y'all did it, you others should call me. Big difference in court between a witness and an accomplice. If any of you saw something that night, you can bring some relief to the dead boy's parents. They're hurting."

They look at each other, start backing away and keep going into the parking lot to climb into what looks like a 1936 Ford pickup truck. It leaves a few minutes later.

* * *

Outside Kirsch's Restaurant the following evening a man named Joe Hanratty tells me a short guy with a knife tried to rob him on the Saturday night before Mardi Gras. That was in February. Couple months before Lloyd's murder.

"He came up on me like you did. Right out here. Pulled out a knife and told me to give him my wallet. I tried to but dropped it and he asked me my shoe size."

I look up from my notebook. "Run that by me again."

He does, adding the man scooped up his wallet and ran across the parking lot.

"What about your shoes?"

"Told him I wore a size nine and he just took my wallet."

I write the description he gives me of the robber—white male, frizzy brown hair, about 5'8", thin, wearing a pea-coat and dark slacks and dirty white shoes.

"You report it to the police?"

"Naw. I only had three bucks in the wallet. I don't want to…you know… the police."

"How big was the knife?"

"Like a Bowie knife."

The blade of a Bowie is twelve inches long with a single sharp edge so I ask if the knife looked sharp on each side of the blade.

"Yeah. Like one of them stilettos."

I go back to My-O-My and run the description past the bartenders and bouncers, who don't seem to notice anyone. I had to re-introduce myself to each except bartender Doug Jenson, who remembers me but doesn't recall any frizzy-headed guy. Claudia D'Amico has not seen any frizzy-headed guys in recent memory.

"Knew one in high school, but he's a priest now in Puerto Rico or maybe Costa Rica."

On my way out, she says, "You keep working at it, Monsieur Caye. I have confidence in you."

* * *

At three p.m., the following day, I pick up the phone, call My-O-My to tell Claudia the killer's in custody.

"You solved it?"

"Not exactly, but I helped." I tell her I'll come by later with details after I tell the victim's parents about it.

A half hour earlier, Lt. Frenchy Capdeville had called me at my office and said, "We caught an armed robber with a .22 last night who asked his victim his shoe size."

"What?"

"He got the man's wallet and turned to leave only a patrol car was passing by and we caught him. Took me four hours but he copped out to your murder."

My murder.

"Can I come see him?"

"He's already booked in Parish Prison."

"Did he have frizzy hair, like I told you?"

"Yep. Floyd Hicks, 5'8", thin build with light brown frizzy hair."

A second later I come back with. "You sure he's the guy?"

"Went back to his place and he gave us five wallets, including Lloyd Vernet's. He said he killed the pretty boy by mistake, slipped on the steps. Lloyd wouldn't give him his shoes. They were new. Two-tone Florsheims. Jackass was wearing them when we caught him."

"Slipped on the steps? There were six stab wounds."

Damn.

"Sometimes, murder doesn't make sense. Just hope the DA accepts the charge and doesn't send me to Jefferson Parish to file. No telling what goes on out there in the country."

"Gotta go," he says.

"Wait. The little boy," I said. "With the hands."

"Yeah. We solved that one too. It was his drunk-ass uncle. The boy was making too much noise."

Before I leave for the Vernet's, I close my eyes and think about what I'll tell them and tell everyone at My-O-My.

What do I tell them?
Murder doesn't make sense?

Ill Met By Moonlight

A Benjamin Enoch Mystery

Luke Deckard

"Truth, reason, and love keep little company together nowadays," I quoted Shakespeare to Michael Finch. Michael was a thirty-six-year-old hedge-fund boy from the city. He was muscular and well-dressed, with a £200 haircut, but had a face like he hadn't slept in days. Dark stubble grew on his cheeks, and purple circles hung under his eyes—for good reason. He had a midsummer wedding planned in four days. The only problem was that the bride had vanished, and he wanted me to find her.

We sat at a corner table at the Oscar Bar and Restaurant on Charlotte Street after twelve. I drank a sparkling water. Michael wanted a glass of Domaine Laurent Roumier: Clos Vougeot Grand Cru, 2013. When the thick-browed waitress said they didn't sell it by the glass, he demanded the bottle without checking the price. I did. That sucker cost £240. It didn't bother me; I wasn't footing the bill.

"Where's this note your fiancée left?" I asked.

"Here." Michael pulled a handwritten note from his cream blazer:

Michael. I can't go through with the wedding. Forgive me. Jessie.

He confirmed it was Jessie's handwriting. I told him to walk me through what happened.

"I came home Tuesday night, about nine, and found that note on the kitchen table. I phoned Jess, but her mobile was off, and her Facebook and Instagram accounts were deleted. I called our mutual friends—they hadn't seen or heard from her. And then called Will Kirk, who produces the play Jessie performs in, and he said she quit without reason that afternoon. The police came, and I showed them the note. They said she wasn't a missing person since Jessie left of her own accord, they can't, i.e. won't, do anything." Michael took a messy sip of wine. A violet line pressed between his lips.

"Tell me about your relationship."

Michael's romance with Jessie Holden was a whirlwind. They met in November at Holy Trinity Brompton, where his father, Rev. Isaac Finch, was the minister. By January, they were in love, moving in together in February, and by March they were engaged and planning a midsummer wedding. Jessie's career was unstable—she sold perfume at Selfridge's while auditioning for plays without luck. As Providence provided, Michael's father was pals with Will Kirk, who got her a role in *Moulin Rouge* as a background singer and dancer. Coincidentally, Jessie was also an excellent dancer with a good voice.

"When did you see Jessie last?" I asked.

"Monday morning. I stayed overnight at the office for a call with my Japanese clients at midnight and two. Jessie texted me that night, around seven, saying she was going out for drinks."

"With who?"

"I don't know, friends." He shrugged.

"Maybe she didn't want you to know?"

"Could there be another man?"

Michael went red, and balled his hand into a tight fist.

"Only entertaining possibilities, not putting ideas in your head."

He huffed and drank more wine.

"What about Jessie's family?" I asked.

"She's an only child and her parents were killed eight years ago in a car accident. She was only nineteen." He paused. "Christ, why did she leave? I must salvage the wedding. You gotta find Jess and bring her back."

I smirked. "Hold on there. I'll look for her, maybe even find her, but if she has a reason not to come back and marry you, I'll respect that. And no amount of money will buy her location. Is that clear?"

There was a slight squint on Michael's face. "Enoch, if there's one thing I know, every man has his price…"

"I don't."

"Then I'll hire someone else," Michael said.

I pushed my chair out. "Okay. Good luck finding your fiancée before Saturday."

"No. Wait. Just stay seated," Michael ordered.

He didn't like being rejected, and I didn't like being told to stay in my seat, so I stood up.

"You need to decide why you're hiring me, Michael."

He leaned forward and rubbed his tired, stubbled face. "I miss her, man. And I just…." he huffed.

"You want an explanation?"

"Dammit, yes. Calling off the wedding will be humiliating. My dad will never let me hear the end of it."

"Give me until Friday, and don't do anything drastic. It's possible she has cold feet and needs to clear her head. I'll head over to the Piccadilly Theatre to the *Moulin Rouge* and ask around now. What are Kirk's details?" I put them in my phone.

"I'll phone ahead and fill Kirk in," Michael said.

"I'd rather you didn't."

After he transferred my retainer, he sent me a few pictures of Jessie, gave me four names and numbers of her friends.

As I rose, Michael said: "And Enoch, if there is another man…I want his balls served to me on a silver platter."

"If you say so."

As I walked out to find his missing bride-to-be, I pictured Michael prepared to eat another man's balls.

* * *

I walked to the Piccadilly Theatre on Denman Street. The sun was high, and the sky was clear. I appraised Michael. He was as sweet as a lemon—obnoxious, flashy, and bossy. If I had the luxury of turning down jobs, I might've done so with him—but I had rent and bills to pay, and virtue never stays off the taxman.

What would Jessie's story be if and when I found her? Another man? Or was Michael overbearing? Neither would surprise me, but getting an answer wouldn't hurt either party.

Looking at the pictures of Jessie Holden on my phone, she had a pretty face, soft features, auburn hair, and a trim build. She wasn't a starring lady, more of a half-decent supporting actress. She looked sweet. This wasn't a woman I expected a power-obsessed hedge-fund boy to go for—I expected fake tan, eyebrows, tits, and lips bursting at the seams with filler. A saline and silicone trophy. Not a flesh-and-blood woman.

At the Piccadilly stage door, a dark-eyed black woman wearing gray leggings and a black V-neck shirt that hugged her shapely figure sucked on a vape pen. The layers of makeup and vibrant red lipstick suggested she was a performer. She stood with a chubby white man in a blue and green tartan suit with leathery skin and manufactured white teeth.

"I'm Ben Enoch, I'm looking for Will Kirk."

"Aye, Mr. Enoch, that'd be me," the chubby man with a Scottish accent said. "Mike said ya were comin.'"

"Of course he did. Can we talk about Jessie Holden?"

The name sparked a reaction on the woman's face.

Excuse us, Kira," said Kirk before inviting me for a "wee word."

The office was small. Kirk sat behind a cluttered desk piled with headshots. Against the wall was a two-seater couch, which I sat on. On the stone walls were posters of the theatre's more respectable plays: *Who's Afraid of Virginia Woolf?* and *A Streetcar Named Desire.*

"Are you Canadian, Mr. Enoch?"

"I'm American."

"No shite. You donae sound it, pal."

"No shit. Mr. Kirk—"

"Kirk," he said.

"Can you tell me what happens on Tuesday?"

Kirk sucked his teeth. "A shame tae lose her. Jessie cleared out her things and was gone. I wish there was more I could tell ya, but that's all I know. This doesnae help Mike's situation."

"Mind if I ask around?"

"Can I be blunt? Performers come and go, aye. Mike's having a rough time acceptin' the situation. Who wouldnae? But Jessie doing a runner should tell him all he needs tae know—she didnae love him. A lass like her isnae the one you marry."

"A girl like what?"

"Leaves you high and dry after givin' her the world! Doesnae take Sherlock bloody Holmes tae deduce it. Mike's better off." Kirk laughed.

"Is Jessie the type to fool around behind Michael's back?"

Will squirmed. "Ah, actors muck around, don't they? I see it this way: if she wasnae, she would've. She'd have broken his heart eventually. Tell Mikey tae cut his losses and drop it, aye?" Kirk looked at his watch. "I've must go, Mr. Enoch. And I'd kindly ask you not to disturb the performers today."

Kirk showed me to the stage door and shut me out. I wanted to get back inside and ask around, but first, I needed to take care of something.

I called Michael.

"Mr. Enoch, hi."

"I explicitly told you not to call Kirk and tell him I was coming," I said.

"He's a family friend. I had to."

"All you did was tip him off."

"I don't appreciate this tone. I've hired you—"

"Michael, you're paying me to do things my way, not yours. Understood?" I scolded him like a bratty child.

There was silence, then: "What did Kirk say?"

"You should drop it," I said.

"Christ, why?"

"Says she would've broken your heart."

"You kidding me? He actually said that? Shit. I'm calling him..."

"Do that, and I'm done."

"I'm just meant to sit here and do nothing?" Michael shouted.

"Yes, dammit. Let me do my job." I hung up.

"Hey, you." The woman from earlier held the stage door open. "Kira, right?"

"Did Kirk tell you about Jessie?" she asked.

"No. Why, do you know something?"

She looked behind her. "Are you a cop?"

"Private Investigator. Do you need a cop?"

"I can't talk now, but I think Jessie's in trouble. Can you meet me at the Century Club at eleven p.m.? Give my name at the desk—Kira Scott. I'll be at the bar."

"See you there."

* * *

It was just eleven when I arrived at the Century Club. I wore a slim-fit powder-blue T-shirt under my dark blue blazer, wool socks with green turtles, and Doc Marten dress shoes. I was clean-shaven, neat, and smelt of Dior Sauvage. I felt like four million bucks.

The club's lounge was dark and intimate. Dance music thumped so that conversations had to be close.

The day had been a bust. That afternoon, I called the four women Michael said were Jessie's friends. The three I spoke with had the same story: they knew her through Michael, weren't close, and didn't know where she went. The fourth wouldn't pick up or call me back. I wondered if Michael knew any of Jessie's real friends. I hoped Kira was one.

Kira sat cross-legged at the bar with a white wine. She wore a red, low-cut summer dress dotted with white flowers. Her shapely legs shimmered in the twinkling fairy lights. She was beautiful.

"I wasn't certain you'd show," Kira said.

"You're all I've got."

"Hope I don't let you down." She smiled.

"Unlikely." My cheeks blushed.

We chatted a while and nursed drinks to loosen up. Kira told me about plays and TV shows she'd worked on, and I told her about my failed attempt at being a journalist, which spiraled into becoming a PI. Then the conversation moved to Jessie Holden.

"So you've no idea why Jessie bailed?" Kira asked.

"Not yet," I said, sipping a double Highland Park.

"Sorry, you're here to ask me questions, huh?"

"That's usually the way it works." I smiled. "Why do you think she's in trouble?"

"Tuesday was mad! Around eleven, I was vaping at the stage door when Jessie stormed up with this big bald-ass white guy. Her eyes were red—definitely crying. I asked if she was okay, but the man wouldn't let her talk. No idea if he was a lawyer or something, but he was an intimidating motherfucker. They were there for less than ten minutes and left with a bag of her things. The guy had her by the arm. I followed them out. She wouldn't bloody acknowledge me. They got into a car, then the jerk-off sped away, and Jessie was gone. I thought maybe she was fired, but when I asked the director, he said Jessie quit because of a family emergency." Kira paused and took a drink. "Whatever the hell I witnessed wasn't a family issue."

"Did you tell Michael about this?" I asked.

"No." Kira deflated. "That's why I'm telling you—I felt guilty not saying anything, but I don't really know him. I'm worried she's in trouble."

"Do you remember the car?"

"I can do more than that." Kira took out her phone. "I have a picture."

It was blurry, but she'd captured the left corner of a silver Tesla and a partial on the license plate: BD51. Kira air-dropped the photo to me.

"This is helpful, thanks."

"So, is this where you run off into the night now that you got what you wanted?" Kira said.

"Who said I got everything I wanted?" I said.

"Another drink?" Kira grinned.

***

Three days before the wedding.

I was at my office on Percy Street at nine a.m. with a black coffee and a cinnamon bun from Pret. My head was groggy from the previous night. Memories flooded back. The drinks, the kissing, Kira and I in an Uber returning to my place. The shower running, a door shutting. I wanted to text Kira to tell her I had fun and would like to see her again. I decided to wait a bit—it doesn't matter how keen you are; the rule is never to show it. I don't know who created that rule or why appearing keen is a turnoff—it's a nuisance.

Tucking into my cinnamon bun, I replied to a string of text messages from Michael asking for an update—I told him there was nothing concrete to report, but I had leads. Well, one lead—the Tesla. And there was only one quick way to ID that partial plate. I made a call.

"DC Roubina Mistri," she said down the line.

"Rubes, it's Enoch—need you to run a plate for me."

"Good God. No good morning, how was your weekend, fancy a drink and a natter—just straight to it. Rude-ass Americans."

"Sorry. It's a time-sensitive case." I explained the situation and gave her the partial plate.

"This Finch guy sounds like a prick."

"He's a hard pill to swallow. But he pays well."

"One of these days, I should go rogue, like you."

"But I like our little team-ups...we're like Thor and Hulk."

"More like Storm and Howard the Duck."

"Ouch."

"Okay, Enoch, so you want me to illegally run the plates and then illegally tell you who they belong to, putting my neck and career on the line so you can find this guy's runaway bride?"

"Bingo! I promise to take you out on the town afterward."

"I don't wanna go out on the town. But a movie night with beer and pizza on Sunday would do."

"Done."

"Fine. Meet at the Picture House Central in three hours."

* * *

It was lunchtime when I met Rubes at our usual spot—the rooftop bar of the cinema, with a straight view down Haymarket and Big Ben. She was sat with a pot of tea and a piece of lemon cake. The weather was overcast, but the air was warm and breezy. She wore a forest green top, a navy blazer, and matching jeans. Her dark pixie cut whipped in the wind. Rubes never wore much makeup except for dark purple lipstick, which matched her brown complexion expertly. Today was no exception.

"This isn't good," Ruby said stiffly as I sat, cracking open a bottle of sparkling water.

"Why?"

"Your Tesla is registered to a shipping company owned by Lawrence Moran—he's a person of interest to us. Suspected of laundering and racketeering. We just haven't landed the proof. The problem is he doesn't match the description of the man driving the Tesla, but I checked Moran's associates, and it must be Jack Powers. He's an enforcer with links to the Clerkenwell crime syndicate and the Brindles. He's been working with Moran's people for a year or two. He's a nasty old dog."

"Why isn't he off the streets, then?"

"Connections, money and circumstantial evidence. If Powers is involved, or Moran, come in, let's talk. Make a proper investigation out of this."

"My investigation is propah," I said, putting on an accent.

"Dammit, Enoch."

"I can't come in without my client's consent. Besides, I only have one witness who claims my person of interest was in the car—but you can't see them in the photos. The Met won't do shit with this. They'll maybe send a cop who's pals with Powers or Moran and call it a day. You know I'm right.

That's why people like me get hired—no one trusts the cops, but they trust what money will buy."

"We're not all on the take, Enoch."

"You're not. But I don't trust anyone else in the Met. Now, are you going to give me Powers's details?"

Ruby fiddled with her teacup. "Enoch."

"Yes or a no, Rubes?"

She looked toward Big Ben.

"Am I really asking too much?" I asked. "If my requests have become too much, just tell me."

"It's not that…" She paused. "I just don't want to lose my friend. Powers is dangerous, with powerful connections."

"I promise I'll let you know before I do anything rash."

"If people thought through their rash behavior, it wouldn't be rash."

"Rubes," I smiled.

"Be careful whatever you do."

"I always am."

Ruby handed over a folded envelope from her jacket pocket. Inside was a picture of Powers. He was built like a rugby player with a sizeable, wrinkled face and saggy earlobes. On the back was a Camden address.

"The address is probably bogus," Rubes said. "But there's a speakeasy in Earl's Court that's Powers's regular. It's in the back of a kebab shop."

"What?"

"Earl's Kebab—near the station."

"Thanks, Rubes." I stood. "What film do you want to watch Sunday night?"

She laughed. "God, I don't know, Enoch—something Eighties. *Lost Boys*. No, wait, maybe *Aliens*. One of those."

"Game over, man," I said.

"Oh, make sure your guest sheets are washed. I'll crash at yours."

"See you Sunday night."

"I hope so."

* * *

It was ten p.m. and raining lightly when I arrived at Earl's Kebab—tucked between a dry cleaner and an off-license. I dressed casually—a jean jacket, dark trousers, and a flat cap.

I went inside.

The dining room, if you want to call a bar with five stools a dining room, was narrow. You couldn't stand in line without bumping into people eating.

Two Middle Eastern men worked behind the counter. One, an older, plump guy with a gray moustache, used a long knife to slice meat off the roller grill. The other, younger and skinnier, shook a vat of chips dripping with oil. A small woman with graying hair ran the till. She handed a drunk man his change and food. He wobbled past me, shoving chips into his face.

"Yes, sir?" the old man asked me.

"I'm looking for the bar."

"Through there." He pointed to a swivel door without hesitation.

I nodded and went through, accepting the easy win. I went down a flight of stairs to a dim basement bar at the bottom. It was busy, with twenty or thirty people squeezed onto leather sofas and the half-a-dozen tall tables dotted in the center of the room. AC/DC's "Dirty Deeds Done Dirt Cheap" played. The dark light made it hard to make out faces, an intentional choice. Two women in tight, low-cut dresses circled the room like predators, flashing their white teeth. I found an empty stool at the bar and ordered a Black Label on the rocks. When I got it, I scanned the room, looking for Jack Powers.

One of the predators came up to me. She was pretty, with crystal-blue eyes and cheap fruity perfume.

"I no seen you here before," she said with a thick Eastern European accent. She wrapped her arms around my neck.

"First time," I said.

"I make it memorable for you, huh? I have room just above."

"Another time, maybe."

She pouted playfully.

"I'm meeting someone."

"Yes. Me." She grinned and laughed.

"If only, sweetheart. No, have you seen Jack?"

"Jack, who?"

"Powers. Big bald guy."

Her eyes went cold, and the playfulness drained from her face.

"He is upstairs with Veronica. You are meeting him?"

"Yeah."

I took a sip of whisky.

Her smile returned. "We can…play…while you wait?"

"How long will Jack be?" I asked.

"Maybe another hour."

"Stay here a moment, I'll be back. I need the loo."

I left the kebab shop, went across the street and watched. Lights were on in the rooms above the shop. I waited for Powers to show himself, which didn't take long. About thirty minutes later, he emerged from a dark doorway beside the shop. He didn't go back inside. He smoked a cigarette and adjusted his trousers. He was bigger in person than I expected. Thicker, meatier, and probably meaner too. I felt bad for the prostitute—must've been like sleeping with a warthog. He tossed the cigarette and walked toward Old Brompton Road.

I tailed him down Earl's Court Square. I slipped a brass knuckle taser onto my left hand. There would be no reasoning with him.

Car lights blinked—it was the silver Tesla with matching license plate. Powers opened the driver's side door.

"Hey, Powers," I said.

The hulk turned. I clobbered him, and he fell into the car, tased and dazed. I grabbed him by his shirt. Powers still had some fight in him. He swung a thick fist. I ducked. He smashed his hand into the car, denting it. My elbow swiped his face, and I zapped him again. He slid to the ground unconscious.

I dragged him out of the road, propped him against the gate surrounding Hands Gardens, and zip-tied his hand to the iron fence. I padded him for the key, but it wasn't on him—it must've dropped when he fell. I couldn't find his phone either.

I sat in the driver's seat and rummaged through the car. The Tesla stunk of spicy cologne mixed with weed. A gun, weed, cocaine, and a user manual were in the glove compartment. Inside the console was a nudie mag with a well-endowed woman on the cover and several boxes of mint Tic-Tacs. I wanted to turn the car on and see the location log. I checked under my seat and around the pedals for the key—nothing. I felt around the passenger side and reached under the chair. I brushed something cool and smooth. It was a phone. I pressed the power button, and the Apple logo lit up on the screen. The lock screen was a selfie of Michael Finch and Jessie Holden—it was *her* phone.

There was a snap outside. As I peered through the passenger window, a meaty hand grabbed me, and I was thrown out of the car. I hit the pavement, and Jessie's phone flew out of my hand and slid under one of the cars.

I scrambled to my feet and backed away. I couldn't find my brass knuckle taser.

"I'ma fuckin kill you, you little bitch!" Jack Powers moved toward me, his face like a devil, snorting. His large feet pounded with every step. My foot clipped the edge of the pavement, and I fell again. There was a click and the sliver flash of a blade in his hand, and he charged at me like a juggernaut. I bolted. He chased me, grunting and growling like a bull. I didn't stop. I knew if I did, I was dead.

I ran out of breath around Brompton Cemetery. Powers was gone. Leaning against the locked gate, I buried my hands in my face. My heart pounded, and my body trembled.

Composing myself, I went back to Hands Gardens. The Tesla was long gone. I hoped Jessie's phone was still there. After checking under three cars, I was in luck. Powers didn't realize it was gone, and now I had it.

* * *

We need to meet, is what I texted Michael Finch at midnight.

I'm in a meeting with my Japanese client, what is it? he replied.

It's about Jessie.

Is she OK?

We need to talk.

OK.

Michael said to meet him at the War Memorial on Tower Hill in two hours, so I did.

It was two a.m., two days before his wedding, when I found him. Michael paced the enclosed war memorial and smoked a cigarette. Under the pale moonlight, I could see the stubble had formed a proper beard. As we walked in circles past the names of dead men and women, I told him what Kira had seen, about finding Jack Powers and locating Jessie's phone.

"You let the guy get away?" Michael snapped.

"Would you rather I let him knife me?" I said.

"I'd rather you beat the shit out of him to get answers. Christ, you nearly had him?"

"This isn't some Jack Reacher bullshit."

Michael walked in circles and lit another cigarette.

"What's Jessie's passcode?" I asked.

"Hell if I know," he said.

"The hell do you know about Jessie, Michael? Seriously? The women you told me to call, these 'friends,' all said they weren't close with her, and one didn't even call back. Do you even know Jessie's close friends?"

"I don't need this shit from you." Michael collapsed on a bench next to the statue of a naked woman and stared at his feet. He sniffed. The darkness hid his face and the tears.

"Michael."

"My dad said we were moving too fast," he said quietly, his voice heavy with humiliation. "I didn't want him to be right. I mean, Christ, he said she wasn't right for me weeks ago and to end it. Why didn't I listen?" Michael stood.

"Look, Michael—"

"No, I'm done. I can't do this. I'll pay you what we agreed…but I'm terminating the contract." He walked off, his hands in his pockets.

"Did you hear anything I said?"

He stopped, dropping his head but keeping his back to me.

"A thug collected her and took her somewhere. Her phone was found in his car. Your fiancée is in trouble, man. She might even be dead. You can't just walk away."

Michael turned his head slightly. "She did." He walked off. I called after him, but he didn't stop.

* * *

I slept on the sofa in my office. When I woke, it was around nine a.m. My right side ached from Powers throwing me to the ground, and my thighs needed a good stretch after that bit of cross-country I did to get away. Michael had emailed a termination of services, and he settled his bill. He was done. But I wasn't. Call it charity, justice, or just plain morbid curiosity…I wanted to know what happened to Jessie Holden. Was she alive? Had Powers killed her?

I needed to get into her phone, and I had just the guy.

Around one, Rooker arrived at my office.

I never know what Rooker is going to look like. His appearance changes every time. Six months ago, he had blue hair, a nose ring, and dressed like a Camden Town cyber-goth. Today, he looked like a preppy hipster—pink trousers, brown suede shoes, and a white shirt with a spotted bowtie. His red hair was slicked back, and his ginger moustache curled up on either side of his top lip.

"Where's the phone?" he said. I handed it to him. He unpacked a laptop at my desk, plugged in external drives, and booted up Pegasus—an Israeli hacking software. "This'll take a while. Come back in an hour."

"Want anything?"

"No."

I wandered around Tottenham Court Road, stopping at Waterstones, but bought nothing. I wondered if Michael would change his mind or how he'd react if I discovered something.

An hour later, Rooker was done and packed. He held up a piece of paper with the four-digit passcode. "Here."

"Thanks," I said as he walked out.

I sat at my desk with Jessie's phone. I punched in the code: 1965. What did this date mean to her? Looking through her WhatsApp, I saw messages from friends—her real ones, I guessed—all asking where she was. No replies. I spotted a message from an unknown contact on Monday. The last message was: *Who the fuck are you?* I opened it. The first message from the sender was a link to Venmo. Jessie replied, saying, *Who are you? Where did you get this?* The sender replied: *Call off the wedding, or it will be sent to every guest.* Jessie said: *Don't! I was a kid it was a mistake. How did you find this?* There was no reply, then Jessie said, *Who the fuck are you?* Then, I clicked the link.

The page came up, and there was a list of videos. All of them were pornographic. They were of Jessie and a man whose face was out of the frame. She looked younger—by maybe eight to ten years. She was taken advantage of in every way possible. At the end of each video, there was a trailer for the production company, offering easy money for girls willing to fuck on camera. It made my skin crawl.

Thinking about Jessie's age—nine years ago was when her parents died. She was nineteen. My heart broke for her. Was she hard up for money? Desperate? Now, a past she didn't want exposed was used to ruin her marriage-to-be. But who was doing it? And why?

I reviewed more of her texts and emails—nothing else stood out until I checked her calendar. She met with Rev. Isaac Finch at ten a.m. on Tuesday, the day Kira saw Powers take her. Michael hadn't mentioned this meeting; I guessed he didn't know. Rev. Finch might've been the last person to talk with Jessie before she disappeared. I wanted to know what this meeting was about.

* * *

Isaac Finch was the pastor at Holy Trinity Brompton in South Kensington. I didn't know him, but I knew the church. A few years ago, I dated a girl who dragged me there. I hated it. It's a gaudy, flashy affair. They have ten services across six sites in Kensington every Sunday, with a concert-grade light show and sound equipment for the professional musicians who put on a faux-rock concert in the name of Jesus. It's a congregation packed with rich frauds and frauds wishing they were rich.

At the church, a pretty young woman with blond hair who loved my American accent showed me to Rev. Isaac's office.

He sat behind a large oak desk. His thin gray head looked up from his notes and studied me curiously over a pair of small, wire-rimmed glasses. The office was spacious, with floor-to-ceiling bookshelves crammed with theological writing, from Ignatius of Antioch to Tertullian and John Wesley and modern-day pop-pastors like Rob Bell and Brian Houston—names I knew well in another life.

"Rev. Isaac, I'm Ben Enoch." I showed him my ID. "Apologies for interrupting you, but I need to ask you some questions about Jessie Holden."

"Jessie?" he said, sitting up straight. "Whatever for?" Rev. Isaac's nasally posh accent screamed Eton-educated.

"I understand you aren't keen on her marriage to Michael."

"I don't see what business this is of yours, Mr. Enoch."

"It's my business because she's missing."

"Missing?"

"Since Tuesday, Reverend."

"But I saw her Tuesday morning!"

"At ten a.m., here?"

"Yes."

Rev. Isaac's cheeks flushed. "Now she's missing? My God. Oh, Michael. He must be shattered. He hasn't said anything."

"He's too afraid."

"My dear boy." Sadness filled his eyes.

"Why did you meet with her?"

"I, well, you're right. I did oppose the marriage, but not because of Jessie.

Because of Michael. He's not ready. I'm ashamed to admit it, but my son is a playboy. He moves through women like a hot knife through butter. Jessie needs a good man, and as much as I love my son, he's a lost soul. I asked Jessie here to discuss the wedding and if she could convince Michael to postpone it a year. Allow them time to go through couples' therapy and get involved with the church. And well…." Rev. Isaac shook his head.

"She wanted to go ahead with the wedding?"

"She said I misunderstood Michael." He laughed. "Are you a father, Mr. Enoch?"

"No."

"Well, as a father, I can tell you, you will never misunderstand your child—even when they think you do. Oh, my poor boy."

"Did Jessie give any hint that she was in trouble?"

"Not at all, why?"

"She didn't mention a threat?" I asked.

"A threat? Heavens no."

"Someone is blackmailing her with explicit content she made years ago. She was told to call the wedding off, or the entire guest list would be sent the material."

"How do you know?"

"Because I have her phone."

"You have her phone? Where did you find it?"

"I can't say right now."

"I truly hope she is okay. This is all deeply disturbing. My wife will be a wreck. I really must speak with Michael." There was a knock on the door. The pretty young blonde poked her head in. "Rev. Isaac, Lord Richards is here for your four o'clock."

"What? Oh, is that now? Yes, thank you," he said, discombobulated. "Mr. Enoch, I hate to end this conversation…if there's anything I can do…I really need to talk to my family."

"If you remember anything, just call me." I gave him my card.

"Thank you, Mr. Enoch."

Not for the first time, I walked out of the church angry and without answers.

* * *

I returned to my office on Percy Street, feeling listless and done with Michael Finch and Jessie Holden. I didn't know what to do. I couldn't call Ruby and hand the case over to the police because everything that happened was protected by client confidentiality, and I didn't care to be sued.

Around nine, I got sick of sitting at my desk doing nothing, so I drove home to do nothing there. I lived in a one-bed flat in Du Cane Court, in Balham. I wanted to get into bed and start fresh in the morning.

Something felt wrong the second I entered my flat. The air stunk of spicy cologne and weed. There was a noise to my left. Storming out of the darkness of the bedroom was Jack Powers with a blade.

"Where's her phone!" he roared.

As his meaty hand reached for me, I dove forward into the long and narrow kitchen. Powers grunted after me. I made the wrong choice; I was trapped.

I grabbed a dirty frying pan from the sink. Powers jabbed at me. All I remember was swinging frantically. Then, Powers on the floor with a broken nose and bloody mouth.

I acted fast. I cuffed him, bound his legs, and gagged him.

He knew I had Jessie's phone. Only two fucking people knew I had that.

I went through his pockets and found his mobile. Luckily, it was an older iPhone that didn't use face ID. While he grunted in pain, I put Powers's thumb to it—the screen unlocked. The last text was from a number giving him my address and saying, *Bring me her phone ASAP.* There was a call from the same number just before the text. I recognized it and checked my phone. It wasn't Michael or Isaac Finch; it was Will Kirk, the producer of *Moulin Rouge*.

I found messages from Powers to Jessie in WhatsApp—he had sent the video and made the threats, but for who? Kirk?

I then opened the Tesla app to check the location logs. The car was at Michael's house Tuesday morning, then it went to Holy Trinity Brompton, the Piccadilly, and then he drove down the M2, stopped at the Queen's Head pub in Boughton-under-Blean, then drove around Blean Woods National Nature Reserve before doubling back to London. My gut told me Jessie's body would be found in the reserve. Something nasty had happened at the pub.

I texted Kirk from Powers's phone: *Got the phone. Where to meet?*

Kirk replied: *The theatre—1 a.m.*

I added: *Little problem. Enoch got my car logs and sent them to Michael.*

Kirk: *How the fuck did he do that? Christ. Tell me Enoch is dead?*

I replied: *Yes.*

Kirk: *OK. Good. I'll talk to Isaac. We might need to take care of Michael.*

That was all I needed, and now, I wasn't bound by my client confidentiality.

* * *

The streets around the Piccadilly were busy at one a.m. Drunks and partiers chased pleasures and escapes under the silver moonlight—I wouldn't find either. I was after justice.

The stage door was propped open. Will Kirk wasn't alone in his office. Rev. Isaac sat with him.

"Ill met by moonlight, proud Titania," I said.

"Mr. Enoch!" Kirk spat.

Rev. Isaac shot up from the sofa, the color drained from his face.

I raised Powers's phone. "Reports of my death have been greatly exaggerated. So what's this, Reverend, you would let Powers kill your son like he did Jessie?"

"Enoch, you don't understand," he said.

"No, I do. You lied to my face. You orchestrated all this. And Kirk and Powers were your lackeys."

Kirk reached into his desk and pulled out a gun.

149

"It's over, man," I said. "Powers is in custody. The police are already searching Blean Woods. They'll find Jessie there."

Kirk looked at Rev. Isaac and me. The gun swung back and forth. The Scotsman's eyes were wild with fear. "Damn you, Isaac. Damn you!"

"Kirk, put the bloody gun down." Rev. Isaac was pale and sweaty. "Don't listen to Enoch; he's trying to frighten us."

"The police will find her. And you'll go to jail."

Kirk's eyes watered. "I'm not goin' down for you, Isaac! I swear tae fuckin' Jesus Christ." The gun shook in his hand.

"There is no way out of this, Kirk," I said.

"Aye, there is. Tell the lad I'm sorry."

"No!" I jumped at Kirk.

BANG.

Kirk's body fell back. The wall and desk were covered in blood.

Rev. Isaac threw up before collapsing onto the sofa, groaning. Behind me, Ruby stood in the doorway with two armed officers. I waved at them to hold off. Rev. Isaac began to talk through the weeping groans.

"I never wanted the poor girl to die. Powers was meant to take her to Dover to the ferry. At some point, she tried to get away and call Michael. Powers had to chase her. He killed her! It wasn't me. It wasn't fucking me!" Rev. Isaac wept. "I had to stop my son from marrying that whore!"

I grabbed Rev. Isaac's collar and hoisted him to his feet. He screeched, and I slammed him against the wall. "Please! Please! Don't hurt me!"

"Enoch!" Ruby shouted. "Put him down!"

"You're fucking scum," I said.

"Enoch," Ruby's voice was tempered. "Let go."

I did and straightened his shirt and jacket.

"Rot in hell." I pushed past Rubes and her men and walked out into the night alone.

There would be no amends between Michael and his father. No escape from the serpent's tongue and offending shadows. There would be no midsummer wedding: just heartbreak and a lonely funeral for Jessie Holden.

And All That Jazz

BV Lawson

The winds were blowing out of the east, and Scott Drayco thought he could just hear a wailing sound carried on the breeze. He continued his run past the Tidal Basin and the Washington Monument heading toward Capitol Hill, but he was so focused on the sound he didn't see the shiny-new red car that came within inches of putting him in the hospital. Or worse.

The shiny-new car pulled into one of the shiny-new office buildings popping up along Mass Ave. The driver hadn't bothered to see if he was okay, not terribly surprising since Capitol Hill was the capital of self-absorption. Drayco stopped long enough to catch his breath and continued toward his target.

It was just a bit after noon, and he now distinctly heard the musical sounds wafting in his direction from their usual place. Being outdoors kicked his synesthesia brain into high gear—with every noise hitting him with an explosion of colors, shapes, and textures—but the music from the saxophone cut a colorful path through it all. To his ears, most saxophones were like fuzzy caterpillars with magenta spikes, but this one was different, better. More like a crumbled azure chalk dust formed into fan shapes.

He drew closer and spied the musician seated against the building, surrounded by his backpack, a lone water bottle, and an upturned cap with a few dollars and some change inside. Not too far away stood a metal shopping cart filled with plastic bags of clothes, another backpack, and the other few possessions the musician pushed around with him from place to place.

As Drayco neared, the musician stopped playing, prompting Drayco to say, "Abiram, you didn't have to stop."

"Well, now, Dee-teck-tive Scott, can't exactly ignore my best customer, can I?" The voice of Abiram Fox also had an unusual coloration, like turquoise gravel. He and the sax were a perfect match in more ways than one.

Drayco shook his head. "I don't know about the 'best' part. But your wailing on that sax is like some kind of saxophone god. Reminds me of John Coltrane."

"Oh, now, you're just being an idle flatterer. But, if you really like it," Abiram picked up the cap and gave it a little jiggle, making the coins inside clink together.

Drayco grinned and tossed in some twenties. When he saw a shadow looming off to his side, he turned to see a ten-year-old boy hanging back and watching. Drayco said, "I see you around here a lot, Fitch. Are you a sax fan?"

The boy nodded. "Used to listen to my granddaddy's Charlie Parker records. Abiram here is better."

Abiram gave a little half-bow from his seated spot, and Drayco asked Fitch, "Do you have a request for our saxophone master?"

Fitch looked from Drayco to Abiram with a shy smile. "'Just Friends' is one of my favorites."

The audience of two, man and boy, stood in admiration as Abiram belted out a note-perfect rendition of the piece, and when he finished, they applauded. The musician bowed again, and Drayco tossed in another twenty.

Fitch said, "You should play at Blues Alley or maybe the Kennedy Center."

Abiram's face grew pensive. "Well, now, I don't know about that. I do recollect when I was about your age, I used to go to Carter Barron over in Rock Creek. Heard the likes of Ella Fitzgerald, Stan Getz, Louis Armstrong,

Benny Goodman, Ray Charles. Always thought I might be up on that stage one day."

"I'll bet you still could."

"Ah, young Fitch, that was another lifetime ago. But I don't mind. I'd play just for myself if nobody else was around." He asked the boy, "You thought of taking up sax playing? Bet you'd be a natural."

Fitch's smile faded. "Can't afford one. And they canceled the program at school. Used to have instruments they loaned to kids like me."

Abiram shook his head. "Well now, that there's a crying shame."

A faint voice in the distance calling Fitch's name made the youth give the two men a wave and dash off into the nearby alleyway. Abiram leaned up against the building. "Yep, a crying shame. Too bad his daddy lost his job. Leastways, the boy still looks up to him no matter what. That says a lot right there."

Drayco didn't have to ask Abiram what he meant because the man had offered up past clues about his own estranged son. They hadn't spoken in years, though Drayco sensed it wasn't due to any lack of desire on Abiram's part. Quite the opposite, since Abiram always had a haunted look in his eyes when the topic of the son came up.

Just then, Drayco got a sudden whiff of hot, sweaty cotton, à la baked Drayco, and took that as his cue to finish his trek back to his townhome and a waiting shower. After he toweled off, he called up a recording off the internet of Charlie Parker playing "Just Friends." Fitch was right—Abiram was better, and Parker was no slouch.

The strains of the piece followed Drayco over the next week as he got involved in another case with its usual long days and late nights. When he finally got a breather, he decided to check up on his favorite saxophone player again and see how he was doing.

But when Drayco arrived, Abiram was sitting against the building, his instrument nowhere in sight. "Taking a break for a few minutes, Abiram?"

The man shook his head sadly. "It's gone, Dee-teck-tive Scott."

"What's gone? Your sax?"

"Was at my usual night spot couple nights ago. The railroad underpass at the Second and L bridge. Hadn't put up my tent. Too hot. Just a blanket. Woke up, and the case and sax were gone."

"You didn't see anyone suspicious hanging around?"

"Just the usual folk, but couldn't have been one of the camp. I'd swear to it on a stack of my mother's Bibles. And she had a dozen of 'em."

"So you weren't alone?"

"Yes and no. We always spread out a little bit under the bridge. Privacy, you see."

With a frown, Drayco said, "You know my offer to help you find a permanent place still stands."

"And that's mighty nice of you, Scott, but I kind of like it the way it is."

Drayco sighed inwardly. It didn't hurt to keep trying. "Has anyone threatened you lately? Followed you?"

Abiram took off his cap to scratch his head. "Can't say yes. Did have a funny dream, though. The night my sax went walking."

"What was it about?"

"Was one of those fancy electric cars, you know? A red one. It smiled at me."

"What do you mean by 'smiled'?"

"Don't know exactly. Just that it chirped and smiled. Maybe that's 'cause its driver was a bird."

Drayco stared at the other man. "You mean the driver flew?"

"No, just colorful like a bird. One of those toucan birds. Had a hawkish nose, too."

Drayco was a victim of hypnagogic dreams, so he guessed it might be something like that. Especially since he knew Abiram never touched drugs. "Did you report it to the police?"

Abiram rubbed his forehead. "The police don't care about us homeless people, especially losing things. Not when they have rich folk paying their salaries."

Drayco thought for a moment. "Your gifts shouldn't go without a voice. Why don't you just let me buy you another sax?"

"Oh, that's right nice of you, Scott. But it wouldn't be the same. My ole sax and me, well, now. We've been together for forty years. It's got character, like me. A little roughed up, dents in both sides. Not so shiny anymore."

Drayco rubbed the back of his neck. "I understand. I don't know what I'd do without my best girl."

"You mean your piano, doncha?"

"Like your sax, she's not the latest model, but you can't beat the sound. Look, just in case anyone has seen your sax, you wouldn't mind if I checked around?"

Abiram gave one of his half-bows. "That would be just fine. I'd be most grateful."

True to his word, Drayco consulted some of his MPD officer contacts, but there weren't any reports of similar thefts. Drayco also did a little research to track down Abiram's estranged son, Franklin. That conversation hadn't gone exactly as Drayco hoped, either. The son had pretty much washed his hands of his father and seemed embarrassed to talk about him.

That left just one other fairly obvious avenue. Drayco called up a list of all the pawn shops in the area and stopped by to visit each one in turn. He struck out with the ones in the District, but when he popped into Bixby's Pawn Shop in Prince George's County, one of the first things he spotted in the window was a saxophone.

He hurried in and approached the man behind the counter who sported a tag that said, "Mitchell." Drayco said to him, "That sax in the window. When was it brought in?"

Mitchell eyed him skeptically. "You a cop?"

"Not a cop, no. Private."

The other man appraised him for a moment. "Seems like it was about a week ago. No longer than."

Drayco went over to the window and picked up the instrument to examine it more closely. It was definitely not new, as the dull finish showed. On each side of the bore lay a matching set of dents. Without asking, Drayco blew through the mouthpiece and keyed a few notes. He was no pro, but his "playing" was enough to tell him this was indeed Abiram's instrument.

It had the identical sound of crumbled azure chalk dust formed into fan shapes.

He looked at the price tag. About what he'd expected, but Abiram could never afford it. Drayco reached into his wallet and pulled out some cash he flashed at Mitchell. "I've got enough for this sax upfront. And if you recall the person who dropped it off, I'll throw in a couple of extra Ben Franklins."

Mitchell's eyes widened at that. He hesitated for only a moment and snatched the bills from Drayco's hand to stuff into the cash register. "I remember the guy. Kind of hard to forget. Reddish hair, kind of a large nose. Think he was driving one of those new Teslas."

Drayco took a stab in the dark. "A red one?"

Mitchell nodded. "To match his hair, I guess. Maybe he spent all of his cash on that car 'cause people who can afford those don't usually need to pawn these," he nodded at the sax. "This stolen from you?"

"No, a friend. A homeless man."

Mitchell frowned. "That's pretty low. Too bad my security camera's on the fritz. Don't have the guy in my books, either, 'cause I gave him cash up front, no questions asked."

Drayco handed over the promised additional C-notes and carried the precious cargo to his car. Once back at his townhome, he made sure it was hidden away in a locked closet. Although he'd prefer not to wait to reunite the instrument with its rightful owner, he had someone else he needed to see first.

When Abiram told Drayco about his "dream" and the "bird man," Drayco was convinced it was just the man's imagination. But only yesterday, when Drayco was on another run through Capitol Hill, he'd spied someone who might match the description of both Abiram's "bird man" and the details from the pawn store clerk—red hair and "hawkish" nose, probably from being broken at one time.

The man had headed into the same ritzy office buildings where the red-car driver who almost hit Drayco had disappeared into a parking garage. So, Drayco had followed his target into the building long enough to see him get into an elevator that stopped at the third floor. Upon checking the directory, Drayco noted the entire third floor was taken over by Carr Legal & Accounting Services.

Armed with this new information and putting two and two together, the next day, Drayco again headed toward that same building, opting to drive instead of run to avoid working up a sweat. He parked in the underground lot, climbed out, and stopped in front of the reserved space labeled "Basil Carr," which sported a shiny-new red Tesla.

On a hunch, Drayco pulled out his cell phone and found a video of that model of Tesla, especially when the remote was used to open the falcon-wing doors. The sound was a little like an electronic "chirp." Abiram had referred to a "flying" car in his dream the night his sax was stolen. Falcon wings, a chirp, the bird man—it all seemed to fit.

After taking the elevator to the third floor, Drayco stepped out into a hallway and made a beeline for the door with the lettering "Basil Carr, JD, CPA." He entered, taking note of the mahogany veneer and gold hand-tooled leather on the front desk and the polished white marble floor. He approached the secretary, asking to see Carr.

When she replied, "Do you have an appointment?" he shook his head. "No, but he'll want to see me. Tell him it's about a saxophone."

She eyed Drayco skeptically but used her inter-office phone and parroted back what Drayco had told her. He could hear a male voice on the other end say, "Send him in," so Drayco didn't wait for her, and let himself into the back office.

Abiram's red-haired "bird man" stared back at him. "What's this about a saxophone?"

Drayco smiled as politely as he could, trying to hold back his anger. "Three words. Bixby's Pawn Shop."

Basil Carr frowned. "I don't understand. Pawn shop?"

"You were seen taking a saxophone into that particular pawn shop several days ago. Funny thing, though. That sax was reported stolen."

Drayco could see the wheels turning in the man's head as he considered his options. Apparently deciding total denial wasn't going to work, he replied, "Why, yes, I did drop off a sax at a pawn shop recently. But it wasn't stolen. I found it lying on a sidewalk."

"Oh, really? Just lying there?"

"I asked around to see if anyone knew who it might belong to, but alas, I struck out. So, I decided to take it to the shop. Finders keepers, I suppose," and he uttered a fake laugh reminiscent of a hyena barking. It hit Drayco's brain with little mud-colored darts that he found particularly annoying.

"You didn't think to report it to the police?"

Carr shook his head. "Why should I? They're very busy with rapes and murders. This seems like such a minor thing."

"There's a musician who plays a saxophone identical to the one you pawned. He's often just around the corner, not too far from here. Surely you've heard him?"

Carr shifted around in his chair. "I suppose I might have. From a distance."

"It never occurred to you that this 'stolen' sax might belong to him?"

The other man's jaw worked side to side, and he grabbed a pen etched with "Basil Carr JD, CPA" in gold lettering that he tapped on the desk. "I don't pay much attention to the homeless people. Especially the street musicians. Except for how they affect businesses around here. People don't like having to step over those dirty types to visit their accountants. Customers will go somewhere else rather than deal with that."

Drayco's eyes narrowed, and he had to count to ten to let his blood pressure die down. "And if one of those musicians could no longer play—say, because his instrument disappeared—they'd move along, is that it? No more nuisance?"

Carr dropped the pen on his desk and tilted back in his chair. He waved his hand at the door and said, "I'm quite busy today. And you just barged in without an appointment. You can let yourself out, can't you?"

Drayco reached over to pick up the pen by the ends. As he let his arm drop to his side with the pen still in his hand, he nodded at a photo on the wall of the red Tesla. "That your car?"

When Carr turned around to look, Drayco palmed the pen into his pocket.

Carr turned back with narrowed eyes. "If anything happens to that car, I'll have your head. Now, are you going to leave, or do I have to call building security to help you with that?"

Drayco just smiled and headed out of the building. He hadn't expected the guy to make a full confession, but at least Drayco got some ammunition from his visit. Later that day, he took the pen and sax to a friend at the MPD and explained the story. Knowing Abiram wouldn't want to get involved, and the MPD couldn't open an investigation without the owner filing a report, he got his friend to agree to run the prints off the books as a favor. But the results were another disappointment. No match between prints lifted off Carr's pen and the sax, meaning Carr probably wore gloves, something he'd have to ask the pawn shop clerk. If so, wearing gloves in summer was another red flag.

Without fingerprints or video proof, Drayco knew he didn't have a case with the guy, at least nothing that would stand up in court. It was the word of a successful accountant-attorney versus a homeless musician who'd "dreamed" he saw someone who "might" have looked like Carr the night the sax went missing.

It was rare Drayco faced a situation where he solved a crime without the perp being held accountable at the end. He was angry Carr wouldn't face justice—at least, not this time. Karma willing, maybe at some point in the future. Sometimes it was a hard fact to swallow, but life wasn't always fair.

But as he stewed about it some more, he decided that no, he wasn't just going to leave it at that. He wanted nothing more than to wipe that smug smile off Basil Carr's face. Drayco returned to the pawn shop and checked with the clerk, who did recall that Carr had worn gloves. Like Drayco, the clerk thought it odd anyone would wear gloves in the summer heat, but he was in the business of not asking questions.

Fortunately for Drayco, that summer heat had been accompanied by a lack of rain. He located the nearest dumpster to the pawn shop and peered inside. And he was in luck—he spied a pair of gloves like the ones the clerk had described—thin, brown leather. He hadn't been dumpster-diving in years, but it was worth it if it would avenge Abiram.

Drayco was afraid his MPD friend would laugh in his face this time, but it turned out that the department had just received a new vacuum metal deposition machine. Drayco had asked the MPD to save the pen, just in case, and lo and behold, the prints on the pen and gloves were a match.

Nothing would have made him happier than to be present when the MPD questioned Carr. But Abiram was right about one thing—to a department facing rapes, murders, and even terrorism these days, the theft from a homeless man wasn't a high priority. Drayco—and justice—would just have to wait a little longer.

He could still look forward to returning the sax to its rightful owner. He'd just gotten home and pulled the instrument out of the closet when he got a call from one of the police officers he consulted when the instrument was stolen.

The tone of Officer Alissa Smoak's voice should have given him a clue the call wasn't good news. "You were asking about that homeless man's stolen sax. Abiram Fox, right?"

"That's his name, yes."

"Apparently, he had a heart attack last night. At least, that's what the coroner thinks. One of the other homeless people who slept under the same bridge told us Mr. Fox had been complaining of chest pains the past week."

"I see." Drayco kicked himself for not checking up on Abiram yesterday. Would it have made a difference? Now, he'd never know.

Officer Smoak continued, "The homeless camp told us about his son, who we called. Apparently, they were estranged. He's not interested in claiming the man's body but told us to contact you—that you could decide what to do with it."

Drayco blinked several times as he considered her words. Guess that made him the unofficial executor. He thanked her and told her he'd pay for a cremation and pick up the ashes when they were ready.

He tossed the phone aside and sat back against the sofa with his eyes closed. Maybe he'd brought Abiram a little bit of justice, but it was too late. And now, Drayco felt an even heavier burden wondering how to handle his new duties. What would Abiram have wanted? How did you honor someone whose life had been filled with such quiet pain but who possessed such a rich musical soul?

He knew one thing he had to do. He jumped up, grabbed the saxophone, and hurried down the stairs of his townhome. After heading to Abiram's former spot, Drayco maneuvered through the back alleyways until he found the address he was after. When he knocked on the door, a woman answered, and Drayco asked to see Fitch Solomon. She hesitated for a moment but called her son to the door.

Drayco explained to the boy, "I'm sorry to bring you sad news, but Abiram Fox passed away from a heart attack. Before that, he told me he wanted you to have this," and Drayco handed over the sax. It was only a little white lie since Abiram had never told Drayco that, at least not in those exact words. But he was pretty sure the musician would approve.

Though his eyes were full of unshed tears, the boy's face lit up like footlights on a stage. "I'll take good care of it," he said. "Maybe one day, I'll be as good as him."

"I have no doubt of it." Drayco fully expected he and everyone else would be seeing the name of Fitch Solomon in the arts headlines in about ten years.

The other part of Drayco's tribute to Abiram was a bit harder. He had to wait five days for the urn with the cremains to be transferred to his care. During that time, he'd wracked his brain trying to decide what would have pleased Abiram the most. Then, he remembered Abiram's words about the Carter Barron Amphitheatre in Rock Creek Park.

It was a hive of summer concerts and festivals in its heyday, but it was currently closed for restoration. Thus, as Drayco stood there now, the only music he heard were the sounds of the crickets, the mourning doves, and the wind whispering through the oak trees.

He turned to his young companion, "Are you ready to do this?"

Fitch nodded. "Sure we won't get into trouble?"

"There aren't any laws against scattering ashes on federal land. And we're not near any trails, facilities, or waterways on this particular spot."

Drayco looked around. The concrete platform and stairs were a little dirty, the audience chairs a little faded, and the whole middle and back part of the stage were missing. But it would be restored in time, and when it did, the atoms of Abiram Fox would dance around along with the musicians.

Drayco and Fitch went to the edge of the stage and scattered the ashes as the winds picked them up and carried them across the grass. Then, Drayco pulled out his cell phone and called up a sound file. Soon, the strains of "Just Friends" were carried on the winds along with the ashes and the music of the universe.

The Singular Case of the Bandaged Bobby

Andrew McAleer

As the celebrated private detective Henry von Stray's official historiographer, I have long held that the singular events occurring on Guy Fawkes Day 1921, led to von Stray becoming recognized as one of the world's foremost criminologists of his day. The baffling affair not only exhibits many examples of his unique insight into the criminal mindset, but also demonstrates his ingenious ability to use his specialized skills in this area to outwit some of the most cunning members of the criminal fraternity and, I am delighted to report, beat them at their own game.

I began the early part of the holiday uncovering what I couldn't help but conclude was an evil plot to ransack the annual awards dinner von Stray and I had planned to attend that evening at the Fraternal Order of Benevolent Walnuts. A celebration I might add in which I would be receiving the Club's most prestigious award—Honored Walnut of the Year.

In preparation of the important festivity I removed my official Club stickpin from my dress jacket's lapel buttonhole for a final inspection and polish. It was then I observed its stick was bent and badly fractured. It would never do if during my acceptance speech the pin toppled off at the foot of the Club's highest-ranking member the Honorable Veritable Walnut

Sir Percy Stonyhurst Berrycloth. Without haste I ran to our telephone to make arrangements with our friend and local jeweler Mrs. Amalasand Omloop to schedule an urgent repair; however, after several attempts to get through, the operator informed me the telephone call failed to reach the intended party.

Unwilling to wave the white flag of surrender I decided on a brisk walk to her shop located at the Piccadilly.

"Von Stray," I said to my dear colleague who was seated comfortably in his sitting-room easy chair studying the art of criminal dialect from his tattered edition of *The Rogue's Lexicon*, "I must dash off to Mrs. Omloop's for an urgent repair."

The great detective said, without lifting his eyes up from his book, "Ahh, Dilpate, I see you are finally in need of having your Benevolent Walnuts gold lapel pin repaired."

"Good Heavens, von Stray how did you know?"

He rose from his chair and explained. "The button hole in your official Club jacket is beginning to look as if it had been tied to a hansom and dragged through an unruly hedgerow. I concluded the lapel stem had been fractured in such a way it snags the delicate silk threads bordering the buttonhole. Really, my good fellow, I warned you against removing the pin too often and subjecting it to your rigorous polishing campaigns. It's 24-karat gold and rather fragile."

"Von Stray," I responded, taking few measures to conceal my pique at my friend's cavalier attitude concerning the emergency, "I take great exception. The Club's pin signifies my full membership in one of London's oldest and most revered institutions. How could I in all decency attend Club functions without putting it in proper order? I would no more mistreat my pin than you would a volume from your vast library on criminology."

He placed a bookmark into his book and gently closed it shut before slipping it back into its assigned slot on the sitting-room bookshelf. "Point taken, Dilpate. I think I've studied enough criminal argot today. It is a beautiful autumn morning and I think I'll join you on your stroll to the Piccadilly to discuss your dilemma with our lovely and friendly jeweler.

She is available to take on your trade I trust?"

I showed my palms. "I tried ringing her, but the shop's telephone must be out of order."

Von Stray flipped on his ancient wool-tweed scally cap. "Then there must be no further delay if we are to have you in ship-shape order for tonight's festivities."

"Splendid!" I cheered. "And with absolutely nothing else on the docket today I suggest we duck into the Nook and Hearthstone Public House for a pint of Haughey Ale and their scrumptious Lancashire hot pot while Mrs. Omloop works her magic."

* * *

As we walked down Berkeley Street I resumed my cross-examination of the great detective. "But how did you know it was my lapel pin and not another piece of jewelry in need of repair—my gold watch fob for instance?"

"A logical conclusion, Dilpate. You are wearing your watch fob and tonight we celebrate your well-deserved selection as the Club's Honored Walnut of the Year. A shoddy lapel pin wouldn't do. As you stated the matter is 'urgent.' A watch fob would hardly receive the same scrutiny your coveted lapel pin will undoubtedly receive on this truly august occasion."

I humbly waved off my dear friend's praise. "Tommyrot, von Stray. There are many members more worthy than I to receive the award."

"You're too modest, Professor. Your discovery of not one, not two, but three rare South American beetle specimens in a single year is I am quite certain the first of such accolades in the Club's history."

As incredulous and utterly amazing as it may sound to readers of these narratives von Stray's reference to my notable discoveries was the absolute truth. While on an infrequent sabbatical from the prestigious Clifford University I toiled for months under dense canopy and constant rainfall collecting mercurial beetle specimens from remote territories of Brazil, Paraguay, and Ecuador. I daresay few men outside indigenous groups have ever sloshed and clawed through such dangerous, predatory terrain as I had done in order to advance the cause of science.

Once again dismissing my friend's praise I said, "You make too much of my efforts, von Stray. The creatures practically waddled into my study."

When we reached Omloop's Master Jeweler and Antique Emporium on Coventry Street I couldn't help but admire the orderly appearance her shop added to the Piccadilly and therefore, all of London.

I said to von Stray, "I must say, old man, foreigners have taken quite a wallop here in old London since the war, but if the detractors could see how tidy Mrs. Omloop keeps her wares I think many would quickly change their tune."

"I quite agree, Dilpate. And when you consider the horrific circumstances leading to her relocation to our fine city she and her fellow refugees deserve our utmost support. Especially when you consider we are all the benefactor of their contributions."

My dear friend's admiration of Mrs. Omloop was heartfelt. When he returned from the war with little more than a case of trench foot to show for his effort, Mrs. Omloop extended him a kindness that even to this day he refuses, at the request of Mrs. Omloop, to disclose. A close friendship soon developed and by extension I had been tacitly invited to join their inner circle, where, over time, I learned of Mrs. Omloop's remarkable journey to England.

The story of her odyssey began at the start of the war in August 1914, and was not unlike 100,000 other Belgian refugees who fled for England after Germany viciously attacked Belgium. Mrs. Omloop's husband Garrin was killed in the carnage making her the sole caretaker of her infant daughter Elise and elderly mother Mrs. Sofia DeWitte. Refusing to leave either behind, she managed to enlist the help of a Belgian soldier, who sacrificed his life escorting them safely across the Sambre River. From there they headed south for France. Surviving on scant rations and kind deeds, they journeyed west for many weeks across France's countryside before securing safe passage to Hastings, England.

* * *

As we opened the door to the quaint shop its shopkeeper's doorbell announced our entrance. After a moment's delay Mrs. Omloop appeared through a curtain separating her back office from the shop. A casual glance of our dear friend would suggest to the untrained observer that she was an established woman who had been practicing her trade in London for generations and didn't have a care in the world. She would fit the description of the quintessential shop owner. A thin woman now somewhere beyond her fortieth year she had brown hair drawn to a tight bun, thick-lens spectacles covering studious brown eyes, and a healthy, colorful complexion complementing her amiable and jaunty disposition. Today, however, she appeared agitated and worried.

"Eh…good morning, my dear friends," she said, twisting her wedding ring and then suddenly looking back at the swaying curtains, "please enter. I must return to the telephone and shall return to my dear friends in one small moment." She turned and rushed back through the curtain.

"Von Stray," I said, *sotto voce*, "it seems her telephone is back in working order, but Mrs. Omloop doesn't appear in her usual jovial spirits."

"I agree, Dilpate. We must find out if all is well without prying too deeply into her personal affairs."

Mrs. Omloop reappeared moments later and made an attempt to greet us with sufficient cheerfulness. "My apologies, *mes amis*, I am always so happy to see my dear friends."

"Good morning, Mrs. Omloop," von Stray said, touching his hat brim while studying our friend. "We're delighted to hear your telephone is back in working order."

"Yes, my dear lady," I added, "I tried ringing you this morning about arranging an urgent repair, but was informed by the operator your line was not in service."

Mrs. Omloop produced a handkerchief, lifted her spectacles off the bridge of her nose and began dabbing her eyes. "It is the most strangest thing. A sergeant from the police asked to use the telephone and it was not until much later I realized he left the receiver disengaged."

"This is outrageous conduct," I reeled. "Not the sort of thing the honest taxpayer should expect of a public servant. We must find out the name of this irresponsible sergeant and report his remiss conduct to his superior."

Von Stray removed his briarwood pipe and began tapping tobacco into it meditatively. "Perhaps, Dilpate, but first I would like to hear Mrs. Omloop explain to us how this mysterious sergeant of the police had occasion to use her telephone."

"Yes, yes gentlemen. I must tell you. Your arrival at this time is most helpful. I am afraid I may have made a *grosse erruer*. This would be a terrible loss to my small shop. I don't know if my business could manage. Terrible loss."

Our dear friend had undoubtedly received a severe shock. I put a hand on her shoulder. "Come, my dear lady, it can't be as bad as all that. Start at the beginning and tells us everything. Von Stray and I will do whatever it takes to help remedy this *grosse erruer* of yours—if indeed one has been made at all."

Mrs. Omloop took a deep breath and after a few dabs to her cheeks began to tell us of the strange events leading up to her shock. "I arrived at my shop at precisely nine a.m. as is my custom and a police sergeant and police constable take a stroll up to me as I unlocked the door. At first I think there must be big trouble, but the sergeant told me it was his good luck that he happened to walk by as I was opening because I would maybe get a handsome *grande* sale first thing this morning."

Von Stray lit his pipe. "Could you describe the sergeant?"

"A big man," she said, lifting her arm to demonstrate. "Tall. The poor man had his right arm held in a sling and his hand covered in a heavy bandage. He had a *grande* moustache with curls at each end. I can say no more about him."

"You've done quite well, my dear. Now, could you describe the police constable?"

"Him not so good. He stood behind the sergeant looking away. I can only say that he was much smaller." She waved the handkerchief at me excitedly. "Perhaps like…my dear friend Professor Dilpate."

I raised my chin. "Yes. Er…what happened next?"

"I opened the shop, and the sergeant and I entered. Then the constable followed behind and when he entered he closed the door, turned around, and remained at the foot of the door looking out its window. Sergeant O'Rourke following me explained that the police were going to buy a retirement gift for their beloved chief, but could not spend more than £19, which he could send for right away if he found the perfect item."

Von Stray cut in. "My apologies, Mrs. Omloop. The sergeant stated his name?"

"Yes. I should have mentioned. He gave his name Sergeant Arthur O'Rourke."

"Splendid, my dear," I said, giving the air a spirited upper cut. "Now we know precisely who to report for his outrageous treatment of your telephone. And after you had shown him so much kindness. If you allow me the use of your telephone I will report the matter at once to the proper authority!"

Von Stray gently rubbed his scar located on the left side of his forehead; what he refers to as his war "memento" from his time in the trenches on the Western Front. "I think, Professor we had better hear our friend's full account of the matter before reporting this alleged sergeant who just happens to be named 'Arthur O'Rourke.' Quite a coincidence indeed."

I cleared my throat. "Yes…yes, of course…a remarkable coincidence. I quite agree. Based on this remarkable coincidence I think it best we continue gathering more facts from your account, Mrs. Omloop."

She nodded. "Thank you, Professor. I then proceeded to show him many items but the sergeant said none of them were right for their nice old chief. Then he approached this gold-plated mantle clock," she said, removing the exquisite piece from a gift box and showing it to us.

Von Stray examined the item with intense concentration. "A rather expensive item even for their 'beloved nice old' chief."

Mrs. Omloop repackaged the clock and continued. "He said this was the perfect gift and that the boys must have it for their darling chief. When I explained to him that this item cost £22 he said this was the most perfect gift and that it was a sorry day that they should have to part without it.

Then suddenly his spirits lifted. He explained that maybe the boys could pull together a few more 'quid' for their dear old chief who had been so good to them like a father."

Von Stray nodded. "I see. Please proceed, Mrs. Omloop."

"Well…he then asked for paper and pen and tried to write a note with his left hand, but his hand fumbled and he couldn't write. He patted his right hand and said, 'Sorry, Miss, damaged in the line of duty, you know. Would you be so kind as to write the note to the boys for me?' I retrieved a fresh sheet of paper and wrote down what he told me. I remember word for word. He said:

A bit of wonderful news. I found an item I know we can use. Only one exists. We must have it and I wish to buy it at once and need a total of £22. Borrow the extra if you must. Please give it to Police Constable Walker straightaway, who I have entrusted with this note to you.

* * *

"The sergeant read the note carefully, took the pen with his left hand, and with great difficulty initialed the note at the bottom. He then walked over to Constable Walker and ordered him to deliver the note."

This time I did a little cutting in of my own. "Excellent work. Thanks to our line of skillful questioning we now have the police constable's name as well. Walker is it! We'll report both names to their superiors. Good thing we waited, von Stray. I'll telephone police headquarters at once."

My dear friend whisked his pipe stem at me. "Hold fast, Professor. I suspect Mrs. Omloop has more to tell."

Mrs. Omloop began twisting her wedding ring again. "Sergeant O'Rourke told him, 'Walker, take this note to the boys and tell them to send me the collection funds and three pounds more. Don't take no for an answer. I found the perfect gift for our dear beloved chief.' Constable Walker opened the note and when he started to read it the sergeant made a fist with his left hand and shook it at the constable. But here I become most confused, gentlemen because I do not *comprendre* all of the sergeant's strange words to the constable. He said very loud, 'Get on with it straightaway autum-diver before I give you a floorer to the bonebox.' Constable Walker touched the rim of his helmet and ran out of the shop. Of course I do not understand all of these English words, but I remember them because they are so strange to me and my English is not yet *parfaite*. Not like my mother who teaches my daughter Elise."

Von Stray clenched the stem of his pipe. "Your English is excellent, Mrs. Omloop. Autum-diver. Floorer. Bonebox. Very strange words indeed. The English language and yet another language entirely. A language an honest woman such as yourself isn't intended to understand."

"What does it all mean, von Stray?" I asked, massaging the back of my neck.

"All part of the criminal dialect, Professor. If my studies from the *Rogue's Lexicon* serve me correctly an autum-diver is a pickpocket who practices his trade in churches and a bonebox is a mouth. Floorer is a word you might recall from your boxing days in the Royal Navy…"

I translated without check, "A pugilistic term of art we used to refer to as a 'knock down blow.' But I still don't see how any of this helps Mrs. Omloop."

"It confirms what Special Justice George W. Matsell held that 'The rogue fraternity have a language peculiarly their own, which is understood and spoken by them no matter what their dialect, or the nation where they were reared.' I'm afraid, Mrs. Omloop you have been cheated by a pair of rogue confidence men. Unfortunately their kind are infiltrating the streets of London in ever increasing numbers and taking advantage of kind-hearted refugees such as yourself. You outwardly show your gratitude toward a nation and its people for providing them with a safe home during the crisis. I'm afraid these men identified your kindness as vulnerability and took full advantage of you knowing you would never suspect a public servant in uniform of foul play. Tell me, my dear lady, were you speaking with your mother by way of the telephone when we arrived?"

She nodded and then slowly bowed her head. "She called greatly excited to hear about the wonderful item I purchased. At first I did not understand, but then I thought it strange that Sergeant O'Rourke was so long in returning. After he gave me engraving instructions for the clock he asked if he could use the shop's telephone to call police headquarters."

"Von Stray," I said, "how would Mrs. DeWitte know about the note?"

"These crooks are quite cunning and ruthless, Dilpate. They undoubtedly did their homework and staked out her home address. I'm afraid the note was intended for the elderly Mrs. DeWitte all along as part of their unthinkable plot to cheat unsuspecting refugees."

"Both of whom are widows!" I added, not hiding my contempt.

Von Stray turned to Mrs. Omloop. "Could you hear any part of his telephone conversation?"

"Yes, I heard him ask for Constable Walker and after short delay I heard him say, 'Keep your flatter-trap to a minimum lest the chief will discover our surprise.'"

I was agog. "'Flatter-trap!' He may as well be speaking another language."

Von Stray smiled. "Precisely, Dilpate. Just as Mrs. Omloop sometimes substitutes French words for English, our imposter is so accustomed to using criminal vernacular he isn't even aware he's uttering them. As a result he leaves us with yet another clue identifying his profession as a member of the criminal fraternity. His purported telephone call to the station was undoubtedly a blind in order to give him the opportunity to leave the telephone receiver disengaged so that no calls could come through. He made no telephone call whatsoever and when he pretended to speak to his confederate he blurted out the criminal vernacular 'flatter-trap' meaning 'mouth.'"

I shook my head. "By Jove these criminal masterminds plan for every contingency. He left the telephone receiver off the hook knowing Mrs. DeWitte might call and question her daughter about the strange note."

"Precisely, Dilpate, but I am not convinced these criminals are the masterminds you credit them as. I am close to identifying their own vulnerabilities that will lead to their apprehension and conviction of this tricky crime." He turned to Mrs. Omloop. "What happened after the telephone call?"

"He said that he would like to remain and chat while we waited for Constable Walker to return, but that he should attend to a few duties in the meantime and would return within the half hour. I waited quite a bit after the half hour and when there was no Sergeant O'Rourke I returned to the back room to see if I could reach him by telephone at the station. This is when I saw he left my telephone…how you say…*kaput*. I thought it strange that a sergeant would be so careless and when I fix his mistake I was about to ring the station when my mother rang. This is when you, my dear friends arrive at my shop. My mother reported that she has given Constable Walker at my instructions £22 pounds. Five she has borrowed from friends. I will have to pay them back with money I do not have. I am ruined!"

"We will do our best, my dear lady to ensure that the only ones ruined will be the scoundrels who cheated you," my companion promised. "I have just one more question. You say Sergeant O'Rourke's right hand was the one in the sling and heavily bandaged around his hand. Did you notice anything unusual about his left hand?"

Mrs. Omloop removed her spectacles and rubbed her eyes. When she was done she shook her head. "I can think of nothing. Wait! When he initialed the note with his left hand I saw that his knuckles all very bruised."

"Thank you, Mrs. Omloop. This bit of information will prove most helpful to the investigation."

"Yes," I seconded, while clearing my throat, "bruised knuckles. Quite important. A very important clue indeed."

* * *

We left our dear friend with instructions to notify the police without delay while we began our quest to track down the confidence men. I must confess that while I thought von Stray had done an excellent job in determining that a crime had indeed been committed, I saw little hope that the information he gathered would lead us to the villains' capture. While von Stray steered us toward the alley behind the Piccadilly shops on Coventry Street I shared with him my doubts.

"I'm a bit foggy, von Stray, on how the information we gathered will lead us to the culprits. Certainly you don't expect to find them hiding out in this back alley cutting up their spoils?"

Von Stray came to a stop. "Not the thieves themselves, Dilpate, but if my supposition proves correct I am certain we will find the remains of Sergeant Arthur O'Rourke."

"Great Caesar's ghost, von Stray, you think his confidant murdered him!"

"Not quite, Dilpate. If I am correct, the alleged Sergeant Arthur O'Rourke has played his final role and will be waiting for us in the wings."

I made a gesture of bewilderment. "Von Stray, you're constantly speaking in riddles."

"My apologies, old man, I have little more to go on than theory at this point and my theory is that the criminal mind can often be beaten by its own game."

"I don't follow."

"Confidence men seek to identify a victim's soft spot and use it for nefarious purposes. Therefore, when conducting an investigation of this kind I make it a habit to ask: What is the criminal's soft spot and how can I use it to my gain? In the case before us I have come to the conclusion that every moment our imposter remains in police uniform he runs the risk of being spotted and detained by a legitimate member of the police. My supposition is further supported by Mrs. Omloop's observation that Walker never partook in the gift selection, but spent his visit instead staring outside. A role more consistent with a look-out man than prospective patron." He began walking and I followed. "According to my hypothesis our imposter would, at first opportunity, shed himself of his disguise, lose himself in the throng of Piccadilly shoppers, and then rendezvous with his confederate at a predetermined location where they will divide the money."

Von Stray stopped at a set of rubbish-bins located behind the shops. He began pulling off their lids and inspecting their contents. I followed his example and on my fifth attempt I uncovered what we were looking for. "Von Stray! A police sergeant's uniform."

"Excellent work, Dilpate!"

"Think nothing of it, von Stray. It's all quite simple really when you use scientific reasoning to dismember the criminal brain and begin to think one step ahead of them."

The great detective removed the uniform from the rubbish-bin and upon close inspection it turned out to be of the same quality one would acquire from a costume shop. Nevertheless, it was enough to fool a trusting refugee still acclimating to her new home.

"Well, here is the whole outfit," I said, showing my palms, "hat, tunic complete with sergeant stripes, costume police badge, and trousers. This all but confirms our sergeant was an imposter but unfortunately it doesn't tell us where he disappeared to."

"Perhaps the uniform does not, my dear fellow, but what is noticeably absent from our imposter's discarded uniform supports my hypothesis of where to look. Come, Dilpate, we must embark for Whitehall Place with all available dispatch!"

* * *

For multiple reasons I have never regretted my decision to keep myself in tip-top condition; not least of which is keeping up with von Stray when he is hot on the trail of a suspect. Keeping to his heels we raced past Trafalgar Square and then made a few cuts over to Whitehall Place where we stopped in front of the Marquess of Queensbury Boxing Chamber.

I caught my breath and said, "Von Stray, what are we doing here?"

"Testing whether my theory on a criminal's habits is correct."

Inside the boxing gym von Stray approached a scrappy looking elderly gentleman who was busy chewing on the butt end of a mangled cigar. "Excuse me, sir, we're looking for a left-handed boxer whom I believe may have an injured right hand."

The old man studied von Stray's forehead. "'E give you that gift on the ol' brainbox?"

Von Stray touched his scar. "I'm afraid that was a gift from the Kaiser."

The old man nodded. "Well, guess no 'arm in tellin' ya. Your man's Tony Capone, but you won't find 'im 'ere for long. Told 'im to clean out 'is bloody locker and beat it but quick. 'E wouldn't know the Queensbury Rules if they 'it 'im straight the kisser. You can find 'im out back."

In the locker-room we saw a big man fitting Mrs. Omloop's description of the imposter—bandaged hand and all. He was in the process of cleaning out a gym locker using his left hand to stuff boxing gear into a draw-string sack.

Von Stray shouted, "Sergeant O'Rourke stand fast!"

The big man's head snapped in our direction. He froze for a second and then pulled a concealed stiletto out from his arm sling and then charged von Stray.

"Knife!" I shouted, pushing my friend safely out of the way.

Upholding the finest traditions of the Queensbury Rules, I put my right hand behind my back to even the odds against the scoundrel. Having had extensive experience in the boxing ring during my days with the Royal Navy, I instantly identified the clumsy bloke as a plodder and didn't bother to remove my spectacles. As the big clod lunged at me I easily parried his downward left blow. My quick bob-and-weave caused him to miss his target and stumble into a locker. With an adroit step backward and nimble shuffle to my left I was able to greet him with a fierce hook to his nut as my attacker turned right in attempt to regroup for a feeble second charge. My one square strike to his bone-box was all I needed to send the imposter crashing to the floor for a clean knockout.

Unbeknownst to me the old man had followed us in the locker-room. "Sportin' match, old man," he said, taking my hand with his own iron grip. "Marquess of Queensbury all the way. Always a spot 'ere for a sportin' gent such as yourself."

"Thank you, sir. This impudent scoundrel is an imposter and is wanted by the authorities for impersonating a police sergeant and swindling two widows."

He took a moment to adjust his cigar before saying, "Villainous! I only 'opes a British jury repays 'im with a bit of 'is own coin and throws the book at 'im, gents because 'e's been imposterin' 'round 'ere as boxer, as well."

***

After placing the imposter Capone into police custody they got a confession and the name of his confederate out of him in two shakes of a lamb's tail. As is usually the case with these lawless types his fellow flimflammer had double-crossed Capone intending to keep all the ill-gotten gains for himself. Fortunately, the police recovered all of Mrs. Omloop's £22.

Walking back to our lodgings I quizzed von Stray on his remarkable discovery of Capone's location.

"How did you figure out Capone was a boxer, von Stray?"

"His use of the word 'floorer' is a term as you know in general use by pugilists and this was enough for me to at least ponder the notion. I then considered that perhaps his right hand really had been injured—in a manner consistent with a boxing match. This was enough for me to make further inquiries from Mrs. Omloop about Capone's left hand and you will recall she said the knuckles were bruised. My hypothesis was further supported when we discovered his complete disguise in the alley with the exception of his arm sling and heavy bandage. If they had indeed been part of his disguise, then there would've been little reason not to dispose of them along with the uniform."

"Brilliant, von Stray. Always making bricks without straw. How did you know he was a left-handed boxer?"

"Much of the confidence scheme depended on his being left-handed. You will recall the name he used while posing as a police sergeant?"

"Arthur O'Rourke," I replied, " I shall never forget."

"Can you think of anyone else with the same initials?"

I thought for a moment. "Good Gad! Mrs. Amalasand Omloop. So when Capone initialed the note he had Mrs. Omloop write in her own hand he could initial it with her same initials."

"Precisely, Dilpate. Adding further authenticity to the note. Not only would Mrs. Omloop's mother see a note written in her daughter's hand, but it would also bear her initials."

"Ingenious."

"The language of the note was not only designed to swindle the intended victim, but drafted in such a way to allow Capone to forge Mrs. Omloop's hand."

By this time we had reached the wrought-iron gate leading into our apartment building. "How so?"

"If we credit Mrs. Omloop's recitation of the note's language, the sentence 'A bit of wonderful news' begins with a capital 'A' and the sentence 'Only one exists' begins with a capital 'O.' This provided our imposter with a handwriting sample of how Mrs. Omloop writes these particular letters. You will recall how she said the imposter read the letter closely. I submit he was really making a quick study of our friend's script. If his intent was to copy her hand this is a strong vote in favor of Capone being able to control his left hand sufficiently enough to accomplish the forgery."

"Well done, von Stray. Who would have suspected that my broken lapel pin would ultimately lead to you solving yet another baffling matter. My lapel pin! I forgot to leave it with Mrs. Omloop." I consulted my pocket watch. "It's quarter to four and her shop will close in a quarter hour."

"Leave it to me, old man. I owe you. Capone's stiletto was meant for me."

I handed my lapel pin to von Stray and he was off like a shot to the Piccadilly. As I watched my friend disappear from my view I shook my head in admiration for his effort, but knew he would never make it in time.

* * *

Other than a slight snag at the close of the evening's events, the Club's ceremony honoring my beetles was a swell affair enjoyed by everyone in attendance. After my brief remarks concerning my discoveries brought thunderous applause, the Honorable Veritable Walnut called the gathering back to order.

"And now," His Honor bellowed, "we complete our ceremony with a time-honored tradition. As a sign of friendship and loyalty this year's

Honored Walnut will exchange his Club lapel pin with a fellow member of his choosing." He spread his arms with a dignified flourish. "Professor…you *have* the stage!"

With dispatch I tore myself from the head table and double-timed it over to von Stray. He had somehow managed to have my lapel pin repaired in time for the ceremony and I told him upon its return how it had never looked better.

I tapped him on the left shoulder in accordance with Club custom and he rose from his chair and stood at attention. I removed my pristine lapel pin and when I pulled his pin in order to conduct the exchange its stick end caught a snag and yanked out a web of silk threads from his buttonhole. It was all I could do to hide my complete shock at the scandalous outcome of the sacred ceremony.

Von Stray said, while collecting my gleaming lapel pin and slipping it into his buttonhole, "Sorry to stick you with a busted lapel pin, old man, but Mrs. Omloop closed shop early today. I swapped out my pin for yours. Seems you're back where you started."

I scooped a glass of champagne from a convenient tray and with a genuine air of cheerful mateyness toasted my friend for the whole Club to hear, "To Henry von Stray, who exemplifies better than any man I know the Club's motto—*Amicus Fidus*—Loyal Friend."

Velda and the Murder Muffins

Ron Miller

"You don't have to sit like that," Chip said, "I'll take you somewhere and feed you."

"I was hoping you'd take me someplace *nice* for a change," I scowled, uncrossing my legs and pulling the hem of my skirt back below my knees.

"Yeah, well," he said, leaning back from his typewriter and digging his wallet from his back pocket. "Here's a couple bucks. Why don't you run across the street to the Automat and pick us up some sandwiches? Coffee, too. I gotta get this story to rewrite by seven or, well, I'll be back working for Slotnik. You wouldn't want that to happen, would you?"

Was he kidding? What did I care? I hopped off the corner of his desk and took his damned money.

"Nobody can ever say you don't know how to show a girl a good time."

"Aw, don't be like that, Velda, you know what I make here…"

"Piffle. You were making a lot better money at Slotnik's and you still only took me to the Automat."

"Say, you were making pretty good money, too—before you quit to become a private eye. How much've *you* made since?"

"Yeah? Well the same to you, too," I said and stormed down to the street, as angry at Chip as I was at myself for having made such a lame rejoinder, let alone one that hadn't made a lick of sense. The Automat was actually a block away and I was still so sore at Chip that I was nearly there before I realized there was a crowd pushing its way around the entrance.

"Hey, Clancy," I asked a cop I recognized, "someone jump off the roof?"

"Oh—howya doin', Velda? Naw, someone croaked inside. Two of 'em, in fact. All I know. I'm just here to keep the rubberneckers movin'."

I knew the food was no great shakes, but this news certainly gave me pause for thought. I'd never heard of the stuff actually killing anyone before.

"You wanna know what's goin' on, you go on in there and talk to the lieutenant."

"Dillinger? Why's homicide interested?"

"Ya gotta ask him that."

I went inside and did. The lieutenant was as happy to see me as he always is.

"How the hell did you get in here, Velda?" he said, warmly.

"I just pushed on the revolving door and here I am. What's up, anyway? Someone finally order the salmon mousse?"

"Naw. It's a plain case of poisoning, see?" the lieutenant said, holding out a plate on which lay a couple of half-gnawed muffins. "Loaded with enough cyanide to kill a horse."

They looked ordinary-enough to me at which thought a chill went down my back. What had I expected? Little skull-and-crossbones on them? I told Dillinger that Clancy'd said a couple of people had died.

"Yeah. One's right over here," he said, pointing to a sheet-covered form on the linoleum floor. "Show 'er the stiff, Ralph."

The cop pulled the sheet aside, revealing a body that'd probably looked no better alive than it did dead. It was a raggedy old lady, about a thousand years old, like you see a hundred times a day picking through ash cans and bumming cigarettes. Dillinger must've seen the expression on my face.

"Anyone you recognize?"

"Yeah. She used to come round Slotnik's all the time, looking for handouts and cadging cigarettes and dimes. Lived in a dump at the end of the alley that ran behind the theater. Shame, I guess, her being bumped off this way and all. She was okay—a nice enough old bird, I guess. I gave her some change now and then, but I don't think I ever said more than two words to her. Never did learn her name. Uh, you said there are two of them?"

"Uh huh. The other one's over here," he said, leading me toward the door to the men's restroom. He turned to me and damned if he wasn't blushing!

"He's, ah, he's in the, ah, men's room."

"Why, that's great, Lieutenant. I can not only see the body, I can finally find out what the inside of a men's room looks like."

"Tsk, tsk. Your dad must never've known what sort of daughter he was raising."

I knew the lieutenant was just kidding around. My dad was the best cop the force ever had—and would still be if he hadn't gotten killed in the line of duty. There was a big scandal around his death—I won't go into that now—and Dillinger was one of the cops that put his career on the line standing up for my dad's name. I owed him a lot for that. On the other hand, there was something to what he said. I know dad wouldn't have approved of my job at Slotnik's, but what was I to do?

I followed him inside, where the police photographer was still taking shots. The body was uncovered and I saw a chubby little man in a nice pinstripe suit. Nice, but not expensive and not new, either. Looked like an insurance salesman, maybe, or an accountant.

"This fellow," Dillinger said, handing me a business card, "we know. According to this, he was Conklin P. Aglet. Got a little import-export business around the corner. Dealt mostly in plastic spatulas."

"Anything to tie the two together?"

"Not a thing, so far's I can tell."

"So what do you figure, lieutenant? Some psycho, maybe?"

"I dunno. Beats me. Who else'd poison the food in a restaurant?"

It beat me, too.

There was obviously little point in trying to get anything to eat at the Automat. Which was okay by me since I hated eating there anyway. I went around to the next block where I knew there was a little coffee shop. I got myself a cheeseburger and black coffee and started thinking. Not about Chip. Let him wonder where his dinner was, I figured. Do him good. No, what I was thinking about was that old lady. I'd kind of liked the old bat and wondered if there was anyone at her place who ought to know she was dead. Maybe a cat or something.

Slotnik's was only about three blocks over, so I hoofed it to the alley behind the theater. At the dead end of it were the rears of half a dozen tenements. The old lady, I knew, had a hole she called home in the basement of one of them. I banged on the door, but didn't get an answer, which is pretty much what I expected. It took me about three seconds to spring the lock. (I've been getting really good at that lately, I'm pleased to say.)

Inside it was an even worse dump than I'd imagined. There was just the one room, an old storeroom or something like that. No heat, no electricity, no water. There was a ratty-looking cot pushed up against one wall behind a bunch of fiberboard barrels. Sitting on an old vegetable crate next to it was a Sterno hot plate. There were empty tin cans—mostly beans and hash—piled on the floor around it. The rest of the room was filled with stuff—nothing but junk and more junk. She must've been like a packrat or whatever they're called, picking up everything she saw and dragging it back here. There were bundles of old newspapers and magazines, broken baby carriages, empty bottles, old mattresses, busted chairs, discarded clothes, bird cages, stuffed animals missing legs and heads, all sorts of lumber, car parts, bicycle frames, old radios, you name it and every bit of it was useless trash.

I poked through it all, not having any idea why—maybe just a kind of morbid fascination—when I spotted a Folger's coffee can sitting on top of a doorless Frigidaire. I don't know why I thought there was anything unusual in that, given how the rest of the place was decorated, but I took the can down and shook it. There was something inside. I pried the lid off and pulled out a zippered leather bag, like the kind people keep toiletries in when they travel.

Oh ho!

It contained a fistful of bank books. Five of them, to be exact. There was also a bunch of other papers, but they were just typed pages, all yellow with age. Old letters or some such, I figured. I was more interested in the books. I spread them out like a poker hand. They were from banks all over the city. I opened one of them at glanced at the first page. Well, at least now the old lady had a name: Lola Momrath. That was something anyway. I flipped through to the last page in each book and did a mental calculation. Oh ho, indeed. The old bat had more than forty-five grand stashed away.

This certainly gave me pause for thought. Could it be possible that *she* had been the intended victim, not the spatula man? But then, why did Aglet die? And if someone'd croaked the old lady for her money, what were the bank books still doing here? The whole thing was making me damned curious.

I walked over to Splittner St., where Aglet had his office according to the business card I'd seen. It was after eight o'clock, but there was a light on in the third floor front, where I figured Aglet's place probably was. I went upstairs. At the end of the hall there was a door with a pebbled glass panel on which was painted: Conklin P. Aglet—Import and Export. There was a light on behind it, so I went on in.

Inside was just a small room with a bunch of filing cabinets, a couple of ratty leather chairs and a desk with a blonde behind it. She had been crouched down digging in a bottom drawer and jumped about six inches straight up when I came in.

She pushed her harlequin glasses back onto her button nose, glared at me over the top of them and said, "Oh. I thought it was the police again. I'm sorry, but the office is closed."

I fished one of my cards out of my purse and dropped it onto her desk. She didn't pick it up. She didn't even look at it.

"My name's Velda Bellinghausen. I'm a private investigator. I was wondering if I might ask you a few questions about Mr. Aglet?"

"Why?"

"Why what?"

"Why are you interested in Mr. Aglet? I really don't see what concern he would be to you."

"I'm not at liberty to reveal my, ah, client. I only have a couple of questions, though. You don't have to answer any of them if you don't want to."

"I probably won't, but go ahead if it'll make you happy."

I glanced around the room and asked the obvious one: "Was Mr. Aglet in any sort of financial difficulty?"

That got her. She snorted derisively. It was a very unladylike sound.

"Was he ever! He was dead broke, the lousy phony! I ain't been paid in two months! And it sure don't look like I'm gonna get paid now, does it?"

"I'm surprised you're still working…"

"Yeah, you'd think so, wouldn't you? Well, I ain't working. I just figure maybe I can find something worth pawning before the creditors start showing up."

"Bad businessman?"

"Naw—he was a great one. A lousy *gambler* is what he was. Made a ton a cash in the business but lost every penny he had on the ponies—and every penny he could borrow, too, near's I can figure. Buncha tough mugs been comin' round lately lookin' for their dough, which I can tell you I didn't like so much."

"You think he welshed on a gambling debt?"

"What do you think? You're the detective. The lousy fink! Now what am I supposed to do?"

I couldn't have cared less. It looked like my next stop was going to be Virgil the Bookie. I found him where he could always be found, twenty-four hours a day, but then it's easy to find a good case of tetanus, too, and who does that on purpose?

I spotted him as soon as I entered the bar. He was a skinny man who'd gone completely bald while still in high school, which gave him a jaundiced outlook the rest of his life. He watched me walk up to his booth with all the expression of a doorknob, which he resembled to no small degree.

"Say, long time no see, Velda! How ya doin'?"

"I'm doing just swell, Virgil."

"Well, you're sure a sight for sore eyes, I can tell you." He meant that, too, being a longtime sufferer from granulated eyelids. "Siddown, siddown, already, have a beer or somethin.'"

I slid onto the bench opposite him and took the drink he offered. It was an ice cold Pabst, so how could I have refused?

"So how's the private eye racket?"

"It's just swell, too."

"You ain't on a case now, are you? 'Cause I gotta tell you I don't know nuthin bout nuthin."

"No, I'm not on a case, not exactly. I'm just curious about something, that's all."

"Well, sometimes curiosity, you know, is a pretty good thing. I mean, you discover gravity and penicillium and things like that, but sometimes curiosity also ain't such a good thing, if you get my drift, you know what I mean?"

"Yeah, I know what you mean, but this isn't anything like that. Like I said, this is just for me."

"I can tell you got a question you're just dying to ask me, so go ahead and shoot."

"You know a guy named Aglet? Conklin P. Aglet?"

"Don't I just!"

"How much was into you for?"

"That piker? Hell, I sold his marker. Wasn't worth keeping. It was only a lousy forty-five centuries. Peanuts."

"Well, someone must've liked peanuts well enough to have croaked him."

"Only one person that hungry—"

Yeah, I knew just whose name he was going to say, too. Spider-eyes Griswold. No way *he* was going to get stuck with anyone's bad debt, peanuts or no peanuts. I thanked Virgil for the beer and left.

Spider-eyes ran his operation from a cubbyhole in the back of what passed itself off as an auto repair shop, but I sure would've been surprised if the owners of any of the cars I sidled past knew they were there since the men working on them were busy filing the serial numbers off the engine blocks. The door to Griswold's office was closed and was kept that way by a thick-necked bruiser the size of a Nash Metropolitan and probably not half as smart. Fortunately, he'd spent a lot of what his boss paid him at Slotnik's box office, so he knew perfectly well who I was. I recognized him, too, since he'd always sat in the front row.

"The boss in, Percy?"

"Hey! Velda!" he said, with a grin that threatened to split his head in half, like a grapefruit. "Watcha doin' here, not that it ain't swell to see ya?"

"Just want to have a little chat with Spider-eyes, is all. Okay?"

"Hey! Yeah! Sure thing, Velda!"

He turned to let me pass and just for a treat for being so nice, I kinda bumped him a little as I went by.

I opened the door, but didn't go more than half a step into the room. Not that I didn't want to, but because Griswold had already filled it to capacity. He was not only the fattest human being I'd ever seen (he made Fifi, the fat lady with Professor Peerpont's Grand Universal Wonder Show, look like a *Vogue* model), he was the ugliest, with a kind of monumental ugliness that was almost supernatural.

"Say! If it ain't my favorite stripper! Little overdressed tonight, ain't we?"

"Not you, Spider-eyes. I see you forgot the paper bag you oughta wear over your head."

"Ha. Ha. Ha"—he laughed just like that; three distinct, mirthless syllables—"You think you're a riot, don't you"

"Yeah, I got 'em slapping their knees at the rest home. So—how's business?"

"It's a livin'. Why the sudden interest?"

"I heard that Harry Aglet was into you for forty-five hundred bucks. Buy you a lot of chicken-fried steak."

"Chicken *feed* you mean. I dint have nuthin' t' do with him gettin' hisself croaked. I heard he just ate somethin what disagreed with him."

"Yeah—like maybe a muffin full of cyanide."

"Look here, kid—yer barkin' up the wrong neck of the woods. You think I'd risk a murder rap for a lousy forty-five hundred bucks? I mighta had the boys mess 'im up a little, but *poison*? That's for sissies. Jesus, Velda, I'd hoped you thought better of me than that."

I walked back to Pith Street, made myself a stiff martini and went to bed.

The papers the next morning were making the most of the story, which I'm sure Mr. Horn and Mr. Hardart just hated. I went down to Joe's for my usual coffee and donuts and he tossed the morning edition of the *Graphic* onto the counter for me to look at while he got my order. He knows I usually prefer the *Graphic* out of loyalty to Chip, but today I opened the paper with only halfhearted interest. I forgot my gripe with him, though, when the headline jumped out at me: *Businessman Kills Self At Automat.* Joe set my coffee and donuts by my elbow, but I ignored them as I flipped to the page with the story. There wasn't much to it. The cops'd found a suicide note in Aglet's office. It was pretty straightforward. He'd been up to his neck in debt and didn't see any way out but suicide. Goodbye cruel world, sincerely, Conklin P. Aglet.

I didn't believe a word of it.

Well, I mean I didn't believe a word about Aglet's checking himself out, though if true it explained, I guess, what happened to Lola. When Aglet felt sick and went to the restroom, she'd glommed onto his left-over muffin like the good little panhandler she was and, well, there you go.

But...

"You're going to get wrinkles, screwing your face up like that."

"I know, Joe, but I'm trying to figure something out."

"About that bozo what croaked hisself over at the Automat?"

"Yeah."

"See? All the more reason you shouldn't oughta eat at places like that. How many times I tell you that? Who knows what's goin' on behind that wall, huh? Here, the food ain't nothin' special, but you see what you're gettin', you know what I mean."

"Only thing might put me off my feed, Joe, is you, not the food."

"That's okey dokey by me. You got a strong enough stummick to take my looks, my grub won't be nothin'."

I told him how I just couldn't figure Conklin P. Aglet for suicide, but couldn't put my finger on why.

"Hell, eating a poisoned muffin in the Automat? You gotta be kiddin' me.

That ain't no way to kill yourself. A guy, he's gonna eat a bullet or jump out a winda—but a poisoned *muffin*? No way. Hell, how many guys even know how to *make* a muffin?"

I had to admit he had a point there. *I* couldn't make a muffin…well, I couldn't make much of anything for that matter, but that's beside the point. Could a spatula importer make a muffin? I had my doubts. On the other hand, it sure seemed even sillier to think of someone going to the Automat, getting a muffin from the window, sitting down and then sprinkling it with cyanide.

I went back to my place and called Sally at my answering service, though I was pretty sure what I'd hear.

"You got about a dozen messages from Chip," she said. "You wanna hear any of them?"

"Hell, no."

"That's what I figgered so I already dumped 'em. Why don't you do the same thing to the bum, Velda?"

"I might just do that very thing, Sally."

"Yeah, sure—you could have your choice of any man in the city, for Pete's sake. Sure could do a lot better than that cheapskate, at any rate."

"No kidding. I'm sure getting tired of take-out Chinese and going to the fights. That's all we ever do."

"Sure thing! Say, Velda…you ever give the bum the rush, lemme know, will ya? I ain't had a date in so long I can't afford to be too fussy. Maybe he goes for the petite blonde type, you know?"

"He might at that," I said, hanging up. I was, after all, three and a half inches taller than him.

A thought had been percolating through my head ever since breakfast, so I called Lieutenant Dillinger.

"Say, Lieutenant," I said after the usual chit chat, "anyone find the container, the one that had the cyanide in it?"

"What container?"

"The one I just said, the one that Aglet had the cyanide in?"

"What the hell're you talking about, Velda?"

"Nothing, Lieutenant. I was just thinking is all."

"Well, it was bound to happen sometime, but don't get overexcited about it—it might be just a fluke."

"Yeah? Well, the only flukes *I* know about are the ones attached to your liver." That was, I thought, a pretty damned good come-back, so I hung up.

I made myself some coffee, thinking: if Aglet poisoned his own muffins, where did the cyanide come from? I poured a big mug full of black fluid, dug Lola's leather pouch out of my purse and took both over to my old easy chair by the window. I flung myself onto it, draping my legs over one of the arms, and took out the bank books again. I flipped through the pages, but they didn't tell me much. She'd made regular deposits for years, like clockwork, every week. Just a few bucks, not much, but it'd sure added up.

I was shoving the books back in the pouch when I remembered the papers that were also in it. I pulled them out and unfolded them. They were soft and yellow and coming apart at the folds, so I had to be careful. There were some typewritten letters, a couple of old newspaper clippings and a document of some kind. I looked at that last one first. It was a birth certificate, of all things. It wasn't Lola's, partly because it was dated only forty years earlier and she'd sure been an awful lot older than that, but mainly because it was for a boy. Jeez, old Lola was a mother. Who would've thought?

Stapled to the back of the certificate was another document. This one was from the state orphanage she'd evidently turned the kid over to. I compared the dates—yeah, they were only a couple of days apart. She'd probably had the kid at the place. It probably said so somewhere, but I'd look for that later.

The newspaper clippings… One was dated about seventeen years after the birth certificate and announced the graduating class of a Brooklyn high school, the other was dated a few years later and listed the graduating class of a downtown trade school. I traced the lines of names with my finger until—bingo—there was Conklin P. Aglet, two times.

Well, well!

I leaned back in my chair and sucked on my coffee. It wasn't too hard to figure out that Lola was Aglet's mother. Somewhere along the line she must've picked up a case of maternal instinct and started keeping track of her offspring.

I'm not sure what inspired me, but I reached over to the window sill, picked up the phone and put it in my lap. With the receiver clamped between ear and shoulder, I opened the first bank book and dialed the branch number printed inside the cover.

"Say," I told the man who answered, "I just got a check here for, ah, fifty dollars from a Lola Momrath and I was just wondering if it was any good."

I gave him the account number and he told me to hold one while he looked it up. He came back on the line a minute later.

"Miss? I'm sorry, but I'm afraid that account's been closed."

"Closed?"

"Yes, ma'am. Mrs. Momrath closed it out just a few days ago."

I thanked him, hung up, and called the other four banks. I gave them the same story and got the same answer. Well, now there was a puzzle, wasn't it? The old lady must've had forty-five grand in cash kicking around somewhere. Where? Why? Especially "where."

* * *

I went back to Splittner St. As I'd half expected, Aglet's office was closed. I made sure the corridor was empty, and sprung the lock. The secretary'd certainly been busy since I'd last seen her. She'd ripped the place apart. I went through the mess, but only found a couple of useful things. One was a metal cash box. It was laying open beneath an emptied bookcase, so I figured it'd been hidden behind some books. I picked it up, but there was nothing in it. Either it'd been empty all along or the secretary had found what she'd been looking for. The second thing I found gave the secretary a name, so now I didn't have to keep calling her "the secretary." I could call her Paula Panda. Better yet, I found out where Paula Panda lived.

I went across the street and sat in the drug store, sucking on a chocolate soda, where I could see the entrance to Aglet's building. I might well be too late, but what the hell. At least I was having a chocolate soda, so whatever happened the afternoon wouldn't be a total loss.

I glanced at the clock above the fountain. It was a quarter of two. Just as I turned my gaze back to the street, I saw the mailman enter the building. I finished my soda in a hurry, which I hated to do, but I figured I'd better just in case. I never know for sure when I'll eat. By the time I got to the lobby, the mailman was just leaving. The place was empty, so I went up to the mailbox for suite 3B and—fully aware I was committing a federal offense, but what the hell—twiddled a bobby pin in the crappy little lock and pulled out the package that'd just been delivered. I shoved it into my bag and scrammed, sweating and my heart pounding like I'd run a mile, as if I'd ever do such a thing. As soon as I was on the street, I flagged the first cab I saw. Fortunately, I never have any trouble getting cabs to stop for me.

I gave the driver Paula's address, thankful we had to go only a half dozen blocks, since I only had a couple of dollars in my purse. As soon as the cab pulled away from the curb, I ripped open the package. Inside was an expandable folder, the kind with a little ribbon tying it shut. I undid it and looked under the flap.

Well, well!

I had the driver stop a few doors past the secretary's address. I gave him everything I had, which didn't make for much of a tip, I'm afraid, so I made sure I showed a lot of leg getting out of the cab.

I walked back to the address I'd gotten in Aglet's office. It was just a narrow apartment building squeezed into a row of exactly identical buildings. I checked the mailboxes. "P. Panda" was lettered on a piece of tape stuck beneath the slot for apartment 5.

The apartment was at the head of the first flight of stairs. I tiptoed up to it and put my ear to the door. Someone inside was very busy doing something. I swallowed hard, opened the door and stepped into the room. It was just a cheap cold-water flat with one room serving for living room and bedroom and a little alcove for the kitchenette. Paula was standing on the far side of the bed, her hands full of the clothes she was packing into a couple of suitcases. She stared at me as though I'd just risen through the floorboards like a magician's trick.

"Mind if I come in?" I asked.

"What the hell do *you* want?" she snarled, her expression of surprise changing to anger. "I already told you everything I know."

"Yeah. You told me Aglet owed you two months' back pay."

"Yeah? And so what's that to you?"

"Nothing—but at twenty-five hundred a month you must be the highest paid key-pounder in the city."

She glared at me for a full five seconds and then her hand dived into the open suitcase. When it returned it was bearing a little nickel-plated revolver. She let me have a good look at its business end, which I found uncommonly interesting.

"Think you're pretty damn smart, don't you?" she sneered.

"I do indeed. Smarter than you, at any rate."

"And how do you figure that?"

"Four reasons. One, Aglet wouldn't kill himself over a lousy forty-five hundred bucks. Two, I knew he'd pulled together the money he owed his bookie. Three, I figured you for taking that money and making it look like your boss never had it. No special reason for thinking that—I just didn't like your looks very much. I found the empty cash box, by the way. That where he'd had the money hidden?"

"That's only three reasons."

"Yeah. Number four: I know enough to take the safety off a gun."

The dummy actually turned the gun to look at it, which is when I leaped over the bed and tackled her. We both went over backward onto the floor, my fall cushioned by her body. Her head bounced off the wall, leaving a round hole in the plaster. I slugged her on the point of her chin, making her teeth clack like a castanet and her silly-looking glasses shoot off somewhere. That felt pretty good, so I did it a couple more times, just to see if it weren't a fluke. Nope. Felt great each time.

I squatted on my haunches straddling her and pointed the gun at her nose while she glared back with myopic hatred.

"You really weren't all that hard to figure out, Brainiac. You just thought that if no one ever knew your boss had gotten the money to pay off Virgil, everyone would assume he killed himself because of his debts. I take it you got the money around here someplace?"

"Why don't you just take a flying leap and—" she growled, finishing the sentence with a very rude suggestion.

"Nice talk coming from someone who just murdered an innocent old lady."

"Aw, how was I supposed to know she'd glom onto one of the muffins after…"

"After you'd laced one with the cyanide?"

She glared at me, knowing she'd just let slip a pretty damning admission.

"So what'd you do, have lunch with the boss and use the poison on whatever first came to hand? Then when he got sick and took off for the restroom, you scrammed—forgetting about the leftover muffin laying there on the plate."

"It wasn't my fault…"

"Then you really didn't have any idea that was Aglet's mother did you?"

"Who? What? Not that old bag? You're kidding me! That was really his…?"

"Uh huh. And look at the birthday present she sent him. You should've waited around for this afternoon's mail."

Keeping the gun pointed at her nose, I flipped open the folder I'd picked up at Aglet's office and showed her the sheaves of greenbacks it contained. Gee, normally I would have said that the expression on her face was just priceless, but under the circumstances I'd say it was worth just exactly forty-five thousand dollars.

The Mysterious Woman in the Lifeguard Chair

Bruce W. Most

The summer night was airless, pitch black, and as sultry as sin. The residential lights of Coney Island huddled behind blackout curtains, the bright boardwalk lights snuffed out, Wonder Wheel and the Baby Incubator sideshow gone dark, while saloon patrons drank by candlelight. Even the moon was afraid to come out.

Weegee, New York City's most famous crime photographer, if he did say so himself, slogged in the soft beach sand in his brogues lugging his 4x5 Speed Graphic press camera. He hadn't come to photograph a crime scene, however. The tabloids were hungry for human-interest pictures depicting how New Yorkers were surviving the city's heat wave.

Or maybe it was a crime scene. While the rich cooled off in their luxury high-rises with new-fangled air conditioning, thousands of less fortunate slept on beaches to catch the cool Atlantic breeze, trying to escape heat stroke in their stifling, breathless apartments.

Weegee zigzagged gingerly to avoid stepping on the sleepers and the couples who'd come not to sleep but to find amorous refuge in each other's sweaty arms.

The sleepers he couldn't see or hear, except for the occasional snore, but the lovers he could zero in on by their bursts of laughter, moans, or the flare of a cigarette tip.

"No, no, Billy, don't touch me there."

"Ah, c'mon, doll, you'll like it."

A slap.

"Damn, what was that for?"

Randomly, Weegee would raise his camera and blindly snap a photo, the camera settings preset at f/16 and 1/200th of a second, focused at ten feet, the flashgun throwing out its light, as he had done so often documenting the city's crimes, fires, and accidents.

These photographs were different, however. He was using the new infrared film he'd been experimenting with the past few months, able to record in dark movie theaters or other low-light situations. The flashbulbs were not standard either. Standard flash would have disturbed the lovers and sleepers, to say nothing of breaking wartime blackout regulations. These special infrared-wavelength bulbs sent out light invisible to the subject.

Few on the beach would even know he was taking their picture.

"Hey, pal, watch where you stepping," snapped a gruff voice in the darkness.

Weegee mumbled apologies around his half-smoked cigar and backed away. He continued slogging through the throng, snapping pictures. Once, he caught a sailor in white embracing a woman in a long white dress. He smiled to himself. A sure seller to the tabs.

As he neared the water's edge, waves slapping against the shore, he stopped to rest against one of the beach's many wooden lifeguard stands. Slogging a heavy Speed Graphic across sand was hard work, and he wasn't in the best of shape.

Something stirred above him in the unmanned chair. No giggles or moans, but he suspected a couple had found their way above the crowd, a place to be intimate in private. He stepped back to get a clear view. He could make out the vague outline of a person. Not a couple. A single person. A young woman, he thought. An intake of breath. Yes, a woman. Restless, edgy movement.

Why was she perched alone on this sultry night atop a lifeguard stand above the lovers and sleepers, staring out at the black sea? Waiting for her lover? Or had he jilted her, leaving her alone with her anger and disappointment and maybe sadness?

Intrigued, he lifted his camera and snapped a picture with invisible light.

* * *

Two days later, knuckles rapped on the door of Weegee's tiny Manhattan room near Little Italy. The photographer stirred from a shallow sleep. He mostly slept during the day—catnapped, really, what with the constant chatter of the police radio by his bed, the crack of gunshots below him from the firing range of the John Jovino Gun Shop, and shouts from across the street as cops hauled suspects into the block-long central police headquarters. The oppressive summer heat made sleep even more difficult.

More raps. Insistent this time. Weegee blinked and glanced at his alarm clock. Twenty after two in the afternoon. Hours before he would normally rise, prepare his equipment, eat at Moran's luncheonette down the street, followed by a beer at Headquarters Tavern, before striking out into the evening to document the dark underbelly of the city.

"Yeah, whaddya want?" he grumbled, his voice still groggy after a night photographing a bread truck hauled out of the East River with its dead driver, a burning apartment building in the Bowery, and a homicide in Chinatown. Another mob guy.

"I wish to purchase a picture from you," a male voice said through the thin door. "I'll make it well worth your while."

The voice was loud enough that everybody on the floor could hear that Weegee the Famous might be coming into money. God knows he could use it.

He rolled off his iron cot and its thin mattress, half-dressed should the fire bell go off or the police radio broadcast a newsworthy crime. He threw on a shirt, shuffled across the linoleum floor in his stocking feet, and opened the door. The voice belonged to a man short like him but far better

197

dressed than anyone living within the surrounding blocks. Hot as it was, the man wore a suit, hat, and brown and white reptile leather shoes, which must have been expensive or stolen, what with wartime leather shortages. Who the hell wore such fancy shoes in this part of town?

The guy bulled into the room without an invitation. He took in the place with disdain in his dark eyes and hesitated, as if having second thoughts about doing business with anyone living in a dump like this. His attention paused at the riot of newspaper photos tacked to the wall above the bed, surrounding a handmade sign that read in large black letters, *Murder Is My Business*.

"Hey, pal, you don't barge into my room," snapped Weegee. "Who the hell are you?"

The man slowly turned his attention from the clippings and focused on their creator. "I saw your pictures in the *Daily Mirror* you took the other night on the beach at Coney Island."

Hard to imagine the guy read the tabs. Seemed more a Gray Lady type. Weegee's photos rarely made the *New York Times*.

"Always happy to meet fans," Weegee said, not bothering to hide his annoyance.

"I'm not a fan," the man said. "I find pictures of people sleeping and guys getting fresh with their women highly offensive in a family newspaper. Taking their picture with some kind of *invisible light*. Creepy, you ask me, stalking people like that."

Something in his voice reminded Weegee of the sing-song patter of grifters on the boardwalk.

"I didn't ask you, pal," Weegee said. "And I'd hardly call the *Mirror* a family newspaper." The *Mirror* had snatched up several of his photos and splashed them on the back-page. Good money. And he'd sold pictures to three other tabs. "What picture you lookin' to buy? One of the creepy ones?"

"You took a picture of a woman sitting in a lifeguard chair. Remember her?"

Weegee closed the door behind him and studied the man. He looked in his fifties, kinda mousy, dark-rimmed glasses, thinning brown hair. How did the guy know he took that particular picture? He'd processed it along with the others he'd taken that night, but didn't make a print. It wouldn't appeal to the editors like the sleepers and lovers. Still, he'd been intrigued by the woman's thousand-yard stare at the sea that night.

Now he was even more intrigued.

"I didn't sell a picture of a woman in a lifeguard chair," Weegee said. "What makes you think I even took it?"

"She saw you."

"I doubt that. I could barely see my own hand that night."

The man began to pace, not that there was much room for pacing. "She heard people around her yelling at you. Stepped on them, I guess. She said she felt someone lean against the stand and thought she saw movement. She heard a click. A camera."

A click. The shutter, yeah, that was possible.

"How many clicks did she hear?"

"One."

That fit too.

"Don't prove it was me," Weegee said. "There's a lotta beach on Coney Island, a lotta of lifeguard stands, and a lotta photographers. Coulda been anybody."

The man glanced at a half-smoked cigar near the bed. "She smelled cigar smoke. Every picture I've ever seen of you, you're chomping on a disgusting cigar."

Well, that was true. Always good that he was being noticed.

"We scoured every tabloid in the city," the man said. "The only pictures published from that night were yours."

Not a surprise. Few freelance photographers or even staff photographers ventured out into the city at those hours. He owned the night.

"How did you find me?" he asked. He made it as difficult as possible for people to learn where he lived.

"You're hardly obscure. Weegee the Famous. Besides, I have friends who have friends."

Weegee tensed. He had friends too. And friends of friends. Maybe acquaintances was a better word, as many of them were mobsters. Bosses and soldiers. Men he'd photographed alive, then later when they turned up dead. Even the police referred to him as the Official Photographer of Murder, Inc.

The mousy man in front of him didn't have the beefy look of a mob soldier or a boss. Or act like one. An accountant for them, maybe? That might fit his demeanor. The contempt and arrogance he'd put on was a front. The pacing had stopped, but his hands trembled and he unconsciously kept shifting his weight.

"Like I said, mister, I don't recall taking that particular photo. And I definitely didn't sell a picture like that to the papers."

"I don't want you to sell it to any of those rags," said the man. "I want to buy it from you."

"Why? Who's the woman?"

"She's my younger sister."

The man's undercurrent of nervousness didn't sell that claim. "What's her name?"

"It's not important. What's important is that she's hiding from her ex-husband. A man who beats her. She doesn't want any pictures of her going public. Especially in some sleazy tabloid."

Weegee didn't buy the boyfriend bit either. "Why? Does she live on the beach and she's worried he'll find her?"

"The reason doesn't matter."

"Why didn't she come see me herself?"

"Because I'm the guy with the money."

"What's your name?" Weegee asked.

"That doesn't matter either. I just want the picture. I'll offer you three times your going rate."

"I get fifteen bucks a photo."

"Okay, forty-five bucks then."

The man didn't flinch at the price. He must have some dough. He also didn't know the value of pictures sold to the tabloids. Weegee was lucky to get five bucks for one.

"The negative too," the man added.

Weegee shook his head. "I don't sell negatives. To the papers or anyone else. Negatives are my creation. It would be like a painter selling his paint brushes along with the canvas."

"I need the negative. My sister and I want to rest assured you can't sell it later."

The photographer paused for a long moment. The police radio crackled in the background. The man glanced nervously at it. An idea emerged of how Weegee could work around this guy. The picture meant a lot to him for reasons other than what he was claiming. Weegee was curious why.

"Okay, thirty for the negative," he said.

The man nodded. Again, not flinching at the price. Should have bargained him for more. Still, seventy-five bucks for a print and a negative he didn't plan to use. Couldn't get that from *Life* magazine.

The man scanned the room. "Where are they?"

Weegee pointed to a large barrel overflowing with film holders and loose prints. "It's still in there. *If* it's in there. Unprocessed, if I really took it like you claim."

"I'll wait." The man searched for a place to sit. A castoff chair hunched by his desk, a brown fedora hanging over one corner. The man stepped toward the chair, then thought better of it. He remained standing, crossed his arms, and began to fidget.

Weegee's suspicions about the man and his story gave him pause. He shook his head. "I'm leaving shortly on a job, plus I gotta find the damn thing and process it. That's gonna take a while, pal. Come back this time in two days. I'll have the negative and a print from it—if I can find it. You pay me then."

"I don't trust you."

"Negatives don't lie. Take it or leave it. There's nothing says I gotta sell anything to you."

"It's good money."

"Then you'll get your negative and print. I like good money."

* * *

After the no-name man left, it took Weegee twenty minutes to find the negative of the woman in the lifeguard chair. He really needed to catalog his work better. He enlarged and processed an 8x10 print, squeegeed it as dry as possible, and examined it with a photo loupe.

Infrared photos don't have the snap and clarity of standard prints. More contrasty and lack of definition. Still, it was enough for him to determine it was a young woman, maybe ten years younger than her "brother." She wore black flats and a dark skirt pushed to one side, legs bare from the knees down, as if trying to catch the ocean breeze.

Why was the mousy man so anxious to buy her picture? Weegee didn't buy the sister bit or the abusive boyfriend. Why the lie? Still, seventy-five bucks was seventy-five bucks.

Yet the more he studied the picture, the more it haunted him. Who was this mysterious broad? Why was she sitting above everyone, alone, in the dead of night? The picture caught her at her most vulnerable. Fingers of her left hand touched her mouth, as if pensively biting her fingernails. But her eyes were the most startling. The infrared made them black dots, as dark and dead as shark eyes. The eyes gazing out to sea with a thousand-yard stare. Staring at what?

Why so pensive? Mere loneliness? Despondent? Or was she contemplating something more drastic? It was only a few steps to the sea.

* * *

The nameless man returned two days later.

"Let me dig up the picture," Weegee said, as the guy fidgeted in the middle of the room.

Weegee fumbled through a stack of prints on his desk. His back to the man, he felt the hidden shutter release cable attached to a 4x5 on the desk casually aimed toward the man, wide angle, ten feet, no flash. He coughed loudly, twice, as he squeezed the bulb release, muffling the shutter click.

"Ah, here it is," he said. He handed the man an 8x10 black-and-white print. The guy examined it through his black-framed glasses.

"This doesn't look like my sister." A forefinger tapped the face. "Those eyes. What's with the eyes? They're eerie."

"People's eyes dilate in darkness," Weegee said. "And let me tell you, pal, it was damn dark that night. The infrared film makes the dilated eyes look like solid black dots. Kind of a milky tone to the face. So yeah, it's eerie. But I wasn't taking fancy portraits. I was capturing people trying to survive a hot summer night in New York."

"I don't need all the photography crap. It doesn't look like her. This is the wrong picture. You tryin' to con me?"

Weegee shrugged. "It's the only picture I took of a woman on a lifeguard stand that night. Take it to your sister to see if that's what she was wearing."

"What about the negative?"

Weegee produced the 4x5 negative. The man held it against the gloomy light filtering through the room's lone window.

"How the hell can you tell anything from this?" he asked.

"The dark portions are the white portions in the print, and vice versa. You can tell it's a woman sitting in a lifeguard chair. Compare her posture, the placement of her legs, all that, against the print. They match."

The man still hesitated.

"Look, pal, if you can't recognize your own sister, then nobody's gonna recognize her. Including her so-called dangerous boyfriend," Weegee said. "Even spread across the front page of a tabloid. I don't plan on trying to sell it, anyway. The tabs won't buy it. They want couples fooling around on the beach. Not some broad sittin' in a chair."

The man stared at the picture, edgy.

"You wanna buy it or not, pal? If your sister ain't convinced it's her, then return the photo and I'll refund your money."

The man finally looked up. "The negative too."

"Yeah, yeah." Weegee handed over the negative and the print, and the man paid him in crisp bills. Weegee counted out seventy-five dollars as the man headed for the door.

The man stopped and turned toward Weegee. "A word of warning, buddy. If I or my sister see this picture published in a newspaper or anywhere else, you'll regret it. I know where you live and I'll have people come for you."

* * *

Three days later, as Weegee prowled the north end of Brooklyn at dusk, a call came over the police radio in his maroon 1938 Chevy coupe. A floater had washed ashore on the beach on Coney Island. Female.

No name, no other description. Weegee immediately flashed on the woman on the lifeguard stand and her distant stare. Had she climbed down and walked out into the water that night and drowned herself?

Yet that didn't match the nameless man who showed up two days later demanding to buy her picture and the negative for a ridiculous sum. How would he have learned from his "sister" that she suspected Weegee the Famous had photographed her shortly before she walked out into the sea?

Still, the floater was worth checking out. A human-interest photo if nothing else. Weegee nosed his car south toward Coney Island.

Twenty minutes later, he parked and trudged across the beach to a gaggle of police and lookie-loos huddled around the floater half a mile from where he'd photographed the mystery woman. Squeals of joy from the nearby amusement park drifted over the solemn yet similarly energized scene.

He popped a standard flashbulb into his flashgun and snapped a picture of the people standing around the body: two cops, gawkers, and two ambulance attendants. Several in the crowd turned their attention toward him when the flash went off. The cops ignored him. Weegee wore his fedora with a press badge stuffed in the band. They probably recognized him anyway.

He popped in a fresh bulb as he changed angles and moved closer for a better view. Now he could see the dead woman's bloated face. Her short, dark hair matched the hair of the woman in the lifeguard chair. But beyond that, he couldn't determine whether it was the same woman, or even the floater's age. Her body was bloated beyond recognition, further desecrated by birds and sea life.

One other observation heightened his uncertainty. The woman was dressed in a black-and-white bathing suit, not a skirt and blouse like the mystery woman wore. Possible she wore the suit under her clothes that night, shed the clothes, and walked out into the sea. But why bother with all that? It's easier to drown wearing heavy clothes.

Had he misread her thousand-yard stare, her restlessness, her aloneness? She wasn't suicidal and never went into the water? Was it mere coincidence that a female floated up on the beach five days after he'd taken the mystery woman's photo?

* * *

The next day, Weegee scoured the city's dailies for news of the floater. The morning papers ran a paragraph or two but offered few details. The afternoon papers, however, provided more information. The dead woman was tentatively identified as Elizabeth Evelyn Johnson, age forty-seven. The identification was made by her husband, Chauncy, a prosperous clothing store owner pushing ambitious plans to construct a grand hotel on the boardwalk in an effort to resurrect what had once been viewed as an enclave for New York's wealthy.

The identification wasn't official yet. Johnson couldn't positively identify the woman, of course. Not in her sea-rotted condition. But the black-and-white bathing suit, dark hair, and a birthmark on her right calf—all of which he'd told the police when he first reported her missing—strongly suggested it was his wife. That and the fact she frequently went swimming in the evenings, blocks from their large Victorian home near Surf Avenue and the Wonder Wheel, close to Henderson's Music Hall where the Marx Brothers once performed.

One paper quoted Johnson saying he'd warned her often not to swim alone at night. No lifeguards. The risk of riptides. Didn't trust the "riffraff" who frequented the long strip of beach. Occasionally he went with her, but couldn't swim well himself. But she was stubborn that way, he said.

205

Johnson sure seemed critical for a guy whose wife just drowned, thought Weegee.

The papers reported that when she didn't return from her late-night swim—the same night Weegee photographed the woman in the lifeguard chair—her husband went searching for her, in vain. Fearing the worst, he reported her missing to the police the next morning. Weegee knew from experience with cops that they wouldn't normally start a search for a missing person for at least forty-eight hours. She could have gone off with a lover, right? Or left her husband because she couldn't stand the man. Yet clearly Johnson carried clout with local authorities, for they'd launched a search that very day.

Nothing turned up until the woman in the black-and-white bathing suit washed ashore, and the police quickly brought Johnson in to see if the body might be that of his missing wife.

Weegee monitored the papers over the next two days, but the story quickly faded. Who cared about another drowning victim? Other than the *Daily Mirror*, which bought one of his pictures of the lookie-loos crowding around her body. The editor liked the one with their faces captured in the flash: two young boys uncertain what they were looking at, adults staring in horror or emotionless curiosity, and most of all a woman staring directly at his camera, a slight smile on her face, as if it were more important that her picture was in the paper than the victim.

The drowning and the mystery woman continued to nag at Weegee, but he was too busy hustling more crime and disaster photos to probe deeper. It wasn't until a few days later, when he spotted the drowning victim's obituary in *The New York Daily News*, her identity confirmed, that he grew convinced the drowning victim was connected to the woman in the lifeguard chair.

Elizabeth Evelyn Johnson's picture caught his attention first. Obviously taken when she was alive and younger than her forty-seven years, it bore a striking resemblance to the younger woman in the chair, even taking into account the distorted quality of the infrared image.

But there was more. The obit revealed the dead woman was born in

Kansas, worked as an executive secretary after moving to New York, and became a housewife after marrying Chauncy Johnson. No children. What caught Weegee's attention, however, was the fact she was survived by not only her husband and both parents, but also a sister. A younger sister named Rose Wilcox, the sisters' maiden surname. Weegee immediately considered attending the funeral services in hopes the sister might show up and he could confirm whether she was the mysterious woman, and Chauncy Johnson was the man who'd bought his "sister's" photo. Unfortunately, services and burial would be private, despite Johnson's prominence as a local businessman.

Thwarted but not defeated, Weegee called Detective Julian Gold.

Gold worked lower Manhattan, and Weegee ran into him frequently at crime scenes. He was a good detective and one of the few cops who treated him with at least a modicum of respect. Perhaps because of their days as young Jews running the streets of the Lower East Side—along with another kid who now ran one of the city's mob families.

"What's on your mind, Arthur?" Gold said with a mix of cordiality and impatience. Calling him Arthur always irritated Weegee. It was a name from his past, a name he wanted to keep there.

"I need you to put me in touch with the detective investigating the death of an Elizabeth Johnson. She washed up on shore on Coney Island the other night. Reach out to him and put in a good word for me. I need to see him."

"I read that in the papers," Gold acknowledged. "Looks like a straightforward drowning. Not even sure they have a detective involved. What's your interest in it? Besides someone being dead?"

"There's something suspicious about her death."

Gold was silent for a long moment. "Suspicious how?"

Weegee gave him a quick summary of the nameless man's visit to his room to buy the picture of his "sister."

"I don't see the connection," Gold said.

"If he's the dead woman's husband, I'd call it suspicious that he showed up at my room desperate to buy a picture of a woman sitting in a lifeguard chair the same night his wife went missing."

"I'm not gonna bother a fellow detective with what sounds like a wild goose chase, Arthur. What's it to you anyway?"

What was it to him? His work was to document the dead and leave the detecting to others. Still, he couldn't get the young woman and the strange visit by her "brother" out of his head. He felt used by the nameless man. He sensed if there were a crime here, he was the only one who could push investigators toward it.

"Justice," he said.

Detective Gold scoffed at Weegee's grandiosity. "You need more than that, Arthur." He hung up.

* * *

The next day, Weegee rose earlier than usual and drove to the *Coney Island Times*, a weekly located in a nondescript building not far from the boardwalk. He knew the editor, having sold him a handful of pictures over the years. Weegee preferred the tabloids because they paid better, but if they turned down something that might fit the *Times*, it was still money. And he never knew when a contact might pay off in unexpected ways. He hoped this was one of those times.

The editor was a crusty old coot named Sam Greenberg who'd been there since Gutenberg invented the printing press. He smoked cigars, which Weegee also enjoyed, so they'd hit it off from the beginning.

"I hope you're not trying to sell me a picture of another drowning victim," said the editor as Weegee approached his desk. He had tried to sell Greenberg a picture of the floater the *World-Telegram* didn't use, but was politely turned down. "They don't care in Manhattan, but we don't want pictures showing dead people on our beach," he'd said.

"No photos, Sam," Weegee said. "A favor."

"What?"

"You got a picture in your archives of the guy whose wife washed up on the beach?"

"Chauncy Johnson?"

"Yeah. I figure you have something, him being a prominent local businessman here. Wants to build a big fancy hotel, from what I read."

Greenberg shook his head forlornly. "Yes, Coney Island's latest huckster."

"Huckster?"

"That's what I call guys like him. Come along every decade or so with a fancy proposal to save Coney Island from its reprobate ways. Turn it into the next World's Fair or Atlantic City. A luxury resort by the sea. Our civic leaders always get suckered into it 'cause they get Coney Island all wrong. Don't realize we got Brooklyn blood in our soul. Amusement parks and honky tonk joints, and nickel hot dogs. A little tawdry but fun-loving. Did you know this place was called Sodom by the Sea in the early 1800s? We're a carnival at heart. But that ain't stopping Johnson from scheming with the city fathers to build another big fancy hotel on the boardwalk, like the Half Moon Hotel."

Weegee knew the Half Moon well. Built in 1927, it, too, was supposed to compete with Atlantic City. Instead, it became notorious after Abe "Kid Twist" Reles, a Brooklyn gangster, took a flyer out of a sixth-floor window. Considering Reles had been under constant police protection for the last year at the hotel while he helped the Brooklyn DA clear eighty-five murder cases, people didn't buy that he'd died trying to escape rappelling with a bunch of poorly tied bed sheets. Especially the day before he was to testify in a Brooklyn court against Albert "The Lord High Executioner" Anastasia.

"Johnson a short guy with glasses? Kinda mousy?" Weegee asked.

"That he is, but don't tell him I concurred."

"Just want to see his picture."

"Why?"

"If I'm right, you'll be among the first to find out."

The editor, who remembered every story they ever published to within a given week or two, led the photographer to the archives and quickly found a feature story on Johnson's clothing store, two stories on his grand hotel scheme, and a photo showing him presenting a major donation to the local Red Cross, one of the paper's favorite charities. The man in the pictures matched the man who'd bulled his way into Weegee's room to buy the photo of the mystery woman.

Weegee turned to Greenberg. "Do you know if Johnson has a sister? A little younger than his wife."

"If he does, even he doesn't know it. He was an orphan in upstate New York. Came to the city when he was seventeen. A regular rags-to-riches story."

"But his dead wife has a sister, right? Rose Wilcox?"

"Yes, but I've never met her. She and Elizabeth were estranged from what I gathered. Hadn't seen each other in years."

"Any idea where the sister lives?

He shrugged. "Kansas, for all I know. Why all these questions, Weegee?"

"Like I said, if my hunch proves right, you'll be the first to know."

* * *

Weegee called Detective Gold from the editor's phone. Gone for the day. The next afternoon, with no phone in his room, he cadged the phone of a neighbor, a retired reporter who served as his answering service in return for various favors and cash. This time, Gold was at his desk. Weegee rattled off what he'd confirmed at the *Coney Island Times.* Hotel-magnate-wanna-be Chauncy Johnson, whose wife washed ashore, was the same guy who showed up at his room pressing to buy a negative and print of a young broad Weegee photographed the same night Johnson reported his wife missing. A woman Johnson claimed was his sister, when in fact he had no sister, but whose wife Elizabeth did have one, an estranged sister named Rose.

"Not exactly convincing evidence for an investigation, Arthur."

"Tell me you've never investigated on less, Julian."

The detective sighed and said he'd put in a call.

Weegee's neighbor knocked on his door an hour later. Gold was on his phone.

"Talk to a detective in the Sixtieth Precinct named Frazer," said Gold.

"He says you're wasting your time, but he'll see you. A straightforward drowning. He's workin' graveyard. Just your hour. Maybe you'll get lucky and photograph him investigating a real murder."

"Thanks, Julian."

"As a favor to me, don't be your insufferable self. He's a good cop."

* * *

The 60th Precinct served the southernmost end of Brooklyn, including Coney Island. Weegee found Detective Frazer around midnight, not hunched over a body in an alley as he'd hoped, but over a typewriter as he two-fingered a report.

"Weegee the Famous, in the flesh," Frazer said, leaning back in his chair without offering a handshake. A cigarette dangled from thick lips. The rest of his face was thick, too, under a head of black hair with a side part and slicked back with a high shine of pomade. Late forties, maybe. "I shouldn't give you the time of the day but Julian asked me to. He and I once worked together in Queens."

"Julian and I go back to childhood," Weegee said.

"Lucky him." He blew smoke toward the peeling ceiling. "Julian gave me a summary of what you claim. I ain't exactly clear what you're trying to make of all this. Even if it was Chauncy Johnson buying pictures from you, it don't sound like he broke any laws."

Weegee paused for a moment. He had to speak aloud what had been nagging him in the back of his mind, based entirely on hunches. But he'd been around enough crime to believe he wasn't crazy for thinking it.

"He broke the law if he murdered his wife."

The detective flicked ashes on the floor. "No evidence of that, pal. The ME said the woman's lungs were full of salt water. No bruising or marks indicating she was forcibly drowned. She was in a bathing suit. She commonly went swimming at night. Accident for sure."

"Not if her husband slipped her a knock-out drug and threw her overboard from a boat."

"For which you have no evidence. The guy's a respected businessman of the community. Hell, you can't even prove he was the guy you claim wanted to buy your picture and negative. He didn't even give you his name, from what Julian told me."

Weegee pulled a black-and-white photo out of a shoulder bag and laid it on the detective's desk, hesitating out of fear it would get lost in the clutter.

"I sneak-photographed him when he came to pay for the picture. I think you'll agree it's Chauncy Johnson. Detective Gold can attest this is my room in Manhattan."

He'd captured Johnson with the wall of newspaper clippings and *Murder Is My Business* sign in the background.

The detective crushed his cigarette in an ashtray overflowing with half-smoked cigarettes and looked at the picture. "Okay, I grant you it's Mr. Johnson. Don't prove you took a picture of this broad in a lifeguard chair. You understand you sold the picture and the negative to Johnson."

"I sold him a negative and a print. Just not the ones he thought he was buying." The photographer laid down another print and a 4x5 negative. "This is the original."

The detective examined it. "You sold him a fake?"

"When he first showed up demanding to buy it, I told him to come back in two days. I'd have it ready then. I didn't trust him. That night I took a woman friend who resembled the mystery woman down to that same lifeguard stand and posed her in near identical clothes. That's the negative and print I sold to Johnson. I don't think even his sister could be certain it wasn't her."

The detective examined the photo. "Not exactly Museum of Modern Art quality. What's with the weird eyes?"

"Infrared film."

"Tell me again how he showed up at your door?"

Weegee recounted how Johnson tracked him down and his desperate willingness to pay a pretty penny for the photo and negative, claiming it was to protect his abused sister. A sister he didn't have.

"Suspicious behavior for a man whose wife went missing the same night

I took that picture," Weegee insisted.

The detective shrugged. "I dunno. Maybe this woman was his lover and he didn't want the picture to go public."

"Why would a picture of a nameless woman perched in a lifeguard chair expose their affair? It's not like he's in it."

"Okay, why *do* you think he wanted the photo so badly?"

"Because I believe that woman is Rose Wilcox. The dead wife's estranged sister. My picture places her on the beach the night her sister drowned. That's no coincidence. That's what worried them."

The detective took a second look at the photos.

* * *

Weegee's retired neighbor banged on his door late one morning. Some guy on his phone wanting to talk to him immediately. The photographer stirred from a sound sleep—he'd been out until four a.m. photographing the city's miseries—and stumbled to the man's apartment. The voice at the other end was a source in Brooklyn's central booking office on Schermerhorn St. He had sources in every borough booking office in the city. Chauncy Johnson was about to be arrested and brought in for the murder of his wife Elizabeth.

Weegee gave his neighbor a buck and dashed out with camera in hand.

Breaking a few speed limits and traffic lights in his Chevy coupe, a press sign displayed in the windshield, Weegee barely arrived in time to snap pictures of Johnson being led from a patrol car, including one of him scowling at Weegee while Detective Frazer and a uniform clamped each arm. That photo would sell! They'd kept the arrest off the police radio, so only one other news photographer was there, a staff photographer from *The Sun.*

"Hey, Frazer," Weegee yelled at the detective moments before they entered the building. Frazer let the uniform escort Johnson inside and approached the photographer.

"Whaddya want, Weegee?"

"I want inside to get a booking photo."

"Well, don't you rate."

"I gave you the tip that got you looking at this guy. You owe me a photo."

"Don't let it go to your head, pal."

Weegee stood firm.

"Okay," the detective relented. "Make it quick."

Weegee grabbed two shots of Johnson being fingerprinted, then persuaded the detective to come back outside with him, away from the hubbub.

"I'm curious what evidence you arrested him on. Was I right about some of it?" Weegee asked.

"It'll all come out at arraignment and the trial."

"I don't want to wait that long. This is personal. This guy tried to buy me off to cover up his crime."

"We won't release details before then."

"I'm not going public with it, detective. I promise."

"Promise all you want. I ain't telling you a thing."

"I got a great photo of you bringing Johnson in. It'll make the papers—if I choose to offer it. I'll even print a nice eight by ten just for you. Stamped Weegee the Famous on the back. Guaranteed the print will be valuable someday. Sell it or frame it and show it off to your grandkids. I don't care. You got grandkids, don't you?"

"Do I look that old?"

"You will someday. Come on, a little trading."

"Detective Gold warned me you were pushy."

Weegee almost grinned.

Frazer sighed. "All right, all right, if it will get you outta my hair. But if you leak a word of what I'm about to tell you, I'll confiscate every damn camera you own, throw 'em in the ocean, and toss you in a cell with Johnson."

To Weegee's surprise, Frazer had followed up on his tips. He discovered that Johnson rented a boat in Brighton Beach the day before his wife disappeared. Acquaintances confirmed their marriage was rocky amid rumors of an affair. Further probing found that Johnson's once prosperous clothing store was struggling financially because he was pouring cash into developing his big hotel on the boardwalk, and that he'd taken out a large insurance policy on his wife without her knowledge months before her death.

Most important, a second autopsy by the medical examiner found traces of chloral hydrate in the dead woman's system. Along with alcohol, it made a fine Mickey Finn. Enough evidence for an arrest, and they expected more once they interrogated him.

Weegee promised a print in a few days and headed straight to the *Coney Island Times* to use their darkroom to process and print the photos of Johnson's arrest. He let editor Greenberg pick the one he liked best and gave it to him for free. The picture of Johnson scowling, naturally. Greenberg was downright ecstatic. Another Coney Island huckster bites the dust. Weegee would sell the others to the big tabs. They'd eat it up. They were growing weary of pictures of mob killings and stupid burglars shot by police. Nothing like a nice domestic murder with a prominent suspect to titillate the strap hangers.

* * *

Weegee stepped onto Coney Island beach shortly after sunset. Another sultry night. Families and couples and singles settling in on blankets with their red-metal Coca-Cola coolers. Lovers already being—well, lovers. He hadn't come to take pictures this time. He carried his camera, to be sure. He never knew what opportunities might present themselves. But for now, his destination was the lifeguard stand where weeks before he'd photographed the mysterious woman. Part of him hoped he might find her sitting there again, staring out at sea, but he knew he wouldn't.

She had vanished into the wind.

Several days ago, he had stopped at the desk of Detective Frazer at the 60th Precinct to drop off a nice 8x10 black-and-white print of Frazer escorting Chauncy Johnson into central booking, one without Johnson scowling.

"As promised," he said, as Frazer stared at it, unable to repress the grin on his face.

"I saw this on the front page of the *World Telegram*," the detective said, puffing out his chest. "Bought copies for all my relatives. You caught me good."

"I read in the tabs that Johnson confessed soon after his arrest. You're a persuasive man, detective."

"Didn't take much. Broke down within hours, bawling like a baby."

The detective spelled out the details, some Weegee had read in the papers, some not. Johnson confessed to drugging his wife, manhandling her body into the small, rented motorboat, and dumping her off Coney Island at one in the morning. He hoped her body would eventually surface and drift ashore, backing up the story he would tell the police that she'd recklessly gone swimming again and maybe drowned.

The twist, said Frazer, was that Chauncy Johnson didn't kill his wife solely for the insurance money. The rumors were right. He was having an affair—with his wife's estranged sister, Rose Wilcox. They'd met by chance the year before in the middle of Manhattan. His wife got wind of their affair and threatened divorce that would strip away half his property if he didn't break it off, destroying his dream of building a boardwalk hotel. Johnson claimed it was Rose who, months into their affair, ginned up the idea of buying the life insurance policy and killing her sister. Rose was a nurse—Johnson knew that from his wife—and Rose said she could easily get her hands on chloral hydrate. Her scheme shocked him, but lust, a badgering wife, and the desperate need for money triumphed.

"You haven't arrested her yet, have you?" Weegee said. The tabs would have shouted that if he had.

A shadow crossed the detective's face. No, she was proving elusive. Her lover said the two of them never rendezvoused at her apartment, supposedly located somewhere uptown. Only various hotel rooms or Johnson's home when his wife was away, so he could not provide them her address. Rose had told him she worked at Lenox Hill Hospital on the Upper East Side. Turned out she'd never worked there. Nor any other hospital in the city.

Investigators discovered a picture of her and her dead sister taken years ago, buried in a dresser drawer at the Johnson home. They'd provided Rose's picture to the papers, and circulated it to every precinct.

When Weegee first saw it, it strongly resembled the mystery woman in the lifeguard chair.

"We'll find her," insisted the detective.

They wouldn't, Weegee mused as he reached the lifeguard stand. He leaned against it, weary from the slog through the sand and bodies on the beach.

His theory was that Rose Wilcox had planned this all along, ran into Johnson as if by "accident," and led him down a primrose path. Revenge against her estranged sister? A gold digger? Who knew? Assuming all went as planned, Johnson had told the detective, Rose would have surfaced publicly months after her sister's death and eventually marry him.

But it hadn't gone as planned. Weegee suspected that upon Johnson's arrest, Rose Wilcox disappeared down the red carpet in Grand Central Station to catch the overnight 20th Century Limited to Chicago, where she could dig her claws into some new sap. Anywhere but Kansas.

Weegee had come to realize why the woman sat in the lifeguard chair that hot dark night, sweltering sleepers and lovers scattered around her, with that thousand-yard stare. Not contemplating suicide as he'd feared. No, she'd sat in that chair because in a twisted way she wanted to bear witness, that somewhere out in the darkness that night her lover was dumping her sister's body into the ocean.

That was his speculation. What Weegee knew for certain was that if Rose Wilcox had not panicked when his beach pictures appeared in the tabloids from that night, she and Chauncy Johnson would have gotten away with murder.

Scamming the Scammer

Marcia Muller

"I lost my life savings to that scammer. Thirty thousand dollars. Everything I had," Ana Emery told me.

"This was an internet scam?" I asked.

"No, Ms. McCone. I don't have a computer, don't much like them. It happened on the phone."

I frowned. Internet scammers are fairly easy to trace; I have an employee at my agency—Derek Frye—who can identify one with a few strokes of his keyboard. But phone scammers are not as simple: they change their number often, re-route their calls deviously, assume identities with the artistry of Academy Award-winning actors.

"Tell me how it happened," I said.

She fiddled with the edge of her Irish-knit sweater, uncrossed and recrossed her legs.

Ashamed of her foolishness, I thought.

My new client struck me as someone who was very concerned with projecting a confident image as an executive assistant in one of San Francisco's high-powered law firms. She'd been referred to me by her boss, my old friend criminal defense attorney Glenn Solomon, who'd called her—in retro-speak manner—"one sharp cookie." But the cookie appeared to be crumbling now as she sat across my desk from me in one of the clients' chairs. She looked around the office at everything but me.

"Ms. Emery?" I prompted.

She roused herself and sighed. "I just feel so stupid."

"No need for that. Thousands of people are scammed every day. Why don't you start at the beginning?"

She sighed again, ran her fingers through her short, feather-cut hair. It was almost as black as my own, except for faint reddish highlights. "This woman called. I don't normally pick up the phone unless I know who's calling, but I was cooking and expecting to hear from my friend Janey, so I did. She said, 'Hi, this is Daniela.' Now, I do have a friend called Daniela, but I was surprised to hear from her since she lives in Paris. So surprised that I said, 'Hey, what's happening?' We chatted; she asked me about my job and my new car and recommended a few investment opportunities, which I decided to take her up on."

"And when did you act on that decision?"

"The very next morning. They sounded too good to pass up."

"Let me guess: these opportunities involved cryptocurrency."

"Yes. I wish I'd never heard that term."

I know a good amount about cryptocurrency. It's been around a few years now, to very mixed reviews. Hailed as the new wave of high-earning investment, it is purely digital, bypassing banks and other financial institutions, and since its inception has been plagued by serious drawbacks. Purchases in such currencies as Bitcoin, Etherium, Litcoin, and SafeTcoin are uninsured, hard to convert, and subject to extreme volatility. Huge price swings can wipe out fortunes in nanoseconds.

"Which crypto exchange did you have your account with?"

"SafeTcoin. Daniela recommended it."

SafeTcoin was the least reliable of all the exchanges.

"Did you talk with Glenn before you invested?"

"No. I wanted to, but he's been involved in a high-profile murder trial, and I didn't feel I should bother him. Plus, I wanted to prove I could do something on my own."

Pride goeth before, I thought.

"When did you realize your funds had been wiped out?" I asked.

"The second day after I transferred them in. I called Daniela's number in Paris. And then I knew."

"It wasn't Daniela you'd been speaking with."

"As soon as she answered, I knew it hadn't been her voice on the phone. The voice had been close but a little off."

I'd expected this. "What information did you share with the fake Daniela?"

"Everything. She said she needed it to help set up a wallet—one of those digital things where they store your information—for me."

"Even your social security number?"

She nodded. "I know they say you should never give it out, but Daniela—the real one—has been my friend forever. I felt safe with her."

I hesitated, doodling on the legal pad where I'd been taking notes. "Okay," I said, "I'll need one of my staff to get in touch with Daniela in Paris so he can get a voiceprint on her. Also copies of your savings and investment statements and any communications with the fraud departments you contacted. And anything else you may feel is pertinent to the investigation."

She nodded and stood up, clearly relieved the interview was at an end.

After she was gone, I moved from the desk to one of the sofas in the conversation area of my office. Stared out at the flurries of late February rain that washed the plate glass window. Thought about how I'd pursue this new investigation. Before I left to go home to my house in the Marina district—and to my husband Hy's great chicken cacciatore—I made a list of additional questions to ask Ana Emery.

* * *

The morning was as gloomy as the day before. I drove my Miata to the McCone & Ripinsky Building in the financial district, parked in the underground garage, and took the elevator to the top floor. Ana Emery was already there, a typed list of the answers to my questions and a sheaf of documents in hand. I poured coffee from the carafe on the table and seated Ana in the conversation area, where—as I'd supposed—she seemed more at ease than in the formal setting across my desk. While we sipped, I glanced over the list. No surprises there; I'd turn it over to Derek for fact-checking.

After a moment I said to Ana, "The voiceprint from Daniela came in last night. I didn't think it could possibly be a match. As you probably realize most scammers don't know their victims, which makes them so hard to trace. But from what you've told me, this woman seemed to have a lot of your personal information. I think we need to take a look at your other women friends."

"Oh, I don't believe any of them could be responsible..."

"It's still a possibility. Who are they?"

"Well, I...I don't actually have many. I'm not what you'd call gregarious. There's Janey Woodman, who I was expecting a call from when I first heard from the fake Daniela. Lee Leveroni. Becca Sissel. That's about it."

"Are they work friends?"

"No. I went to high school with Becca. Lee I met at a book group about three years ago. It bored me, so I quit. Janey used to live in my old building on Arguello; we've kept in touch."

I wrote down the names and contact information, then asked, "Any male friends?"

"No." She colored slightly. "I used to date a guy named Mark Evans, but he moved to Silicon Valley a few months ago. Besides, aren't you looking for a woman?"

"Or a man who put her up to this scam."

She pressed her fingertips to her lips. "I hadn't thought of that."

It seemed to me there were a lot of things she hadn't thought of.

"Besides," she added, "Mark doesn't need money. He's independently wealthy."

"To some people, any amount of wealth isn't enough." I made a check mark beside the next item on my list. "Okay, Ms. Lewis, what do you do for fun?"

"Fun?" She made it sound like a foreign term.

"Do you play sports? Take classes? Take photographs or paint or travel?

You mentioned a book group—anything else like that?"

"Why do you need to know those things?"

"Just trying to get a picture of your life."

"Oh. Well, I did take a cooking class at Le Ecole a while back, but it didn't work out so well. Turns out I've got no talent as a cook."

"What about going to nightclubs?"

"I don't drink."

"Not even to listen to music? Or dance?"

"Well, I went once to Jude's Tavern—that place on Van Ness—with Janey, but I hated it. It was crowded and hot, and the music was loud. I never went back."

I wanted to snap, "Is there anything you do do?" but I held back. The client, I always proclaim to my employees, must always be coddled and cosseted.

* * *

"Your administrative assistant," I told Glenn, "is a real nothing woman."

We were seated over drinks in Rosanna's, on the 31st floor of Embarcadero Three, his favorite after-work venue. The rain had worsened, slashing at the windows, and neither of us had cared to venture out.

"I said she was a smart cookie, not Miss Personality."

"More appropriately—in your vernacular—Miss Wet Blanket."

"Give the girl a break."

"I'm trying to. But what the hell is wrong with her?"

"Difficult childhood."

"How so?"

He frowned, ran his fingers through his thick white hair. "Her father left the family when Ana was ten. Went to live with a friend of her mother's down the street from them and later divorced the mother and married the new woman. The mother became an alcoholic and died of an overdose of sleeping pills three years later. The father took Ana in, but his new wife treated her badly. Ana left at sixteen—underage, but her father didn't try to stop her."

"And after that?"

"Surprisingly, Ana pulled herself together. Moved in with a friend's family and exchanged babysitting services for her room and board. Graduated high school early and attended paralegal classes while holding what she calls 'a string of nothing jobs.'" Came to me two, two and a half years ago. She's been an excellent employee."

"I see she gave her address as a studio apartment south of Market, not too far from the M&R building."

"Singles place. She could have afforded better before this scam occurred, but she said she was saving to buy a house."

"She's still there?"

"Rent is paid up until the end of the month."

"And then?"

Glenn looked embarrassed, as he always does when caught in a kindness. "I'll cover it until this mess is cleaned up."

"I notice none of the three friends whose names she gave to me live at that address. I'd have thought she'd connect with more people in a singles place."

"Friends don't seem to be big on her agenda."

"Nothing else does, either."

"McCone, you seem to have taken a dislike to Ana."

"Not a dislike. It's just that passionless people irritate me."

He considered that. "Come to think of it, me too."

* * *

I spent a couple of hours setting up appointments to interview Ana's three friends: Janey Woodman, Lee Leveroni, and Becca Sissel. Before I'd called the women I'd listened to the voiceprint of the real Daniela: the register was low, but strong, with a silent French accent. The women's voices were all low and strong, but none had an accent. Of course, accents can easily be faked.

Becca worked at home in interior design. Her office was in a spacious condo on Scott Street, crowded with three drawing boards for her assistants. She took me into a glassed-in conference room and gave me coffee. From her surroundings I assumed she was affluent and worked hard at it—I doubted she had the need or the time to pull off a complicated scam.

She seemed genuinely concerned about Ana's problem. "I wish she'd let me know. I could easily have helped tide her over. Is there any way she can recover the money?"

"It's doubtful. Scams like this—especially ones involving cryptocurrency—are designed to move funds very quickly. What I'm primarily concerned with now is to prevent any more losses, and we're monitoring her few existing accounts—like credit cards—on an hourly basis. She provided information to the scammer that might make it possible for her to tap into whatever little remains."

"I'm going to phone her, see if there's anything I can do."

"I'm sure she'll appreciate that."

* * *

Ana didn't; she called me shortly before I left for home, railing at my invading her privacy. "I brought this problem to you because Glenn stressed your high value on confidentiality!"

"The women you named are your friends."

"They won't be if they find out what a fool I've been."

"Becca sounded as if she was anxious to help."

"Anxious to look down her nose at me! She's already wired five thousand dollars into my bank account, as if I were some poor relation."

"I'd say that was a very kind gesture."

"The hell it was! You don't know Becca."

"I guess not. Ana, do you want me to go on with this inquiry?" I'd have been delighted if she'd said no.

But instead, she said grudgingly, "Yes, of course—go ahead."

Damn! I told her I'd be in touch.

* * *

I met Janey Woodman the next morning at a coffee shop on Haight Street. The neighborhood—long ago known as the birthplace of the hippie movement—has undergone various changes over the past few decades and is now gentrified. The coffee shop was shiny with chrome and plush with leather, an oasis from the rain that still pelted the city.

Janey Woodman, who lived upstairs from the shop and clerked at a nearby bed-and-bath store, reminded me of the quintessential earth mother: long brown hair gathered at the nape of her neck; no makeup; plain shapeless clothing. Her earrings were clusters of some kind of seed and matched a double strand around her neck. She ordered a cinnamon latte while I opted for black coffee.

"Ana and I went to parochial school together—Saint Mary's," she told me. "Actually, we lived together the last two years after she moved out on her father and new stepmother. She traded babysitting services with my folks in exchange for room and board."

"So you've been close a long time."

She frowned. "Not close, actually. Ana doesn't get close to anybody. Never has. But we've kept in touch. I've tried to be a friend, and the past couple of years, I've concentrated on breaking her out of her shell—getting her to do stuff like take classes, go to concerts, go clubbing. I haven't been real successful."

"She mentioned not liking Jude's Tavern very much."

"She hated it. Even though she met Mark Evans there."

The boyfriend who moved to Silicon Valley. "That was a serious relationship?"

"He wanted it to be, asked her to marry him and move to Santa Clara. She refused. He still comes up to the city, and I see him around Jude's Tavern now and then. He always asks about her."

I'd try to contact Mark Evans later.

"Anything else you could tell me about Ana?" I asked.

Janey considered, spooning up the last of her latte. "Not really. I've given her gifts from the store where I work, even offered her a place to stay till she gets on her feet. But to tell the truth, I've soured on the friendship. You go out of your way to try to help somebody, and they don't appreciate it—that's kind of a losing situation, isn't it?"

* * *

So Becca Sissel had helped to the extent of five thousand dollars. Janey Woodman hadn't been successful in bringing her out of her shell and was cooling on the friendship. Had Lee Leveroni been similarly repulsed? I'd have to ask her, but Lee was a flight attendant and I couldn't meet with her until after her four o'clock return on Southwest. I hadn't visited my office in the M&R building yet that day, so I stopped there and spent a few hours going over the numerous operatives' reports that were clogging my inbox.

Missing persons: two of them, no progress. Easy to get lost in this city. Check forgery, but the family didn't want the police involved, just wanted to confront the cheating son and probably beat the hell out of him. Petty thefts from a small clothing store; owner merely wanted photographs of the light-fingered employee. Missing grandchildren of legal age. Threatening calls in the Sunset district, probably from a neighbor. Car vandalism. Missing electric bike. Graffiti on sidewalk. Surveillance on Pickleball courts as a possible basis for a nuisance suit. Missing Pickleball paddles....

Finally, it was time to meet Lee Leveroni at her apartment on Russian Hill. It was in a small wood-shingled building sandwiched between two nondescript high-rises that must have provided good views of the Bay. Lee—blond, well-groomed—had changed from her airline uniform to blue sweats and seemed to be glad to be at home. She offered me a glass of wine—which I gratefully accepted—and seated me on a black sofa whose fabric was shot with gold threads.

"So Ana's up to her old tricks," she said.

"I'm not sure what you mean by that."

"Poor mouthing."

"She's been the victim of a scam—"

"Ana is a perpetual victim."

"Her entire assets have been wiped out in a cryptocurrency confidence scheme."

"What assets?"

"Stocks, bonds, pension fund, bank accounts."

Lee Leveroni looked surprised. "I didn't think she was so prudent with her money. I've never known her to save. Ana spends and spends. Always has. Always will."

* * *

Somebody was lying to me.

Lee Leveroni? She was a distant friend from a book club she and Ana had once attended. I'd questioned her more thoroughly about that. The club had focused on how-to volumes about finance. "Ana didn't seem to grasp the concepts," Lee told me. "She took detailed notes, but the questions she asked didn't address the issues we were all talking about."

"Did she attend for very long?"

"Three weeks, maybe. Frankly, I'm surprised she gave my name to you as a reference."

Janey Woodman? She'd known Ana the longest. Their high school years were long behind them, so why had Janey recently taken an interest in breaking Ana out of her shell? Janey hadn't struck me as a woman who needed old friends in her life; several people had greeted her enthusiastically in the coffee shop, and she'd introduced one of them to me as her "bestie." Of course, Janey also seemed to be the type who liked to be helpful.

Becca Sissel? She seemed sincere about scanting to help Ana, had indeed sent her the five thousand—unappreciated—dollars. But Ana had been upset with me for contacting Becca, claimed she would be "looking down her nose" at her. Why? Was there some dynamic there that I was missing?

* * *

Seven o'clock. I'd called Mark Evans earlier and when I'd mentioned Ana's name, he'd eagerly agreed to meet at Jude's Tavern. The club was on Van Ness Avenue, sandwiched between a new car dealership and a bank. Rock music filtered out onto the sidewalk, and the interior—as Ana described it—was hot, crowded, and noisy. Big-screen TVs showed reruns of football games in three corners. I asked the hostess for Evans, and she pointed me to a booth near the rear.

Evans was sandy-haired, one of the baby-faced men who would never look old. He rose, asked what I would like to drink, and signaled to a waitress for my glass of wine. Then he asked eagerly, "Ana—is she all right?"

"She's had some difficulty." I explained about the cryptocurrency scam.

"Damn!" He slapped a hand on the table. "I should've warned her about investing in stuff like that! I'm an analyst for Citibank. I know the risks. But it never occurred to me that she would take that kind of plunge. Why did she?"

"Bad advice. Tell me, do you know anything about her friend Daniela?"

His mouth turned down. "The expatriate? Oh sure. Ana adores her. So free, she says. So worldly. But I can't imagine Daniela would set her up like that."

"Apparently, she didn't. But someone who could mimic Daniela convinced her to move her money."

"Someone who could mimic Daniela." He stared into the distance for a moment. "Let me check with a buddy of mine." He took out his phone, got up, and moved toward the door. "Be right back."

While I waited, I studied the crowd. They were a mixture of young and middle-aged, dressed in casual business attire. Long blond hair predominated among the women; the men favored shorter cuts and were mostly clean-shaven. From the quality of their clothing—to say nothing of the prices on the drink menu—I assumed they were fairly affluent. They gathered in large booths or at long tables, calling out to friends and newcomers. At a nearby table, I spotted a pair of men, one at either end, holding an enthusiastic conversation with each other via their cell phones.

Mark was back in about five minutes. "Had to go outside; it's hard to make yourself heard in here. I was calling a friend of mine who's a sound engineer with one of the cable companies. He says it's easy to mimic a person's voice if you vary the levels and introduce enough background noise to distract the listener."

"Ana told me the connection was 'spotty'—one of the reasons she actually thought she was talking with Daniela in Paris."

"That could have been done deliberately."

"Did you ever meet Daniela?"

"No. Ana's always been very guarded about her friends."

"Someone also has told me that Ana never saved money."

"That I wouldn't know about. From her clothing, I'd say she spent a lot."

"She furnished my office with copies of statements from the various accounts that were looted."

Mark was looking bored with the conversation. "What I really want to know," he said, "is if there's a chance she'll come back to me. Money doesn't matter; I have plenty of my own."

"Why don't you ask her?" I surveyed the crowded bar, then blinked in surprise.

"How can I do that when she won't see me?"

"Look right over there." I gestured at a space near the hostess stand where Ana had suddenly appeared.

As I rose, Mark turned. When I reached the hostess, Ana had already slipped out the door.

* * *

She was nowhere on the street—not that I could have spotted her through the driving rain. I ran around the corner to where I'd parked my car, fumbled with my keys, and slipped inside, squeezing water out of my hair and reaching for a cap I kept in the back carrying space. I was severely pissed off at my client—so angry that normally I would have dumped her case on the spot. But not yet; it had piqued my curiosity, and I had too many questions to let them go unasked.

From the car I called Derek Ford. Still at the office, the unceasing workaholic. When I asked about the documents Ana had provided us, he said, "Can you come over here? There's something I want to show you."

Traffic from Van Ness to the financial district was slow on a rainy late afternoon. I drummed my fingers on the steering wheel and grumbled. When I was finally seated across the desk in Derek's office, I pulled off my cap and used it to wipe moisture from my face. "So what have you found?" I asked.

He slid a sheaf of papers over to me. "Take a look at the numbers on these accounts," he told me.

They were the account statements showing zero balances that Ana had provided. I scanned them, shook my head. "They look okay to me."

"They're not. An extra zero has been added to each. No such account exists at any of the financial institutions. Someone's faked them to show no balances."

"Ana?"

"Most likely."

"But why?"

"Think, Shar, of what she's gained since she claimed to have been cleaned out."

I considered. "Glenn Solomon plans to pay her rent. Her interior decorator friend sent cash. Her flight attendant friend is offering frequent flyer miles in case she needs to travel to look for a new job. Her pal Janey gave her gifts from the store where she works and also offered her a place to stay. Her old boyfriend is determined to marry her."

"To say nothing of her getting free investigative services from M&R."

Dammit, I'd been had. Had like the most gullible victim of a simple scam.

I gritted my teeth, growled something along the lines of wanting to kill her.

Derek tried to hide a smile, but didn't quite succeed. "Don't get murderous," he said. "Get even."

We went to the conference room, met with my operatives Patrick Neilan and Julia Rafael, as well as my nephew Mick Savage, Hy, and a couple of operatives from his side of the business. Officer manager Ted Smalley obliged with a couple of pots of coffee. He also sat in and contributed avidly as we began to plan what we called Scamming the Scammer.

***

Ana called around noon the next day. "Sharon, I think I may have a line on the scammer."

"You do?" My surprised tone was disingenuous, given what I now knew.

"Yes. A man phoned this morning and claimed he knows who the woman is. He wants money before he'll tell me anymore."

"How much money?"

"He wouldn't say."

"Who is he?"

"He wouldn't tell me that either. He wanted to arrange a meeting."

"Where? When?"

"You know the Grove?"

It was a parklet near our building. An appropriate place, since the rain had yielded to a brilliantly clear day.

"Yes, I do."

"He'll be there at four-thirty. Can you come too?"

"Yes, but I may be a little late. Don't let that bother you, though; it's a perfectly safe location."

"I won't agree to anything till you get there."

You bet she wouldn't.

***

Our office manager, Ted Smalley, had volunteered to play the role of blackmailer and made the call to Ana last night. He'd really gotten into it, so much so that I'd had to ask him to tone down his villainous pose. A wiry, goateed man with streaks of silver in his dark hair, for years he'd indulged in periodic changes of costume: grunge, Edwardian, hip-hop, Botany 500, Hawaiian, caftans. You name it, he'd tried them all. Fortunately, under the influence of his husband, antiquarian book dealer Neal Osborne, he'd settled on more normal attire, although today, I'd had to restrain him from trading his coat for a cape worthy of Jack the Ripper.

I watched from the corner of our building as Ted crossed the parklet. Awnings had been let down over the little tables scattered there, and he approached the one where a slumped figure sat. Ana. From her posture, I assumed she wasn't taking the news of her "recovered money" well.

Ted's voice came over the open line between our cell phones. "Ms. Emery?"

"Yes."

"Ted Smalley. May I sit down?"

"If you wish."

Scraping of a chair as he sat.

"I understand you've been the victim of a cryptocurrency scheme."

"—One that you perpetrated."

"I'll neither confirm nor deny that."

"So what do you want?"

"To return your finds to you—for a percentage, of course."

"How much percentage?"

"Fifty."

She was silent.

I crossed the street, entered the parklet.

Ted went on, "I have here the most recent statements from your bank and brokerage accounts. Would you care to look at them?"

Grudgingly: "All right."

Rustle of papers.

"These aren't mine."

"It's your name on them."

"But they show the full balances that were scammed! They must be outdated."

"Look at the date—it's yesterday's." Yesterday's, when Derek had created them using actual statements as templates.

"But I gave my investigator the most recent statements."

"The most recently doctored statements."

"What does that mean? I don't know what you're talking about!"

More rustling of paper.

Ted said, "Look at the numbers on the statements you gave, er, your investigator."

Silence. Then: "Oh. There's an extra zero."

"Meaning the documents were faked."

"But who would do such a thing?"

I stepped up to the table. "Who, Ana? You."

She twisted in her chair, eyes wide with shock. "It's about time you got here. Who is this Ted Smalley person anyway?"

"A member of my staff. He volunteered to pose as a scammer."

"Why? And what's this about me faking those documents? Why would I?"

"To prove you'd been a victim of a scam."

"But why?"

"Because of the things you collected or are about to collect from people who care about you. Rent subsidies, cash, gifts, frequent flyer miles. And I've wasted a hell of a lot of my valuable time chasing around on your so-called case."

She pushed her chair back.

"Stay right where you are," I said. "There's no use rushing out and cashing in your accounts. I've already contacted the district attorney and he's put a hold on the funds."

She sank back, shaking her head. "I don't see why what I did was a crime. It was a game, that's all. Just a game."

"My agency has been playing a game, too. It's called Scamming the Scammer."

Aim

A Finn Teller Story

Twist Phelan

Finn Teller sat on the trattoria's terrace, trying to pay attention to the waiter's description of the appetizers.

"*Cipolla dorata al cartoccio* is an onion cooked in a cartouche," he said.

Whatever that is, Finn thought. She looked across the table at Luc Barthez, her boyfriend, who shrugged and nodded.

"We'll share one," she said in English although she was fluent in Italian. The waiter took their orders for main dishes and left. Finn resisted looking at her watch.

You're on vacation, she reminded herself, sipping her wine. It had become her mantra, like something she'd say before a yoga class, if she were the type to do yoga. She closed her eyes and tried to let the sounds of Florence—the peal of church bells, the sputter of a Vespa motor, the murmur of other diners—calm her.

The waiter returned with their starter, a large onion encased in cellophane cinched with a red string. With a flourish he untied the string and folded back the plastic, then nodded approvingly as Finn peeled away the outer skin with a knife and sliced into the tender layers.

"There's a visual metaphor," Luc said as Finn took a trial bite.

"I don't get it," Finn said when she'd finished chewing. The onion tasted pretty good.

"You sliced that onion like you work a case, peeling back the layers."

Finn was a corporate spy for Strategic Information Associates. SIA operatives did a lot of the same work for individuals, companies, and governments that the CIA did for the US government.

Finn plunged her knife into the center of the onion and drew the blade swiftly toward her. Onion juice spilled onto the tablecloth as the white orb fell apart into smooth-edged halves. "Sometimes I prefer to cut to the heart of things."

"You have the manners of a cavewoman," Luc said, emphasizing his French accent.

Finn forked a piece of onion. "Of course. I'm American."

After lunch Finn and Luc strolled through narrow streets toward their hotel. End of the day sunlight set the terracotta-colored buildings ablaze, while a breeze rippled through the white flags marked with red fleur-de-lis hanging from balconies. The Red Lily, official emblem of the city of Florence, was ubiquitous, emblazoned on everything from jewelry and dishes to tote bags and T-shirts.

Luc paused at a small tailor's shop to photograph its window display of a half-stitched suit. A freelance photojournalist based in Paris, he regularly won awards and his work was featured in prominent publications and websites.

The shop's door stood open. The stocky man sitting inside at a sewing machine looked up at the sound of the camera shutter. Smiling, he beckoned them inside.

Finn and Luc entered the cluttered room lined with vintage cabinetry, bolts of fabric, and yellowed tailoring patterns. The man introduced himself as Gabriele.

"My great-grandfather opened this shop in nineteen eleven," he said in accented English. He showed them what he was working on, a dark green moleskin hunting jacket with a pouch on the back to carry a rabbit or pheasant. "The pocket—it is only for fashion now," Gabriele said.

Finn fingered the compartment, lined with leather as soft and gold as poured honey. It was just the right size for her Ruger.

"How long would it take you to make me a jacket like this?"

Gabriele beamed. "I can tailor this one for you." He quoted a price.

"Deal," Finn said, handing over her credit card to pay the deposit. The jacket was pricey, but it would mean not having to wear a holster or carry a bag when she needed to be armed.

Gabriele took her measurements, noting them in a ledger that looked old enough to have been used by his great-grandfather. "The jacket will be ready tomorrow, three o'clock," he said.

When she and Luc were outside again, Finn tilted her face to the sun. "I guess I could get used to this vacation thing."

Luc looked amused. "Are you talking to yourself or me?"

"Both," Finn said as her cell phone vibrated in her pocket. She checked the caller ID. "Sorry, I need to take this."

Luc kissed her cheek. "I'll check out the cheese shop."

Finn hit the green ANSWER button on the screen, realizing she was not totally unhappy to do so. "I'm on vacation."

"I don't believe you," Jon McAuliffe said.

Finn imagined her boss sitting behind his desk at the DC office—though he could be at any of the company's locations around the globe—shirtsleeves rolled up, steel-rimmed glasses pushed up into thick gray hair.

"It's true," Finn said. "Today I sliced up an onion in a cartouche."

"I'm sure the onion never had a chance. Listen, last night there was an incident at an embassy. The ambassador wants our help and he's willing to pay for it." In addition to working for individuals and corporations, SIA often did for governments what they couldn't do themselves for political or legal reasons.

Finn felt her pulse amp a few beats. "Just a sec."

She caught Luc's attention through the wavy glass of the shop window, held up an I'll-be-a-few-minutes finger, then found an empty bench and put in her earbuds.

"Which embassy?"

"It's the…" McAuliffe paused for a second, long enough for Finn to interject.

"Nope."

"What do you mean, *nope*? You don't even know where I'm talking about."

"But I know you. That pause is your tell. It means you want me to go someplace where people already want to kill me."

"Given your track record, there aren't that many places I can send you where they don't feel that way. For the record, I don't think anyone from Kazjakistan is still looking for you."

"Kazjakistan? I can't go there!"

Kazjakistan was one of the countries south of Russia that Finn privately referred to as the Ickystans. Her work on a prior assignment had exposed corruption by Jalad Kerimov, the son of Kazjakistan's president. The son had gone underground to avoid prosecution after vowing retribution against SIA, specifically Finn.

"You're not. Well, not really. The call came from the Kazjakistani embassy in Slovakia."

"An embassy is legally considered the territory of the country it represents. So I'd be in Kazjakistan."

"The ambassador asked for you. Said he was impressed by your takedown of Kerimov, compared you to Lady Abernathy."

Finn blew out a dismissive breath. "Doesn't he know she's a myth?"

When Finn was a CIA agent-in-training, her courses at Langley included case studies of the famous British spy's operations against the Eastern Bloc. If half the stories of Lady Lillian Abernathy's quick thinking and bravery were true, the woman was the OG of Western spies.

"She's a living legend. At least let me tell you the assignment."

Finn sighed. "Fine."

"There was a party last night at the embassy, a send-off for a recalled diplomat. Things got out of hand."

"By 'out of hand,' are we talking about embarrassing viral videos?"

"No, we're talking about a dead diplomat and a missing girl."

"So it really was a going-away party. Why was the diplomat being recalled?"

"He's a sleaze—two attempted rape allegations over the past year. The victims were Slovak. Kazjakistan refused to waive his diplomatic immunity so he could be prosecuted."

"Gee, what a surprise."

"But they also didn't want the bad press of Slovakia expelling him. Apparently the two countries are finalizing a potash deal worth billions, and this diplomat was Kazjakistan's point man in the negotiations. So they settled on recalling the guy."

"What the heck is potash?"

"Google says it's potassium-rich salts vital to crop nutrition—in a word, fertilizer. According to the ambassador, whoever controls potash controls the global food supply. Slovakia produces a lot of the stuff. Until now, Russia handled its transport and sale to Europe. Under the new deal, a Kazjakistani company will do it instead."

"That should make Russia unhappy."

"Very. Last year potash more than doubled in price. The deal means billions of dollars in revenue for Kazjakistan."

"If the deal is essentially done and the minister was being shipped home, why was he killed?"

"Leopards and spots. The ambassador said he made a pass at the missing girl last night. Apparently she was better prepared than the other victims."

"She killed him?"

"Looks that way."

"Why doesn't Kazjakistan handle it internally?"

"The missing girl is Slovak."

"Which means involving the local police. Hello, bad press."

"Yep. The ambassador wants us—you—to find the girl so he can plan the next moves."

"Which I'm sure will include payoffs and cover-up."

McAuliffe said something in response but Finn wasn't listening, her attention caught by the sight of Luc walking toward her. He smiled and held up a small brown parcel. She smiled back, her thumb unconsciously rubbing the ring on her right hand, a gift from Luc. She refocused on what

McAuliffe was saying.

"…the background info is waiting for you on the plane. So, we're good?"

"I told you, I'm on vacation."

"You hate vacation."

The thin gold band was warm under her touch. It wasn't an engagement ring. That was fine with Finn—she liked their connection undefined. Lately, she wasn't sure Luc felt the same.

"You're the best op for the job," McAuliffe said. "Give Luc my apologies and go back to your hotel. A car's already there to take you to the Florence airport."

"Wait a minute—I didn't file an itinerary before I left! How do you know where I am and who I'm with?"

"What else do you expect from the spy who trained you?"

Finn had worked for McAuliffe at the CIA before a job gone wrong resulted in the end of her government career. When McAuliffe went private not long after and founded SIA, he'd reached out and she'd come aboard.

"I don't have any gear with me," Finn said.

"I had Tech load a shoulder bag with what you might need. There's a Ruger in there, too."

Finn stopped rubbing the ring. "Okay, I'll go. But you owe me a five-hundred-euro deposit on a jacket."

"Five *hundred*?"

"It comes with a pocket to carry dead animals."

"Of course it does. Just get on the plane." McAuliffe ended the call. He was superstitious about saying good-bye.

Finn wouldn't admit it, but she was, too. She dropped her phone into her bag as Luc joined her.

"I have to go," she said. "Work."

The arctic blue of his eyes dimmed as though a cloud were passing, although the sky overhead was clear.

"Have to?" he said. "Or want to?"

"Have to. It's Kazjakistan."

His jaw tightened, sharpening the angles of his face. Luc knew about her history with Kerimov. "You can't possibly—"

"I'm not going in country," Finn said quickly. "Just to one of their embassies." She ran her fingers down his forearm, feeling sun-warmed skin, the tickle of fine hairs. "I'll be back before you know it."

Luc blew out a small breath, then abruptly wrapped an arm around her shoulders and pulled her into his chest. "You'd better be."

* * *

According to the file that was waiting for Finn on her seat, the missing girl was eighteen-year-old Iolanda Albescu. There was only one photo, apparently a school headshot. Finn took in the tight, tense face: watchful dark eyes under swooping brows, lower lip jutted out while the top one pulled tight. Brunette curls strained to spring free from their bobby pins.

Iolanda's mother worked as a cleaner at the Kazjakistani embassy. The diplomat who was killed was Gregor Zima, Kazjakistan's minister of commerce. He had been found dead in a small room upstairs from the reception hall where the party was being held.

Finn skimmed the preliminary forensic pathology report. Cause of death was a single high-velocity rifle wound to the chest, with a muzzle-to-target distance estimated at greater than twenty feet on a downward trajectory. Particles of fine-ground stone and sand were found in the bullet's track through the body's soft tissue, likely the result of the projectile grazing a plaster or cement wall while in flight, or contamination of the projectile prior to its insertion in the firearm. The bullet was too deformed to enable matching with a particular weapon.

Forty minutes after her flight touched down at Bratislava Airport, Finn stood in front of the Kazjakistani embassy on the pedestrian walkway that fronted the city's embassy row. The four-story monolith was prototype Cold War architecture—concrete, windowless, walled. She gave her name to the guard at the door and was shown to the Kazjakistani ambassador's office.

In his mid-forties, Jozef Dobromil wore a white shirt, forgettable tie, and a brown suit in need of Gabriele's attentions. His pale eyes were bloodshot and he hadn't shaved. The odor of cigarettes hung in the room.

Finn sat in the chair closest to the door. It didn't feel like a setup—payback for what happened to the president's son—but she was nonetheless wary.

"I'm familiar with your company, your work in particular," the ambassador said. "It is why I want you to look for the girl." He lit a cigarette with a lighter fished from his suit pocket. "You read the materials we sent?"

"I did. Tell me more about the potash deal."

Dobromil blew out a stream of smoke. Finn, an ex-smoker, sniffed appreciatively.

"Russia traditionally handled the transport and sale of Slovakia's potash to Europe. Under the new deal, a Kazjakistani state trading company will do it. We will charge Slovakia less for transportation and take a smaller sales commission than the Russians."

"And still your revenues will be in the billions. Sounds like a win for both of you. Who's the loser?"

"Ruspotashi, the Russian company that used to have the contract. It's been a cash cow for the Russian government." He spread his hands. "Now, decamillions in tax revenues and hundreds of jobs, all lost."

"If this deal is so great, why would killing a sleazy diplomat derail it?"

"Kazjakistan and Slovakia are historic enemies. The president's political opponents don't think we should be doing business with the Slovaks, despite the potential for profit. The same belief is held by a faction in the Slovakian government. If Russia uses the news of a Slovak woman claiming assault by a Kazjak diplomat to sow disinformation and confusion about the deal, it could spark protests, even an uprising against our president."

Not necessarily a bad thing, Finn thought, recalling her encounter with his son. "Why was Iolanda at the party in the first place? Was she someone's date?"

"No, she was working as a server—passing canapés, that sort of thing."

"Has she worked events here before?"

"This was the first. One of the regular girls was sick and Iolanda took her place."

"Does she have a job here?"

"She helps her mother with the cleaning. The head of staff says she does okay—not late, no stealing, cleans good."

"What about the minister who was killed? What's his story?"

The ambassador looked at her through a haze of smoke. "It is because of Gregor Zima's efforts Kazjakistan and Slovakia reached the potash agreement. It will be his legacy."

"Along with at least two, maybe three, attempted rapes."

Dobromil ground out his cigarette. "The man is dead. Don't insult his memory."

"The preliminary report said cause of death was a single shot to the chest. Do you have the weapon?"

Dobromil shook his head. "The girl must have taken it with her."

"How would she even get a gun? The laws here make it pretty impossible for an average citizen."

"It would not be hard for her."

"Why? Do you know that she has criminal connections?"

"No. I am saying it would be easy because of who her people are."

Finn leaned forward. "Her people?"

"The girl is Roma. She lives with her mother behind the wall."

The Romani, or Roma—often referred to by the pejorative *Gypsies* because it was thought they came from Egypt when in fact they originally hailed from India—were targeted for extermination during the Holocaust because of their itinerant lifestyle and supposed mystical power to see the future, and their "flexibility" regarding private property. Nowadays they were still shunned by their fellow European citizens for the same reasons. Many Romani resisted assimilation and lived in remote self-contained villages or segregated ghettos within cities, sometimes behind walls erected by their town ostensibly to contain their thieving and scams, despite EU laws to the contrary.

Finn was familiar with their unique language and culture distinct from the European norm. Her mother, Zara, was half Romanian. While it wasn't something Finn made public, she wondered if it was why the ambassador had asked for her.

"The report also said Zima was found in a small room, shot at a downward angle from twenty feet away," Finn said. "Tough for Iolanda to pull off if she were in the room with him."

Dobromil shrugged. "But not impossible."

Finn pursed her lips. "What happens when I find her?"

"There will be justice for Gregor," Dobromil said.

"What about Iolanda?"

The ambassador offered an empty smile. "Of course."

Right, Finn thought. But big money was at stake in the potash deal, really big money. It was probably safer for Iolanda if Finn found her rather than someone else sent by the Kazjakistani ambassador…or president.

Finn stood. "I'd like to see where the shooting happened and speak to Iolanda's mother."

* * *

An aide summoned by Dobromil showed Finn down a hallway to where it passed through a medium-sized octagonal room from the west to the east. Tall rectangular windows were cut into each wall, giving the space the feel of an open-sided gazebo. There was no furniture.

All six of the windows were cranked open. A flowery scent hung in the air and Finn heard voices of people in the garden below. The floor was covered with handmade rugs, save for an area near the center of the room where the exposed tile was still damp.

"You've already cleaned up the scene?" Finn said, surprised.

The aide nodded. "The ambassador wanted it done as soon as Minister Zima's…as soon as he was taken away."

Finn walked the perimeter of the space, looking out the six windows as she went. All allowed a view of the embassy gardens and perimeter wall. From the northwestern and northern windows she could see the upper floors of the British embassy next door; from the northeastern and southeastern windows, the tops of the trees in the park on the other side of the embassy row pedestrian walkway. The southern and southwestern windows looked at the brutalist facade of the neighboring Belarussian embassy.

According to the file, the minister was alone when he was shot. Given the lack of furniture, he was likely walking through the room rather than standing still. Finn timed herself walking from hallway portal to hallway portal, a distance of about twenty-five feet.

Four seconds, she wrote on her copy of the preliminary report, less than three to the center of the room. It was unlikely a sniper—even one set up and waiting in an elevated position in the garden—could have gotten off an accurate shot in time. Given the entry wound, Zima must have somehow ended up on the ground, with the shooter standing in the east or west hallway. She walked the distance again to double-check the time.

"You know, Minister Zima did not walk like that," the aide said.

Finn turned to him. "What do you mean?"

The aide tapped one of his legs. "His leg, it was bad. He used a cane."

Finn walked across the space again, this time with a limp. It took her twenty seconds—more than enough time for a sniper to take a shot.

She used her phone to take photos of the room and the view from each of the windows, then turned to the aide.

"Would you take me to Iolanda's mother now?"

* * *

Finn led Elena Albescu to a far corner of the walled garden. The embassy was undoubtedly full of listening devices, and Finn wanted to be outside where the jamming device in her bag wouldn't be as readily detected.

"*O čom to je?*" Elena said when they were by themselves. *What is this about?* She was dressed in clothes Finn remembered her grandmother wearing—full pleated skirt, white bell-sleeved blouse, *diklo*, or kerchief, holding back her hair. The necklace of gold coins around her neck jingled softly. Romani women traditionally wore their wealth as a sign of good fortune. Finn recalled the stack of thick gold bangles her mother always wore. Several were now her sister's, with the rest stashed in a drawer at Finn's condo in the States.

"*Povedz mi niečo o svojej dcére,*" Finn said. *Tell me a little about your daughter.* Finn had spent a winter in Jasná on a CIA assignment. Her local contact, a ski instructor, had taught her conversational Slovak as well as off-piste technique.

"*Je to dobré dievča!*" Elena said.

"I'm sure she is a good girl. But I know she is also in trouble," Finn said, switching from Slovak to Romani.

Elena gasped. "You are Roma!" she said in Romani, tears welling in her eyes. "People are talking about Iolanda, but she did not do what they say. She did not kill that man!"

"Do you know where she is?"

Elena shook her head. "I have not seen her since she went to work at the party."

"The ambassador has asked me to find her," Finn said. "It would help me if you would answer some questions."

Finn went through the basics. No, Iolanda had never run off before. No, she didn't have a computer, just an old mobile phone. When Finn asked about social media accounts, Elena looked at her blankly, her naiveté almost painful for Finn to observe.

With no cyber footprints to follow, Finn tried the human route. The trail was similarly scant—Iolanda had no boyfriend, past or present, and her father had left before she was born.

"Who's Iolanda's best friend?" Finn asked.

"Catina Popescu. She lives next door. She and Iolanda have been close since they were girls."

"Do you own a gun, Elena?"

The other woman looked shocked. "No! You cannot without a license."

"Do you mind if I take a look at Iolanda's room? Maybe I can find something that'll give me an idea where she's gone."

"I cannot leave work. I will lose my job." Elena produced an old-fashioned brass key from her skirt pocket and gave it to Finn. "But please, you go now."

Finn saw how stretched she looked, a mother worried about her missing daughter, from a people with centuries of threat and loss laid down in their bones.

"Please," Elena repeated. "Find my daughter."

* * *

Finn drove her rental car to the Roma section of the city under an eggshell-hued sky. She couldn't help but think of the Jewish ghettos of the last century as she passed under the arched stone gateway marking the area's entrance. She knew the tide of nationalism was rising in Europe, including Slovakia. Here was an egregious example spilling over the dike of decency.

Unlike the streets near embassy row, the streets inside the walled neighborhood were unkempt. Finn's rental car rumbled over rough pavement and bucked through sections of missing roadway. Housing was either tiny concrete apartments stacked five stories high, or haphazardly painted bungalows shouldering for space on small lots.

People were everywhere—kids played in the street, young people smoked and clustered on corners, men in undershirts sat on wooden chairs in front of drab cafés or conferred under upraised hoods of old cars while women in aprons hawked homegrown produce from their stoops. Most flicked eyes— some stared, a few gawked—at Finn as her car passed, and she resisted the urge to self-consciously tug at her collar.

The Albescu house was on the outskirts of the quarter. Bricks showed through crumbling stucco and tar paper weighted down by tires where tiles were missing from the roof. Finn parked in front, her car and a black sedan halfway down the block the only vehicles that weren't a set of bald tires and another winter's rust away from being junkers.

The air hung silent, and the slam of her car door reverberated like a clap of lightning. Save for a white-haired woman pulling a shopping trolley, the street was surprisingly empty. Finn glanced up at the flat gray sky. Even it seemed dingier on this side of town.

She knocked on the front door. No answer. She made a quick circuit of the dwelling, peering in windows and trying doors. It appeared empty.

Using the key Elena had given her, Finn let herself into the dim interior. The house was small—two bedrooms, one bath, a kitchen, and a living room. There was a faint, furtive smell, a combination of overcooked vegetables, mildew, and stale dust—odors of poverty. But Finn sensed resilience, too, in the Saint Sarah icon tacked to the wall and the blouse embroidered with traditional chain-stitching draped over a chair. The Romani had endured enslavement in medieval times, forced assimilation throughout the 1800s, attempts at extermination during the twentieth century via Hitler's gas chambers and Czechoslovakia's forced sterilization, and still they persevered. Finn liked to think her grit came from her Romani heritage.

Her search of Iolanda's room didn't take long. The chest held several T-shirts, a cheap pair of jeans, and some underwear. Finn couldn't tell whether the drawers had been cleaned out or the girl didn't own many items of clothing. There was nothing hidden in the narrow single bed, but on the floor underneath it Finn found a plastic bag. Inside was a stack of school books—computer science, computer programing, German I, calculus, physics—and composition notebooks. Finn flipped through the latter. The pages were filled with equations and coding notes.

She returned the textbooks and notebooks to where she'd found them. Were they stored there because they were no longer needed? Or because they were valued and needed to be hidden?

Finn quickly looked through the rest of the house. Elena's bedroom was similarly spartan, save for an ancient foot-pedal sewing machine and a shiny bolt of white satin in the process of being transformed into a dress. Finn guessed Elena did sewing on the side. Romani women were recognized for their needle skills, just as the men were known for their metalwork.

The kitchen cupboards held two plates, two bowls, and two drinking glasses, along with a large pot and a frying pan. A bunch of carrots, a head of cabbage, and a small piece of meat wrapped in butcher paper sat in the refrigerator, while the larder shelf held four eggs, an apple, and a sack of potatoes. There was a tin of paprika on the sideboard, its pungent smell bringing Finn back to childhood meals of peppers stuffed with seasoned rice.

Finn locked the door behind her and walked to the house next door. It, too, was small, but better maintained than the other houses on the block, a bulwark against the decrepitude. The dirt walkway showed rake marks and was lined with an uneven row of pansies, faces bravely tilted upward. Thin curtains, blindingly bleached, hung starch-stiff at windows that were clean and unmarred, except for one pane covered with a fresh piece of plywood.

The metal front door was painted burgundy. Finn rapped on it.

A dark-haired woman in a navy dress cracked the door. She looked at Finn with trustless eyes. Gold coins attached to a thick chain jangled at her wrist. "*Čo chceš?*"

"I am with child welfare," Finn said, also in Slovak. "I'm looking—"

The woman barked a mirthless laugh. "You are lying. There is no organization like that, not for Roma children."

"I'm looking for Iolanda Albescu. Your daughter is Catina Popescu, yes? I understand she and Iolanda are good friends. Is Catina here? May I speak with her?"

"Catina is not here." The woman started to close the door.

Finn held out a hand to stop her. "Iolanda is in danger," she said in Romani. "Please, could we talk?"

The woman considered Finn, lips pursed. "Okay, I see it, in your face," she said, switching to Romani. "Your mother or your father?"

"Mother." Her mother was Roma; her father, Croatian.

The woman scrutinized Finn for a few more seconds, then opened the door. "Come in."

Finn followed her into a small front room. A hot pink cropped top and jeans trimmed in sequins were drying on a clothes rack by the woodstove in the corner. Beside it, a backpack leaned against the wall.

The woman sat on a faded sofa with thick wooden legs. Finn chose a bench by the woodstove.

"I am Magda," the woman said. "Who are you really and why are you looking for Iolanda?"

"My name is Finn Teller. I work for a private security company. Iolanda disappeared during a party at the Kazjakistani embassy last night and I've been hired to find her. I'm hoping Iolanda said something to Catina that might give me an idea where—"

"Catina does not know where Iolanda is. They are not friends."

Finn frowned. "Iolanda's mother said the girls have been close since they were young. And don't they go to the same school?"

Magda shook her head. "Iolanda stopped school two months ago, when her mother announced her engagement. Catina and I have not seen her since then."

Finn knew in Romani culture boys and especially girls married and began having children at an early age. She also knew while most Romani children attended primary school—which ran through ninth grade in Slovakia—a large percentage, again especially girls, didn't go on to high school. Those who managed to succeed in mainstream society typically did so by turning their backs on Romani society.

"Who is Iolanda engaged to?" Finn said.

"Vasile Lungu."

"A boy from school?"

"No. A man fifteen years older and already with one wife."

The reference to an existing wife didn't surprise Finn. Polygamy wasn't uncommon among the Roma. "Catina is still in school?"

"Of course! She is serious girl, third grade in gymnasia, studying computers."

Finn knew gymnasia—nonvocational four-year high schools—explicitly prepared students for university and were often highly selective.

Magda tilted her chin. "Not every eighteen-year-old Roma girl is illiterate with baby on her hip and another in her belly." As she spoke, Finn saw the something she'd seen in her mother's eyes when she talked about Romani culture—pride, but at the same time the knowledge it was something she had to leave behind. It was the first time Finn realized a thing could be both good and bad.

"That's true," Finn said. "My mother graduated from university and didn't marry until she was in her twenties."

"That will be Catina's future, too. So I do not want her involved with Iolanda's problems." Magda stood. "I have work to do."

Finn nodded at the broken window patched with cardboard. "What happened?"

Magda's lips tightened. "They fire shots in the night, yell things."

"They?"

"People who don't like Roma, don't like immigrant, don't like girls to be in school—take your pick. There is much hate here. It is why Catina must do well in gymnasia, so she can get out."

Finn extracted a business card from her bag, wrote her local number on it, and laid it on the bench. "If you see or hear from Iolanda, please call me."

"I will think about it," Magda said without conviction. She showed Finn to the door and stayed propped in the doorway, as though wanting to make sure Finn left.

As Finn approached her rental, the black sedan up the street pulled away from the curb and rolled toward her, a faceless man behind the wheel. By habit, Finn watched it approach as she felt for her keys in her bag. When the car was four houses away, the driver's window lowered.

Intuiting what was happening even before glimpsing the gun barrel, Finn dove behind her rental. She was pulling her Ruger from her bag when a blast punched through the air from behind her, followed by the ping of bullets hitting metal and a familiar ratcheting sound.

Magda threw herself down beside Finn and laid the barrel of a shotgun over the trunk of the rental car, readying for another shot. As soon as it had been hit, the black sedan had shifted into reverse. It now sped backward down the street, a bloom of shotgun spall marring its glossy paint.

Finn cupped her hands around her eyes and squinted at the car's license plate.

"Double E, nine, six, three, one..." she said under her breath.

The car swung into a J-turn at the end of the block and disappeared. Finn hit an autodial entry on her phone.

The call went through. She identified herself and repeated the two letters and four numbers. "I missed the last number. Slovenia, blue plate with yellow letters. Black four-door sedan. Everything you can tell me. I'll ring back for the info." She ended the call and looked at Magda.

"Thanks," she said in Romani. "And what the hell?"

Magda got to her feet. "Come with me." Finn followed her into her house.

"Catina told me a man in a black car talked to her and Iolanda last week," Magda said as she set about reloading the shotgun. "The girls were walking home from the park. The car pulled up beside them and the driver asked if one of them was Iolanda. Iolanda said she was. He said there was an emergency at the embassy and both girls should come with him. Iolanda said she wanted to call her mother first. The driver said there was no time and started to get out of the car." Magda set the reloaded shotgun in the umbrella stand by the front door. "Catina thinks he is going to take them and tells Iolanda to run. At the same time, some other kids show up, so the man, he got back into the car and drove away."

"Could the girls describe him?"

"No. He wore one of those face masks."

Finn nodded unhappily. The pandemic had given criminals and those looking to stay anonymous an easy way to hide their identities from public and CCTV scrutiny.

"Did you call the police?" Finn said.

Magda snorted. "We are Roma. They would do nothing. And I do not want to embarrass Catina at her school, have people there think she is a bad girl men want to pick up."

Finn met Magda's eyes. "Did you or Catina see Iolanda yesterday?"

The other woman's shoulders slumped. "Yes. She came over last night, very late, very upset. She asked if she could spend the night with Catina. This morning when I call them for breakfast, they were both gone."

"What was Iolanda wearing when you saw her?"

Magda shrugged. "White shirts, black pants."

"Did she have anything with her?"

"A backpack, like Catina's." Magda nodded at the backpack, red with a white cross, like the Swiss flag. "This is why I am worried. Catina always has her backpack. I cannot imagine her going anywhere without it."

"Can I look inside?"

Magda nodded. Finn picked up the bag and searched it. She found a Bluetooth microphone and speaker; school books—computer science, information technology, coding, and German; several composition note-books; a plastic wallet with eighteen euros in change; two hair scrunchies; and a sweets wrapper. The notebooks contained a few class notes, and lots of what looked like poetry or maybe song lyrics. Finn skimmed the pages of one—unrequited love, falling in love, falling out of love.

"Did Catina have a boyfriend?"

"She is not permitted. I do not want her distracted from school. Studying computers is very hard."

Finn held up the microphone. "Is Catina a singer?"

Magda rolled her eyes. "My brother in Berlin sent that to Catina two years ago. Always Catina is watching the TikTok, the Instagram on her friend's phones. She thinks she can be famous." Magda made a face. "She sings Western songs, not Romani. She was making videos instead of studying until I told her no more."

Finn put the microphone away, then took a photo of the backpack. "Is there someone you can stay with in case the guy in the black car comes back?"

Magda indicated the shotgun in the umbrella stand. "This is only company I need."

"I thought those were hard to get."

A smile tugged at Magda's mouth. "License, yes. Gun, no."

"Can Elena stay with you tonight? I think you'd both be safer if you were together."

Magda nodded. "I will bring her here after she is home from work."

Finn pointed at the card she'd left on the bench. "Call me if you hear from Catina."

Magda put the card in her pocket. "Even with the man shooting, you will keep looking for Iolanda?"

"Yes," Finn said. She understood what the woman was really asking. "Catina, too."

* * *

Finn hit redial on her phone as soon as she was back in her car. The SIA researcher told her the blue-and-yellow license color scheme meant the plates were from Slovakia's diplomatic series. A double E meant the car was assigned to a diplomat; a double Z indicated the car was driven by administrative or technical staff. The pair of numerals after the double letters denoted the embassy the plate was issued to—*nine seven* was assigned to Kazjakistan—and the last three numbers were unique to the particular vehicle.

Finn drove toward the Kazjakistani embassy. When she was four blocks away, she parked and continued on foot, cutting through the park that edged embassy row. Stopping in a stand of trees near the Kazjakistani embassy, Finn removed a pocket surveillance drone from her bag. About the size and shape of a swallow, the device was equipped with a camera that sent real-time video to her phone.

She launched the drone. The sky had blued out and visibility was good. Two aerial circuits over the Kazjakistani compound revealed neither the shot-up black sedan nor a set of plates with three and one as the third and fourth numbers.

Finn had just put the drone back into its case when a silver BMW emerged from the treed section of the park and stopped not far from her. Curious, she ducked behind a tree to watch. Less than thirty seconds later, the Kazjakistani embassy's main gate opened on the other side of the pedestrian mall. A young man in a purple sweater emerged, carrying a small duffel. He jogged across the walkway, entered the park, and made for the BMW. When he reached the car's nose, he dropped to the ground out of Finn's sight.

253

Finn waited. Purple Sweater didn't reappear. No one got out of the car. She was considering launching the drone to check out what he was doing when Purple Sweater came into view again.

He moved to the rear of the vehicle, where he unscrewed the car's license plate and replaced it with one from the duffel bag. The license plate he removed was white with black letters, similar to the ones on most Slovak cars. The one he replaced it with was blue and yellow, its first four characters, ZZ 96—plates from a Kazjakistani embassy staff car.

Finn knew diplomatic missions sometimes loaned out their vehicles' license plates, even though they weren't supposed to. Embassy plates meant parking wherever without being towed, high-speed spins sans speeding tickets, and border crossings without Customs hassles.

His task finished, Purple Sweater went to the driver's window, where he was handed what looked like a handful of euro notes. He stuffed them in his pocket as the car started up. Finn snapped a photo of the car and its new plates, then moved to intercept Purple Sweater, who was walking back toward the embassy.

She grabbed him by the arm from behind. "I have a few questions," she said in Slovak.

Purple Sweater tried to jerk free. Finn pulled him close and knocked his feet out from under him with a quick side sweep. She pulled the duffel from his grasp and tossed it out of reach.

"Let's talk about license plates," Finn said, her knee in his back keeping him prone.

Purple Sweater struggled to get free. "Let me go! I have diplomatic immunity!"

Finn pressed down harder. "Maybe you do. But I wonder if my new friend the ambassador knows about your side gig."

Purple Sweater went still. "You know the ambassador?"

"Jozef and I chatted this morning. Want me to call him?"

"No!"

"Then talk to me." Keeping a hand on his collar, Finn helped him sit up. "What's your name?"

"Laszlo."

"Do you work at the Kazjakistani embassy?"

"I'm in charge of the auto pool."

"Gas, maintenance, that kind of stuff?"

Laszlo nodded.

"How many different sets of plates have you rented out?"

Laszlo picked a twig off the cuff of his sweater. "Two."

"Is the other set a diplo one, double E, nine six three one something?"

Laszlo frowned. "Yes—double E, nine six three one eight. How did you—"

"Who has them now?"

"Peter Sazbó."

"Who's he?"

"Some Russian. He came to the embassy last week, demanding to talk to Gregor Zima, the minister who was killed last night. The guards wouldn't let him in."

"Did you hear why he wanted to talk to Zima? Or anything else about him?"

"I heard the minister call him 'the damned Russian trying to kill the potash deal' after he left."

"When is Sazbó supposed to get the plates back to you?"

"An hour ago."

"What happens if he doesn't?"

"I report them as stolen off the car they are assigned to."

Finn snapped a photo of Laszlo, then released her grip on his collar. She took a photo of his bag and its contents, too. She handed him the bag along with her card.

"Call me when Sazbó shows up and your rent-a-plate secret is safe with me."

"Yeah," Laszlo said sourly. He slung the duffel over his shoulder and jogged toward the embassy.

Finn googled Sazbó on her phone. She stared at the results, surprised.

Peter Sazbó was the chairman of Ruspotashi, the company that up to now brokered Slovakia's potash. What did a Russian oligarch want with Kazjak diplomatic plates? And why was he sniffing around Iolanda?

* * *

Finn bought a map of the city at a kiosk and walked to the pedestrian mall. Strolling at tourist pace, she passed the tall wrought iron gates fronting the Kazjakistani embassy, then turned down the alley between the Kazjakistani compound and the larger British embassy next door. There were no doors or windows in the concrete wall on the Kazjakistani side.

At the end of the alley she turned left and walked the length of the rear of the compound. At the far end was another alley on her left, this one separating the Kazjakistani embassy from the Belarusian one. Again, no openings on the Kazjakistani side. Behind all three embassies was an expanse of mowed field.

Finn backtracked along the rear wall of the Kazjakistani compound. There were two points of access: a loading dock protected by two metal doors, and beside them a set of wrought iron gates matching the ones at the front of the embassy.

One of the loading dock doors was propped open. Finn glanced inside as she passed, seeing a wide corridor that led to what appeared to be a commercial-sized kitchen. The metal gates opened onto a paved courtyard where several cars were parked.

If Iolanda hadn't left the compound last night via the front entrance, that left the rear vehicle entrance and the loading dock as her escape routes. Finn was surveying both, weighing possibilities, when an older woman walking a black Scottish terrier approached. Both wore red-and-navy plaid coats.

As the pair passed, the little dog jumped up without warning, pawing Finn's leg, stumpy tail metronoming furiously, head bumping against her hand.

The woman tugged at the leash. "Angus! Mind your manners!" Her accent was upper-class British. She looked with dismay at Finn's pants, now marked with dusty paw prints. "Oh, dear. I am terribly sorry."

Finn brushed off the grit. "No worries. They're washable."

"Oh, you're American." The woman nodded at Finn's map. "Would you like directions?"

Finn slipped the map into her bag. "No, thank you. I'm with child welfare." She nodded at the Kazjakistani embassy. "I'm looking into something that happened here last night."

"You mean the shooting at the party?"

So much for the ambassador's plan to keep it under wraps, Finn thought. "Were you there?"

"Oh, no. The United Kingdom and Kazjakistan do not enjoy diplomatic relations."

"You work at the British embassy?"

"Human resources, at least until the end of this week. Then it's back to London."

"Then how did you know—"

"I heard the shot when I was walking Angus." The little dog perked his ears at the sound of his name. "I picked him up and ran for cover."

"That was smart."

"More likely reflex." The woman's gaze went to the empty field, and Finn had the sense she was seeing another place in another time.

"Do you remember what time you heard the shot?" Finn said as Angus sniffed one of her shoes.

"Just past nine." The woman cocked her head. "Why is child welfare interested in a shooting at an embassy?"

"A local girl went missing during the party. I'm trying to find her."

"Really? What's her name?"

"Iolanda Albescu."

"Iolanda? But I've met her! She waits for the bus where Angus likes to walk. She plays fetch with Angus and we chat."

"Did she ever mention anyone bothering her, like a stalker or someone harassing her at work?"

"Oh, no. Our conversations were casual—what she was studying, places she'd like to visit, acting…"

"Acting?"

"I've done some theater, and Iolanda has a friend who wants to be a singer. They make videos in the park."

"You've met Iolanda's friend?" Finn asked, feeling as though she were two steps behind in the conversation and still losing ground.

"Catina. Lovely girl. She has quite a nice voice. And her arrangements are original—contemporary songs set to a Romani beat." The woman smiled. "I can see how she could be successful."

"And when you talked with the girls, neither mentioned having problems with anyone?"

"Iolanda did say she wanted to be going to school instead of working at the embassy. She wants to be an app developer. Of course, there's no chance of that if she marries that man."

"She told you about the engagement?"

"If that's what you want to call it. She barely knows him and he's almost twice her age." The woman made a face. "Archaic misogyny is what it is."

"Did Iolanda ever mention Gregor Zima?"

"No. Who is he?"

"A minister with the Kazjakistani mission. The party last night was in his honor."

"Well, Iolanda wasn't there."

More like ten steps behind. "And you know this because—"

"Because I saw her and Catina leave the embassy before I heard the shot."

"You were walking your dog?"

"No, I was on my balcony." She nodded at the British embassy. Victorian gables, turrets, and rooftop finials rose behind the red brick wall. "It's the corner one, top floor."

Finn saw the window offered a clear view of the Kazjakistani compound. "Do you remember what time you saw them?"

The woman thought. "Around eight o'clock. It was when I took my break." Seeing Finn's questioning look, she added, "I sculpt; marble, mostly. That's my studio. I go out on the balcony to look at the view and smoke."

She sighed. "I know it's not good for you, but so many fun things aren't, are they?"

Finn thought of her recently kicked Gauloises habit. "True that. Did you see anyone leave the embassy after you heard the shot?"

"No, but I was focused on keeping Angus safe and getting back to the embassy."

"Did you see where the girls went after they left?"

"I believe they ran across the field. In any event, Iolanda couldn't have shot that minister."

"I don't recall saying the victim was a diplomat," Finn said.

"Oh, when you said minister, I assumed that was who'd been shot." Angus strained against his leash and whined. The woman checked her watch.

"You'll have to excuse me. It's almost time for Angus's tea."

"Thank you for your time."

Finn watched the woman and Angus start toward the British embassy before she turned and walked through the alley that separated the Kazjakistani and Belarussian embassies. She crossed the pedestrian walkway and entered the park, thinking about what the woman had said. If Iolanda had left the embassy an hour before the minister was killed, did that put her in the clear? Or had she returned and shot Zima—without being caught on the security cameras and knowing nothing about guns? Was Catina involved?

Finn reached her car and got behind the wheel. Had the minister tried to sexually assault Iolanda? Or was it another kind of attack? Did the Kazjakistani ambassador want SIA to find Iolanda because he truly thought her guilty of the minister's murder, or was there another reason?

If Iolanda stayed missing, other people could benefit, including Peter Sazbó. If the minister's murder were made public, the Russian disinformation corps could use it and Iolanda's disappearance as part of a campaign to doom the Kazjakistani potash deal, which would be to Ruspotashi's financial benefit.

Finn thought about her visit to Iolanda's and Catina's houses. Two very different households, yet both had one thing in common. One thing that didn't belong in either.

She called SIA research. When the text with the answers she expected came back ten minutes later, she started her car.

* * *

Magda opened the door. "Catina is still not here."

"I know," Finn said. "She's on her way to Germany with Iolanda."

"What? Why do you think this?"

"Let me in and I will show you."

Magda moved aside. Finn crossed the room and picked up the backpack. She unzipped it and took out one of the books. "Because of this." She held up the German textbook. "Iolanda has one, too, in the schoolbooks she hid under her bed."

"So? The girls take language classes in school."

"Not German," Finn said. "I had their class schedules checked for this term and the previous year."

"I don't understand—"

"You said your brother in Berlin sent Catina the microphone. They are close, yes?"

Magda nodded. "He spoils her."

"Iolanda wants to study computer science, not get married. Catina wants to be a singer, not go to university. I think the girls were studying German because that's where they planned to run to. I bet they're on their way to Berlin right now."

Magda took out her phone. "I am calling my brother!"

The call went through but was unanswered.

"Text him," Finn said. "Tell him Catina and a friend may show up, and that he should let you know ASAP if they do, but without them knowing. We don't want them to take off again."

Magda tapped on the screen. "Okay, it's sent. But what if they aren't going there? Or if something has happened to them on the way?"

"That's why I'm going to keep looking for them," Finn said. "Someone went to a lot of trouble to plant the story that the minister tried to assault Iolanda and she killed him. Assuming that isn't what happened, that means Zima was killed by someone else, for another reason. And we still don't know why someone tried to shoot us this afternoon."

"They tried to shoot *you.*"

"They had eyes on *your* house." Finn ran a hand through her hair. "You and Elena should stay in a hotel tonight."

"No," Magda said. "I want to be here in case Catina comes back. I know she will feel the same way."

"At least be sure Elena comes over here after work so neither of you is alone. And call me if you hear from your brother."

Magda nodded. "Fine."

Once in her car, Finn called SIA's Eastern European headquarters to ask for a contact at the Bratislava morgue. The text came five minutes later; a "friendly" assistant to the coroner waited to hear from her. Finn never wanted to know why people became an SIA "friend"—blackmail, a return favor, a way out of debt, just plain greed. It was a sordid but necessary part of the business she preferred to ignore.

The coroner's assistant sounded young and nervous. "The preliminary autopsy was sealed," she whispered into the phone.

"By whom?" Finn said.

"Someone from the police. He said if anyone asked to see it, we were to say *no* and then call him with the person's name."

Damn, Finn thought. She'd have to boost a copy of the report. She was about to ask the assistant about the morgue's layout and work hours when the young woman continued.

"But I saw it before they sealed it."

"What did it say?"

"Not very much. Only that the minister was shot from far away."

"Far away? What does that mean?"

"The estimate was thirty meters."

Finn could see it. Air conditioning wasn't big in Europe like it was in the United States. Summer weather meant open windows.

"Did they recover the bullet?"

"Yes, but I don't know the caliber."

Finn knew a bit about firearm range. A bullet shot from a 9mm handgun could travel 1.2 miles; one fired from an AR-15 rifle, just over two miles. But maximum range wasn't effective range. The farther away the target, the longer the odds of a hit. Long-range shooters had to calculate the deviating effects of gravity (bullet drop) and wind (drift), among other factors. Military snipers typically operated at ranges of one third to two thirds of a mile.

Finn drove back to the Kazjakistani embassy and parked behind the compound. Assuming the woman from the British embassy was right and Iolanda and Catina had left through the loading dock door, there were only a few ways for the girls to get out of town. Private jet? Ridiculous. Commercial flight? Unlikely. Private car? The girls weren't old enough to have licenses and didn't seem to know anyone with a car. Rideshare? Finn doubted either had a credit card or bank account to link to an account.

The embassy's metal gate slid open and a woman in a maid uniform exited. She started across the field and Finn watched her go, noticing she followed a well-worn shortcut across the dirt. Finn got out of her car and followed.

A few minutes later, the path dead-ended at a paved road, where the woman stopped beside a pole with a metal sign that read BUS STOP.

Finn jogged back to her car, found the address on the map app, and drove to the town's main bus station. There had to be CCTV. She'd have SIA work its magic to get a copy of the recordings. At least she'd know which bus the girls had gotten on.

She parked a block from the station. Walking toward the terminal, she passed a crowd listening to a busker. The singer had a great voice, and Finn heard the clink of coins dropped into a receptacle.

The onlookers shifted and Finn glimpsed the singer, who was in her mid-teens. The girl had a lilting mezzo-soprano, made distinctive by her incorporation of Romani syncopation and phrasing. Her accompanying dance moves were contemporary with a suggestion of flamenco, a dance said to have originated with the Romani. The audience was enthralled, with more than a few members filming her with their phones.

Beside her, sitting cross-legged on the pavement behind a plastic cup of coins, was another girl of similar age wearing a bright red-and-pink camo hoodie. Leaning against her knee was a backpack—red, with a white cross. Finn pulled out her phone and checked her photo library. The backpack matched the one in Catina's house.

Finn looked closer. Even though the sitting girl's head was bowed and the hood of her pullover drawn close around her face, Finn glimpsed the dark eyes, saw the tendrils of brown curls. It was Iolanda.

The other girl stopped singing. There was a smattering of applause and a few more coins were tossed into the plastic cup. As the crowd dispersed, Finn moved closer to the girls.

"Do we have enough?" the singer asked in Slovak.

"Almost," Iolanda replied in the same language. "Can you do one more song?"

"I need an Orangina first. My throat is sore!"

Iolanda twisted a piece of her hair. "Catina, I am so sorry I lost the money."

Finn wasn't surprised to hear the name. Ten feet from the teens, she pretended to be texting as she surreptitiously snapped their photo.

"You didn't lose it! That boy stole your belt bag."

"How am I going to pay for school? How can you do your videos?"

"I told you, my uncle will help us."

"Are you sure we can't go home before we leave?" Iolanda said. "I want to get my books."

"And I want to get my backpack and my microphone and speaker. But we can't. My mother almost caught us this morning." Catina tugged at Iolanda's sleeve. "Let's get an Orangina and I will sing some more. We'll be on the bus to Vienna tonight and the train to Berlin tomorrow, I promise!"

Finn put away her phone and stepped up to the two girls. "Excuse me, can you tell me where to catch the bus to the airport?" she said in Slovak.

Catina pointed. "You go to the end of the block—"

As Finn looked where the teen pointed, a black sedan with a constellation of shotgun blast on its driver's door turned the corner and started down the street toward them. Its front license plate was diplomatic blue with yellow trim.

Finn grabbed Iolanda's hand and wrapped an arm around Catina's waist.

"Come on! Hurry!" she said in Slovak, steering the girls toward the terminal. "The person in that black car is looking for you."

Iolanda tried to pull free. "Let me go!"

Catina began, "Who are—"

Finn tightened her grip. "Your mothers sent me," she said in Romani. "I mean it—move!"

The black sedan accelerated, bumping over the curb as Finn and the teens reached the terminal building. The car sped toward them on the sidewalk as pedestrians screamed and ran.

Finn pushed the teens behind a large metal dumpster. "Get down! Make yourselves as small as possible."

Catina and Iolanda did as they were told, hugging each other and crying. Finn pulled her Ruger from her bag. She heard a loud crash, followed by more screams. She peered around the edge of the dumpster.

The black sedan had hit one of the metal bollards that ringed the bus station. As Finn watched, the driver's door opened and a man wearing a hoodie and black pandemic mask got out holding a rifle. The scream decibels rose at the sight of the weapon as the remaining pedestrians sprinted for safety in the terminal or cowered behind the nearest vehicles.

The man crouched behind the car door and aimed the rifle at the dumpster. Finn squeezed off a shot, then pulled back out of sight. The crack a millisecond later told her she'd hit the car's window.

There was a sharp metallic ping as a bullet hit the dumpster. Catina cried out and Iolanda hugged her harder. Sirens keened in the distance.

"Stay down!" Finn said in Romani. "Don't move." She lay on her belly, legs V-ed behind her, the Ruger extended in a two-handed grip. The dumpster was on wheels, elevated off the ground about eight inches, giving her a view of the lower third of the car.

Right cheek pressed against her right upper arm, Finn lined up the shot. The screaming had stopped and she heard the *ch-chunk* of the rifle being racked, followed by another metallic ping. Catina whimpered.

Finn focused on the shooter's shoe and ankle, exposed under the open car door, and squeezed the trigger. The bullet hit its mark. With a yell, the shooter fell out of his crouch onto his side.

Finn sprang to her feet and ran toward where the shooter lay clutching his ankle, the rifle on the ground beside him. She grabbed the rifle and cleared it, stowed her Ruger, and took a handful of zip cuffs from her bag.

As she reached to secure his arms, the shooter backhanded her across her cheek. Finn kicked him in the groin and he screamed in pain.

"I know, not nice," she said as she cuffed his wrists together. "But neither was the drive-by at Magda's."

The shooter donkey-kicked with his uninjured leg, connecting with her shin.

"You're really starting to irritate me," Finn said. She looped a cuff around his good ankle and threaded it though the set, pinning his wrists, and fastened it.

"Perfect hog-tie, emphasis on the hog." Finn pulled off the shooter's mask. She'd never seen him before. She took out her phone and snapped his photo.

Finn got to her feet. Only then did she glance into the sedan and see the other man. He sat in the backseat, staring at her.

She grabbed her Ruger and aimed it at him as the man raised his hands. They were empty.

"The young ladies have something that belongs to me," the man said. "I want it back."

"And you thought your man shooting them was the way to accomplish this? How would you get it back if they were dead?"

"You're right, of course," the man said. "My driver can be a bit… impulsive."

A siren whined from a block or three away. Finn took a photo of the man.

"They can keep the money," he said. "I just want the envelope that was in the bag."

A patrol car squealed around the corner. Finn turned and sprinted for the dumpster where Iolanda and Catina cowered.

"Let's go, let's go!" Finn said. "Hurry, but don't run. And don't look back."

Finn followed a zigzag course through the city's streets for ten minutes until they were at the edge of the park that fronted embassy row. She bought three Oranginas from a kiosk and led the teens to a secluded bench.

Catina twisted the cap off her drink and gulped the sugary liquid. Iolanda held her bottle, unopened. Both girls wore cheap jeans and off-brand sneakers, but Finn saw Roma touches. Gold hoops hung from Catina's ears and Iolanda's hair was held back by an embroidered headband.

"Who are you?" Catina asked in Slovak.

"Someone hired to find you," Finn answered in Romani.

"By Vasile Lungu?" Iolanda said. "I don't care if you drag me back. I'm not marrying him!" She stared at Finn, her dark eyes lacking the softness of her mother's acquiescence to tradition, instead hard with resolve to set her own course.

"Not by him. Your mother, the people at the embassy—they were worried when you disappeared after Gregor Zima was killed."

"Minister Zima is dead?" Iolanda said. "How?"

"Someone shot him at the party."

"Iolanda and I left right after it started," Catina said. "We don't know anything."

"Iolanda, did Zima or anyone else at the embassy ever bother you?" Finn said.

"Bother me?"

"She means did he hit on you," Catina said.

Iolanda made a face. "No!"

Finn took out her phone and showed the girls the photos of the shooter and the man in the car. "What about either of those guys?"

Catina pointed at the photo of the shooter. "That's the guy who was shooting at us? He was driving the car!" She turned to Iolanda. "You know, last week."

"The other guy was in the car, too," Iolanda said. "I saw him in the backseat."

"Pervs trying to pick us up." Catina made a dismissive noise. "As if we'd get into a car with them."

"I don't think that's what they were looking for," Finn said. "That man in the car is Peter Sazbó, a Russian who wants to kill a trade deal Minister Zima helped broker. He isn't cruising the streets in a car with borrowed diplomatic plates to pick up teenagers." She looked at Iolanda. "What did you take from him?"

"You are Roma and ask that?" Catina said, outrage in her voice. "Iolanda did not steal anything!"

"I think she did, at least from Mr. Sazbó."

Catina grabbed her friend's hand. "Tell her, Iolanda! Tell her you are not a thief!"

Iolanda wouldn't meet her friend's eyes. "It happened so fast," she said in a small voice.

Catina dropped her friend's hand. "What did you do?"

"I was waiting for you in the park. The man and Lazlo were there, too. The man was in the car and Laszlo was switching the license plates." Iolanda's words tumbled out like water rushing over river stones. "Then the man got out and asked Laszlo where was the toilet. Laszlo told him and the man left. He didn't shut the car door all the way and it swung open. There was a paper bag on the floor. It was open and I could see it was full of money. Laszlo was busy with the license plates, the man was gone…so I just took it." She clasped her hands together, pleading. "Catina, it was so much money! Enough for us to go to Berlin and get an apartment, enough for me to go to school and you to make your videos!"

"I thought you made that money working at the embassy!" Catina said.

Iolanda gave her friend an exasperated look. "It would take years to earn that much! Anyway, it doesn't matter now. That boy stole my belt bag. It's all gone."

"Was there something else in the paper bag?" Finn said.

"An envelope. I didn't open it."

"Do you still have it?"

"I put it in my school books."

"The ones under your bed?"

Iolanda stared at Finn. "How do you know about the books under my bed?"

"Never mind. I'll get the envelope. We need to get it back to Sazbó."

"What about us?" Catina said. "Are you going to make us go home?" She crossed her arms. "Even if you do, I am not going back to school. I am going to be a singer. My grandmother, my great-grandmother—they were famous Roma singers. I have their voice."

"Home isn't the best place for either of you right now. Sazbó was there this morning, looking for you. He might come back."

"Sazbó was at my house?" Catina said. "But my mother, she—"

"Can take care of herself," Finn said. "Trust me." She turned to Iolanda. "How did they know you took the bag?"

"I don't know! Maybe Laszlo saw me run away with the bag?"

Finn binned her empty Orangina bottle. "Let's go. I'm taking you someplace safe, then I'm getting that envelope to Sazbó."

It took Finn an hour to stash the two teens in a hotel—after extracting a promise from them not to leave, in return for access to room service and movie rentals—and retrieve the envelope from the physics book under Iolanda's bed. She then drove to the Kazjakistani embassy and asked for Laszlo. He was working in the front garden.

"Call Sazbó," she said, squeezing his shoulder under the purple sweater for emphasis. "Tell him I've got what he's looking for."

Twenty minutes later the black sedan rolled into the spot in the park where Finn had watched Laszlo switch plates earlier. Sazbó was alone in the car. He got out, showing empty hands. Finn stepped out from behind a tree, Ruger in one hand, the envelope in the other.

* * *

"How much money was in the bag?" McAuliffe asked.

On the other side of the desk, Finn swiveled her chair so she had a view of the Eiffel Tower. SIA's Paris office was one of her favorites. "Around a hundred grand. Sazbó's side hustle is money laundering. It was the weekly take from a local drug dealer."

"Why the license plate switching?"

"He did it whenever he had a big cash pickup. The police never stop anyone with diplomatic plates."

"So when the girl stole the money—"

"Let's go with *made an impulsive decision* rather than *stole*. Iolanda was desperate to stay in school and not get married. The money practically fell into her lap."

"And Sazbó apparently was just as desperate to retrieve it. How did he know the girls were at the bus terminal?"

"Luck and TikTok. Iolanda wore a distinctive hoodie the day she took the cash. Sazbó kept checking local social media, looking for someone wearing it. When people livestreamed Catina singing at the terminal, he spotted it in the background. Anyway, Sazbó didn't care about the money. There was a list of his money-laundering clients in the bag—names, bank accounts, balances, transfer histories. Either he was old school or worried about hackers, because he kept everything on paper." Finn smiled. "I made a copy before I returned it to him."

McAuliffe nodded in satisfaction. "I'll pass the info on to my friend in the GOPAC task force."

Finn knew he was referring to the global anti-corruption organization's anti-money laundering group. McAuliffe had connections everywhere.

"The ambassador was pleased with your work. He's releasing an official statement today," McAuliffe said. "Sazbó had Zima taken out in a last-ditch attempt to kill the potash deal. His driver—the guy you shot at the train station—used to be a sniper in the Russian army. He set up in a tree in the park across from the Kazjakistani embassy and took the shot from there."

"Pure fiction. I went over the findings in the prelim report. The shot that killed Zima was fired from the upper floor of the British embassy."

"That's why the report was pulled from the file. The last thing the president of Kazjakistan wants is to get into it with the Brits, even if they don't have diplomatic relations."

"It's also why the ambassador started the story Iolanda killed the minister in self-defense, and why he hired us to find her. They were setting her up to take the blame, until Sazbó made a better fall guy."

McAuliffe spread his hands. "Easier to deal with a #MeToo scandal—or a disgruntled businessman—than an assassination by a foreign government."

"And Sazbó and his driver aren't around to say otherwise because Russia claimed diplomatic immunity for both and scooped them up. Does money laundering without Kremlin approval get you prison or a Siberian work camp?"

"Where are the two girls?" McAuliffe said.

"In Berlin, with their mothers. I tracked down the pickpocket that took Iolanda's bag and, uh, suggested he turn over what was left of the cash. It's enough to give them a fresh start."

McAuliffe looked amused. "Suggested?"

Finn waved a hand. "Whatever. I still don't get why the Brits wanted Zima dead. The potash deal was done, and besides, they didn't have any interest in it."

McAuliffe absently picked up a flat piece of marble from his desk. Finn knew he wasn't a memento man—no brag wall of photographs, no tchotchkes from round-the-world travels gracing his work space—except for the white stone the size of a deck of cards he now held. It was a fixture in whichever SIA office McAuliffe was currently occupying, transported via a faded red velvet bag tucked into his briefcase.

McAuliffe fingered the piece of marble, and Finn realized the design carved on top was the fleur-de-lis she'd seen all through Florence.

"What did you think of Lady Abernathy?" he said.

"I didn't—" Finn caught his grin. "No *way*."

McAuliffe's grin widened. "I understand you met Angus, too."

Finn's mind went back to the woman and the little dog in matching plaid coats. "What's she doing in Slovakia? I'd expect her to be assigned someplace like Spain or the Caribbean, maybe the States if she likes to shop."

"I'm sure she has her pick of postings," McAuliffe said. "Anyway, she let me know she'd run into you."

"How'd she know who I was? And why would she call you?"

"The Brits ID everyone who goes into the Kazjakistani embassy. And I met her when I was with the Company; she was my MI5 counterpart on a joint op. So when you came up as SIA on their surveillance, she called me."

"You *worked* with Lady Abernathy?"

"We were tasked with picking up a Kazjak human trafficker who was smuggling girls into Europe via shipping containers. When the guy got a tip we were after him, he left his last load—seventeen girls—locked in a container at the Genoa port." McAuliffe traced the pattern on the piece of marble with his thumb. "I'll never forget opening that container. Eight days in the summer heat without food or water. An awful way to die."

"Jesus. I hope you got him."

"We traced him to a villa outside Florence. Our orders were live capture. We set up a sniper's nest in a nearby abandoned apartment building and Lilly—she wasn't her ladyship back then—dug in."

Finn was surprised. "Not you?"

McAuliffe shook his head. "She's one of the best distance shooters I've ever seen. Patient, too. She waited four days to take the shot. Brought him down with a through-and-through to the knee."

"Did we keep him, or did the Brits?"

"Neither. The guy had a lot of names to drop—human trafficking, drug smuggling, money laundering. He got full immunity, ended up becoming a successful businessman." McAuliffe paused. "I recently learned he was even an advisor to Kerimov."

"A human trafficker is a member of the Kazjakistani president's inner circle?"

McAuliffe met Finn's gaze. "His most recent minister of commerce, if I'm not mistaken."

The pieces fell into place so quickly, Finn felt almost lightheaded.

Particles of fine-ground stone...contamination of the projectile prior to its insertion in the firearm...I was on my balcony...it's the corner one, top floor...I sculpt, marble mostly...one of the best distance shooters I've ever seen....

Finn now understood Lady Abernathy's choice of a posting to the British embassy in Slovakia. She got to her feet.

"If you speak to her ladyship again, please tell her it was an honor to meet her." She smoothed the front of her new jacket. "Thanks again for having this sent. And for covering the tab—really not necessary."

The pocket in the rear fit her Ruger perfectly. As a surprise, Gabriele had added an extra one hidden under the lapel, sized for "the other kind of stiletto every woman should own," according to the accompanying note.

McAuliffe grunted. "Aren't you supposed to be at the airport?"

"Sure you're good with me finishing my holiday?"

"Go see Luc. Enjoy yourselves." McAuliffe held the carved marble piece for a moment as though gauging its weight, then set it back on his desk, fleur-de-lis side up.

"You know, Paris gets all the attention, but it's really Florence that's the city for lovers," he said.

The Shandiclere

Neil S. Plakcy

One Saturday afternoon, my next-door neighbor knocked on my door. She and her roommate were flight attendants, and I had a soft spot for both of them.

"Hey, George," Patti said, standing in my doorway. "Sandi has a crush on a singer named Jimmy Fowler, and she wants to go see him perform at this bar in Miami tomorrow night," she said. "We heard the bar is kind of sketchy, so we were hoping you would come with us."

"Which bar?"

"The Shandiclere," she said. "It's right on the other side of the Miami River from downtown."

"I know where it is," I said. "It's a place where shady people conduct drug deals or find a hit man. The cops are all over it." Sending the two of them unescorted to the Shandiclere was like thrusting Daniel into the lions' den.

In addition to running my own private detection agency, which usually teetered on the edge of bankruptcy, I worked as a bouncer five nights a week at a gay bar called the Cockpit. Though the last thing I wanted to do on my night off was hang out at a skanky bar full of straight men, most of them criminals of one kind or another, I agreed to escort the two of them.

We drove over the causeway from Miami Beach in my 1958 lime-green Chevrolet Bel Air and navigated our way through downtown Miami. It was about nine o'clock on a Sunday evening, and the city was as dead as a vampire with a wooden stake in his heart. The storefronts on Biscayne Boulevard were dark, and the only people on the street were either ladies of the evening or workers on their way to midnight shifts guarding the doors of the rich or cleaning their toilets.

"How'd you hear about this singer?" I asked, as we drove.

"He was on a flight from New York, and Sandi flirted with him," Patti said.

Sandi elbowed her friend. "I was just being sociable," she said. "As soon as I heard his accent, I pegged him as from Tennessee, and I wanted to be extra nice to him."

"He told us he was playing at this bar and invited us to come," Patti said. "He is pretty good-looking." She looked over and smiled at me. "Who knows, maybe he's playing for your team, George, and we could hook you up."

"I have my own man, thank you," I said.

* * *

The Shandiclere was in a two-story building nestled against the entrance to the South Miami Avenue bridge over the Miami River. Because so many of the local roads in the neighborhood dead-ended into the waterway, which snaked from the Everglades to Biscayne Bay, it had become a hangout for the kind of illicit characters that kept to the shady parts of this sunny city.

Patti and Sandi both wore cotton peasant blouses with flowing sleeves over long skirts. Both were pretty and blond, with shoulder-length hair and long beaded necklaces, and Patti had stuck a peacock feather in her hair.

I was surprised when I walked in to see Cliff Galanis at the bar. He was a regular at the Cockpit, and if he was hoping to get lucky at the Shandiclere he was in for a world of trouble. I tried to hurry Sandi and Patti past him, but he reached out to me.

"George Clay," he said. "Wouldn't have pegged you for a fan of Jimmy Fowler." He leaned in close to my ear, and I smelled the cheap beer on his breath. "He's straight as an arrow."

"Then what are you doing here?" I asked.

He puffed up his chest like a peacock getting ready to spread his wings. "I'm his manager." He looked over at Sandi and Patti. "You going to introduce me to your friends?"

Reluctantly, I did, and Patti was excited to ask, "Can we meet him afterward?"

"I can make that happen." He put one arm in Patti's. "I have a table right up by the stage. Why don't you ladies join me?"

There was nothing I could say to stop him, so we followed him to his table.

Jimmy Fowler was a striking figure, standing at six feet tall with a lean, athletic build. His sun-kissed, wavy hair fell just above his collar and framed a chiseled, square-jawed face. His voice had a country twang, and he sang songs about drinking down by the bayou, holding his baby close under the midnight sky. I saw his appeal—and if I wasn't getting everything I wanted from my sweetheart, and Jimmy was so inclined, I wouldn't have minded taking him out behind the bar for a quickie.

But instead, I shifted my legs to cover my interest, and focused on the music. After his set, Cliff waved Jimmy down to join us. He was just as handsome a guy in person as he was on the stage. His piercing blue eyes seemed to hold a depth of emotion that was reflected in his heartfelt songs. A well-groomed mustache and a hint of stubble on his chin added to his rugged charm.

"I promised Jimmy that if he'd come down here to Miami Beach for a while, I'd get him on *The Jackie Gleason Show*," Cliff boasted.

"You can do that?" I asked.

"I'm a close personal friend of Rich Fazio, who books all the musical and variety acts. He was supposed to come here tonight to hear Jimmy, but I haven't seen him yet. Jimmy still has another set to perform, though."

Sandi joined my conversation with Rich, leaving the way clear for Patti to chat with Jimmy, and by the time he left to go back on stage, I could tell from the glow on her face that the two of them were getting along.

The girls had a noon flight the next day, though, so we couldn't stay for the second set. I wished Cliff luck and led the girls outside, to the accompaniment of some hoots and catcalls from guys at the bar.

The girls just waved gaily at the men and took my arms, one on each side.

* * *

I was in my office the next morning when I got a call from Frank Coyne, an attorney I had worked with in the past. He was a prominent figure on Miami Beach, gay and wealthy, though very discreet. "I understand you know Cliff Galanis," he said. "I'd like to hire you to work on his defense."

I sat up in my chair and grabbed a pen and a legal pad. "What's he accused of?"

"First, you have to agree to work for me, so that everything we say is covered under attorney client privilege."

"Sorry, I knew that. Yes, I'll work for you on your defense of Galanis."

"Excellent. He says you saw him last night at the Shandiclere, is that correct?"

"I did." I explained how I'd come to be at the bar, and how Sandi, Patti and I sat with Cliff to listen to Jimmy Fowler's first set.

"Then what?"

"Jimmy got back on stage, and the girls and I left. Cliff was alone at the table, though he said he was expecting Rich Fazio, who he said books the musical and variety acts for *The Jackie Gleason Show*. You still haven't told me what Cliff's accused of."

"Fazio was seen at the Shandiclere with Cliff for Jimmy Fowler's second set. Then he turned up dead in a dark corner of the parking lot with his pants down around his knees."

"Shit. And Galanis?"

"Galanis was arrested for the murder. He called me, and when I met with him at the police station downtown, he told me he'd been with you for part of the evening and suggested I hire you to prove he's innocent."

"I can try."

I arranged to head over to Coyne's office in the middle of Miami's growing financial district, to sign the paperwork and get my retainer, and take a look at what Galanis had said. I signed the appropriate paperwork and received a check for my retainer.

Coyne's secretary handed me photocopies of his handwritten notes of his interview with Galanis that morning. Galanis said that after Jimmy's second set, the three of them had talked. Then Jimmy left for his hotel, and Cliff and Fazio walked out to the parking lot together.

Cliff said he'd gotten into his car and driven away. That was all he knew.

I drove back over to Miami Beach and deposited the check into my business account. Show business was off my path, but I knew one woman who might be able to get me started. Helen Cantrill was one of the June Taylor Dancers, the group that opened each show with specialty dance numbers and concluded with a high-kicking tap chorus line.

I'd helped her with a problem a year before. When I called and told her about Rich Fazio, she suggested I talk to Eddie Kelton, a rock and roller she'd dated briefly. "He told me Fazio wanted him to pay to get booked on Gleason."

"Is that normal?"

"Not at all. Fazio worked for Gleason, and he was supposed to find the best talent. But the whole music business is still mired in payola, despite the scandals from the fifties. From what I understood, Rich took in a nice chunk of change in exchange for bookings."

"And Gleason didn't know?"

"Either he didn't know, or he looked the other way."

When I left my office for lunch, I picked up a copy of the *Daily Planet*, a free alternative newspaper that listed live music. Eddie Kelton's band would be playing that night at Churchill's Pub—a British-themed bar that also served dinner. Which worked out well because it was my night to have dinner—and often something more, with the guy I was seeing, Alex Reyes. So, I called him. "There's a musician I want to talk to playing tonight at Churchill's," I said. "Eddie Kelton."

"Eduardo!" he said. "He's not very good."

"Do you know every Cuban-American in Miami?"

"Only the interesting ones. What do you want to talk to him about?"

"I'll explain when I see you. How open can we be there?"

"I won't kiss you, but I might feel you up under the table."

"Alex Reyes!" I said. "Kelton goes on at nine. If you come to my apartment at seven…"

"Say no more, *mi amor*," he said. "I will see you then."

* * *

We didn't end up leaving my apartment for Churchill's until eight-thirty. The bar was dim and decorated with a dartboard, wooden booths and tables, and a very fake replica of a red telephone booth in the corner, which was covered with names and phone numbers and nasty messages. The air was smoky and smelled of spilled beer and fried food.

We took a table near the stage, and our fish and chips arrived as Eddie Kelton strutted on stage. He was slim and saturnine, with the pasty skin of someone who spent his nights in dive bars. He wore torn jeans and a very tight T-shirt.

He was marginally more talented than Jimmy Fowler, at least in my opinion, but I preferred Fowler's laid-back sound to Eddie's hard-core rock and roll. After he finished his set, Alex waved him over, and he joined us.

He was dripping in sweat, and the server immediately brought him a tall glass of ice water, a beer, and a clear shot. He drank the water first, then the shot, then most of the beer. "What brings you out this way, *compañero*?" he asked Alex, after he'd hydrated himself.

"This is my friend George Clay. Private investigator."

I reached out to shake Eddie's clammy hand. "What's up?" he asked hesitantly.

"You know Rich Fazio?"

"That *cabrón*? Why?"

"Somebody killed him Sunday night in the parking lot behind the Shandiclere," I said. "I've been asked to look into his murder."

"You won't find a shortage of suspects in this town," Eddie said. "Fazio ripped off a dozen musicians and talent agents, promising to get their acts on the Gleason show." He spit on the floor. "Nobody watches that show anymore, not even my parents."

"Did he approach you?"

Eddie nodded. "Wanted a thousand bucks to get me in the lineup. And even then, he couldn't guarantee I'd play if another act ran longer. I didn't pay."

The waitress brought him another beer and shot, and I waited until he'd downed them to ask, "You know anyone he cheated? Who paid to get booked and then didn't get on the show?"

"It was the out-of-town acts he screwed, the ones he'd convince to fly down from Atlanta or New York." He leaned close and his beer breath enveloped my face. "You didn't hear it from me, but I heard the mob is moving into music in Miami. Using their connections at bars to push musicians." He got up and walked away to forestall any further questions.

"You think that's true?" I asked Alex. "That the mob is moving in?"

"The mob is already here, you know that," Alex said. "I wouldn't be surprised if they were muscling into music."

Alex drove us back to his house in Coral Gables after we left the bar, and we took a shower together to wash off the grunge, then picked up where we'd left off earlier that evening. I had begun to leave clothes and toiletries at his house, and he'd throw whatever dirty clothes I arrived in with his own laundry, and his maid never said anything.

* * *

The next morning, he dropped me at my office, and I wrote up notes on my conversation with Eddie Kelton. I didn't know much about the mob in Miami, but I had one contact, a guy I'd once helped out of a jam.

Pinky Feldman wrote book out of the back of a Brazilian restaurant on the north end of Miami Beach, and that afternoon I drove up there to see him. All I knew was that he was connected to the Bonanno crime family, and I didn't want to know more.

He was a short, balding guy in a bad suit, sitting at a table with a telephone, a calculator and a thick binder of paperwork. I slid into the chair across from him. "Hey, Pinky, how's it going?"

He glared at me. "What do you want?"

I leaned in close so no one else could hear. "How are things going with your wife?"

He didn't change his expression, but he said, "Interesting."

I leaned back. "Good. I've been hired to defend the guy accused of murdering Rich Fazio behind the Shandiclere on Sunday night."

"What's that to me?"

"A little bird told me that the mob is moving in on the live music business in Miami." I held up my hand before he could speak. "I know you're a law-abiding citizen. But you're also a smart guy with your ear to the ground. You heard anything that might help me?"

He continued to glare at me. "You know, with what I know about you and your fairy pal, I could get you put in jail and out of business."

"That's true. But I swore that I'd never use your name and 'up the ass' in the same sentence. And I haven't."

He finally laughed. "You know something, Clay, I kind of like you. You may like to ride the Hershey Highway with your boyfriend, but you're all right."

I laughed with him. "I'm glad you feel that way, Pinky, because I kind of like you, too. So, what do you know about the music business?"

"The Bonanno family is not involved," he said. "To be honest, we've got too much trouble going on with the Feds to be expanding." He reached over for his glass of club soda and took a swallow. "Now, the Gianellis, they're another story."

"I don't know that name."

"Small-timers out of Newark. Got a boss who thinks he's the shit. Looking for ways to edge their way into other families' territories. You didn't hear it from me, but they've got a piss-ant enforcer named Vito Iovine in Miami these days. He came by to see me last week, a courtesy call, he said. Courtesy my ass."

"He threatened you?"

Pinky shook his head. "Too smart to. Just let me know that he was around, if I need any help with anything."

"You know how to reach him?"

"He said he's staying in the Everglades Hotel on Biscayne Boulevard. Front desk can take a message for him. I gave him my message before he left."

He held up his right fist, then slapped his left hand on his right biceps and pulled his right arm back. I knew that gesture. In my Master-At-Arms training in the Navy, we'd learned it was called the *bras d'honneur* or the Iberian slap, and we were told not to engage with anyone who used it on us.

I laughed. "If I run across Iovine, any easy way to recognize him?"

"He's like a bantamweight rooster," Pinky said. "Maybe five-six, walks with his chest puffed out. Dresses like a Jersey thug, jackets with big lapels. And he's got a scar on his right cheek."

I thanked Pinky. From his office, I drove over to Frank Coyne's office in downtown Miami and was able to get the very important man to break away from whatever he was doing in his office to talk to me. He always seemed oily, and I wanted to wash my hands right after shaking his.

But he was paying the bills. I sat across from him, the breadth of a polished mahogany desk between us. I had the feeling that my chair was pegged a little lower than his, so I was in a position of supplication.

I relayed everything I had discovered. "Interesting," he said, his hands steepled in front of him. "Will Mr. Feldman confirm that information to a police detective?"

"I doubt it. He specifically used the words 'You didn't hear it from me' and if I sent a cop his way, he'd never talk to me again. I'm still building my network here in Miami and I'd hate to lose anyone."

"Then the best thing you can do is tail Iovine for a couple of days and see if you can catch him doing something the cops can pull him in for."

"I'll have to get somebody to sub for me at the Cockpit if I'm working nights," I said. "There'll be an extra charge."

"Galanis is good for it."

I stopped at a pay phone in the lobby of Coyne's office building, called a buddy of mine from the Fifth Street Gym, and arranged for him to cover my shifts for a few days.

I left my car in the garage at Frank's building and walked over to the Everglades Hotel. I walked into the lobby and bought a copy of the *Miami News* from the stand. The room was ringed with tall white marble columns which supported arches, with a carpeted walkway between the columns and the walls that allowed one to circumnavigate the room.

I did so, making sure there was no one resembling Iovine in the room, and settled myself in a plush green armchair and pretended to read. People came and went around me, families on vacation, businessmen with leather briefcases, and guests on their way to luncheons in one of the hotel's banquet rooms.

Either Vito was up with the larks and had already left the hotel, or he was a night owl and sleeping in. I had no way of telling which was correct unless I sat there all day and into the evening.

So I did. My stomach grumbled and my throat was dry, but I knew if I ate or drank anything, eventually I'd have to visit the john, and it was just my luck that Iovine would take that opportunity to show up.

Not that he had any way of knowing he was under surveillance, but my limited experience of guys like that told me he'd be aware of everything around him.

Around six o'clock he came strolling out of the elevator, his gait reminding me of the bantam rooster Pinky Feldman had compared him to. He walked into the swanky bar, where a curved wall held a mural of the eponymous Everglades, a heron taking flight over sawgrass.

He ordered at the mirrored bar and leaned against the bar to look around. Waiting for someone.

Somehow, I wasn't surprised to see Eddie Kelton walk in. He was wearing the same kind of outfit he performed in, a colorful T-shirt, torn jeans, and steel-tipped boots. He looked out of place among the suits and nice dresses of the rest of the clientele, and I wondered if he cared.

He walked right up to Iovine, as if he already knew him, and they shook hands. Kelton ordered a drink, and they moved to a table by the wall.

I used that opportunity to head to the restroom and relieve my aching bladder. I wasn't going to be able to get close enough to them to hear anything anyway.

By the time I returned, their conversation had turned less than amicable. Eddie was scowling, and Iovine was leaning across the table, getting into his face. Eddie picked up the crystal glass that held Iovine's drink and spat into it.

Then he got up and stormed out.

I really wanted to know what had caused Eddie to get so angry, but I could find him the next day to ask. Iovine waited a couple of beats, then got up from his table and walked out.

I followed him to the cab stand and lurked in the background so I could overhear him tell the doorman where he wanted to go. When I heard Churchill's, I walked past him, got my car, and drove up there.

I hoped Iovine would be there for a while. I got myself a table, ordered a burger and a glass of water, and ate and drank as he did, listening to the opening act, a young woman with long blond hair who sang a bit like Joni Mitchell.

Only a bit, though.

Vito Iovine paid close attention to the next act, a female rocker with a raspy voice and a full head of blond hair that she swung around as she sang.

Iovine got up to leave when the blonde finished, and I tailed him outside. Once again, I lurked in the shadows until he was able to hail a cab, and when I heard him say he was going to the Everglades Hotel I gave up my surveillance and drove home.

* * *

The next morning, I finished up some paperwork for other cases, putting together bills and doing some research for a new client. I ate a solid lunch, then went back to the Everglades Hotel lobby to wait for Iovine.

He met with the pretty blonde rocker from Churchill's for dinner in the hotel restaurant, and I followed them outside. They argued for a few minutes while they waited for a taxi, and in the end the woman got into the first taxi that arrived, leaving Iovine on the sidewalk. He told the next cabbie who pulled up that he was going to the Shandiclere.

Once again, I retrieved my car from the parking garage and drove to the Shandiclere. I parked under a streetlight and walked over to the club.

The first act was a young guy with shaggy hair who sang a couple of John Denver covers to mild applause from the audience. He was followed by a trio who resembled the Monkees, in funky clothes and goofy haircuts. Neither of the acts seemed to interest Iovine, who finished the last of his whiskey and stood up.

I was surprised to see that he went out the back door to the parking lot, since he'd arrived in a taxi. I waited a beat, then went after him. Wrong move, because I felt an arm around my neck as soon as I did.

"You've been following me," he said.

I had years of experience in street fights by that point, including how to get out of a simple arm hold like that. In a moment, I ducked his grip, twisted around, and faced him.

I hadn't counted on the knife, though. I should have; I knew whoever killed Rich Fazio had used one. With a quick move, Iovine had a hunting knife with a wicked blade out of his pocket, had ditched the sheath, and was facing me with it.

He had the look of a predator, one I'd seen often enough in the Navy. His eyes narrowed, his lips pursed. I danced back a few steps. "That the knife you used on Rich Fazio?" I asked.

"Stupid prick wouldn't listen to reason," he said. "I made him a decent offer. He could keep scamming the musicians and all he had to do was pay me a twenty-five percent commission."

"Protection money," I said. "To protect him from you."

"That's the way of the jungle," he said, and he lunged forward, trying to slice the knife into my abdomen and then up, the way he'd done with Rich Fazio. I was too quick, though not quick enough, and he hit the left side of my stomach.

The pain was sharp, and I smelled my own blood. That enraged me enough that I darted to his side, wrapped my arm around his neck as he'd done with me, and put pressure there. Hold it long enough, you cut off a guy's airway.

Iovine started to panic, grasping at my hands, but this wasn't my first time subduing a rowdy guy. I'd practiced this hold enough on drunken sailors that I knew how long to hold until Iovine passed out—but not long enough to kill him.

One of the bartenders stepped out the back door with a pack of cigarettes. "Do me a favor, call the cops, will you?" I asked. I pressed one hand against my side and then held it up, covered in blood.

* * *

The cops arrived and called an ambulance that took me over to Jackson, the public hospital nearby, where an ER doctor stitched up my wound. "Lucky cut," he said. "Didn't do any major damage. But it's going to hurt like a bastard for a while."

I didn't bother to tell him it wouldn't be my first scar.

By the time he was finished, a detective showed up who wanted to talk more about Vito Iovine and what had happened at the Shandiclere. He was the same guy who'd caught Rich Fazio's murder, and he was very interested in the knife Iovine had used on me.

"You told the beat cops you went out back for a smoke and Iovine asked you for money, then attacked you," he said. "Now tell me what really happened."

"Frank Coyne hired me to look for evidence that would exonerate Cliff Galanis," I said. "Based on a tip I had, I put Iovine under surveillance for a couple of days, hoping to turn something up. And I did."

"Where did the tip come from?"

"I believe that's covered under my employment with Coyne," I said. "You'd have to confer with him."

He was kind enough to give me a ride back to the Shandiclere, where I'd left my car. I drove home, took some of the painkillers the ER doctor had given me, and went down for a nice long sleep.

Everybody was Kung Fu Fighting

William Dylan Powell

Houston, Texas, 1978

"How many?" asked the ticket lady. She sported round, oversized glasses and an enormous Afro, leaning out of the ticket box to see inside the gold Ford Elite. But the car's interior was all shadow and smoke.

"Five," said the driver, not looking at her but scanning the drive-in's ocean of cars.

"Five dollars, please," the woman said.

"Jungle Boogie" played on the car's radio as the man handed over a five-dollar bill and took his tickets.

"Enjoy Chopsocky Saturday."

On the big screen, *Five Deadly Venoms* was projected fifty feet high—Lo Mang and Wei Pai battling to the death as fists and feet flew. The Elite crept up and down the lines of parked cars like a bull shark. Windows down, the men heard the on-screen action come and go from the speakers clipped to each car.

"Thought you'd find my weak spot," said the man on screen, his lips moving out of sync with the sound. "But still, you've failed."

The driver of the Elite stopped behind a two-tone brown Oldsmobile Cutlass. The men poured out and surrounded the Olds. "Jimmy Chin," one of the men said. "You're a thief and a coward. Come out and face us."

On screen, Lo Mang was being placed in an iron maiden, his screams falling on deaf ears.

A young Asian man stepped out of the Cutlass, bag of buttered popcorn in hand. "Derrick Lau? Is that you?" he said, squinting through the darkness. "What kind of jive y'all talkin' man?"

"Shut up, fool." The man flicked open an expandable baton. "You crossed the line. Now it's time to pay."

* * *

Gene lit a cigarette, took a drag and set the pack and lighter on the table, which was covered with half-eaten roast duck, Mandarin pancakes and spring onions. "Look, I've got my license now. At six clients you're groovin.'"

The waitress set Dan's *Tsing-Tao* on the table.

Dan loosened his tie. "Okay, Lew Archer, do you have six clients?"

"I just got my license last week," Gene said, tapping his ash into the nearest plate.

"Would you like a job?" Dan said.

Gene blinked. "What? A PI job?"

"No," Dan said. "A real job. Offshore. One month on, one month off. Ridiculous money, and you'd be great at it. Basically, just problem solving."

Gene held out his hands. "What have I been saying? I'm starting a business, growing a client base. How am I going to do that if I'm turning wrenches offshore?"

Dan took a long pull of his beer and leaned forward. "Goddamnit, Gene. You owe me a lot of fucking money. And you owe my sister more than that after y'all's clusterfuck of a marriage."

Gene rubbed his forehead. "Look, this thing is going to work. I can feel it. But not if I change the plan every few months. Just be patient."

"Jesus Christ," Dan hissed. "I'll be your boss's boss's boss. Pay me back in a month and buy a house for cash at the end of the year. What the fuck is there to talk about? You still going to meetings?"

Gene took a drag on his cigarette, glaring at Dan. He exhaled. "Yes, I'm still going to meetings. Look, thanks. Really. But I'm a grown ass man. I gotta square my life my way."

The waitress appeared with the check. "Who's the lucky winner?"

Dan drained his beer, slamming the bottle onto the table and standing. His face was red as sweet-and-sour sauce. "Give it to the grown ass man over here," he said, tossing his napkin in his chair. "The grown ass man who'll be at our Galveston heliport in forty-eight hours for deployment if he knows what's good for him."

* * *

The waitress was in her seventies, gray hair in a bun. She wore a mustard-yellow blouse, polyester slacks, and an orange ascot. She handed Gene the check and raised her eyebrows.

He sighed. "Ma'am, I'm sorry but I can't cover that. When my doofus ex-brother-in-law invited me, I just assumed..."

Gene had been eating at Hong Kong Palace since Sandy divorced him, and he'd never seen the old lady smile. Not once. In his mind he saw her pick up the red phone by the hostess station and call the cops. Cops meant charges. Charges meant no PI license. But, instead, she took Dan's place in the opposite chair.

"You're a private investigator, right?" she said.

Gene nodded. "Yeah. Gene Kuykendahl." Gene reached out his hand and she shook it.

"Maggie Chang," she said. "Pleasure."

"Likewise."

"One year now you've come every night. Ordered the cheapest menu items and read all those private investigation books. Get your license yet?"

"Uh, yeah. Last week."

"Perfect. Come take a ride." Despite her age, she hopped off the chair with the agility of a child and smoothed out her slacks.

"Excuse me?"

"C'mon. You're on a case."

"Just like that?"

"You got eighty-two dollars to cover the Space City Peking Duck Special?"

Gene swiped his keys off the table. "I'll drive."

* * *

The caramel tan Plymouth Volaré was the only thing that had survived Gene's gambling, a loan shark named Big Bubba Valentine, and his ex-wife, Sandy. It had a dent in the hood after an unfortunate incident at Gilley's, and a cracked windshield.

Smoke erupted from the slant six as he cranked the ignition. Maggie Chang directed him from Hong Kong Palace and down the street. The heat was oppressive, the Volaré's underpowered air conditioner struggling against a coastal breeze that felt like it was blowing from the back of an overloaded clothes dryer.

"We're looking for lions," Maggie said. "Hundred dollars now, two hundred when the lions come home."

"Lions? Like, live lions?"

"Yeah, you have a whip handy? No, dummy, stone lions. From the kung fu school. Somebody stole them."

Maggie pulled a pack of Chunghwas from her purse and lit one. "We reported it to the police, but you know." She shrugged.

After Maggie pointed Gene down Leeland and over a few blocks, they pulled up to a brick building with a glass storefront. "My brother and I bought this place for a song when we moved from California ten years ago. Built in nineteen twenty-five. Maintenance is a nightmare, but it's paid for."

"It's a great old building," Gene said, shutting the car off as they hopped out and walked to the entrance.

"Used to be a soda shop back in the day. Then it was a jazz hall, then a dance club. Today, it's a Wing Chun school."

"Wing what?"

"Wing Chun. Kung fu. You know, like Bruce Lee?"

"Ah."

Inside Gene saw men in white T-shirts and black cotton pants punching, kicking and doing various exercises. A few plonked on wooden dummies or hit punching bags.

Just outside the front door Maggie gestured at the ground. "Well, Perry Mason, here's the crime scene."

Gene looked around. "Where?"

"Some detective," Maggie said, pointing at the ground.

On either side of the door, Gene now noticed two dark rectangles where the bricks were a rich maroon. Elsewhere the brick was pink, faded, dirty, chipped and cracked. The patches looked around two-by-four feet.

Gene kneeled and inspected where the lions had been. "Perry Mason was a lawyer. Paul Drake was his investigator."

"Whatever," Maggie said. "When a new school opens, your master paints the eyes of lions guarding your door. So, they can always watch over you. Dig?"

Gene stood, wiping his hands. "How tall were these lions? They must have weighed a ton."

Maggie put a hand to her waist. "About like so. Yeah, weigh a lot for sure. Must have brought a pickup or something."

The front door flew open. A slim man in a white T-shirt stepped out. He had shaggy, black hair and was out of breath, hands on hips.

Maggie said something in Cantonese and gestured at Gene.

Gene smiled and extended his hand. The two shook.

"This is Derrick Lau, my nephew. Derrick, this is Gene. He's going to find our lions."

"Nice to meet you," Derrick said. Then he said something else in Cantonese, pointing at the spots where the statues had been.

Maggie rolled her eyes.

"Do you have a copy of the police report?" Gene said. "That would help me catch up more quickly."

Derrick looked at Maggie, whose eyes narrowed.

"Fine," Derrick said. "Make it fast, though. We do kung fu here, not Kojak. You dig?"

As they walked inside, Maggie said: "Derrick thinks he already knows who stole the lions."

"Who?"

"Iron Mantis Fist Society," Derrick said.

Sweat popped from Gene's forehead as soon as they stepped into Cheung's Martial Arts, where it felt twenty degrees warmer than the summer heat outside. He removed his fedora, wiping his forehead. None of the students paid them any attention as Gene followed Derrick and Maggie into a small office. Traditional Chinese music played from speakers in the ceiling. The plonk-plonk-plonking of men hitting the wooden dummies echoed through the space, which Gene thought cramped for a gym now that he was inside. Those who talked whispered, as though in a library.

The office held a small brown couch, a metal desk with piles of papers and a glass case containing bottles and jars. Derrick opened a desk drawer and pulled out a pink can. "Tab?"

Maggie sat on the couch.

"Is it cold?" Gene asked, wiping his forehead again.

Derrick smiled. "Air conditioning makes you weak." He took a folder off the desk and handed it to Gene. "I want that back. Sifu needs to see it when he returns next week."

"And who is Sifu, exactly?"

"Sifu Cheung," Derrick said. "Our teacher. This is his school."

"Sifu means like master," Maggie said, lighting a cigarette.

How can she smoke in this heat? Gene thought.

"Sifu is in Hong Kong," Derrick said.

Gene scanned the police report. "So, he was gone when the theft occurred?"

Derrick nodded. He opened his Tab and dropped the pull top into the trash. "Never would have happened if he were here."

"That's not the only thing that wouldn't have happened." Maggie said, taking a draw off her cigarette.

Derrick glared at her, then looked at Gene. "Look, this was all Jimmy Chin. We worked it out. Far as I'm concerned, it's done. I'll replace the lions before Sifu gets back."

"What makes you think this Jimmy guy took the lions?"

Derrick took a sip of his Tab. "Man, he's always talking trash about the Wing Chun style. Not to my face, you dig, but out in the street. You know what a praying mantis is? An annoying little bug."

Gene looked at the police report again. "You left around midnight and the lions were here, then gone when you came in the next day around noon?"

"Yep. Two days ago."

"Mind if I look around?" Gene asked.

Derrick shrugged, drinking the rest of the Tab and throwing the can in the trash. "Free country. Now, if y'all don't mind, I've got work to do."

Maggie stood.

"Thanks for your time," Gene said, shaking Derrick's hand again.

"No sweat."

"Bullshit," Gene said, "everyone in here is sweating."

Gene followed Derrick into the main room. There wasn't much to the place, mostly empty space with framed photos and Chinese prints on the wall. A rack of sticks and swords stood in the corner. In the middle of the room near the ceiling was a clock built into the wall. A recessed rack of shelves sported trophies, metals, and trinkets. A tiny decorative fountain sent the calming sound of trickling water throughout the room.

A man and woman stood chatting by the fountain. Maggie joined them and waved Gene over.

"Mary, this is Gene Kuykendahl, private investigator. He's going to get our lions back. Gene, Mary Fung and Matt Yu."

"Hello," Gene said, nodding. A drop of sweat fell off his forehead and onto the hardwood floor.

"Mary is Sifu Cheung's Disciple," Maggie said.

"Nice to meet you," Mary said. Gene thought she seemed sad and a bit detached, her expression blank and voice robotic.

"I don't know anything about kung fu," Gene said, "other than the movies. Disciple means you're good, huh?"

"That's one way to look at it," Mary said.

A few feet away Derrick began pounding a punching bag. The building shook.

"It means she'll learn everything Sifu knows," Matt said. "Hey, come workout with us. You can protect yourself while you're doing all that PI jive."

"Yeah," Derrick said, pounding the heavy bag. "We'll make a man out of you."

"We'll see," Gene said as Mary Fung excused herself and walked over to a wooden dummy, her ponytail flopping back and forth as she struck the polished wood.

"Her fists must be pretty tough after hitting on that thing," Gene said to Matt.

"Oh, it's not about that," Matt said. "In Wing Chun the goal is to dominate the center of your opponent." Matt stood in front of Gene, placing a fist in front of his chest. "These cats on the wooden dummies are practicing various hand and foot positioning to take the centerline. Feel me?"

"Must take a lot of time to learn," Gene said.

"Yeah," Matt said. "*Kung fu* translated actually means work time. Gotta put in the work to get the skills."

"Interesting," Gene said. "I didn't know that. I'm going to poke around a bit."

"Later, gator."

The first door he opened revealed just a toilet and sink. Opening a second door, the smell of vinegar radiated from a small closet with a mop, broom, and bucket. The only other door was thicker and clearly the back door.

The door led to a small alley, pocked by mud-filled potholes. A gold Ford Elite and a black Datsun 280Z with racing wheels were parked next to a pair of metal garbage pails. It was a longshot, but he lifted the lid off the nearest can. Again, Gene smelled vinegar. A pile of rags covered the bottom. The other can held only a dead flower bouquet, which he inspected. Tulips, mostly, the card attached mostly disintegrated. The only legible word was "congratulations."

Maggie Chang stepped out of the back door, lighting another cigarette. She and Gene walked around the building as they talked. At the entrance, they stopped where the lions had been. Gene looked up and down the street.

Either side of the school held vacant lots but across the street stood a strip mall with a dry cleaner, a bank and a dentist. The signs were in both English and Chinese. Gene took out a handkerchief and wiped his forehead.

"You know," Gene said, "some random person probably just pulled over and threw them in their truck. Hell, they could be at a frat house."

Maggie Chang dropped her cigarette onto the pavement and mashed it with her espadrille. "Really? This is what my eighty-two dollar Space City Peking Duck special bought me? And my hundred? A 'guess we'll never know' attitude?"

Gene's face reddened. "I'm just saying random, stupid crime happens. Not everything is Sherlockian." *But she has a point*, Gene thought. *If this is the line of work that will help rebuild my life, and maybe even allow a little self-respect, I have to give my all.*

He took a deep breath and looked around again. That's when he noticed the camera.

"That bank," Gene said. "Think their security camera works?"

"What am I, Maggie the Mind Reader?"

"Right. C'mon, let's ask."

* * *

Gene held the door for Maggie as the two went inside Hang Seng Southwest Bank of Houston. He heard no English as the tellers served customers from behind a counter. Cantopop music played overhead.

A woman in a gold beret and jumpsuit sat by the front door watching a chunky black-and-white television. On screen, JR Ewing was having a serious discussion with Bobby and Sue Ellen. The subtitles were in Chinese.

"Excuse me," Gene said. "Could I speak to the manager?"

Maggie lit another cigarette.

The woman looked up from the TV for a split second but didn't respond and went right back to watching.

"Uh, miss?" Gene said. "Sorry to disturb you but could I have a moment?"

The woman ignored him all together. On screen Bobby Ewing's office was under construction as he tried to work.

"Hey," Maggie said. "Lemon tart." She walked around the desk and turned off the television. "This man is asking you a question."

The woman's forehead wrinkled. "Can I help you?"

"Yes," Gene said. "My friend was the victim of a burglary two days ago. We'd like to see outside security footage from out front that day. Thursday."

"Mr. Lee isn't here," the woman said, clearly pleased she couldn't help. "He is the only person authorized to share such a thing and he's fishing. In Corpus Christi."

She reached to turn on the television, but Maggie cleared her throat. "When are you expecting him?"

"Tomorrow," the woman said.

"Fine," Maggie said. "Have him call Mr. Kuykendahl as soon as he returns. This is urgent."

Maggie looked at Gene.

The woman looked at Gene.

"What?" Gene said.

"No business card?" Maggie said.

Gene shrugged. "You're my first client."

Maggie tore a page from a *Have a Nice Day* notepad on the woman's desk and handed it to Gene. "Write your name and number down for the nice lady."

Gene wrote down his information. The teller let the paper fall on her desk and turned her TV back on without another word.

* * *

Smoke erupted from the Volaré as Gene cranked the engine. The Groove Line was on the radio singing "Heat Wave." Despite the swelter from the summer sun, the interior of the car was still cooler than inside Cheung's Martial Arts. Gene backed out and dove into stop-and-go traffic. "So, what's with this other kung fu school?"

Maggie rolled her window down and rested her arm on the door. "Iron Mantis Fist Society."

"Right. Think there's any truth to what Derrick said? That guy take the lions?"

Maggie slid on oversized round sunglasses and stared back at him. "I don't know."

"There's bad blood between the schools?"

She shrugged. "Kung fu schools always talking jive about one another. There's an old saying that a kung fu master will beat a karate master, but one karate master can beat five kung fu masters at once. You just wait for them to kill each other."

Maggie looked at her watch. "I have to get back. Some friends are picking me up for a show at the Alley. *Echelon.*"

Gene nodded, turning on Chartres Street. "So, Derrick took matters into his own hands?"

Maggie frowned. "I don't like it. He caught Jimmy Chin at the movies and beat him with a club. He's still in ICU, no visitors. My brother's gonna be furious."

"Is that common? Actual fighting between schools?"

"No," Maggie said. "Back in the day people would challenge rival masters. If they won, they'd prove their kung fu was better and take all the students. But today? Everyone stays in their lane."

A farm truck cut Gene off at Leeland, running the light. Gene mashed the horn. A middle finger shot from the window of the truck, waving back and forth.

"Nobody stays in their lane around here," Gene said.

* * *

The Iron Mantis Fist Society wasn't a secret lair from a Bond movie like the name implied but rather a small, wooden-framed house just off Dowling Street. The time was past eight when he'd dropped Maggie off, eaten a complementary bowl of Crossing the Bridge Noodles and hit the streets again. A dozen cars were parked in front.

The smell of cigarette smoke and the sound of music strengthened as Gene walked to the entrance. A mural on the building featured dragons, praying mantises, and fighting Shaolin monks. The closed double front doors featured a painting of a lion on each door.

Smoke spilled out from around the doors. Gene was about to knock when they flew open, toppling him onto the walkway. A skinny kid who'd been hurled out of the building lay alongside him.

A long-haired, elderly Asian man stood in the doorway smoking. He wore black cotton pants without a shirt. A jagged scar like lightning zig-zagged his chest.

"What did I say?" said the man. "Don't keep weight on your front foot. If you're going to keep doing that, I'm going to keep making you look like an asshole."

The kid stood, brushing off his pants and limping back inside. The shirtless old man slapped him on the head as he passed, then squinted at Gene. "What's happenin' my man? You sellin' vacuum cleaners or something?"

Gene got to his feet, brushing off his corduroys.

"Sorry," Gene said. "Didn't mean to intrude."

The man turned and went back inside, leaving the doors open.

Gene followed. It looked a little like Cheung's Martial Arts, with racks of weapons and framed photos. But it felt more like a clubhouse—a giant praying mantis painted on the polished concrete floor. About fifteen students in all black practiced the same techniques in lock step—punching, kicking, and making mantis-like hand gestures. Sweat poured off their faces. Black Sabbath's "War Pigs" played from a stereo in the corner and the room was thick with cigarette smoke.

"Let me guess," said the old man, leaning against a wall. "You saw *Drunken Master,* now you wanna learn kung fu. No beginner class until Saturday." The man waved Gene away as though he were an opossum that had wandered in from the bayou. "Go. This ain't open casting, baby."

"Actually, I'm here to talk about Cheung's Martial Arts."

One of the students on the front row shot Gene a glance between punching and kicking.

The instructor's eyes narrowed. "Who the hell are you?"

"Private investigator," Gene said. "Maggie Cheung hired me to find the stone lions taken two days ago."

The instructor shook his head. "Nobody here knows what happened to those lions. Derrick Lau is a dolt. Cheung can't control his students and now the whole thing will be a tragedy."

Taking a draw off his cigarette, the man walked to a framed photo showing five unsmiling men in front of a temple. "Cheung is an all-right cat," he said, stabbing at the photo with his cigarette. "I've known him a long time. I respect him, even if the Wing Chun style is inferior to the Iron Mantis Fist."

"When you say tragedy," Gene said. "You mean what happened at the movies?"

"James Chin is a solid kid. Studies kinesiology at Rice. Now he's having seizures. That ain't right."

"He's your student who got attacked at the drive-in?"

"He's my student who got *ambushed* at the drive-in by a man *with a weapon.* Five on one. Girlfriend terrified in his car." The instructor shook his head. "Lau is a punk."

He turned back toward his students. "Stay low," he told the group as they practiced. "Remember, low center of gravity. Low center of gravity. Don't make me show you why."

"That is a tragedy," Gene said.

"Well, yeah," said the instructor, "James is in bad shape. But the tragedy I meant was Master Cheung."

"What do you mean?"

He shrugged. "I got a student in the hospital. I know Derrick Lau went rogue, but there's no other way my man. I'll give Cheung a few days for jet lag when he gets back."

"I'm sorry, you lost me," Gene said. "Give him a few days for what?"

"The death match, of course."

* * *

Death match. The phrase rattled around in Gene's brain as he steered the Volaré up Dowling toward Navigation. *Should I call the police?* Gene thought. *I could ask Sandy to help.* But what could the police do until after the fact? His hands were sweaty on the Volaré's hard plastic steering wheel as he pulled into Sunny Horizons Apartment Homes.

The crickets in the apartment's patchy brown lawn droned on as Gene retrieved his mail from a rusty lock box. He thumbed through the envelopes as he walked toward his apartment. Water bill. JC Penny flier featuring a comely woman in bell-bottoms vacuuming maroon carpet. A postcard declaring *Vote for John Luke Hill for Governor* and *Say No to Nuclear Power!*

He opened the front door and flicked on the dim yellow lamp. Tossing his keys onto the table next to the ashtray, he kicked the door shut behind him and gasped.

A man in a black hood, mask, and cotton pants stood in his living room, hands out like knives.

"What the fuck?" Gene said, grabbing the heavy ashtray. He turned to swing at the intruder, but the shadowy figure struck Gene's hand, the ashtray falling to the carpet. His hand numbed with pain.

"Halloween's not for two months yet," Gene said, shaking his hand. "And I'm out of Zagnuts." He reached to unmask the attacker, but the figure parried, Gene grabbing nothing but air.

"Wassah!" cried the man, driving a series of punches into Gene's stomach, chest, and face. The room spun as Gene felt his body crumple, the floor rushing up to meet him.

Gene's lungs fought for air. He landed face-down, the coarse blue fibers of the shag carpeting rough on his cheek. His stomach lurched, the Crossing the Bridge Noodles almost crossing back the other way. The ashtray in front of him lost focus as the shadow man stepped over his broken body and fled. Gene closed his eyes, the droning of the crickets outside carrying him into dark, comforting nothingness.

* * *

The knock rattled Gene's head. Swinging his legs over the side of the couch sent a wave of pain throughout his body. "Coming," he croaked. "Hold your horses." The steak he'd put on his eye earlier now lay on the floor.

Daylight blinded him as he opened the door.

"Jesus, what happened to you?" Dan asked.

"My first kung fu lesson," Gene said as his eyes adjusted. He squinted at his Timex: 2:34 p.m.

Dan leaned in and sniffed.

"I'm not drunk," Gene said. "I got jumped. What's up?"

Dan held up a thick envelope. "Onboarding papers. Tax forms, next of kin, life insurance…"

Gene reached for the envelope, but Dan held it out of reach. "Ah, ah, ah. That's not all."

Dan turned and walked away. "C'mon, Rocky. Get that eye of the tiger working and follow me."

Gene stepped into the afternoon sun, the humidity like a rice cooker. He licked his busted lips and tasted blood as he followed Dan to the parking lot.

Dan stopped and turned around, smiling. Next to him stood a black Pontiac Firebird Trans Am, complete with gold phoenix decal and dealer's sticker still on the windshield.

"Mag wheels, T-Tops, performance package and, most importantly, a 403 cubic inch V-8. Bootleggers still use these things to run moonshine."

"I don't get it," Gene said.

Dan shrugged. "Signing bonus."

He tossed the keys to Gene, who winced in pain as he caught them.

"Yours free and clear after sign-on. Let's face it, that old shit pile has one foot in the grave." He jammed a thumb at Gene's old Volaré.

Gene opened the Trans Am's door and sat. The interior smelled like new leather and carpet. In the mirror he caught a glimpse of himself—one eye purple and swollen almost shut. He started the engine, the V8 roaring to life. Rod Stewart's "Do Ya Think I'm Sexy" played on the radio.

"I appreciate this," Gene said, shutting off the engine. He got out slowly. "Really. I'm lucky to have this kind of opportunity."

"Don't answer now," Dan said. "Fill out the paperwork and come to the helipad tomorrow even if you turn me down." He held out the envelope. "Please. This could change your life."

Gene nodded, taking the paperwork. "I'll give it some thought."

"Uh…" Dan said. "Do I need to be worried about you?" He pointed to Gene's face.

Gene shook his head. "Nah, my first PI case isn't going great. Do people get their asses kicked offshore?"

"Absolutely," Dan said. "Just not when their former brother-in-law is the Vice President. Two o'clock tomorrow at the Hexagon helipad. Galveston. Paperwork in hand."

***

Gene heard his lime green kitchen phone ringing as he walked back into the apartment. "Hello?"

"This is Gloria from Hang Seng Southwest Bank of Houston."

"Who?"

The woman sighed. "The lemon tart at the bank, genius."

"Oh, right. How are you?"

"Just peachy," she said. "Mr. Lee returned and has copies of the security tapes at our front desk. He told me to say the system uses a new technology called a Video Cassette Recorder and that if you don't have one you could review the footage here."

"Thanks," Gene said. "I've got one. Sort of." But the woman had already hung up.

* * *

The weather was sweltering but sunny, and Gene removed the Trans Am's T-tops. KC and the Sunshine Band's "I'm Your Boogie Man" playing as he gunned the engine. The wind whipped around him as he weaved through traffic, first to the Hang Seng Southwest Bank of Houston and then the Houston Police Department's downtown station.

* * *

"My God, what happened to your face?" Sandy said.

Gene touched his eye. "I wish you could see the other guy."

"Really?"

"Yeah, like in a lineup or something. Sorry to barge in but I need a favor."

The twenty-eight-story HPD headquarters bustled with people coming and going, phones ringing and the *click-click-clacking* of typewriters. In the hallway a man in rust-color bell-bottoms and a red hat with an oversized feather wrestled two uniformed officers.

"This for your PI business?" Sandy asked.

"Dan told you?"

Sandy nodded. "Coffee?"

"Sure."

They stopped in a breakroom where Sandy poured scorching tar-like coffee into two Styrofoam cups.

Coffees in hand, they got on the elevator where Sandy hit the ninth-floor button. The elevator chimed as it climbed.

"You don't approve either?" Gene said. "The PI gig?"

"What?" Sandy said with a shrug. "I didn't say anything."

"Yeah, but that look. You get this line in your forehead."

"Oh, Jesus," Sandy said. "I'm not your wife anymore, you don't need my approval."

When the elevator opened, she took the lead. "This way."

"Ah, that's right. I forgot. For you, marriage means dictatorship. Everything must be approved by *mein Fuhrer.*"

She opened a door and turned on the light in what looked like a classroom. Rows of school-style desks stood in front of a hulking gray television with a silver block of buttons and dials beneath it. Sandy stopped and put her hands on her hips.

"Yeah, and for you, marriage is fucking anarchy whereby you never know—"

Gene held up a hand. "Sorry. That was shitty. Really. Sorry. I'm just having a bad day. Thanks for doing this."

Sandy glared at him for a moment before turning on the television. She powered up the VCR and inserted the bank's tape. He couldn't tell if the room was cold or if it was just them.

On screen a blurry, black-and-white image of the parking lot of the Hang Seng Southwest Bank of Houston appeared along with the road and a view of half the Cheung's Martial Arts building. In the bottom corner a time stamp clicked up hours, minutes, seconds and microseconds in white block letters. You couldn't see the entrance or the lions from that angle, only the road and part of the building.

"Our AV nerd says these VCRs are catching on and that one day people are going to rent movies in their houses instead of going out."

Gene snorted. "Who the fuck wants to go to a movie at their house?"

Sandy took a yellow pad and pencil out of her satchel.

"They don't know what time they were hit," Gene said. "But according to one of the owners he left at night and when he came back Friday the lions were gone."

The time stamp at the bottom read 5:32 p.m. last Thursday.

"What kind of car does the owner drive?" Sandy asked as she fast-forwarded the tape.

"A gold Ford Elite."

At 11:47 p.m., the shape of a Ford Elite cruised past the school. "There's the owner leaving," Gene said.

The two sat in front of the TV watching cars come and go, fast-forwarding through most of the footage until cars approached—Sandy scrawling down plate info of each passing car.

"Wait, go back," Sandy said. "Did you see that?"

"What?"

At 3:14 a.m. a car slowed as it approached the school, rolling past the view of the camera.

"Look how everything reflective gets lighter just for an instant." *True,* Gene thought. A street sign reading McKinney Street and a group of mailboxes lit up just after the car passed. *Brake lights,* Gene thought, *just off camera.*

"Looks like a Cutlass," Gene said. "Two people in it."

"Is that a ponytail?" Sandy asked, pointing to the passenger.

At the end of the tape, Sandy tore a sheet out of her legal pad. She had a list of seven cars and their license plates, plus Derrick Lau's Ford Elite.

She stood, "All right. I'll go run these."

"I owe you," she said.

"As usual."

* * *

The deadbolt in back of Cheung's Martial Arts was an ancient Yale. After a few minutes the lock gave with a *thud.* He knew this was a gamble. Knew if he got caught, he could kiss his private investigation career goodbye. But he had to know he was right.

Gene stuffed the lock picks into his pocket, opened the door and flicked on a red flashlight. The inside of the building was still hot, even at almost midnight. The fountain sat unplugged and silent. The instructor's office, bathroom, and supply closet all shared brick with the exterior wall, as did the back wall. But the east side of the building...

Gene faced the east wall. The swords in the rack glowed crimson. Photos and knick-knacks cast long shadows as he walked up and down the wall, knocking. Solid brick. The Art Deco style clock in the wall read 11:41 p.m.

There were no switches or plugs or sconces. He went to the bookshelf. If this were a Hardy Boys novel rather than a real-world felony in progress, there would be an old leather-bound book somewhere that did the trick. But there were no books on the shelf, only trophies and metals, small jade buddhas and a few framed photographs. One by one, he lifted each up, moved it around and looked beneath—glad he'd worn gloves. The top shelf was more than eight feet high.

Remembering the supply closet, he fetched an empty bucket. Flipping it he stepped up and inspected the trophies on top. Nothing unusual. On a whim, and since he'd explored everything else on the wall, he moved the bucket under the clock. Stepping up he used his finger to swirl the clock forward. A tingle ran across Gene's scalp when he felt a click as the hands reached midnight.

He heard a latch release to his right and, shining the red light on the bookcase, saw it swing out like a door. "Yes!" Gene hissed. "Yes, yes, yes. I knew it. I fucking knew it."

Leaping off the bucket, he ran to the bookshelf door and opened it wider. Four red eyes glowed back at him in the reflection of his flashlight. The stone lions snarled in the shadows, all teeth and claws yet silent and still.

Clap.

Clap.

Clap.

Gene turned.

The lights flicked on. Derrick Lau entered the room from the office and crossed his arms. "Gotta hand it to you, that was a good guess."

As Gene's eyes adjusted to the light, he tried to swallow but his throat felt like sandpaper.

"But for a detective you sure can't take a hint."

"And for a warrior, you sure can't lose gracefully."

Derrick scowled. "You don't know shit."

"I know you were probably jealous when Sifu Cheung passed you over as

Disciple in favor of Mary Fung. Someone sent her flowers congratulating her. I'm guessing it wasn't you."

Derrick took a few steps closer, the polished wooden planks creaking beneath his footsteps.

"I know some people use vinegar to clean hardwood floors. I'm guessing you used a dolly or something and the wheels left marks. I'm just struggling with why."

Derrick waved his hand. "It's ridiculous. A girl as Disciple? Makes us look weak. If he'd chosen me, a rival would have never done this."

"Yeah, but the Iron Mantis Fist Society didn't do it. You did." Gene lifted his shirt. "Wing Chun focuses on the center of the body." Black and blue bruises ran up Gene's stomach and chest. "So, it had to be someone here. And you seem to be the only asshole."

Derrick's face darkened.

I am going to die, Gene thought. But he kept talking.

"The age of the building, the space feeling off and someone mentioning bootleggers to me yesterday. It all sort of just clicked—this was an old speakeasy. Sometimes they built them like this, with hidden rooms."

Gene pulled out the printout Sandy had given him. "Jimmy Chin stopped by the school the night the lions were stolen, but I'm guessing he wasn't stealing lions. I'm guessing he was dropping Mary off after a night out. She was the girl with Jimmy when you put him in the hospital. So, what, you're jealous of her because she was made Sifu Cheung's Disciple, and jealous of him because, let's face it, you like her, huh?"

Derrick stepped forward, hands out like knives. "Your bones will rot in that secret room!"

He leapt at Gene, reaching a paranormal height, black cotton uniform rustling as he flew—foot chambered for a flying sidekick.

Gene closed his eyes.

At the last minute, Gene heard another flutter of cloth, a wet-sounding smack and a grunt of pain. When he opened his eyes, Maggie Chang stood before him, a small strand of gray hair hanging in front of her face. Derrick was on the ground, scrambling to stand.

"You young fool," Maggie said to Derrick. "Your pride has caused a lot of trouble."

"Old woman, you're going to die." Derrick launched himself at her, fists flying. Blow by blow, Maggie Chang adjusted her position, slapped the young man's fists just off-center and took big steps backward to stay just out of his reach. *Thwack, thwack, thwack-thwack* went Derrick's punches against Maggie's blocks.

Maggie's face was calm and expressionless. After blocking several blows, she grabbed Derrick's fist with perfect timing, stepping in between his legs and making an elegant sweeping motion with her arms.

Derrick flew backward, slamming his head on the hardwood floor. Blinking hard, he screamed in fury. Getting to his feet he charged and swung wildly. Parrying like a bullfighter, Maggie tripped Derrick—who fell forward into the open bookshelf. His head slammed into one of the lions, going limp like a robot unplugged.

"Shit," Gene said. "We have to call an ambulance."

Derrick lay crumpled on the floor, blood pooling from his head.

Gene ran to the phone.

Maggie knelt at Derrick's side and stroked his hair, fingers coming away bright red.

Derrick moaned.

In a moment Gene returned. "The ambulance is on the way. Thank you. You saved my life. You were…you were incredible."

"Of course," she said. "Sifu Cheung is my little brother. Who do you think taught him?"

"How did you even know I was here?"

"You tripped the silent alarm. I'm part owner, they called my house."

"Did you know about that secret room?"

Maggie shook her head. "No. But, truly, who cares about the lions? I see now it's the people in this family who need to do a better job of watching over each other."

* * *

Seagulls flapped around Gene, begging for a handout as he leaned against the Trans Am. Dan came out of the trailer that served as Hexagon's helipad office. "Well?" he said.

Gene held out the keys.

Dan let his head drop, then took the keys. "Really, man? You'd be great offshore. What can I say to change your mind?"

Nearby, a Sikorsky's turbines whined to a crescendo, blades chopping faster and faster as the helicopter lifted its nose and thumped away over the green-brown waters of Galveston Bay.

Gene shook his head. "Just because I can do something doesn't mean I should."

"What does that mean?"

"It means I just wouldn't have been into the job. It would have gotten me down, and I'd probably have started gambling again and I could just feel the cycle coming on. But this? This I'm into."

"Getting your ass kicked playing private detective?"

Gene held up a small piece of stationery with Chinese writing. "Hey, I've got skills. My first case and I turned a death match into a wedding invitation for Jimmy Chin and Mary Fung."

Dan turned to look out over the water. "Well, I tried," he said, tossing Gene the keys.

Gene caught them, confused.

"Rockford had a Trans Am right? Keep the Volaré for stakeouts."

"No shit?"

"No shit," Dan said, turning to look out over the water. "Actually, I need to ask you a favor."

"What kind of favor?"

Dan rubbed the back of his neck. "What do you know about Worker's Comp cases?"

The two talked as Dan led Gene into the trailer. Another Sikorsky wound up its turbines and lifted off the ground, *thump-thump-thump*ing into the sun as Gene took out his notebook and bit the cap off his Bic pen. Ready to listen. Ready to get the facts. And ready to put in the work.

Drop Dead Gorgeous

M.E. Proctor

"He'll want her done with, Harry. His kind ruminates on vengeance like a heifer chews the cud."

Harry McLean wedged his back in the corner of the velvet-upholstered booth and stretched his long legs on the seat. Now, without having to turn his head, he had a good view of the bar and the knock-out blonde perched on the central stool.

"He wants his money back, Luis. He doesn't want her dead."

"Keep telling yourself that, maybe you'll sleep better at night." Luis Garcia took a sip of his Canadian and Seven. "Mama didn't carry me in her belly all the way from San Salvador to see me working for Ray Castellan."

"You're not working for Castellan, you're working for Diana."

Somewhat true. When Diana Galindo told Harry DG Investigative had been hired by Castellan to find the woman who had conned him out of three million dollars, Harry's first reaction had been: Good for her! Anybody smart enough to hit the cartel lawyer in the wallet, where it hurt the most, deserved his heartfelt admiration. Then, what Diana said sank in.

"He hired us?"

In his previous life as a cop, Harry had spent countless hours trying to nail Castellan. The thought that part of his salary would come courtesy of the slime lawyer was enough to sour his whiskey without adding lemon juice.

"Would you rather he ask his south-of-the-border buddies to track her?"

"Once we find her, he'll call them anyway," Harry said. "We'll just make it easy for them to chop her head off. Drop the case, Di. Let the woman run and take her chances."

They argued. Harry threatened to quit. Diana compromised.

"We find her, we get Castellan's money back, and we set her on her merry way. Is that acceptable, Harry? You realize recovering the money makes the case a lot more complicated."

The case was complicated from the start. It might have been the toughest Harry ever worked on, and that was without even considering retrieving the money. The woman had a talent for changing names and appearance. She also found gullible marks with baffling ease. Some of them went to the cops to lodge a complaint—which is how Harry caught the trail—but most stewed in anger and silent humiliation. And she raked in the dough. She could have hopped on a plane and enjoyed her hard-earned wealth in the sun, but she was greedy. Castellan's millions got company.

Harry set eyes on her for the first time two months earlier in a posh suburb of Chicago. Her hair was short and brown then. He thought he had time to build a trap, but she skipped town before he could spring it. Then he missed her by a hair, a bright red hair, in Atlanta. Here, in Miami, she went by Charlotte Wainwright, was ash blond, and affected a British accent. She wore the name, the hair, and the plum grammar well. Vowing he wouldn't be caught flatfooted again, Harry asked Luis Garcia, the agency's Miami associate, to lend a hand. At this point, another line item on the bill wasn't likely to make Castellan squeal. He'd been paying through the nose for months.

Luis waved at the server and ordered refills. "How do you want to play it? We let her work the con and catch her when she collects? It looks like she's got a bite."

Charlotte had been getting more bites than she could handle from the moment she hoisted her perfect butt on that stool. Marks had been circling, mouth open and teeth bared. No surprise. She was an appetizing long-legged morsel in a cocktail dress that didn't come from the outlet mall.

With what she netted she could afford haute couture. The men thought they were sharks when they were chum. They came in all sizes and were mostly middle-aged. The club had fake retro Rat Pack vibes, done in chrome and glass with a generous helping of sleaze and hard liquor. Charlotte rose above it all like a pagan idol in a corny B-movie. The set was cardboard, but the technicolor was luscious. It matched her heartbreak of a smile, Marilyn before the fall. Harry felt pangs of impurity. He feared he was falling in love. Or lust, rather.

"Let's see what dude she picks." Harry wished he was wearing his nice suit. Draped in it, he would run rings around these doofuses. The Hawaiian shirt and khakis dumped him in the tourist drawer. He should have planned better. Luis could step in, however. His good looks and dark blue silk suit were yacht club ready. Or wiseguy. Or narco in a *Miami Vice* episode. Harry hadn't put the suggestion to Luis yet. He didn't have to.

Luis smiled. "If you want me to put my natural modesty on the line, just say the word."

That was the biggest bonus of working with true professionals. They didn't need a road map or an instruction manual.

"It looks like she's zeroing in on the baldy with the red tie," Harry said.

"Flat ass and a beer gut. Does she go horizontal with them?" Luis lit a cigar in cocky disregard of the rules. Nobody objected because nobody cared.

"She's pitching hedge funds and real estate deals for serious money. When she opens her legs, she loses credibility."

They nursed their drinks and watched the show at the bar. Charlotte hit the perfect temperature. It was miraculous how she skated between high-society Ice Queen and Hot Cookie. Real talent. The more Harry watched her perform, the more impressed he was. If he hadn't known she was baiting a line, he would never have guessed it. What did she tell these guys, that she was waiting for her date and he was late? She'd been there since eleven. It was inching toward midnight. Something would happen soon.

"He'll take her back to the hotel," Harry said. "If I'm right, he won't stay long."

Harry had a hotel room on the same floor as Charlotte. For five days, Luis and he had been watching her door. Stakeouts were boring, by definition. At least, they weren't in a car. They had access to coffee and a bathroom.

"How long does it take her to work a mark?" Luis said.

"A couple of days. She's efficient."

Charlotte never stuck around after a con. She hit fast and ran even faster. Harry knew he missed an opportunity tonight. He should have worn the suit and made a move. His desire to pitch his brains against hers, and challenge her at her own game, was so acute it hurt.

The bald guy with the red tie's entire body leaned toward Charlotte. She might be talking financials, but the dude had something else on his mind. She flashed him a bright smile and slid off the stool. Heads turned to watch her walk to the restroom. There was no swaying of hips. Harry thought she must have practiced that straight walk before a three-sided mirror.

"Maybe they give her the money in the hope of getting laid," Luis said.

"Obviously it works." Harry slipped out of the booth. "I'll settle our tab. It's wrap up time. Better if you leave first."

Luis was out of the club before Charlotte emerged from the restroom. Harry was hunched over the bar counter, signing his credit card slip. She came so close to him that he could smell her perfume. Something expensive, enticing. A hint of cherry. Is that what she tasted like? He lingered, got another whiff of her scent, and shuffled to the exit, with regret. He was halfway there when a man walked in. A thought flashed through Harry's mind: That's him. Charlotte's date. The guy who made her wait. It was complete nonsense. Charlotte didn't have a date. It was the excuse Harry imagined she gave for being at the club. And yet. The man was perfect. Tall, dark, criminally handsome, brushing forty, in a pale linen suit wrinkled just right, a glint of gold on the wrist. As if he'd been cast and costumed for the role. Harry had stopped in his tracks and forced himself to move. He glanced at the scene one more time as he opened the door. The man was at the bar. Charlotte had swiveled on her stool. She faced the newcomer. The guy in the red tie was forgotten.

* * *

Harry called Luis as soon as he set foot on the sidewalk. "Change of plans. It looks like she's going to dump the mark."

"For the fashion plate with the Porsche?" Luis chuckled. "Hey, it can't always be work. Girl's allowed to have fun."

Harry bit back an acid retort. Charlotte awoke his worst possessive tendencies. He had been hunting her for too long. There always came a moment in a protracted chase when he started to believe the prey belonged to him.

"He drives a Porsche?" Harry didn't see the car in the parking lot.

"Gave the keys to the valet who didn't waste a second taking it for a spin," Luis said. "I called the plate in. It could be a rental. Guy splurging on cool wheels for a weekend, getting his investment back in chicks."

Harry groaned. He wasn't in the mood for waiting another hour in his car, just to watch Charlotte wrap herself around that hunk. "Can you handle it? Stay on her. I don't give a shit about the man."

"*Sin problema.*"

A long shower, maybe a little nap to look forward to. Harry swore he would wear the suit next time. No more portly pigeons. He could act the part and handle Charlotte. If he had moved in tonight, he would have bagged her before the sexiest man alive swaggered in. Diana didn't like it when he injected himself in a case, but they had wasted too much time already. Their client was bound to lose patience and call in the muscle.

Harry hummed under the hot shower. I'll seduce her to save her life. Damn, she was a gorgeous piece of woman. And damn, he couldn't get her out of his head.

He was checking email—Diana wanted a status report, she was getting impatient too—when his phone rang.

"He's parking the car in the hotel garage," Luis said. "Looks like he plans to stay the night."

Harry spat out a curse. He opened the laptop camera app showing images from the hallway, deserted this time of night. He saw the couple leave the elevator. The man had an arm around Charlotte's waist. She leaned against him. Very romantic. She swiped her room card, and he pushed her through the door. His hands went up her skirt.

Harry leaned back in his chair. His fingers trembled on the keyboard, and he made a fist to stop the shaking. He was angry. And furious at being angry. The click of the door opening brought him to his senses.

"The Porsche is not a rental," Luis said. "It's leased to a business in Coral Gables. Diamond dealers. Looks like our girl has lucked out again, even if she has to put some skin in the game this time."

"I need a drink."

Luis poured two stiff whiskeys. The bottle was half full. Booze made watchers sleepy. They tried to stay away from it. "She's a thief, Harry. You know how the story ends. She'll be arrested and locked up. Or she'll trick a nasty chump and get hurt. Or despite what you're trying to do, Castellan won't forgive and will send in the cutthroats. She's the wrong crush, buddy."

"Yeah. Sure." He took a long swallow, and let out a snicker. "I'm glad we didn't bug the room."

"Now you're putting ideas in my head," Luis said. "You mind taking the first watch?"

Harry straightened in the desk chair. "I'm too hyped to sleep anyway." And he wanted to see the Porsche playboy leave. The faster he got out of there, the better.

No such luck. When Luis took over at three in the morning, the man was still in the hotel room.

* * *

"Harry, wake up."

Luis was grabbing his shoulder.

"She's leaving."

"What?" Harry was at the computer in two steps. He saw Charlotte, dressed in jeans and a sweatshirt, standing by the elevator at the end of the

315

corridor. She carried a leather bag. Her purse was slung over a shoulder. The time was five-thirty. "The Porsche guy?"

"No sign of him. He must still be asleep."

Maybe. Maybe. "You go after her." Harry felt a shiver between his shoulder blades. "Keep your distance. Traffic is minimal. She'll spot you in no time. She's good, Luis, very good."

"We have the tracker on her car anyway."

"Yeah, and if she takes the Porsche, we're screwed."

Luis was out of the door at a run. That left Harry pondering. The sensible thing to do was go to reception, show his detective license, and get somebody to open the hotel room. All that took time he didn't have. He rummaged through his travel bag and exhumed his lock pick set. He slipped on a pair of gloves.

A blast of cold air hit him in the face when he opened the door of Charlotte's room. The air conditioning was cranked to the max and fighting the morning dampness that came from the open terrace doors. It didn't completely mask the smell.

The man was on the bed, face down, naked. The ivory handle of a knife stuck out the side of his neck. He must not have struggled much because the bed sheets were still tucked in. They were soaked red. A fresh kill.

Harry went around the bed, careful to step over the dead man's clothing and shoes. A gun lay on the floor, dropped on the man's jacket, on the right side, near the night table. Harry peeked in the bathroom. The shower looked pristine. It was an illusion. Charlotte must have been covered in blood. Luminol would paint the stall blue. She had removed all her personal items, and the closets were bare. It was doubtful she had managed to wipe off all the fingerprints she'd left during her extended stay. And the DNA. On the dead guy. There was no doubt who he was. Ray Castellan had lost patience indeed. He had sent a hitman.

Harry went back to his room to pack and called Luis.

"She took the Ford," Luis said. "I have it on screen. She's heading north."

"Fuck caution. Get closer. She's going to ditch the car. How far is she from the airport?"

"Fifteen minutes at most. You want me to stop her? She's sticking to main roads, Harry. I can't shove her off the shoulder."

A beat. What was the plan? "If she's going to the airport, you'll have to intercept her in the parking garage or the terminal. Grab a tracker when you leave the car so I can find you."

Luis was a pro, but Charlotte had an edge. An airport was a good place to get lost, and she wasn't running blind. She had stayed in that hotel room with a corpse long enough to clean up, pack, and check early flights out of Miami. There wasn't anywhere she needed to be, meaning she could go anywhere, and then anywhere again from there. All before a maid found the body and the cops started scrambling.

Luis did well. He caught up with Charlotte in the parking garage and followed her to the North Terminal. She stood in line at check-in and dropped her bag. Luis caught her before she went through Security. He was charming and a fast talker, and it served him well. Charlotte didn't make a scene. She didn't want police attention any more than he did. He handed her his phone.

"Harry wants to talk to you."

"Who the hell is Harry?"

"An admirer."

Harry was running through the parking garage, a few minutes away. "I've tried to have a conversation with you since Chicago."

"What for?"

"I don't want you to miss your flight, Ms. Wainwright, or whatever name you're using now."

That silenced her.

"There must be a coffee shop nearby," he said. "I'll meet you there."

* * *

Her make-up was much lighter than the night before and there was a slight shadow under her eyes that had not been there. Stabbing a man and watching him bleed to death could do that to a girl. She was still drop-dead gorgeous.

Harry smiled. "You made me run, Charlotte."

"I didn't ask you to, Harry. Who are you working for?"

"A detective agency. Ray Castellan hired us."

She paled under her light tan.

"You need to get him off your back, Charlotte. You can't deal with him and the cops at the same time. You can't keep the money."

She pouted. "He tried to kill me. That's worth something."

Harry laughed. "You want a discount? What about your life as the gift in the kiddie meal?"

She leaned on the small bistro table, closing the distance between them. There was that whiff of perfume again. "What guarantee do I have?"

"None. But if he has you killed after you make restitution, the entire world will know he's a vengeful piece of shit. You will hold the moral high ground."

She burst out laughing. "Six feet under. How come you didn't try to entrap me?" She pointed at Luis who stood discreetly to the side. "Or him. He's cute."

"We missed our chance last night." Harry handed her a piece of paper. "An account number and a phone number. If you call the number, you'll get confirmation that the account belongs to Castellan. I won't stop you from getting on that plane, Charlotte. What you do when you get to your destination is your choice."

She pocketed the note. "You trust me to return the money?"

"There's always another con." Harry stood up. "Choose your targets more wisely. You know the saying. When it's too good to be true…"

She shouldered her bag, gave him an ironic little nod, and left the café.

Harry watched her go through the security screening. She was wearing flats, not the high heels of the night before, and she wasn't keeping her hip swivel in check like she did at the club. Harry had a feeling she knew exactly the effect she had on him. After all, he'd been watching her for a long time. Why would he stop watching her now?

The Kratz Gambit

Mark Thielman

A Ford Fairlane with its windows lowered rolled along Third Avenue North. From the 8-track, Alice Cooper blasted the chorus of "School's Out." Spilling from an NYU dorm window, Elton John sang "Rocket Man." Dimitri's transistor radio sat alongside our table. A commentator offered his analysis. I ignored the words, but the incessant noise sounded like a bee buzzing around my ear. A woman in a pink angora pantsuit, sitting on a park bench, tore small bits of bread from her lunch and threw them into the grass. The wax paper sandwich wrap crinkled with every movement. Cooing pigeons crowded around the castoff crumbs. Others clustered on the pedestal of the George Washington statue and watched. Across the park, a couple of kids hung upside down from the monkey bars, shouting that they were trapped. They played like they were the stars of the *Poseidon Adventure*. Everybody added to the cacophony. In front of me, I had Greenwich Village, then the East River. I'm sure they were making noises too, Nehru jacketed hippies and lapping waves. I wanted to shush them all. Didn't they know I was trying to concentrate? I had a chance to win.

I advanced a pawn.

Dimitri repositioned his knight seemingly without thought. "Is your move."

I had started reading *Chess International Magazine* to improve my game. I remembered an anecdote from a recent column written by a grandmaster. He told about the time Klinkov, the world's sixth-ranked player, started a game one day still suffering a hangover from the night before. Right off, he made a horrible move. As his opponent reached to seize the advantage, Klinkov looked him in the eye and said, "haven't you heard of the Kratz Gambit?" His opponent reconsidered and overthought his next play. Klinkov bluffed his way out of disaster. I tried my variation of the Kratz Gambit.

"What do you think of this Watergate mess, Dimitri?"

He raised a finger to quiet me while the man on the radio updated us on the game in progress. Reaching to the other board, Dimitri moved the black queen to the appropriate square, studied the board for a moment and nodded. Then he turned back to our game. "I pay no attention to government troubles."

I almost laughed. If you asked Blackie seated over at table number one, he'd tell you that Dimitri had been in the Soviet Ministry of Agriculture. He had to defect when the Russian wheat harvest failed to live up to the five-year plan. At table two, Hector pegged him as a submarine captain who had jumped ship in a Mexican port carrying a bag full of rubles and some technical manuals which he later sold to the CIA for dollars and asylum. By table three, Everett swore that Dimitri and his KGB comrades had masterminded the Kennedy assassination over vodka and rye bread. That story didn't explain how he ended up playing chess every day in Washington Square Park, but Everett never let details get in the way. Everybody agreed Dimitri had a dark past, they just differed on the specifics.

I slid queen's rook up the file and scanned the board. I winced, expecting the worst. Reluctantly, I released my fingers and cupped my chin in my palm, my fingers touched my sideburns. "Check."

Dimitri looked surprised. He drummed his fingers against his lips. His hand moved forward and then paused. His chin dipped slightly. "You play well today, Robert." He moved a knight to defend his king.

Then he said those Russian words that always sounded like he was coughing up phlegm, but I'd learned they meant "very good."

"How are your eggs, Robert?"

I attacked with a pawn. "Over easy."

Dimitri cocked his head.

"It's a way to cook eggs," I said. I knew he hadn't been asking about my breakfast. The Hellerman Gallery was about to stage an exhibit of Fabergé eggs, those treasures of Tsarist Russia. An outer shell gilded with gold and jewels; each egg opened to reveal a spherical yolk. The yolk held a surprise, an exquisitely decorated inner scene. The gallery needed a crack PI to oversee security. But they were all busy. So they hired me.

"An American joke," he said and repositioned his king.

I snorted. "You must have a head cold coming on, Dimitri. You're not on your game."

He dipped his head toward the transistor radio. "I am, perhaps, distracted."

On the companion board, Dimitri had set up the game currently being played by Boris Spassky, the Russian grandmaster, and Bobby Fischer, the American. The Spassky side of the board faced Dimitri. I had Fischer's white pieces on my side. The Cold War was being fought by chess pieces in Reykjavik, Iceland. The contest captivated the nation. The radio station ran live updates and offered commentary. The broadcaster on the Magnavox got breathless describing the personal contest between these two men. I like chess as much as the next guy, but I had trouble picturing a board game being covered like a boxing match.

Many of the other chess hustlers in the park followed the big game as well. They each had a sideboard set up to mirror the game's progress. On Blackie's, Spassky's side was marked with the hammer and sickle flag of the Soviet Union while Fischer's showed our red, white, and blue. Everett and Hector had the commie's side marked with the letters CCCP, the Russian spelling of USSR. Fischer's side had USA, spelled the way God intended it.

I supposed that Dimitri still had some warm feelings for his mother country, so I kept my opinions to myself.

He rubbed the pad of his thumb against his index finger. Then Dimitri advanced his bishop to shield his king.

I quickly reached out to make the obvious move, then stopped. "You ain't that distracted, Dimitri. I've seen you play three guys here in the park. Sometimes you make moves without even looking at the board. You're bluffing."

Dimitri frowned and shook his head. "One cannot bluff in chess. It is not like bungling political burglars in the night. The board is visible to all." He seemed to flinch.

"Something bothering you, Dimitri?"

He made a very small shake of his head. "*Nyet.*"

I made my move. Dimitri's mouth sagged.

"I'm glad nothing's wrong, Dimitri. Because I think checkmate is on the horizon." I sat up a little straighter in my chair. "I thought you were bluffing me. Like Fischer in game two against Spassky. He didn't show up, took a forfeit. But I think he was trying to get inside of old Boris Spassky's head. That's what maybe is going on here."

"Robert, there is no such bluffing in chess."

"You can't deny that Fischer crushed Spassky in the next game."

"We will see how it plays out over time. It is long tournament." Dimitri's eyes swept the board. He pushed out his lip in a frown, then turned over his king in surrender.

"Wish I'd brought my Polaroid camera. I'd like to get a picture of this," I said.

I didn't want to rub Dimitri's nose in it, but we'd been playing chess regularly for two months. Since I moved my office to the Village, I've been coming down to the park to eat my lunch. One day, the Russkie and I struck up a conversation. I admired his elegant chess pieces.

"It is from Jaques of London, the same type Spassky will use in World Championships." He pointed at the empty chair. "Do you play?"

He whipped me that day. We started playing regularly and he consistently won. But I could feel myself creeping closer, the gap between us narrowing. I studied the magazines. The effort paid off. Today, I finally beat him. Can't blame a guy for savoring the success for a moment.

Still, the victory felt a little too easy. "You ain't sandbagging me are you,

Dimitri?"

He looked at me through his black-framed glasses. "I don't bag sand. I play chess. Today, you win."

I smiled. I should never forget he ain't from here. Dimitri still wears a plaid jacket with narrow lapels, a thin black tie, and a white shirt. The outfit looks like something he bought at Brezhnev's Basement.

"Something's eating you, Dimitri. I can tell."

He glanced down at his pant legs, searching for ants. He shook his head. "I am not being eaten."

"What's bothering you?"

Dimitri frowned. "In our games, I have grown to trust you, Robert." He reached into the inner pocket of his jacket. He laid it on the chessboard.

I unfolded it. Someone had cut letters from a magazine to assemble a message.

Do Not sTand op i will Shoot

I looked at him. "And you think?"

"My instincts tell me that it is genuine."

My eyes widened.

The transistor announced that Spassky had made a move. Dimitri reached over and adjusted the pieces accordingly. As his hands moved, he spoke in a whisper. "I believe he is in the buildings behind me. I would assume he has rifle. The message sat on chessboard when I arrive. Folded. I thought the paper was from you, leaving a note to say that you could not come today. Busy with case or whatever you American private detectives call your adventures. At least that is what they call them on *Hawaii Five-O*."

"You're pretty calm, Dimitri."

He shrugged. "It not my first time to be threatened."

I looked again at the message. "Do not stand up I will shoot. You just gonna sit?"

His eyes widened slightly. He too glanced at the message. "I fear I have little choice."

"What do they want?"

Dimitri shrugged. "*Ya ne znayu.* Maybe angry about the past. Perhaps mad about the present. I do not know."

"You should run," I said.

He shook his head. "Too many souls in the park. I will wait. One cannot avoid that which is meant to happen."

"Russian fatalism," I said. "Any clues at all?"

"This morning, I had call on telephone. I was told to meet a man at the World Trade Center construction. I say no, I'm not going. Then when I get to park. I have note on chessboard."

Before I could ask, he continued. "The caller did not give name. He was anonymousness."

"Looks like I'm going to the center of your trouble." It was the best line I could think of under the circumstances.

Dimitri didn't smile. He put his hand atop mine. If Dimitri wore a mood ring, his would be colored black. "Robert, I cannot allow you…"

I gestured to the board. "And I can't allow anything to happen to you now that I've got your number."

"I have no numbers."

I couldn't stick around long enough to teach him the American idiom. "I'll be back," I said and stood up from the table. "You just keep up with Fischer's moves. I want to know what's happening when I get back."

Keeping my head down, I focused my attention on the shadow George's statue threw across the grass of the park. In truth, I didn't want to alert anyone watching from the windows that I was aware of his presence. Mumbling greetings to Hector, Blackie, and Everett, I walked to the street. There, I hailed a cab and directed the driver to take me to Radio Row.

The cab had a Puerto Rican flag hanging from the rearview window. The driver rolled south, weaving in and out of cars, maintaining a running commentary in Spanish. I ignored him and looked out the window. We passed by the Hellerman Gallery. I was making good money doing background checks and providing specialized security for them these days. The gallery's paycheck was the reason I'd relocated my office to Greenwich Village. Fortunately, I was caught up with my work. The employees had been checked and the extra security was in place. I could miss a day and spend it trying to keep Dimitri alive.

The hack let loose a burst of Spanish profanity and turned sharply, cutting in front of a garbage truck. They traded angry honks.

Just a few hours earlier, I thought a chess victory represented my day's excitement.

He stabbed his hand toward the street we'd just veered from. "City closed street," he said, turning his back to the windshield to explain.

I waggled my finger, silently expressing my preference that he watch the road rather than update me on New York City's street repair. He hit a pothole with a teeth-jarring thud. The taxi's suspension creaked almost as loudly as the cussing.

Three blocks down, another blocked street had us driving back toward Washington Square. The driver let loose another fusillade of cussing. The detour again took me past the Hellerman Gallery. I watched as workers suspended banners from the nearby lamp posts promoting the exhibit of jeweled Fabergé eggs. The gallery was closed today, setting up for the opening of the new exhibit. Although focused on Dimitri's troubles, I made a mental note to mention to the director that I'd seen the men working. I needed the Hellerman's money, and I wanted the boss to know I was on the job, even when I wasn't.

At the World Trade Center, I pushed the hack a Lincoln and got out of the car. The Center, the world's tallest building, had opened earlier in the year. Construction, however, continued as parts remained unfinished. A fence blocked vehicle traffic.

Hardhats milled about the jobsite. I couldn't ask them if they'd seen anyone who wanted to shoot a Russian; I'd likely be inundated with volunteers. Instead, I picked my way along the fence line looking for anything suspicious.

About twenty-five yards down, I came to a small Soviet flag wired to the fence. An envelope dangled from it.

GuESS wHeRe now—cEntrAL pArk

Again, the letters looked cut from a magazine. I studied the message, mentally comparing it to the one Dimitri had shown me. A theory formed in my head. Dimitri's assailant had to be a recent arrival in the Big Apple, new and unfamiliar with the details of Manhattan. Anybody who'd visited Central Park would know I couldn't just wander the perimeter. That search would take days. I assumed, therefore, that his adversary was an old foe, someone bearing a grudge from his Soviet past. I turned Blackie, Everett, and Hector's stories around in my head. When I got back to the park, I'd press Dimitri for the facts.

Another thought struck me. The Russian Tea Room was located just south of Central Park. As an ex-pat, maybe Dimitri frequented the place. I decided to visit there, ask if they knew him. Maybe they had an envelope taped to the samovar. It wasn't a great idea, but it beat anything else I could think of.

Still, I didn't like it. The phrase "needle in a haystack" came to mind.

To clear my head, I walked into the Trade Center. The place smelled like new paint and clean floors. The South Tower had a newsstand. The kid behind the counter chewed bubble gum and listened to Bill Withers singing "Lean On Me." I perused the magazines. I didn't want to buy anything to read. Sometimes I see best when I don't look straight at something. I was trying to organize my thoughts before I jumped into a cab and raced to Central Park.

Behind the current magazine, the newsstand carried back issues of *Chess International*. Three months earlier, the cover story featured one of the Fabergé eggs we would display in our exhibit. The yolk contained a miniature chess set including delicate pieces crafted from ivory and black onyx. The chess pieces could be moved about the board, except you'd need a pair of tweezers and a jeweler's loupe to see what you were doing. The photographs were good. They had closeups of the egg's detail. The gallery's director would like a copy. I paid the clerk for the magazine. He popped his gum, then Bazooka Joe pushed the change across the counter.

Outside I grabbed a taxi to take me to Central Park. I hadn't come up with a better idea than the tearoom. The afternoon sun was beginning to dip. If Dimitri was going to make a move, he needed to do it soon.

I opened the magazine and glanced at the column by this month's grandmaster. He gushed about the Sicilian Defense. My eyes rode down the column without reading the words. I was trying too hard to think about Dimitri's problem. The story served as a distraction.

The driver cursed his fellow motorists in a linguistic mix of American and…Arabic, I guessed. I didn't know much about other languages. They confused me. Like Russian, I had no idea why they tried to spell USSR with three Cs and a P. It made no sense.

I had a sudden thought. The hairs on the back of my neck started to tingle.

"Stop the car!"

Maybe we'd have stopped sooner if I yelled something in Arabic. The driver let me out half a dozen blocks from the Hellerman. I worked my way back, dodging stoned heroin addicts, their backs against walls tagged with graffiti, their legs sprawled across the sidewalk.

I ran into the gallery and looked around the floor. I hustled into the employee-only area. A few of the guys looked up and nodded. Most kept their heads down working.

I took the stairs two at a time to the second floor and stuck my head in a couple of offices until I found an empty desk. I made a call to a buddy of mine, a private dick who officed out of Brooklyn. Then I went to find the director.

I caught a ride back to Washington Square. The hack leered at a coed in hot pants, an NYU T-shirt, and a macrame vest roller skating in the park. If I was being honest, I'd admit that I'd rather watch her skate than deal with Dimitri's sniper. I didn't know what would happen. I looked straight ahead and concentrated on the job.

For a moment, Dimitri's eyes widened in surprise when I sat down at the chessboard. They quickly lowered and he looked at me. "Fischer won," he said. "He rebuffed the Nimzo-Indian Defense."

"I'm surprised you are still here."

He shrugged. "With you working on problem." Here, he paused and tilted his head to the windows behind him. "No need in trying to run. I trusted you, Robert."

"And I trusted you, Dimitri. May I see the note?"

He reached into the pocket of his jacket and fished out the letter.

I flattened it on the empty chessboard. "You looked surprised when I read the note. 'Don't stand up I will shoot.' You read the note to say, don't stand up OR I will shoot." I emphasized the 'or.' "A Russian R looks like a P to an English speaker. I read it one way. A native Russian speaker might see it differently."

"This hunter is from my past then," Dimitri said.

I shook my head. "No professional assassin would take the window facing the western sun unless he absolutely had to." I pointed in each direction of the compass. "We've got windows all around us. This was a bluff."

"A bluff?"

"You wanted me running up and down Manhattan Island trying to save you from your assassin, cashing in on the whispered reputation you have here in the park."

Dimitri grunted a laugh.

"You really going to make me spell all this out?" I asked.

"You tell stories better than Tolstoy."

I took the letter I recovered from the World Trade Center and laid it alongside his. "Notice the typeface on the letters. Someone used the same magazine to make both messages. Look at the groupings, *and* as in grandmaster, *ESS* as in chess, *AL* from international. You made both notes from a back issue of *Chess International*. The same magazine with the photo spread of the Fabergé egg exhibition at the Hellerman Gallery. The same magazine, Dimitri, that was sloppy. You should have thought two moves ahead."

He looked at the notes and frowned.

"You knew I did security and background checks for the gallery. If you wanted to substitute a couple of your guys to pull off a heist, I had to be away. I'd recognize the replacements. With me walking circles around the Trade Center and then Central Park, you knew I'd be gone long enough for you to pull this job. I stopped by the gallery on my way to the park. The new employees didn't recognize me, and I didn't know them." I paused before my next move. "By the way, the director fired them all on the spot. None of them will be working when the armored car with the Fabergé eggs arrive."

"Very clever, Robert. Too bad all that intelligence is not displayed in your chess game."

I ignored the insult. "Called in a favor from a private detective who works around Brighton Beach. He says in Little Odessa you're known as a chess hustler who is always dreaming of the big score. You like to think you're Marlon Brando in the *Godfather* only with borscht instead of linguine. Likely you know a rich Russkie who would want a Fabergé egg tucked away in his private collection." I paused. "Hector will be disappointed to learn that you're not a sub commander."

Dimitri dropped a Russian cuss word.

I wished I'd been keeping notes. After today, I'd be able to swear in four languages.

Dimitri shrugged. "One cannot avoid that which is meant to happen."

"Russian fatalism again," I said. "I hope you're as calm when all of those fired security guards come by to get paid. Or when the rich guy in Little Odessa asks whatever happened to the money he likely paid you upfront."

Dimitri dropped another word not found in most dictionaries.

"I don't know that one," I said. "But here's a phrase I do know. *Shak i Mat*. I think it means check and mate."

Here's Looking at You

Victoria Weisfeld

My office, Monday morning. Drinking the sludge from the coffee machine, feet up on the desk I'd rescued after the shady tax accountant next door left one night via the window, six stories up. Porcupines playing nine-ball in my skull. Why'd I feel like this? Better not to know.

My secretary Darleen stuck her head in my office, her voice like a slipping fanbelt. "Someone to see you." She was new. She let her surprise show.

"Client?"

"Maybe. A guy." Great. Just what I needed. Someone who'd feel obliged to tell me how to solve his problem. "Handsome dude," she added.

"Give me a minute." I shooed her out. I swept the desktop debris into a drawer. Empty cardboard cups from Theo's, last week's newspapers, overdue utility bills, and a bottle of Maker's Mark, the better part of which I'd drunk from one of those cups after another slow week at Cole Investigations.

Darleen showed him in. I wasn't expecting much, so it would have been hard to be disappointed. But the tingle I felt assured me I wouldn't have felt let down, even if I'd been expecting Brad Pitt. An aura came off this guy like he'd just been polished and buffed. Not a hair, not a thread out of place, except maybe in his life, since he looked like he hadn't slept since last week. Spoiling the illusion, he pulled a tissue out of his pants pocket and blew.

"Allergies," he said.

Uh-uh, baby. Whatever happened to the starched, discreetly monogrammed linen handkerchief? Someone uses a throwaway tissue, makes me think I could be thrown away too. Get dirty for you, then good-bye.

I half-stood and reached across the desk, hand out, causing one of the porcupines to hit a powerful bank shot that almost knocked me back into my chair. "Frankie Cole," I said. He didn't take the hand. Instead he fumbled for his wallet. I sat down.

"And you are…?" to remind him about "conversation." I talk, then you do. Then I do, but only if I feel like it. Increasingly, I didn't.

"Vincent Pane," he sniffed. He laid a business card on my desk that read: "Vincent L. Pane, PE, Structural Engineering." I heard the name as "pain," and so far, it fit. Still. The way he filled out his polo shirt a sneeze might rip it down the middle, and the biceps started me wondering how much he could bench press. He could probably explain all the engineering forces involved too. While I wouldn't turn down a closer look at his structure, it was hidden under that pesky polo.

"You said 'Frankie.' That for Frances?"

Right off, a personal question.

"Francine. How'd you hear about me?"

"Guy who works for my dad said you'd help."

If he wanted me to know who his dad was, he'd have said. Didn't matter. Who he was just clicked into place.

My pleasant smile froze. I was sitting across the desk from a hand grenade.

"How can I help?" I leaned my chair back, putting my fingers together in a prayerful way.

The opening scene of his story played out yesterday at the Metropolitan Museum, where he was chaperoning a field trip for his four-year-old's co-op preschool. In the Egyptian exhibit, due to some combination of staff laxity and youthful chaos, a valuable carnelian scarab had gone missing.

The loss was noticed immediately, and the poor teachers, frazzled parents, and hapless tykes were grilled at length by the head of museum security. My potential client admitted he lost it. He berated the museum staff for accusing a member of their group, as there were plenty of other people around. Kids crying. Desperate teachers. The security chief finally released the class in disgust, and everyone went home unhappy.

Retelling the episode upset Vincent all over again, and I could see why they let the kids go. Impressive temper. He probably didn't realize anger made his dark eyes flash most provocatively, and his face colored to the roots of his wavy black hair, one curl coming loose in the excitement.

After his kid—a terror named Joey—went to bed last evening, Vincent gathered up clothes for the laundry and found the scarab in the boy's cargo shorts.

"Give it back?" I suggested with scant enthusiasm, knowing it wouldn't earn me much of a fee. But, he nixed that. After the fit he threw at the museum, he was too embarrassed to fess up. "Anonymously?" I suggested.

"That sounds simple," he said, "but while I was still looking at the damn thing in amazement—our upstairs neighbor phoned. His son and mine are in the same class, and he was a chaperone yesterday too. He said he saw my son take the scarab, got it on his cell phone camera. He wants a hundred thousand dollars."

I tsk-tsked. "Or...?"

"He'll go to the museum and the newspapers, and my son will never get into Blessingham Academy." From Vincent's alluring lips, the name was a sacrament.

"What's his mother say?" Something unstated was going on here, but I was too foggy to figure it out. Blessingham Academy was a ritzy Upper East Side school, but was it worth a hundred thousand to get in there? Maybe Vincent thought so. Or his neighbor did.

"My wife died in a car accident last year. I'm a single dad."

"I'm sorry," I said, frowning as hard as I could to beat back a smile. "This neighbor have a name? What's his angle? He need the money?"

"Charles Collingwood."

I recognized Collingwood's society-page name. Friend to all. Lover of boats and horses and dogs. Owned many of each. Houses in Bar Harbor, Palm Springs, and Manhattan.

Vincent continued. "And no, he doesn't need the money, per se. It's more a matter of decreasing my assets rather than increasing his own. He wants his son to go to Blessingham, just like we want Joey to go there. They take only a certain number of kids from each preschool, so his son and my Joey are competitors."

"They're preschoolers."

"Exactly. Now's the time. Set him on the path to success."

I consider it a mark of professionalism that I didn't roll my eyes. Yikes!

He derailed this train of thought by crossing his nice long legs. I liked the legs, despite the wacko value system. Of course, I've never had kids, so I probably don't understand.

"Couldn't you just as easily damage his rep, by exposing the blackmail attempt?"

"First of all, no witness, whereas I *do* have the scarab. Second, who'd believe it?" He got that right. Collingwood was wealthy as sin. Not a plausible blackmailer.

Before my next question, he said, "I'd like to get this solved quickly, before my family hears about it and decides to step in."

"Your family?" I figured he couldn't hide it any longer, and he didn't.

"My dad's Joey Pane. Like my son."

"Oh." Earlier, he'd pronounced his name like window-pane, but when he referred to his father, it was PAH-nay, Italian for "bread." Looked to me like Little Joey was following right in Big Joey's dirty footsteps, though Big Joey long ago moved up from simple theft to more lucrative crimes. I didn't blame Vincent for wanting to keep clear of that bunch.

What Vincent didn't know was that Big Joey thought I owed him. And he was willing to—I should say, planning to—make a point of it, eventually. I'd done free work for his legitimate businesses, but not nearly enough to cancel my obligation. I saw a pretty bright line there, and I'd never stepped over it. My little brother Larry had. Drowning in gambling debts, Joey's minions helped him out, right onto the path to the poorhouse or prison.

To clean up that mess, I had to eat a lot of crow and sell some assets I'd been saving. At least Big Joey did forgive the vig. Kind of. I still hear his "Don't forget you owe me."

"Another thing," Vincent continued, "the scarab story was all over last night's news. And on the front page of today's paper. I want to get rid of it!" The eyes flashed.

"So, where do I fit in?" Somewhere, I hoped. I wanted more chances to gaze at the wide shoulders and narrow hips of Joey Pane's dad.

"Here's my plan. Tell me what you think of it."

Ah, here it was. Telling me my business. But, how would I turn this problem into billable hours? So far, it didn't sound like a money-maker. "You still have the scarab? You could give it to me. I'll mail it back to the Met, and the story will simmer down pronto. Once it's found, people won't care what your neighbor says." I thought another moment. "But there's still the blackmail."

"I'll give the damn thing to Collingwood this evening, along with an address in Brooklyn, where one of my fa—my associates will exchange it for the money."

"So, you'll pay him the hundred grand? You have that kind of cash on hand?"

"I want him off my back."

"And he's taking the scarab with him to Brooklyn, why?"

"So they give the money to the right person."

"So, by the end of this transaction, you'll have the scarab again." I was thinking out loud now. "You don't want to be handling stolen property, even if…" I started to say, "the thief is a four-year-old child," but instead said, "the theft was a silly and expensive mistake."

He frowned.

"You wanna know what I think of this plan?" I asked.

"Do I?"

"You're here." His look allowed that was so, and he nodded.

"First of all, this won't be the end of it. Your Joey and Collingwood's kid are still competing for a scarce resource. He recorded the theft on his phone. As we said, people know he's rich, so won't believe he'd squeeze you for a hundred K. Any time he wants, he can play this card again. No chance you'd consider another school for Joey?"

"My wife had her heart set on it."

No arguing with the dead. "Let me think." I worked the problem over from several directions then told him what I thought he should do. I also mentioned the matter of my fee for the consultation and my role in developing and carrying out the plan.

"Don't worry about it," he said. "I'll pay you."

I had an idea of what currency I'd prefer, because, as he stood to leave, the sun hit his belt buckle and reflected back into my eyes like a lightning bolt. I could so easily imagine grabbing that belt, unbuckling it, running my fingers under his waistband to undo his khakis, and slowly lowering the zipper. I'd like to see those pants slide down what would surely be strong, shapely legs, and puddle on the floor around his feet.

I licked my lips and ushered him to the door. I refrained—barely—from patting his tight little ass.

Then he was gone. I wandered to the window and lifted a broken slat of the venetian blind to watch him depart. He emerged from my building and crossed the intersection below, taking the stairs down to the Lexington Avenue subway.

Darleen interrupted my musing. "Phone call. Some guy named Pahnay."

That didn't take long.

"Say, isn't that the same name as—"

"Shut the door on your way out."

"Good morning, Francine." The unmistakable gravelly voice.

"Joey."

"What did my son want? I'm told he visited you."

"Spot of bother. We have it covered."

"Yeah? Tell me about it."

Big Joey hoarded secrets, but he didn't like other people to have them. Some arm of his business would come up with the hundred thou, and he'd hear about Vincent's predicament eventually. I described it in full. Little

Joey's misdeed elicited a grandfatherly chuckle.

"A lot of fuss over some little piece of shit," he said.

"A very *valuable* little piece of shit." I'd been wondering about something, so I probed. "Your son has a fancy address. He must be doing well. Fancy neighbors, too."

"Yeah. I bought him that apartment when he and Carla got married. He does all right. Helps not to have a mortgage. So, Francine, how will you help my son?"

Naturally, I told him.

* * *

Vincent was in my office bright and early the next day, but when he took off his dark glasses, I could see he still hadn't slept. He wore a gray knit shirt that matched his complexion nicely. It was unbuttoned at the top, and dark chest hairs curled over the edges. I could almost feel them under my fingertips.

"So?" Before I've had enough caffeine, I'm short on preambles. "You gave me the gist last night, but I want the details. Starting with your visit to Collingwood."

According to our plan, he went to Collingwood's apartment about nine to give him the scarab. Collingwood grabbed it, then showed Vincent an envelope tucked into the inside pocket of his sport coat.

"My insurance policy," Collingwood said. "It has a full description of what I saw Joey do, how you talked our way out of the museum. And how, as of this writing," he tapped the envelope, "you haven't returned it." He held the translucent red-brown scarab up to the light and peered through it. "As we can see."

Vince said the man's tone was infuriating, but he kept it together. He told Collingwood where he should be at ten p.m. last night—the Starbucks at East 77th and Lexington Avenue. It's the only one in the area open late, maybe because Lenox Hill Hospital is right across the street. Someone would contact him there with the details on how to get the money. "If you think you can manage that," Vince said, per the script we'd worked out. People like Collingwood don't like sarcasm, especially directed at them.

Starbucks had been my idea. I wanted Collingwood out of his apartment and, more important, with his phone and its incriminating photos. I was counting on his having only the one phone, at least for personal matters. When he left the apartment building, Vince discreetly followed.

My plan didn't give Collingwood much time. Under an hour to get to the coffee shop. Not enough to formulate a lot of doubts and questions. Certainly not enough to prepare some elaborate plan of his own.

When Vince phoned to tell me Collingwood was approaching Lex—and alone—I sent him home.

Later that night, I called him to say his problems were solved. Details tomorrow, I said, but mostly I wanted to see him again. Now it was morning, and I had to fill in my part of the story. I arrived at Starbucks well before ten and went upstairs to the mezzanine, which has a clear view of the comings and goings below. I leaned against the wall, sipping a double mocha latte, until a table became available. Then I settled in, opened my tablet, and fired up a mobile security camera app. I got pix of Collingwood's arrival and filmed his pacing, waiting for the ten o'clock contact. I let him wait.

He became increasingly nervous as the appointed hour came and went. Finally, at 10:15, I phoned him. In the most businesslike voice I could muster, I told him to grab a cab and gave him the Brooklyn address Vince had provided.

"I reminded him not to use an Uber," I said. "And I said he should tell the taxi to wait for him at the other end."

"How helpful," Vince said, displaying a charming smirk.

"I needed to focus him on what he'd do *after* the meet-up, not what might happen during it. And I didn't want him thinking about the problem of finding a cab that late in the rain. Insulted, anxious, wet—it would throw him off his game."

"Blackmail isn't easy."

"Yeah, well. After the call ended, I headed outside and popped open my golf umbrella just as Collingwood stepped out into the street to flag down a cab. Big puddle he had to navigate."

"Lex is one-way southbound, so taxis would be coming from where? Harlem?"

"Farther uptown, anyway. But then the plan went out the window."

"Huh?" For the first time, Vince sounded nervous.

"A big black SUV came outta nowhere, squealed around the corner onto Lex, and hit Collingwood before he could jump back onto the curb."

"You're kidding," Vince said.

I'm sure he knew I was not.

"Within seconds, it turned east on 76th and disappeared. The way Collingwood's arms were flung out, a leg crumpled under him, even with the streetlight out, I knew your pal would never blackmail anybody again."

"You're kidding."

I told Vince that a couple of bystanders were taking an interest, and I yelled at them to run across the street to the hospital emergency room. "Get help! Don't just stand there!" Another guy positioned himself in the street facing uptown to try to wave traffic around the body.

"That big umbrella was a godsend. People thought I was protecting the body from the rain, but of course I was hiding it from them. I grabbed the phone out of his right hand and found the scarab in his coat pocket.

"A couple of busybodies still lurked about. I distracted them by pointing across the street where two men in scrubs were wheeling a gurney. Then I reached into Collingwood's inside pocket and grabbed the envelope."

"You got everything."

"Yep."

"No cops yet?"

"They did finally arrive and look the situation over. Too bad for them, the bystanders' descriptions of the SUV, including mine, were so generic they weren't much help. In the dark and with the rain, nobody caught the license plate number. New York plates, they thought. I admitted to moving Collingwood a bit, his arms—I said I thought he was still alive. They seemed satisfied. They even congratulated me. Good Samaritan and all."

"You're k—. Amazing." I could guess what he was really thinking.

"A tragic accident. But timely. Now I'll give you the letter."

Blessingham Academy must be some school, I thought, looking at the handsome man relaxing across from me. How much more lucrative it would be to be this guy's lawyer rather than his private eye, although I didn't think he would need either, not long-term. Little Joey—that's who I pinned my hopes on. I just had to wait about fifteen years.

"You have it?" he asked, breaking my daydream.

"Right here." I pulled it out of my top drawer.

"You didn't open it?"

"It's yours. You do it."

"No. You."

I slit the envelope with a paper knife. "To whom it may concern" the envelope read. Right. At this point I guess the contents did concern me. I removed the two sheets of expensive stationery, unfolded them, took a quick glance, and turned them so he could see. Completely blank.

"Son of a bitch," he said.

"I'll say. And since his phone with any incriminating pictures is in several pieces in several city trash cans, it looks like you're done. I'll mail that scarab back to the museum today."

"It's cursed," he said. "I know it."

"So, back to yesterday's question. What can I do for you?"

He thought a long time. "Unless another letter's floating around, I think the problem is solved."

I had to agree. I doubted there was a second letter. Collingwood was too full of himself to believe he'd need a backup plan. If the police ID'd the hit-and-run vehicle, they might link it to Vince's family, but that was another doubtful proposition. The traffic cameras on East 76th point downtown. They wouldn't have caught the SUV. It was a professional job, and professionals try not to leave a trail wide enough for the cops to stumble upon. There would be some fuss, because of who the victim was, but because of who he was, no one would figure his death involved anything sordid. Just a tragic accident.

The upshot of this brief engagement was that Vincent Pane discarded me like one of his damn damp tissues. He walked out of my office that day without offering to contribute a dime to the financial health of Cole Investigations. But he must have valued my assistance after all, because before I could even explain to Darleen what an invoice is and why they are important, someone slipped a $10,000 check under the door while she and I were having lunch at Theo's. Now did that check mean "thank you," or "keep your mouth shut"? Both, I figured. Even better, Big Joey called to say we are square.

I put the check in my briefcase and called to the outer office, "Darleen, bring me a box and some tape." I put on a pair of latex gloves and carefully wrapped the scarab in its own story from yesterday's front page.

Through Thick and Thin

Andrew Welsh-Huggins

Hayes was accustomed to the confidentiality demanded by clients, to say the least. You didn't hire a private eye in the hopes of trending on Twitter. The whole business was an oxymoron if you thought about it: revealing secrets discreetly. But even by his standards, the agreed-upon meeting place was unusual. A small picnic shelter deep inside Battelle Darby Creek Metro Park and well past Columbus city lines. Nine on a Thursday morning. As deserted a spot and as quiet a time as possible. A welcome addition to Hayes's only other job at the moment, which involved identifying who among an insurance company's employees was poisoning geese on his or her lunch break. But a head-scratcher regardless. Hayes parked his Odyssey in the shelter's adjacent parking lot, looked around, and settled for a seat on the shelter picnic table. Five minutes passed, then ten. He pulled out his phone to be sure he had the right spot. He did. At fifteen he decided to give it another five and call it a day. Getting stood up was also something Hayes was used to; cold feet were endemic among those needing his services. He was the professional equivalent of a dentist on the morning of your root canal. Three minutes later he watched a small four-door red sedan move slowly down the hill before the driver pulled into the lot beside his van. Nothing happened for a full minute. Then a man emerged, looked in the direction he'd driven from, looked in the opposite direction, shut the car door, and walked toward the shelter.

"Mr. Hayes?"

"You've got him. Call me Andy. I thought you might not be coming."

"I thought so too."

Jarrod Rodgers appeared as nervous in person as he'd sounded on the phone a day earlier. He crossed to the far corner of the shelter without shaking Hayes's hand and stood with his arms crossed over his nylon Ohio State windbreaker, all that was needed against this morning's cool April temperatures. He peered up and down the road again. He looked lost, Hayes concluded. No, more than that. He looked like a man awaiting an interview for a job he knew he'd never land.

"This is a little embarrassing," Rodgers said at last.

"Take your time."

"The thing is, I made a mistake."

"Mistakes happen. Why don't you tell me about it."

"I'm not sure where to start."

"Try the beginning. Always works for me."

The attempt to lighten the moment flew past Rodgers without recognition. Nevertheless, after some fits and starts, he told his story.

"I'm happily married. You have to understand that. This wasn't about Missy."

"Missy's your wife?"

"That's right. She's great. I don't know what I was thinking."

They usually didn't, Hayes thought. He said: "Go on."

"I was at a bar, after work. With some friends. A Friday-night thing. I'd had too much to drink. I started talking to this girl. We were, you know, flirting. Somehow, I ended up with her number. Couple days later I texted her, just messing around. The next thing I knew I was at her apartment."

"What happened?"

The question seemed to startle Rodgers and he made eye contact with Hayes for the first time since his arrival. Neatly trimmed goatee. Fit and trim in jeans and the red golf shirt under his jacket. Early forties or so—the short-cropped hair retreating fast off his forehead the only sign of his age.

Good-looking guy.

"What happened was I slept with her. Biggest mistake of my life." He laughed, short and hollow, like a man laughing by himself in an elevator car stuck between floors. "Make that second biggest. Which is why I called you."

"Second biggest?"

Rodgers looked skyward and shook his head in disgust. "I left my wedding ring in her apartment. I took it off when I got undressed. My one noble act." A count of three, and another laugh. "I need that ring back. I need—"

"Have you asked her?"

"What?" Rodgers seemed startled again.

"Have you asked her for the ring back?"

"That's the thing. I can't find her. She won't answer her phone. I snuck over to her apartment when I figured she'd be there, but no one answered. Her car's not in the lot. I'm afraid maybe she moved."

On the park road, a ranger drove past in a green Metro Parks pickup truck. Hayes waved casually, as if being in the shelter so early on a Thursday was the most natural thing in the world. The ranger waved back. Probably had seen it all, and more.

"You need me to find her? Is that it?"

"I just need to know where she is so I can get my ring back."

"I take it you haven't told your wife what happened."

"God, no. It would destroy her."

"Why?"

"Are you serious?"

"Not every affair ends a marriage. Healing is possible—hard, but possible." Except in Hayes's case, though he left that thought unspoken.

Rodgers looked taken aback by this. A moment later, as if recovering from the shock of someone's unexpected arrival at the door, he said, "Her parents split up when she was in high school after her dad had an affair. Times were tough for her and her mom, for a long time. If she found out history repeated itself? I can't even imagine."

"She hasn't realized you're not wearing the ring?"

"Not so far. I take it off occasionally when I mow the lawn. Or sometimes at work."

"Which is where?"

Rodgers explained that he worked at the YMCA on the west side. One of his jobs included regular lifeguarding stints.

"I'm afraid it might slip off and I'd never find it. Once or twice I forgot it in my locker. But the truth is I have it on most of the time. It won't be long before she notices."

"If you're being honest with me and this really was a mistake—"

"It was. I swear."

Hayes held up a hand to stop him. He said, "Assuming that's true, and assuming you're never going to see this girl again, why not tell Missy a version of the truth? You lost the ring and you can't find it. Buy another one, keep your wife in flowers and jewelry going forward, and keep your pants zipped when you're out of the house. All that's a hell of a lot cheaper than divorce." It wasn't that Hayes didn't want or need the work. But half the time it was easier just to point out the obvious, pocket a finder's fee, and move on.

Rodgers didn't say anything for a second. Hayes was left with the impression he'd thrown a stage actor for a loop by going off-script. Rodgers recovered a moment later. "It was her grandfather's wedding ring. Passed down to me. It's a family heirloom. I have to get it back. I have to."

* * *

In the end, Hayes accepted five hundred for a retainer and another five hundred to cover three days of work, with a promise of a refund if he found the girl, and the ring, quickly. Hayes had his doubts. Locating Lainey Perkins—the name of the one-night stand—was one thing. It was a lot harder to disappear nowadays because of the electronic tracks that people left, often without realizing it. Most human beings, even those who prided themselves on their independence, lived their lives trailed by a spectral cloud of ones and zeroes. It was after finding Perkins that the degree of difficulty intensified. Best-case scenario, she parked the ring at a pawn shop where chances were fifty-fifty of retrieving it in time. Worst-case—and more likely, in Hayes's experience—she was holding onto it as collateral. In which situation, separating it from her would be more or less as easy as persuading her to remove a tattoo. She would not be the first woman to turn a keepsake from her married lover into an occasional ATM machine. Want to keep our little secret safe? Time to pony up. Yet one more reason Hayes questioned whether he could help his new client.

He stayed in the shelter house until Rodgers, shoulders slumped, pulled away and drove out of sight. When he was alone, Hayes took out his phone and searched for his new client on Facebook. After a couple of minutes he concluded that Rodgers was the rare sane individual without a social-media presence. Missy Rodgers, it turned out, was more in line with the rest of humanity. Her profile picture showed a sunny, smiling, attractive blonde who looked, like Rodgers, to be in her early forties but with a few more lines around her eyes. Her timeline a long string of upbeat comments accompanying happy pictures of their tween-age children, a boy and girl, a golden retriever apparently called Tanner, a raft of vegetarian recipes and photos accompanied by at least one "Meat is murder" post, several memes about hardworking nurses, and a bunch of outdoor selfies of her jogging and hiking. A picture-perfect life, so far as Hayes could tell. For his part, Jarrod was a ghost on her page—a background image in the photos, rarely showing his face. Jarrod was also largely invisible on the greater Web, almost belying Hayes's belief in the ubiquity of people's e-life. The only picture Hayes found was a handout photo that a local suburban weekly used earlier in the year after Jarrod won a staff award.

Over the years, Hayes had determined that affairs were rarely about physical attraction, at least after the first spark. He confirmed this observation looking at the photos of Lainey Perkins he found next, on her far more stripped-down Facebook page. Heavily made-up, her green eyeshadow the color of something you might skim from a pond in late summer. Hair a bright red found in nature if the nature happened to be on

Mars. Not fat, but a heavy girl, as the saying went. A line of silver earrings starting in the lobes and marching up the cartilage. A nose ring to match. Pale skin with some doughy cleavage. Despite the youthful vibe she strove for, not all that much younger than Jarrod or Missy, Hayes realized. Her last post a week ago: a late-night picture of a raccoon crouched on a sidewalk, its eyes glittering from a streetlamp, a warehouse of some kind looming in the background. The caption: "Traffic blocking my commute, LOL." He could see the bad-girl affinity that might have appealed to Rodgers, but comparing Lainey to Missy gave him pause. He was reminded of something his cousin said to him years ago, after Hayes left his first wife, Kym, for Crystal, the woman who would briefly become his second bride. Thrusting Kym's wedding-day photo at Hayes, his cousin said, "Are you nuts? You traded in sirloin for hamburger."

Hayes had been nuts. Putting the beef analogy aside in deference to Missy's vegetarianism, he saw that Rodgers had been too. Lainey over Missy? Not even close. For his part he could pretend to blame domestic strife for the straying, but Rodgers hadn't hinted at any. She's great. I don't know what I was thinking. So, absent that, was this really a one-night stand? Or did Lainey fulfill something in him that Missy couldn't? Missy struck Hayes as a go-getter: it was possible Rodgers was just worn out and attracted by someone more willing to spend all her energy on him. But something still didn't add up. Maybe it was Hayes's own longing for life with an attractive, maternal, dog-loving vegetarian nurse that made him skeptical. Because at this point, all he had was the dog.

* * *

Lainey Perkins lived just off 3C Highway on the outskirts of Grove City, the same suburb Jarrod and Missy called home, her apartment the middle duplex in a three-unit building, one of two matching structures set back from the street and fronted by resident-only parking lots. Exterior walls a gray stucco that could have used a power washing or three; landscaping limited to a line of shaggy shrubs whose untrimmed branches crept above the lines of several front windows. Hayes considered the manicured lawn that the Rodgers's dog Tanner romped upon in Missy's Facebook photos, in front of a standard-issue suburban split-level, trimmed bushes and all. Talk about trading sirloin for hamburger. No one answered the first, second, or even third time Hayes knocked on Perkins's door. He crossed to the door to his left; no answer either. He crossed to the door on the right. After a minute, an elderly East African woman answered but shook her head politely at his questions. "No English," she said. Hayes thanked her, walked up to the donut shop on the corner, bought a small black and a Boston creme, and returned to his Odyssey. He pulled the brim of his Otterbein University ballcap over his eyes, settled back, took a sip of coffee and a bite of the donut, and pretended to study his phone.

Surveillance was a lot like foreplay, Hayes found. Occasionally, a short stint earned you a favorable outcome. But more often than not, the longer it lasted, the more likely you got what you desired. Today's vigil fell into the latter category. The complex was quiet for a Thursday morning, and for several long minutes nothing happened. Eventually, the door on the right reopened and the East African woman emerged trailed by a couple of young girls wearing bright orange dresses and jackets. They walked around the corner to a playground. Ten minutes after that, a minivan pulled in and parked in front of Hayes, momentarily blocking his view of Perkins's entryway as the driver lifted a phone to her ear. "My kids are straight-A students at Lakewood Elementary," the bumper sticker read, below one of those rear-window happy-family stick-figure decals. Screw you, Hayes thought, still smarting from the reminder of his own hamburger-over-steak failures. Fortunately for his surveillance, the driver's call ended, the van left a minute later, and his sight lines were restored. A good thing, because that's when his wait finally paid off.

He heard it before he saw it, a car with a muffler a week overdue for replacement. He watched as a man parked the beater two spaces to his left, cut the engine, and walked to the duplex to the left of Lainey's. He unlocked the door and went inside. Hayes was opening the door of his van when the man reappeared, looked out over the parking lot, approached

Lainey's door, and used a key to let himself in. Interesting.

"Help you?" the man said, eyes narrowed in suspicion as he answered the door moments after Hayes's no-nonsense knock.

"Hopefully. I'm looking for Lainey Perkins."

"She's, ah, not here," the man said, unable to contain his surprise.

"Do you know where she is?"

"I'm not sure. I think she might have moved out."

"When?"

"Why are you asking?"

"Because I'm curious."

"You a cop?"

"Do you want me to be?"

"I just don't want any trouble." He seemed like the type who wouldn't. Eyes darting back and forth from Hayes to the parking lot and back. Even less hair on top than Jarrod Rodgers, and what there was would have benefited from both shampoo and conditioner. An undergrowth of facial stubble like soft, white mold spreading across leftovers. Further down, a fold of belly fat peeking out from where his Cincinnati Bengals T-shirt didn't quite meet his jeans. T-shirt so suffused with stale cigarette smoke that Hayes felt his breath catch in his throat.

"In that case, I'm not a cop and I'm going to make your wish come true." He dug out a card and handed it to him. "Back to my question."

"What's a private investigator want to do with Lainey?"

"He wants to know where she is so he can ask her a question. But you think she moved?"

The man hesitated, eyeing Hayes's card. "I'm not exactly sure, tell you the truth. I haven't seen her around the past few days."

"Why do you have a key to her apartment?"

"Listen, what's this about? Is she in trouble?"

"Not yet. How about we talk inside?"

"I'm not sure about that."

"Would you be sure if I gave you twenty bucks and promised I won't leave any marks on her carpet?" Hayes opened his wallet and removed one of the bills Rodgers had handed him.

The man didn't look sure but took the money anyway. Hayes seized the moment and pushed past him, ignoring a cry of protest. A moment later the man followed Hayes inside, shutting the door behind him.

Hayes looked around. He'd expected a place that had been cleared out, according to the man's contention a moment earlier that Perkins might have moved. Instead, he saw a cluttered living room, a dining-room table covered with papers, and a kitchen counter crowded with dishes and boxes of unopened food, as if Perkins had walked away in the midst of preparing a meal.

"This doesn't look like the apartment of someone who left."

"I know," the man said, a hint of worry in his voice.

"So, is that why you came in here just now? To check if she'd really gone?"

"I'm not sure how that's any of your business."

Hayes sighed and took out another twenty. He didn't hand this one over but let the man's eyes focus on it before placing it on the kitchen countertop and setting a not entirely clean coffee cup atop it. "Let's start from the beginning, shall we? Who are you, and why do you have a key to this apartment?"

It took a little more back-and-forth, but at last the man relented. His name was Shayne Townsley. He'd lived in the duplex next door for three years. Perkins arrived maybe six months ago.

"We got to be friends. I'd help her out from time to time, give her a ride to work if the weather was bad."

"She didn't drive?"

"Her car wasn't the most reliable. I can do some basic stuff, helped her keep it running. But Walmart's less than half a mile. She said it was just easier to walk."

"Isn't Walmart down on Stringtown Road?"

"Not a store. A distribution center. She worked the overnight shift."

Hayes recalled the photo of the raccoon on Perkins's Facebook page. The quip about the commute suddenly made sense.

"And she didn't say anything about leaving?"

"That's what's strange. I feel like she would have told me. Plus, her dog."

"Dog?"

"I'd feed it from time to time. Let it out if she had to work overtime. Then the other day I heard it barking late in the morning, even though I hadn't heard from Lainey. Her car wasn't in the lot so I figured she'd walked home as usual, then maybe gone someplace. But after a few hours, I knew something was up."

"No idea where she is?"

The man shrugged. "She's from Indy. Said this job paid more, which is why she moved here in the first place. But maybe she went home."

"Without her dog?"

"That's why I'm a little worried."

Hayes did some math in his head. "You watched her dog, gave her rides, fixed her car, and you have a key to her apartment. Sure you're just friends?"

The man looked away. "I'm sure."

"What you're describing is a boyfriend. Or am I missing something here?"

Eyes darting again, this time from Hayes to the stairway leading to the second floor and back.

"Not boyfriend, exactly."

"What then?"

"I still don't see how any of this is your business."

"Let's assume it's not. But let's assume it's weird she disappeared without telling you and left her dog here to boot, at least according to you. You and I both find that strange. The cops might too. We could get them involved if you want."

"There's no reason to do that."

"Then answer the question: Are you her boyfriend?"

"It wasn't like that, okay? I'd help her out with stuff and she'd, you know, pay me back sometimes."

"In bed?"

Townsley nodded, discomfort etching his face, which suddenly looked older and more tired, like a face seen in the full light of the sun after days inside.

"Who suggested that arrangement? You or her?"

"I don't know. It just sort of happened."

"You sure about that? Maybe her car's on the fritz, she calls, you name your price before you'll help her out?"

"It wasn't like that. You make it sound bad, like I was raping her or something."

"Were you?"

"I told you no. It was, what do you call it, consensual. That's all. I swear."

Hayes studied Townsley. The man's eyes had gone soft, and he was no longer staring furtively at the staircase. He looked lonely and confused, Hayes realized, like a man who finds himself lost in an unfamiliar city on a busy street with no idea which way to turn.

Not unlike Jarrod Rodgers, come to think of it.

"Listen up," Hayes said. He retrieved his phone and pulled up the picture of Rodgers from the suburban weekly newspaper, the one they ran after he received the YMCA staff award. "Ever see this guy?"

Townsley looked at the photo for a good five seconds without recognition. "No. Who is he?"

"Never seen him here? With Lainey?"

"Never."

"He says they had a one-night stand. Couple weeks ago. He met her at a bar and then snuck over here one day for a quickie."

Townsley looked as if he'd been physically struck. His shoulders sagged, followed by his entire body, which he folded onto Lainey Perkins's couch.

"You okay?"

"I'm not sure. It—it doesn't seem like Lainey, what you're telling me."

"You said yourself you traded sexual favors with her for household chores. What's not to believe, under those circumstances?"

Now Townsley looked as if he might burst into tears. "When was this? That they, you know, hooked up?"

"They met at a bar on a Friday night, about a month ago."

"Friday? You're sure?"

"What he said. It was an after-work kind of thing."

Townsley looked up at Hayes, curiosity momentarily replacing the misery brightening his eyes. "Like I told you, Lainey worked overnights. Wednesday through Sunday, every week. Eleven p.m. to seven a.m. She made extra, 'cause it was such an unpopular shift."

"And she always walked?"

"Unless the weather was bad. Then I might give her a ride."

"Might?"

"There were times she said she didn't want to bother me."

"Or maybe she didn't want to have to pay you back," Hayes said.

"It wasn't like that," Townsley said, slumping even further down on the couch.

* * *

Hayes took a tour of the apartment, upstairs and down. He didn't like what he found. Lainey's bed was unmade, her closet still full of clothes, her bathroom cabinet jammed with toiletries and makeup. If she'd left town, it had been a snap decision. Townsley told Hayes that Lainey drove a blue 2009 Honda Civic. It wasn't in the duplex parking lot. In the end, Hayes thanked Townsley for his help and asked him to call if he heard from Perkins. He wasn't sure he fully believed the story of consensual favor-trading. But the man's misery over Lainey's disappearance on top of her apparent betrayal of their arrangement with Jarrod Rodgers seemed real enough. After leaving the apartment, Hayes drove around the corner to the Walmart distribution center and then drove around the massive parking lot for ten minutes. No sign of Perkins's car. He parked by the entrance and approached the security booth outside the door.

"Had a question about one of your employees," Hayes said, handing the guard his card.

The man eyed Hayes's license as if it confirmed a positive COVID test. "So?"

"So, I was hoping maybe you could help me. Her name's Lainey Perkins. She might be missing."

"From where?"

"From home. But maybe work too, which I thought might interest you."

"You'd be wrong. But it might interest my boss, which is all I care about. Okay, let me ask you this. Shopped at a Walmart recently?"

Hayes thought about it. "Bought one of my boys some mittens for a ski trip this winter. School took a bunch of kids over to Mad River."

"Close enough. I'll put it down as an inventory query. What's this girl's name again?"

Hayes waited while the guard two-finger typed Perkins's name into a tablet. The man studied the information that scrolled down the screen.

"Found her. What do you need to know?"

"Has she been to work recently?"

"Doesn't look like it. Missed three days in a row starting last week. Fired on the fourth."

"Nothing about why she missed work?"

"Zilch. But it's pretty common, actually. All the opioid stuff going on, we get a lot of dopeheads here. They work long enough for a paycheck or two and then leave and piss it into their arms. That this girl's problem?"

"I don't think so."

"Well, she's gone either way."

"I appreciate it. Oh. One other thing."

"Always is."

Hayes asked about her schedule. The guard touch-typed for a few seconds and studied the screen again. "Yup. Every Wednesday through Sunday. And I thought my schedule sucked. Actually, this girl was reliable right up until the end. No sick days or anything. We'll be lucky to replace somebody like her."

* * *

Hayes spent his lunch hour with his camera trained on suspected goose poisoners. By the end of the surveillance, he was pretty sure the round guy with the funny hair part was having an affair with the lady with the bright pink sneakers, but beyond that he was no closer to catching the culprit than when he started. He put the camera away and texted Rodgers and suggested they meet. They arranged another trip to the park, the next day, at the same shelter house as before. If anything, Rodgers looked even more nervous than the previous day. Hayes explained the little he'd learned. How he found Lainey Perkins's apartment but she was gone, though oddly she left her dog behind. That she hadn't been to work and was subsequently fired. That she appeared to already have a boyfriend, of sorts, in the form of her next-door neighbor. Examining Rodgers, he left out the Friday-night discrepancy for now. Rodgers listened, his face falling as Hayes spoke. When he was done, he unlaced his fingers and cupped his cheeks in his hands.

"So, that's it?" he said. "She's gone?"

"Looks like it."

"And there's no way to find her?"

"Could be hard, at this point. I can keep looking if you want. Though I'm not sure I see the point."

"What do you mean?"

"I mean, you having found your wedding ring and all." Hayes gestured at Rodgers's left hand, where a band of gold encircled his ring finger. A ring that hadn't been there two days earlier. Rodgers didn't say anything at first. Hayes waited for the cry of protest, the explanation about a misunderstanding, a fabricated gasp of surprised delight. Instead, after a few seconds, Rodgers said, "Shit," and placed his hands over his eyes. Hayes gave him a moment, and two more for free, and then said quietly, "So, what's really going on here?"

* * *

Through the still-greening trees, Hayes watched a pair of cyclists glide along the park's fitness trail. Startled by their approach, a white-tailed deer bobbed briefly out of the woods and onto the grass where it stood for a moment, eyeing its environs suspiciously. A couple of seconds later it faded gracefully back into the trees. It was a nice moment. Hayes wished it would have lasted longer. Slowly, Rodgers talked.

"It happened twenty-five years ago. In Indianapolis. I was fifteen. Bored and stupid. And drunk. Thanks to my buddy. No," he added quickly, shaking his head so violently Hayes was afraid his glasses might fall off. "Thanks to me. It was my decision to drink that night."

Hayes didn't say anything, wondering where this was going and if he really wanted to go along for the ride.

"There's a street running over I-65 we used to walk back and forth on. Sometimes we'd stand and watch the cars go by. Maybe pump our arms to get a truck to blast its horn."

"Sure."

"One night we found these bricks in an alley. Leftovers from some guy's patio project. Not that it matters. We grabbed a bunch and went to the bridge and started chucking them over."

"Okay," Hayes said. It sounded plausible; something similar had happened in Columbus not that long ago.

"Hitting a car's actually harder than you think. You have to calculate your throw carefully. Finally, my friend caught somebody's trunk. I realized he was hesitating a second too long. So, I timed my next one just right. I nailed a windshield. The car skidded off the road and we took off, but not without a bunch of high-fives first. It wasn't until the next day that we even heard."

"Heard?"

"She died," Rodgers said, staring into the woods where the deer had disappeared. "The passenger, I mean. Major head and brain trauma. Cheryl Stevens. She was a middle-school principal. She and her husband were on their way back from their wedding-anniversary dinner. It was all over the news. The police were everywhere in our neighborhood. My friends and I were freaking out. I made up my mind to tell my mom and get it over with, but before I could, somebody busted us. The police came to the door, hauled me away. The prosecutor wanted us tried as adults, but the judge wouldn't allow it. I ended up in juvie for six years, until I was twenty-one.

I would have been out earlier, but I got in a couple fights and they kept extending my stay."

Hayes nodded, encouraging him to continue.

"I had nothing when I was released. My parents had divorced. My dad moved out of state and my mom blamed me. It wasn't hard to see her point. What I did put them through hell. The calls and the threats they got because of me. And afterward, I was useless. No one would hire me for anything. Soon as they saw the name and put it together, forget it. I was homeless for a while, it was so bad. Eventually I hired on to a construction crew as a day laborer. I met this guy who'd done time. He told me there were ways you could disappear. Taught me a few things. It took a couple of months, but the day came when I wasn't the person I used to be anymore—by name, I mean. I became Jarrod Rodgers."

"And ended up in Columbus?"

"I followed the construction crew to a job. They couldn't put up apartments and condos fast enough over here. There was so much work. I liked the money, don't get me wrong, but it was hard. I started looking around for something else. One of the guys on the crew had a brother who worked in a gym, said they were hiring. They needed a night cleaner. It was half the pay but I didn't wake up every day feeling like I'd fallen off the roof. One day the weight-room supervisor quit without any notice and they asked if I could cover his shift. I did okay and they gave me more shifts. Before I knew it, I was running classes. Next thing you know, I'm a gym guy. I had a reputation for being good with the younger crowd, and not long after that I got an offer to go work for the Y, this program they have for troubled teens." He let out a deep sigh. "Guess they picked the right guy for that, without even knowing it. Long story short, that was fifteen years ago. Been there ever since."

"So, what happened?"

He lowered his arms and dug his hands into his pants pockets. "Somebody figured out who I was."

"Somebody?"

"Lainey Perkins."

* * *

Hayes remembered what Shayne Townsley told him, about Perkins moving over from Indianapolis to take a job here at Walmart. He told Rodgers the anecdote. He nodded in confirmation.

"Who is she?" Hayes said.

"She's a nobody. Except in this case she's a somebody who recognized me from that stupid picture the paper ran after I won that award. I asked them not to put anything out, but it was too late."

"What's she want?"

"Money," he said. "Money or she'll tell the world about me. Starting with Missy."

"Your wife doesn't know about Indianapolis."

He shook his head.

"There was no one-night stand. No missing wedding ring."

Rodgers shook his head again.

"How much does Perkins want?"

"She wants more, is the problem."

"More?"

"The first time, it was a thousand dollars. She said she'd leave me alone after that. Like a fool, I believed her. It was hard as hell to find that much money without my wife knowing. Of course, that wasn't enough."

A twinge of guilt as Hayes considered the money Rodgers paid him to look for Perkins. "How much now?"

"She wanted five thousand this time. By this past Monday, or else."

"I take it she never got it?"

"Only because she disappeared. She wasn't answering her texts. I snuck over there one day after work, but like I told you, she wasn't answering her door."

"Why not just leave it be and count yourself lucky? Dodged a bullet and all that?"

"And not know if she's really gone or just planning her next move? No thanks."

"That's why you hired me. To figure out what happened to her?"

Rodgers acknowledged it with a nod.

"Here's the thing," Hayes said. "Blackmail's illegal. I'm not saying it would be easy, but why not just go to the police? Let them handle it."

Rodgers's eyes widened as if Lainey Perkins herself had appeared around the corner of the shelter. "Are you crazy? I do that and the world knows. And once my wife finds out…"

"What?"

"It's over. She'll be out of there. Everything I built will be gone. Everything I've tried to do, to make amends with the universe, down the toilet."

"Last time you said she'd leave because her father broke the family up with an affair. Was that a lie too?"

"No. That really happened. She's estranged from her dad and her mom died shortly after Missy graduated high school. Cancer, but she blamed her father, as irrational as that sounds. She's got trust issues, either way."

"Forgive the question, but how do you know that's what she'll do? Maybe she'd surprise you."

"I just know."

"Meaning?"

"She has a strong sense of right and wrong. Stuff she sees on her job."

"Which is?" Hayes said, though he already had a good guess from her Facebook page.

"She's an overnight ER nurse. At Grant. Eighty percent of what she sees are shootings. It's got her kind of jaded about crime."

"Is that why she's a vegetarian?"

Rodgers stared at him. "How do you know that?"

Hayes explained the social-media snooping he'd done.

Rodgers relaxed a little. "I'm not online much, for obvious reasons. And to answer your question, she's always been a vegetarian. Since she was a kid. Always hated the idea of animals being killed. It's not my thing but, you know, you adjust."

"How'd you meet?"

"She worked out at the Y a lot. We got to talking and hit it off."

"And you're sure her personality isn't the type that would forgive you for what you did?"

"For what I did, and the fact I've lied to her from the day we met? That I've hidden my entire life from her? That's one of the..." He trailed off.

"What?"

"That's one of the things we promised each other, when we got married. No secrets, through thick or thin."

"Admirable," Hayes said, trying not to dwell on the number of lies he told both ex-wives in the first week of marriage alone. Instead, he said, "Like I said, healing can happen."

"Maybe. I thought about it, especially after Lainey came at me the second time. But then I realized I was well and truly screwed."

"Why?"

"It happened again. Few days ago. Kid throwing rocks onto the highway—just east of downtown. The driver wasn't killed, but they're talking permanent brain damage. He was a pastor—worked with sick kids or something."

It was the story that piqued Hayes's interest earlier as Rodgers talked. He knew it was too big a coincidence.

"That triggered something?"

"We were watching the news. They did a segment on it. That's when Missy said it."

"Said what?"

"She was furious—you could see it in her eyes as she watched. When they cut to a commercial, she shook her head and looked over at me and said, 'So much good destroyed by such a vile person.' I just about ran out of the house. The way she said it. I didn't need to guess what would happen if I told her the truth. She told me then, without even realizing it."

Hayes had to admit the scenario didn't bode well for any thought of Rodgers coming clean.

"Back to Lainey Perkins. Assuming I find her, what are you going to do with that information?"

"Give her the money. And try to talk her out of asking for more."

"And that's it?"

"Yes."

"You're sure? You haven't thought about maybe shutting her up? Like for good?"

Hayes saw right away he'd struck a nerve.

"I'd be lying if I said it didn't cross my mind," Rodgers said. "I made a horrible mistake. I paid for it three times over. I rebuilt my life, tried to do some good in the world, and then along comes this loser trying to take everything away from me. What gave her the right? She was ready to crap all over twenty-five years of redemption. Would you blame me if I did what you're talking about?"

"So, the answer's yes?"

"Yes, goddammit," Rodgers said. "The answer is yes, I fantasized about putting my hands around her stupid, fat neck and squeezing until the lights went out."

He spoke so forcefully that it took Hayes aback. He thought about the sorrow he'd seen on Shayne Townsley's face as he wrestled with the fact that perhaps the one person in the world who showed him some human kindness, even if it came wrapped in a twisted sex-for-chores arrangement, was possibly out of his life and gone.

"Sure you didn't already do that?" Hayes said. "Take matters into your own hands, then hire me to cover your tracks? Who'd believe you murdered her if you paid a private eye to find her? You wouldn't be the first to try that stunt, just so you know."

"No. I swear it."

"If that's the case, how'd you know where she lives? Or what her car looks like? You said it wasn't in the lot."

"She drove the car to our first meetup."

"Which was where?"

"The parking lot at Kroger, off Hoover Road. I followed her home from there."

"And that's it?"

"Aside from going back and knocking on her door, and then sitting in the parking lot and running through that fantasy I just told you about, yes, that's it. You have to believe me."

"Why should I? You've been lying this whole time."

"I've been down that path, remember? I've already killed someone. I've lived with that pain my entire life and trust me, I wouldn't wish that hell on anyone. I know how this looks. But I'm telling the truth. I just wanted to talk to her. To see if I could explain to her what losing all this would mean to me. That's all." His last words faded into a choked-off sob.

Hayes leaned back and gave Rodgers a second. He considered the turn the case had taken. He tried to decide if he believed the story. You met a lot of prevaricators in this business. There was an old saying among private investigators. How can you tell when clients aren't telling you the whole truth? Answer: when they open their mouth. The wife looking for dirt on her cheating husband neglecting to mention she had a thing going on the side herself. And on and on. So long as the iceberg of reality below the tip of truth didn't get him killed, and he still got paid, Hayes was happy. He made a snap decision and decided Rodgers was being upfront. Sometimes a stupid reason for hiring a private eye is really just that. Plus, the need for the remote meeting place now made sense. There were secrets, and then there were secrets.

"Two choices here," Hayes said.

"Choices?"

"I can take your word for your good intentions and keep looking for Perkins. Or you can count yourself lucky that your problem's resolved itself one way or the other, forget this ever happened, and move on."

"Assume I do that. What if she calls me again?"

"Cross that bridge when you come to it?"

"So, I just spend my life waiting for the other shoe to drop?"

"No offense," Hayes said softly. "But how is that any different from the last quarter century?"

* * *

Later that morning, Hayes sat at his kitchen table staring at his laptop. Though the case was officially concluded, he needed proof that this time Jarrod Rodgers was telling the truth.

The Indy brick incident that killed Cheryl Stevens happened right before the movement to publicize juvenile names took hold, so there was less information about the guilty teens than you'd see now, including a paucity of booking photos. But eventually Hayes pieced it together. Jarrod Rodgers had been someone named Brad Hilburn. The lone picture he found of Hilburn was a skinny, sullen-looking kid angry at the world. The resemblance to his twenty-five-years-older self was there, but between Rodgers's now-muscular build, his thinning hair and goatee, and his glasses, it was hard to see. As disappearing acts went, it was nearly foolproof.

Hayes checked Lainey Perkins's Facebook page again. No change there. Her last post the same he'd seen the first time he stalked the page: the late-night picture from her walk to work. Just to satisfy himself, he found the number for Perkins that Jarrod provided him and dialed it. It went immediately to voicemail without a ring. He hesitated a moment, then left a message with his name and number, asking for her to please return the call. A moment later he texted the same request.

Finished, he flipped back to Missy Rodgers's page, still not entirely trusting Jarrod, and wondering if he'd learn something new. But all he found were updated pictures of the dog, a splash of color from front-yard tulips, and an artfully displayed plate of falafel tacos cross-posted from Instagram. He scrolled back a few posts, double-checking that Jarrod wasn't suddenly showing up in photos. He wouldn't be the first person to breathe easier with a nemesis out of the way. But he was still nowhere in sight. Hayes idly looked through the long list of Missy Rodgers's friends, just to be sure he hadn't missed anything. He felt a twinge in his stomach as he considered what a happy life Missy had for herself, at least measured by so many friends on Facebook, compared to Lainey Perkins's spare, lonely page.

He was about to click off the site and stake out the goose poisoner once again when something caught his eye. One of Missy's friends was someone named Steve Thayer. But that wasn't what captured his attention. Thayer's profile picture was a store logo. Friedmann's Meats. Hayes knew it well. An independent butcher off South High Street. An old-school business still hanging in there thanks to the loyalty of multiple longtime customers, himself included. Odd, Hayes thought, scrolling back up Missy's page, past the multiple vegetarian recipes, until he landed on one of her most recent "Meat is murder" meme postings.

On a whim, and because he was out of brats anyway, Hayes left the house and drove the mile down to the store, where it sat just north of the old Buckeye Steel complex. As he entered the shop, his regular butcher, a middle-aged man named Darnell, waved him over.

"Hey, Andy. Got a nice rump roast you might be interested in."

"Normally, you might be right. But I'm half on the clock. You got somebody named Steve Thayer working here?"

"Steve? Yeah—that's Mr. Friedmann's nephew-in-law. But he's off today."

"Maybe I'll catch him later. Well, hang on. How long have you been working here?"

"Me? Seems like forever. Almost thirty years next month."

Hayes pulled out his phone and found Missy's profile picture.

"You know this lady by any chance?"

Darnell studied the phone. "Looks a little familiar. Who is she?"

Hayes told him her name and the fact she was Facebook friends with Thayer.

"Yeah, yeah. It's not Missy, though. And not Rodgers. I remember her now. Melissa Mullins. Worked here a couple summers in college, I think. Sweet girl. Good worker too. Lot of those kids, you put half a cow in front of them, tell 'em to take it apart, it's suddenly break time. Not her. She was a whiz with the knife."

"Really? She's a vegetarian now."

"That's a shame. I always feel bad for vegetarians. They think they're doing animals a favor not eating them, but all they're doing is putting a bunch of hardworking cows and pigs and chickens out of work." He crossed his arms and grinned at Hayes. "And don't even get me started on vegans."

"Maybe it's a health thing."

"Could be. Got a cousin like that. Used to smoke these killer ribs, and now all he eats is cauliflower steaks."

"I know this sounds crazy, but is it possible she didn't eat meat when she worked here? Just did it for the money?"

"Nah."

"Why do you say that?"

"It's coming back to me now, Andy. Mr. Friedmann does an employee picnic, every August. There's an eating contest goes with it. I used to be the reigning champion."

"Used to be?"

"You know that Black Men Run club I'm in?"

"Sure." Hayes had even joined him for a couple of jogs in recent years.

"You didn't know me before that. In the old days, I tipped the scales at three hundred and fifty. And man, could I eat. But this one year, that girl, Melissa, she smoked me. She was on her fifth or sixth hot dog while I was still looking for the mustard. She wasn't a vegetarian back then, tell you that much."

* * *

Hayes wasn't a betting man. He took the position that in general the odds were against him, and just lived with the consequences. He certainly wouldn't have placed a wager on the likelihood of Jarrod Rodgers and Lainey Perkins crossing paths again, one way or the other. So, he was surprised when Jarrod called him later that day to tell him the good news.

"Which is?"

"Lainey texted me. Told me to just forget it. Said she was moving on."

"Really?"

"What she said."

Hayes set his camera on the seat beside him and squeezed his eyes open and shut. He was now definitely sure that Weird Hair Part and

Pink Sneakers were having an affair; he'd caught an illicit kiss by the willow on the far side of the retention pond. But still no luck on the goose poisoner, though he wondered if it really mattered. He'd decided the company probably already knew who it was and had a different reason for jettisoning the employee, one they didn't want getting out. But the size of his retainer precluded too many questions about their real motives. Plus, Hayes didn't care much for people who poisoned geese.

"Can you read it?" Hayes said.

"What?"

"Read me the text she sent."

"Hang on." A pause, and then a switch to an echoey background that told Hayes he'd been put on speaker mode.

"It says, 'Sorry I bugged you. Wasn't in a good headspace. Forget I said anything.'"

"That's it?" Hayes said after a second.

"That's it."

"When did she send it?"

"I'm not sure. There's no time on it."

"Pull the text toward you. Swipe it left, I mean."

"I didn't know you could do that."

"No charge for the tip. So, what's it say?"

"Ten oh five a.m."

Hayes thought about it. He thumbed over to his recent calls. Seven minutes after he'd called and texted Lainey's number after re-checking her Facebook page.

"Did you text her back?"

"Just 'Okay, thanks.' Do you think that was all right?"

"I'm sure it was fine."

So, that was it, Hayes thought, disconnecting. Lainey Perkins grew a conscience in the end. Jarrod Rodgers was scot-free. Case closed. He raised his camera and watched as an unassuming, bespectacled man reached into the right pocket of his windbreaker, pulled out a pair of blue latex gloves, snapped them on, dipped his right hand carefully into a plastic bread bag, and just as carefully lobbed a red-tinted chunk of bread toward a hissing pair of geese. Hayes clicked off a round of pictures and examined the results in the viewfinder. Bingo. Satisfied, he placed the camera down again, picked up his phone, and tried Lainey's number himself. Still nothing.

Hayes tried the number again after he returned home and transferred the photos of the goose poisoner to his computer. He compiled his report for the insurance company, embedding the photos into the document, and sent it off. The poisoner would be punished. If the company had another reason for dismissing the man, no one would be the wiser. Secrets would stay buried, along with the dead geese. He tried Lainey again to no avail, grabbed Hopalong's leash, and walked him down to Schiller Park and back, the Labrador moving slowly with age but not so slowly that he didn't alert to each and every squirrel they passed on the way. Back in the house, Hayes tried Lainey's number once more without results. Was it odd that she'd texted Jarrod not long after Hayes called and left a message, but wouldn't pick up for him? Maybe he was overthinking this. Maybe Jarrod Rodgers really had won the lottery.

But he couldn't stop thinking about the defeated, lonely look on Shayne Townsley's face; not the look of a man who'd expected his girlfriend—or whatever she was—to just up and disappear. And what to do with the lived-in apartment and the abandoned dog? Hayes thought back to Jarrod's confession in the park shelter house, and his protestations of innocence when Hayes asked what he planned to do with the information. Then he considered Jarrod's story of the night he and Missy watched the news about the pastor injured by the brick thrown over the bridge, followed by Missy's reaction. So much good destroyed by such a vile person. Hayes pondered the most random detail of all, sticking out like a muumuu at a formal black-tie dinner: Ardent vegetarian Missy Rodgers had worked a couple of summers at a butcher shop where many years later she was remembered for her knife-handling skills. A stint it sounded like Jarrod didn't know about. Yet what was it they promised each other on their wedding day? No secrets, through thick and thin. He thought again about Lainey's apologetic text message to Jarrod. Sorry I bugged you. Wasn't in a good headspace. Forget I said anything. Why send that? Why not just drop off into radio silence for good? Unless the text itself was another fabrication, part of a ruse Rodgers was maintaining to disguise the fact he really had taken matters into his own hands. And if that was the case, where was Lainey Perkins, for real?

* * *

Just past seven the next morning Hayes parked two houses down from Missy and Jarrod Rodgers's place. A mile and a quarter from Lainey Perkins's duplex, though light years in terms of per capita income. The irony: If Perkins had lived one town over, she might never have seen the photo in the suburban weekly serving the town and made the connection with Rodgers and his past.

The magnetic sign that Hayes had affixed to the outside of his van read Dry Basement Doctor, with an illustration of a physician pressing a stethoscope to a cinder-block wall and an accompanying 800 number. Amazing what you could have made online. Despite the hour, the neighborhood was already full of life: kids waiting for buses, dogs getting walked, joggers padding down the sidewalk. The fake business sign a must, since surveillance in a place like this was like an opened jar of mayonnaise left out in hot weather; it had a very short shelf life.

Fortunately for Hayes, Rodgers's garage door slowly rose on schedule. He watched him back out in his red sedan. Hayes prepared to start his van and follow. But then Rodgers stopped in his driveway and cut the engine. Puzzled, Hayes wondered if Rodgers had made him. But before another minute passed, a minivan approached the drive and turned in. It stopped beside Rodgers's car. Of course. His wife, Missy, home from her overnight ER shift. Ships passing in the night. Hayes watched as Missy left her car and opened the door of Rodgers's car, smiling at the children inside. Hayes watched the scene with envy. Secrets aside, the couple appeared to carry off a complicated life with compassion, respect, and love. An approach Hayes seemed incapable of. As the couple bid each other goodbye and Rodgers slowly backed out of the drive, Hayes thought back to the window decal on the van he'd seen pulling into the parking lot the day he surveilled Lainey's place, the happy nuclear stick family, and how much that had bothered him. That and the van's bumper sticker: "My kids are straight-A students at Lakewood Elementary." But here was the problem. He'd just seen that same van again, with the stick-figure decal and the elementary-school bumper sticker. Driven by Missy Rodgers as she pulled into her driveway.

* * *

Hayes gave it five minutes, and five minutes more, and then departed his van and walked up to the Rodgers's door. He wouldn't have been surprised if Missy were on her way to bed after working an all-night shift. Instead, she answered the bell after a minute dressed in exercise clothes and wiping perspiration from her face.

"Yes?" she said, her face showing annoyance at the interruption of her workout.

"My name's Andy Hayes. I'm a private investigator. I'm here about Lainey Perkins."

Missy froze in place.

"Who?" she said a second too late.

"I think you know who I'm talking about."

"In that case, you're mistaken."

"Am I?"

"That's what I just said."

"I can always come back another time. Say when Jarrod's home?"

A skirmish of emotions briefly played out on Missy Rodgers's face before what appeared to be stoic resignation claimed victory. "Come inside, why don't you," she said.

She showed Hayes into the living room but didn't invite him to sit. Tanner, the handsome dog from Facebook, padded into the room and collapsed with a sigh beside Missy. Hayes handed her a business card. Missy examined it, folded it in half, and tucked it into the waistband of her shorts.

"So, what exactly is it that you want, Mr. Hayes? Money? Is that it?"

"I just want to know where Lainey Perkins is."

"I have no idea."

"Really? You were parked at her apartment complex two days ago, right in front of me."

"That's not true."

"We both know it is. Why were you there? Making sure no one was missing her? No one who might interfere with you and Jarrod? Or should I say, Brad Hilburn?"

She flinched as if Hayes had slapped her.

"Well?"

Missy looked down, like a person in prayer. She looked up and said, "You really don't know the extent of the damage you're causing, do you?"

"Meaning?"

"Meaning my husband's a good man."

"I can see that."

"A man who deserves to live his good life unimpeded. For his sake. And for our children's." A pause. "And for me."

"You know about Indianapolis," Hayes said.

She didn't speak, but the look on her face gave Hayes the answer anyway. In that moment, the story Jarrod told Hayes about the Columbus pastor injured by a similar prank came back to him. What was it Missy said? So much good destroyed by such a vile person.

Such a vile person.

No wonder Jarrod panicked. He heard the vitriol in Missy's voice and assumed the worst.

Except Jarrod got it wrong. His wife wasn't talking about the person who hurt the pastor at that moment.

She'd been talking about Lainey Perkins.

"How did you find out?" Hayes said.

"Do you have children, Mr. Hayes?"

He told her about his two boys.

"Our son is twelve. Sometimes he uses our computer for school projects. When he's finished, I always check the browser search history."

"And?"

"He likes to look at photos of women in bikinis. It's kind of cute, actually. Nothing more harmful than that."

"You found a search about Lainey Perkins."

She nodded.

"And what happened in Indianapolis," Hayes said. "Something Jarrod had been looking up."

"I'd rather have found porn, believe me. Or pretty much anything else."

"You didn't confront Jarrod?"

"Maybe I should have. Maybe I would have. But then I picked up his phone one day when he was in the other room and I saw a text, asking about money. We share each other's passcodes, in case of an emergency. It wasn't hard to track her down after that."

"Is that how you knew Jarrod hired me?"

"I saw a number I didn't recognize and looked it up on Google. When it came back to you, I knew something was up."

"And you followed me that day I went to her apartment?"

"That was a coincidence. I just went by to be sure nothing was happening, given that Jarrod had called you. I knew who you were by then. I left as soon as I realized."

A bad feeling came over Hayes. He remembered Perkins's last Facebook post. The picture of a raccoon, with a description of her "commute." The inadvertent admission on a public social-media page that she walked to work late at night. He considered for the first time the odd coincidence that both Lainey and Missy worked overnights.

"Where is Lainey Perkins, Mrs. Rodgers?" Hayes said.

She stared through him as she spoke. "I believe in justice, Mr. Hayes. Criminals should be punished. Wrongdoing shouldn't be rewarded. But I also believe in forgiveness. Retribution is meaningless if rehabilitation isn't honored. My husband paid his dues. He owes no one anything."

"He kept a secret from you."

"There are worse sins. Don't tell me you never hide things."

"I hide plenty. Everyone does. For example, a committed vegetarian disguises the fact she once worked at a butcher's shop and won hot-dog-eating contests. So much for the two of you never keeping secrets from each other." Hayes thought of Missy's carefully curated, always sunny Facebook feed; the posts cheerful and upbeat even in the days after she'd learned of Jarrod's past. How did the old saying go? The grass is greener on the other side because of all the bull crap it grows in.

Missy didn't say anything for a moment. When she spoke next, Hayes expected a note of resignation. Instead, her voice exuded defiance.

"We all make mistakes we'd rather forget."

"And keep from our loved ones?"

"It's time for you to leave, Mr. Hayes."

"Lainey Perkins," he said, not moving. "That wasn't her texting Jarrod, was it?"

"I'm begging you."

"You saw that I called her phone, which I assume you have, and figured you'd better drop one more clue. Is that right?"

"Please."

"Can you just take me to her? Or tell me where she is?"

Missy Rodgers lowered her head and didn't speak for a moment. Her shoulders drooped in defeat. When she looked up, her eyes were bright, and not with perspiration.

"I'll be just a minute," she said, slowly leaving the room and walking around the corner. Hayes heard the clink of dishes being moved. The act of a woman seeking familiarity as her life implodes before her. He felt no relief now that he knew both Jarrod's and Missy's secrets. He felt nothing less than disgust at his intrusion, regardless of its necessity. Because the problem was, he agreed with Missy. Crime needed punishing, but rehabilitation needed honoring. At what point do we stop penalizing each other for the past? Maybe it all depended on the depth one buried one's secrets.

Jarrod Rodgers's carefully constructed alternative life had evaporated thanks to Lainey Perkins's greed. Missy Rodgers's own obfuscations tripped her up as she stumbled onto the lie Jarrod had been living. But was it a lie if she never probed the life story of the man she loved? More importantly, what action had she taken to protect that love, regardless of the facade that stood behind it?

A sound interrupted Hayes's thoughts. From the kitchen, as though something heavy had fallen. Another sound followed by a woman's soft cry. He moved toward the sound. "Missy? Are you all right?"

A moment later he backed up as she rounded the corner. He stared at her face; blood trickled from a cut on her cheek, which was red and already starting to swell.

"What happened? Are you—"

"Stop," Missy said, taking a step closer. As she did Hayes watched as she raised her right hand. In it gleamed a long steel kitchen knife. "Stop."

"What are you doing?"

"You came in here, made all these accusations, then attacked me. I begged you to stop but you just kept hitting me. I barely made it to the kitchen in time. I had to defend myself."

"Put the knife down, Missy."

"I had to protect myself. For my sake, and for my family."

Faster than Hayes would have thought possible she charged him then, knife rising as she ran. He backed up but not fast enough and stumbled against a coffee table. He lost his balance and fell, hitting the carpeted floor hard and sending Tanner skittering across the room, barking loudly. Hayes raised his hands to shield himself as she came upon him. The knife rose high. Then a sound distracted her; the front door was opening. Hayes kicked hard with his right foot, striking her off balance. Enraged, she tried to stab him but her equilibrium was off. The flat of the knife struck his arm. He tried to wrestle it away but her grip on the handle was too tight. He scooted back and kicked at her again and she raised her hand and then lost her balance for good and fell with a shriek.

"Missy?"

Hayes turned. Jarrod stood in the doorway, gaping at the scene.

"Stay where you are," Hayes said.

"Oh my God," Jarrod said.

"I said—"

"What did you do? Look at her—she's bleeding. Missy? Angie forgot her homework. I was just—"

Sentence unfinished, Jarrod ran across the room. Hayes turned and stared at Missy. The blade had buried itself deep in her abdomen as she stumbled and fell. Blood pumped from the wound around the knife, reddening the carpet. She gasped, breath coming short and shallow, her eyes moving from the knife to her husband and back.

"Jarrod," she said.

"Oh, Missy. Oh God oh God oh God."

* * *

The coroner called it a freak accident. The knife severed an artery, and the internal bleeding was worse than the exterior wound. Missy Rodgers died in the ambulance on the way to the hospital. Hayes spent the rest of the day in an interview room in the Grove City Police Department and the night in the Franklin County Jail. It wasn't until late the next afternoon that a combination of Jarrod's testimony, Hayes's own account, and grainy video obtained from the donut shop across from Lainey Perkins's apartment complex that showed Missy Rodgers moving Perkins's car in the middle of the night confirmed the truth of what happened.

The last Hayes heard, Jarrod Rodgers lost his job and had to sell his house. But he got a new job at another gym and a new house in another suburb. He kept his new name, but he was done hiding too. Hayes learned all this right around the time a fisherman's hook snagged on something big in a quarry off Trabue Road. He watched the divers like everyone else, in a clip on the six o'clock news. The body was identified as Lainey Perkins two days later. Her throat had been sliced clean through, the cut strong and true. As far as detectives could figure, Missy confronted her walking to work one night, tipped by the Facebook post of the raccoon. Jarrod none the wiser thanks to a white lie Missy told about having to work an additional overnight shift that week. The problem of Lainey Perkins resolved, permanently, Missy moved Lainey's car down the street where it sat, undetected, until news broke of Perkins's murder and police cast a dragnet for evidence.

Hayes did some research and found out about a memorial for Lainey in Indianapolis. He called Shayne Townsley to see if he wanted to go over for it, but Townsley—when he finally reached him—said he just wasn't up for it. Hayes couldn't blame him. Some things, some memories, were better left in the past.

Broken English

Sam Wiebe

The photo of Tim Garber on the Tri-Cities College faculty page suited an instructor of English. A boyish round face with a healthy complexion, clean spectacles, hairline on the verge of retreat. An expression equal parts good humor and impatience. Garber held degrees from Brown and McGill, had a book and several articles to his name. "An often-cited scholar of the mid-nineteenth century novel of manners," according to his self-authored bio.

The man next to me at the ramen bar looked more like a punk drummer on stop thirty of a fifty-city tour. In person, Garber was bedraggled and wan, his shapeless gray hoodie infused with burnt tobacco. He fidgeted with the porcelain sake jar, refilling our cups before placing the death threat on the bar.

A printed off email from an anonymous sender, it read:

Mr. Tim I'm soon kill you.

"How do I gauge if this is genuine?" Garber asked.

"Time," I said. "If they follow up, it's usually pretty genuine."

"Sorry if I don't find this amusing, Mr. Wakeland."

The email had been sent two days before. A server I'd never heard of, the account a seemingly random string of characters. Difficult to trace.

"It's best to treat it as serious until we can write it off," I said. "Do you recognize the account, have you received anything else from it?"

"No."

"Anyone come to mind who'd maybe want to threaten you?"

"Only one or two hundred," Garber said.

He tipped out more sake. Spun his cup clockwise on the bar, once, twice.

"I'm almost surprised I haven't gotten one of these before now," he said. "I teach four classes a term, three terms a year. Thirty-eight students per class."

"All first-year English?"

He nodded. "The pressure these kids are under—that the government puts them under—it would make anyone snap."

Given the haunted look to his face, the way he drank, I believed him.

"Explain to me this pressure," I said.

"Did you go to university?"

"Community college. Briefly."

"Lecture halls, a student union, loads of extracurriculars?"

I shrugged. College had been a means to get on the police force, a career which thankfully hadn't worked out. I'd spent my time drinking in libraries, making the minimum effort to study, and whittling a sizable chip for my shoulder against all things academic. For a private investigator, a healthy distrust for inherited wisdom isn't the worst attribute.

"Tri-Cities College has zero in the way of amenities," Garber said. "What we are is a business designed to take money from the families of broke kids overseas. We pretend to teach them, and in exchange, they pretend they're going to school."

The ramen bar was all but empty at eleven a.m., the two waiters watching a Korean soap on the bar's TV. Through the tinted glass I could see a looming office tower and a ribbon of Skytrain track. More malls and more towers in the background.

The door chimed, a trio of young women entering. Garber greeted them each. "Hello, Ranveer. How's your mother, Eunice? Sara, I'm looking forward to your PowerPoint today." The students nodded and took a table in the far corner. Garber hunched over the bar and spoke quietly.

"Presentation week," he explained. "Everybody's a bit stressed."

"You were talking about the college."

He nodded. "The school recruits from rural areas overseas. Pakistan and India are big right now. Before that it was Mongolia, Mainland China. The schools partner with a recruitment agency that works out the visas, sets the kids up with a place to live while they're over here—and also a place to work."

"Doesn't sound like a bad deal," I said. "Make some money between classes. The North American way, isn't it? Unless you're rich."

"I'm not talking about washing a few dishes, Mr. Wakeland. These kids are working forty-, sometimes fifty-hour weeks. Night shifts much of the time. Warehouse jobs, fulfillment centers. They're so overworked they're falling asleep in class."

Our waiter swapped sake jugs, asked if I wanted more tea. I held my hand over my cup, still good.

"It's their choice to work, though," I said, still not understanding.

Garber filled his cup again, quaffed it, wincing at the heat. "The families scrape together everything they have, sometimes taking out mortgages, to get the kids over here. The kids work themselves silly for minimum wage, which is big money back home. The school gets rich off international student fees, and the government wets their beak and gets to tout how well the economy is doing."

"And you get a job out of it."

He nodded. "True, I'm no innocent, but I'm not teaching them, either. They're not learning. The placement tests for English are a joke, and instructors are, let's say, 'encouraged' to pass as many students as we can. As long as the kids keep a C average, their visas are good, they can stay, and the whole corrupt enterprise keeps moving."

"What's the class dynamic like?"

"Resentful, and rightfully so. Students come to class unable to write a sentence, let alone a five-paragraph essay. And I'm supposed to mark their research papers. These are good kids for the most part, but by midterms, when they're either flunking or on the precipice of doing so, they get desperate. They cheat, or they plagiarize, or they buckle down and try their best. Whatever they do, I fail a great many of them. The system fails us all."

I tapped the death threat. "But what's any of that got to do with this?"

"Have you any idea how many students I've failed? Say ten per class, which is conservative. Forty a term. A hundred twenty a year. How many of those don't wish me dead?"

The question lingered after Garber left to teach, not quite rhetorical but impossible to answer. It was my job to answer it. I read over the note again. *Mr. Tim I'm soon kill you.* Despite the grammar, or maybe because of it, the sentiment was clear.

* * *

Tri-Cities College was stuffed into a floor of one of the office towers I'd spied from the restaurant. The lobby looked like the waiting room of a prosperous dental clinic. Students lined the hallway, groups of them laughing or discussing classwork with life-and-death gravity, the few loners on their phones. A polyphonic gauntlet of Punjabi and Mandarin, Korean and English, Cantonese and Spanish and Russian. I picked my way through the ranks to the front desk.

The school's vice president, Jane Campbell, escorted me to a cubbyhole office with a sliding door. Campbell was in her late fifties, slender and well dressed. A Blue Jays pennant and a business degree from Carleton hung behind her.

"The school doesn't have a dean per se," she told me. "The head of Tim's department is on leave, so I guess, yes, technically I'm his supervisor."

"Good employee?" I asked.

"We've had no serious friction. Many students appreciate Tim's approach."

"But some don't?"

Campbell studied me before answering. If I'd known I'd be studied I might have dressed better—more collegial, anyway. A flannel shirt and reasonably clean jeans would have to do.

"Let me put it this way," Campbell said. "We give our instructors great latitude in how they manage their classes. If the students are happy, generally so is admin."

"Does that mean encouraging teachers to pass students who might not make it through the same class at a"—I scanned my brain for a euphemism, found none that I was happy with—"a real college?"

Campbell set her mouth in an approximation of a smile. "Every uni in the Lower Mainland has an international college attached to it. Ours happens to be private. Which means we have to be twice as good, and we get none of the government assistance those public institutions rely on."

"So a teacher failing, say, ten students a class, is that high?"

"It's not unheard of."

"But is it high?"

"Of course, we'd prefer zero failures," Campbell said. "What self-respecting postsecondary wouldn't? But we deal in reality here. And the reality is, some students are ill-equipped. We cut them what slack we can, keeping in mind they're being educated in their second or third language. Our classes are small."

"Thirty-eight is small?"

"Compared to the two or three hundred in first year English at a uni? Absolutely. More facetime with the instructors is one of our selling points. We know our students."

And they know you, I thought. "Has anyone else received threats?"

"This office deals with emotionally charged students all the time."

"Have the police ever been involved?"

"Not that I'm aware."

"This threat that Tim Garber received doesn't seem to bother you."

"Mr. Wakeland," Campbell said, "this morning I spoke with a student who missed her Spanish midterm because her mother had died. She was busy viewing the funeral over Zoom. The school requires proof to reschedule an exam, so the student had her hometown's coroner send me a video of the cremation in process. Would you like to see that?"

I declined.

"Tim's situation is serious, of course it is. But there's only so much bandwidth administration can spare. We try to reserve as much of it as possible for our clients."

"You mean students," I said.

Campbell smiled. "Yes, students, that's what I meant."

* * *

I poked around the college in the late afternoon. The impression I came away with was of a once efficient machine, now straining to keep pace. The classrooms were small and low-ceilinged, converted from office space with partitions. The department offices were repurposed storage rooms. Tri-Cities College had leased some square footage on the floor above, and classes continued over the whine and drone of drilling from upstairs.

In college I had worked at a butcher's and been shocked that a fresh side of beef smelled like an animal. The meat-smell of supermarkets was something artificial, created by the absence of hot blood and viscera, the presence of cellophane. Tri-Cities College gave me the same feeling of shock. I'd never taken to college, but I'd gone to one with a large cluster of concrete buildings, with fields to walk, with a cafeteria and a proper library. Hell, I had a locker. The closest these students had to lockers were the trunks of their cars, if they could afford cars.

I was supposed to meet Garber again at four, after his office hours ended. He wasn't in the office, or the break room, or any of his assigned classrooms. The lone security guard hadn't seen him. I took the elevator down to check if Garber's car was still there.

The underground parkade held the Datsuns and Accords of the poorer students, the BMWs and Audis of the wealthier satellite kids, and the sensible mid-priced sedans of the faculty. Tim Garber drove a maroon Kia. He was sitting in the passenger seat, no seatbelt, head lolling back. I called. He didn't answer.

The passenger door was unlocked, the window cracked. Up close I saw a bib of dark crimson clutching his throat. In his lap was a butterfly knife.

Looking down at the dead man, that butcher's smell of hot blood rolled back at me.

* * *

"No prints on the handle of the knife except Garber's own. No prints on the door. There's a camera above the gate showing Garber keying in the faculty code and driving in, probably right after your lunch meeting with him. No cameras inside the garage, unfortunately. A rough break for us."

Sgt. Grant Wong from IHIT, the Lower Mainland's homicide task force, had caught Garber's death. About thirty, stout, with an expression between perplexed and amused, Wong entertained my questions from the courtyard of the mall opposite the college. I'd given him a copy of the email.

"You think it was suicide?" I asked.

"Can't say for certain just yet, but that would be consistent with what we know."

"C'mon," I said. "The same day Garber hires me to look into a threat on his life, he cuts his own throat?"

Wong gave me a shrug, what can I tell you? "All we can go by is the evidence we have. Which doesn't rule out murder, but it sure doesn't point to it, either."

"No suicide note," I said.

"Some people don't leave them."

"A PhD of English wouldn't pen a few lines? Recall a John Donne poem or something?"

Wong didn't volunteer a response.

"Garber was sitting in the passenger's seat," I said. "His window was rolled down. You need a key in the ignition to activate automatic windows. So where were Garber's keys?"

"Turned into the lost and found this morning." Wong sipped his Starbucks and consulted his phone. My question held the remaining third of his attention. "Our theory is the keys fell out of the deceased's pocket and were kicked under one of the other vehicles. When the driver of that

381

vehicle left, the janitor or whoever found the keys and turned them in."

"And sitting in his car, Garber didn't notice that he'd lost them?"

"He was distraught. As you said yourself."

Wong wouldn't treat this as a homicide until the lab analysis was complete. A sensible approach, but it left me with nothing to go on. Maybe Garber had been killed, and maybe, if the forensic lab was prompt and didn't muss up the chain of evidence, I could expect a clue within the year.

Or sooner, if I decided to meddle.

* * *

Garber lived near Burnaby Lake, about ten minutes from the college. His condo was on the ground floor of a low-rise building with a mansard roof and a high weathered fence. A man and woman were dollying a washing machine through the gate, getting pelted by March rain. I slipped past them, through the propped open door of the building.

The police had gone through Garber's flat yesterday. The door was locked, a seal affixed to it, but by going out the building's back entrance I worked around to Garber's patio. A Maxwell House can full of cigarette butts caught runoff from the drainpipe. The ancient sliding door was easy enough to jimmy open.

I didn't know what I was looking for, or why I was risking a trespassing charge. Any information I could glean wouldn't be of much use to my deceased client. But Tim Garber was a client, and I'd found him dead, and I held strong opinions on how he'd ended up that way.

The closets first. The kitchen drawers. The file cabinet of tax forms and papers. I moved thoroughly, thinking the killer might have taken Garber's keys and come here after the crime. Why? To remove something? What?

I was looking for an unknown—worse, an absence of an unknown. If I'd been here directly after the killer, maybe this object would be easy to locate. But the police had moved and removed Garber's things as well. I saw a rectangle of dust on the table where his computer had been.

This was hopeless. I gave up. And the moment I did, I found something.

Garber was a bachelor, tidy but working with limited space. On the top of the fridge was a fruit bowl repurposed to hold odds and ends. Paperclips, gym pass, USB cable, a pair of off-white ear buds, coins, a stamp book with one last portrait of the Queen inside. A condom. An Allen key. And lighters, four of them, Bics of all colors.

Make that three. One of the lighters was a bit too squat, its sides flat where the others were rounded. The striking wheel was plastic and lifted off. Below was the connecting port of a USB drive.

* * *

At home on my couch, in my own ground floor palace, I loaded the drive into my MacBook. No password. In a folder labeled SCHOOL, Garber had backed up his grading and correspondence with his students. The files went back a year, spreadsheets showing thirty-six failures in the spring semester, twenty-four the previous fall, and forty from last summer.

An even hundred failed students. Were all of them suspects? How many were still in the country?

The correspondence was just as bleak. Students begged, cajoled, deployed flattery and veiled threats, hinted at the certain doom which would befall their families if the good professor didn't bump them up from thirty percent to fifty, from fifty-four to sixty.

> *Dear Sir I need C for my to remain in this Vancouver.*
> *As you might not aware my Mum having trouble with her breath.*
> *Because of car accident I am late for presentation and am not concentration very much. Please to do make up this Thursday?*
> *Mr. Tim I am so grateful if you are helping me achieve C I need C I am BEGGARING!!!!*

The grammar of most emails was proof its claim was undeserving. English is an art; art is subjective; but nothing is that subjective. Students raised on the rules of texting now had to write formal requests in a second language, pleading their cases as sincerely as they could, but rarely on the grounds of merit. These were pleas for mercy.

I shut the laptop for a moment and thought of what that kind of gatekeeping would do to a person. Who devotes years of their lives to earning a graduate degree, forgoing better pay and sunshine to stay inside hacking through whacks of Victorian prose and post-structuralist theory— who becomes a college instructor in order to ruin students' lives?

Judging from his replies, Garber had done his best to tread the middle path, cutting the students what breaks he could, without making the grading process ridiculous. The one time I'd met Tim Garber he appeared scooped out, hollow inside. Now I understood why.

Saved on the drive among the presentation schedules and attendance sheets was a text file, UNTITLED-2. A letter Garber had started writing to the president of the college, concerning a student named Arliss Cho.

...At the end of the exam I said 'Pencils down.' The student did not comply. I repeated my request. The student hurled her pencil in my direction, storming out of the classroom, and slamming the door forcefully...I believe Ms. Cho's final grade of 33% is more than fair.

A name.

* * *

Arliss Cho had made a lateral shift, flunking out of Tri-Cities College, enrolling at The New Cambridge, a strip mall institution on Terminal Avenue. New Cambridge had more room to work with than Tri-Cities, including a canopied courtyard in front of the building. Even so, it didn't seem like it would be giving the old Cambridge an academic run for its money.

How many of these schools are there? I wondered.

Cho was in the computer lab, playing the kind of top-down shoot-'em-up that makes video game battle look like televised lacrosse. She clicked a cursor and a phalanx of armored warriors rushed at the walls of a castle. Cho scowled when I held up Garber's threat but didn't deny writing it.

"He only pass the boys," Cho said. "The boy behind me? He pass. The boy here?" She indicated to her immediate left. "He pass. Not many girls. Not fair."

"Other students feel that way?"

"Everybody."

In sentences fired off between castle assaults, Cho explained that yes, she'd been pissed at Garber. Her car had broken down on the Patullo Bridge, a frightening experience. Try calling a tow truck while stranded on a narrow bridge at the height of rush hour, in a community you've only lived in for four months. Cho had arrived at school only thirty minutes late. Garber hadn't given her additional time.

When Cho petitioned to rewrite the final, Garber refused, sending her through the labyrinth of administration, to the president of the college, and finally a conference with all parties involved. This felt to her like a mob sit-down. Cho pressed her case and was allowed to retake the exam, improving her score from thirty-three to forty-six. Garber bumped this to fifty, but that was still ten percent below what she needed.

"Why threaten a former teacher?" I asked.

"Still angry."

"Did you kill him?"

She didn't even look up.

"Where were you yesterday?"

"School. Home. Here." Meaning the computer lab.

"Proof?"

Cho shrugged, immersed in her clan's scaling of the battlements.

"Can you think of anyone who hated Garber more than you?"

"Ajit."

"And who's he?"

She didn't say. On the screen, carnage raged outside the castle. I left her to the wars.

* * *

Ajit Singh Sodhi had been registered in the same block of English as Cho. Ajit was no longer a student. He'd repeated the class three times, twice with Garber, each time bettering his grades only marginally. He now worked at the Braid Station Fulfillment Center, a windowless complex with a guard at the gate. Employees were bussed in and out of a gate with an advertisement for Jack Reacher on it. Ajit was on graveyard shift, would come off work at eight. I parked by the gate and waited.

Imagine this is your experience of North America. An apartment near nothing but malls and other apartments. A company bus which takes you to the warehouse where you slip garden gnomes and action figures into brown envelopes. Your piss breaks are timed. Your meals are eaten at yet another mall. And in the afternoons, dog tired and aching, you go to college in a renovated office space and try to stay awake.

Not slavery exactly, but you couldn't call it much of a life.

At 8:04 Ajit Singh Sodhi came through the gate with the others, still wearing his high-vis vest. The bus awaited. Before he boarded, I approached him, earning a baleful glare from the driver.

"Step away, sir," the driver said to me.

"Permission to speak with one of the prisoners, commandant?" I snapped off a salute that earned me another scowl. The laborers only looked confused.

"Can we talk a bit?" I asked Ajit. Suspicion, fear—I don't know if he understood he didn't have to speak with me. To my shame I didn't inform him of his right to refuse.

As I drove him home, puttering along behind the bus, Ajit looked around my Cadillac's beat-up interior. He ran his hand over the cracked dashboard. I told him about Garber's murder and asked for Ajit's thoughts.

"Mr. Tim was very nice."

"He failed you, didn't he? A couple times?"

Ajit shrugged. "I'm sad he's dead."

"Did you feel he was unfair?"

"No."

"Treated you different from other students?"

"No."

"What do you remember about him?"

Ajit worked the automatic windows up and down, letting in the right amount of breeze. Eyes closed, enjoying it.

"He make us laugh," Ajit said. "Nice man."

I tried several approaches but couldn't pry loose a disparaging word for the dead man. No longer in a position of power, Garber no longer mattered. Ajit would work another month before his visa expired. Double shifts when he could get them, as much money as possible to take home.

"Anything you're planning to do before you leave?" I asked. "Trips, tourist stuff?"

"Work."

"Nothing you want to see?"

He thought about it. I pulled into the roundabout behind the bus, a crescent of six identical apartment towers. Card swipe entrances and one potted tree per tower. Ajit undid his seat belt.

"Water," he said. "I'd like to see the what do you call it. With sand."

"Beach," I said.

He nodded. "Before I go, I'd like to see a beach."

* * *

Over the next week I spoke with two dozen more students who'd failed Garber's class—or been failed by him, however you wanted to put it. Some had tried again and passed, moving on to a proper university. Others had resigned themselves as Ajit had, to work as much as they could before their visas ran out. Still others had litigated their grades and were in the process of dispute resolution with the school. I gathered Tri-Cities College wanted to keep its customers happy, or at least within the cycle of failure and reapplication.

The classrooms of the college were continuously in use. Instructors left nothing behind other than dry erase markers and reams of composition paper. The English department office was similarly busy. Garber's personal effects were in a bankers box under the table he shared with six fellow instructors. Inside, some lecture notes and overhead slides, a box of granola bars, annotated copies of *Wuthering Heights* and *A Christmas Carol*.

Garber's colleagues shared their own horror stories. The school had scant resources for its students, next to none for mental health. Two academic counselors, both with business backgrounds, only one of whom spoke a second language. There had been suicides, workplace accidents caused by lack of sleep. Car crashes.

As a result, the instructors had issues of their own. The department head, I was told in confidence, was on extended medical leave. Some fought depression, anxiety. Others found the role of gatekeeper so repellent they simply passed every student who showed up. A few had doubled down, calculating grades to a maddening level of precision. This essay garners a 56.25 mark and no higher.

As far as I could tell Tim Garber was liked by his colleagues and had done his job unremarkably but with decency. He smoked and drank too much, but he wasn't alone in either. Garber hadn't acted maliciously. He hadn't deserved to die.

From the perspective of Arliss Cho or Ajit Singh Sodhi, though, Tim Garber had been the face of a system that was duplicitous, uncaring, and corrupt. A system set up to extract labor from them and money from their parents. A system which had worked on them exactly as designed.

Step back from the question of who. Why was Garber in the passenger's seat? Why were his keys missing and then handed into the lost and found? And was the knife his, or the killer's?

You might sit shotgun in your own car if someone else was driving. Or if you were sleeping, reclining the seat. But there was no indication that anyone else had driven the car, and Garber had been sitting upright.

I thought about my meeting with the dead instructor, and about the students I'd interviewed. The impossible situations they all found themselves in. Combatants rather than partners in learning. To kill Garber required rage, motive, a reason to be close and alone—

And then there it was.

***

Sara Kang volunteered at the school library, a small cloakroom with one shelf of books and a photo backdrop for snapping school IDs. The temple of knowledge was empty save for Kang, whom I recognized. She and two friends had been in the ramen bar while I'd spoken with Garber.

I eased the door closed and told her I knew what happened.

"Do you want to tell me about it?" I asked.

Sara Kang didn't look like a murderer. A useless thought, since who does? Slender, short, a bit older than the average student, maybe twenty-four. She wore a pearl-colored blouse with washed-out ink stains visible on the left cuff, a button at the throat that didn't match the others. She was perspiring. Sara Kang looked like the type of person who'd sit with her back to the lobster tanks at a seafood restaurant.

"How did your presentation go?" I asked her.

She gnawed her bottom lip and shook her head.

"What was the topic?"

No answer. I felt foolish. The Great Detective, ready to explain just how he'd brilliantly deduced the identity of the culprit, and I had no idea if my audience would understand.

"You did your makeup presentation for Mr. Garber. A PowerPoint slideshow. But the school is too busy, so where could you go to find ten minutes in a quiet space?"

Sara Kang looked over at her feet. I peered over the counter. A few textbooks and a MacBook peaked out of a green Herschel backpack. Her laptop looked no different from my own.

"No free classrooms and a department office full of others. So you presented in the car. With Garber in the passenger's seat and the laptop in front of him on the dashboard. Not exactly ideal. How badly did it go?"

"Very bad," she whispered.

"Was the knife yours?"

"I took from the lost and found. For protection. I walk home at night."

"And what happened with Garber? Did you finish your presentation?"

"No. He stop me."

"Why did he make you stop?"

She inhaled, remembering, the desperate anger flooding back. "Mr. Tim said it wasn't my words. He said I plagiarize. But I didn't. I only ask my friend to help with the language."

"And then what?"

"He told me my grade…"

There were tears now, for Garber and what she'd done to him, and for her own shattered future. One moment of lashing out and two lives smashed to bits.

Her laptop had been open on the dash when she'd stabbed him in the throat. Garber had been in shock, hadn't struggled, had died looking at a presentation slide. Particles of his blood would have settled on the keyboard and screen.

In the moments after her outburst Sara Kang had the presence of mind to wipe the knife, the seatbelt clasp, the door. She'd taken out the keys and wiped them, too, pocketing them absently, only realizing later what she'd done and dumping them in the lost and found. She explained how she'd done this in a daze, outside herself.

"The authorities need to know what happened," I said.

She nodded, mute.

"Assuming you burnt the clothes you wore, the only physical evidence is there." Pointing at the laptop.

She looked at it, at me, and nodded. I stepped outside to phone Sgt. Wong.

Why handle it that way? Why help her? My own tender-hearted foolish nature. A pushover for kids, small dogs, and murderers under the age of twenty-five. Maybe I'd done it because I guessed that's what Tim Garber might do. I very much doubted the justice system would cut Sara Kang more breaks than the educational system had. Welcome to North America, now pay up.

Mercy was in short supply these days.

Contributors' Notes

Tom Andes wrote the detective novel *Wait There Till You Hear from Me* (Crescent City Books, 2025). His stories have appeared in dozens of publications including *Best American Mystery Stories 2012, Ellery Queen's Mystery Magazine,* and *Santa Monica Review.* He lives in Albuquerque, where he is a working musician, performing solo and with several bands. He's taught writing privately and at a bunch of places and also works in catering. His two acclaimed EPs of original songs were rereleased on vinyl by Southern Crescent Recording Co. in 2025. He can be found at tomandes.com.

*To a considerable extent, "Deadhead" is a love story about a vanished time and place, which is the odd corner of New Orleans called Uptown where I lived in the late 1990s. A lot of the story is set in the area of Magazine Street between Nashville and State, where I worked in a restaurant during and after college. That restaurant appears in slightly altered form in the story, as do two apartments where I lived, and not a few people I brushed elbows with back in those hazy days, though of course, I made the rest up. The best and worst part of Uptown is how time there stands still: it never changes. Yet it does change, and that place where I did so much of my growing up and learned so much about the world is gone.

I nearly always submit to *Cowboy Jamboree*'s anthologies and themed issues. As well as a writer, I'm a working musician, and they often publish themed anthologies and issues as tributes to particular country musicians. This story had received an Honorable Mention in a contest from the Arizona Mystery Writers of America, and I'd done a little more work on it. When CJ put out a call for their tribute to another country musician and writer, the late Kinky Friedman, "A Case of Kink," I thought this story might be a fit, so I looked it over one more time and sent it in.

Pete Barnstrom is an award-winning screenwriter and filmmaker whose projects have played at theaters and film festivals all over the world. He wrote a segment of the horror-comedy anthology *Satanic Hispanics*, which went into theatrical release in 2023. He's shot documentaries in Greenland for the National Science Foundation, made movies with the Blair Witch guys (not that one), and seen one of his films screened at the Smithsonian. His experimental short films earned a grant from the Artist Foundation, and Amazon Studios bought a family film screenplay from him. He's on a plane with a camera about four times a month. He doesn't sleep much. When he's at home, Pete lives quietly in the south end of Texas. You can find him on most of the socials as @mistah.pete or something like it.

*First, drive through El Paso, where your phone decides you've crossed into Mexico and so loses streaming services. Radio is dominated by stations that actually are south of that tenuous border, providing a heady mixture of Spanish and American pop and rap, with Spanglish commercials and announcers to test your rudimentary language skills. It brings to mind those stations from the middle of the last century, the ones they called "Border Blasters"; signals so strong they could be heard in Canada, and with deejays (and advertisers) more tailored to gringo teeny-bopper tastes.

Then fold in friends and acquaintances whose ancestors so thoroughly assimilated that their names adapted to be pronounced Loaps, or Noons, or Marteens, and who struggle to find a place in their heritage.

Add a dash of your fascination with the 1960s "swinging dick" private eye, with a cool car, narrow tie, and a Mancini soundtrack.

Bake for about 4,700 words, top with an earworm of a title (thanks, Wall of Voodoo!), and serve to publisher Kerry Carter in the February 2024 issue of *Mystery Magazine*.

Buen provecho!

Robert J. Binney, a Seattle screenwriter, has written about Joe Strummer, James Bond, joyriding with the Salt Lake City police, and his relationships with Peter Frampton and President Jimmy Carter (though not together) for the *Los Angeles Times*, AtwoodMagazine.com, and other fine publications. His crime fiction has appeared in anthologies from Down & Out Books and Starlite Pulp, and he has written for the "Mysteries to Die For" podcast. Binney is a member of the Northwest Screenwriters Guild and the Mystery Writers of America. He holds an MBA from Emory University and an MFA from University of California, Riverside. For more, see www.ThirdActMe dia.com.

*My current hometown was hosting the annual Left Coast Crime conference and put out the call for Seattle-inspired mysteries for its anthology. At this point, I'm unpublished, just trying to get a toehold in a new career. I figure the only way to compete is to go over the top. Something outlandish… So I take Seattle's most prevalent citizen and turn him loose.

I'm really proud of my "Two-Minute Mysteries with Detective Eddie Vedder," but the copyright lawyers were a little suspect. So "Sasquatch, PI" it was—with a locally flavored villain whose resemblance to an actual person is entirely coincidental.

Once I sold myself on the idea, I had to figure out how to sell it to you, the reader: Where does Bigfoot get office space? What does he drive? *Can* he drive? What's his relationship to his community? Most important, how does an eight-foot-tall, fur-covered hominid detect clues without getting noticed?

I received the publication acceptance—my first, obviously—the week before presenting my MFA thesis. There are still moments I question the sanity of leaving behind my status as a Titan of Industry (and my frequent-flier status), but I took the welcoming of Detective Sasquatch as a good omen.

Alec Cizak is a writer and filmmaker from Indiana. His most recent collection of short stories, *Nobody's Coming Home*, is available from ABC Group Documentation. He is also the editor of the digest magazine *Pulp Modern* and a co-producer of the *Pulp Modern* series of motion pictures.

*The Tom Boyle mystery stories are my attempts to capture Indianapolis in the 1990s. The city has changed quite a bit in less than thirty years, and I want readers to know what it was like before the turn of the century. The title "Genius in a Bottle" came to me one night and I sketched the outline involving a chemist at Daisy (a fictitious name for a Big Pharma company that may or may not exist in Indianapolis) getting bumped off because he discovered an actual cure for a disease the company had already decided would be more profitable to treat instead.

Libby Cudmore is the author of *Negative Girl* (Datura, 2024) and *The Big Rewind* (William Morrow, 2016) as well as the Wade & Jacks PI series in *Ellery Queen's Mystery Magazine*, *Alfred Hitchcock's Mystery Magazine*, and *Tough*. Her work has been published in *Smokelong Quarterly*, *The Dark*, *Stone's Throw*, *Dark Waters*, *Shotgun Honey*, *Orca*, *Monkeybicycle*, and *The Coachella Review*, as well as the anthologies *At the Edge of Darkness*, *Burning Down the House*, *120 Murders*, *Shamus & Anthony Commit Capers*, and the Anthony Award-nominated *Lawyers, Guns & Money* (which she co-edited with Art Taylor). She is a five-year Barrelhouse Writer's Camp alumni, and the recipient of the Eleventh Hour Inaugural Short Story Prize, the Shamus Award, the Black Orchid Award and the Oregon Writers Colony prize.

*"Alibi in Ice" was written as a way to introduce Valerie Jacks's POV into a series that began in *Ellery Queen's Mystery Magazine* in 2020. Though Valerie herself is a POV character in the novel *Negative Girl* (Datura, 2024), her first appearance (in "Wait for the Blackout" in the May/June 2023 issue of *Ellery Queen's Mystery Magazine*) was through Martin's perspective. This novella—loosely inspired by the Cherry Poppin' Daddies song "The Lifeboat Mutiny"—was written for the 2023 Black Orchid Novella Contest and took home the award.

O'Neil De Noux is a retired police officer, a former homicide detective and private detective, with forty-nine books published, over 400 short story sales and a screenplay produced in 2000. His writing has garnered a number of awards including the United Kingdom Short Story Prize, the Shamus Award twice, the Derringer Award and Police Book of the Year (awarded by PoliceWriters.com). Two of his stories have been featured in *The Best American Mystery Stories* (2003 and 2013). He is a past Vice-President of the Private Eye Writers of America. For additional material, go to: www.oneildenoux.com.

*Club My-O-My was famous when I was a teenager, as famous as the other clubs on Bourbon Street (where it had moved from its original place along the lakefront). It hung around until the end of the 20th Century. I visited once after a friend became one of the dancers. It was a cool club, one of those unique New Orleans places I thought should be the setting for a mystery, even more so when I learned how it had been on the lakefront when my private eye Lucien Caye was working the city.

Luke Deckard is an American writer and podcaster living in London, UK. He has a master's and a PhD in creative writing and mentors creative writing students. His novel *Bad Blood*, under the title *Wasteland*, was shortlisted for multiple awards, including the Amazon New Voices Award. He's penned short stories and essays, co-edited anthologies like *Virtual Noir at the Bar*, and written scripts for gripping docu-drama podcasts. He is also the co-host and producer of the film noir discussion podcast Mean Streets.

*"Ill Met By Moonlight" was originally written for the CWA (Crime Writer' Association) anthology *Midsummer Mysteries*, edited by Martin Edwards. The challenge: craft a crime story with a Shakespearean twist. While I wouldn't call myself a Shakespearean scholar, knowing that many of his romances are doomed or derailed by family conflict was perfect fuel for blending Elizabethan drama with hard-boiled crime. Plus, it allowed me to play with my love of the cynical American PI in Britain.

BV Lawson started out with two degrees in music before turning her hand to writing full time. The author of eleven novels and over 250 short stories, poems, articles, and essays, BV is a Derringer Award winner and four-time finalist, and her stories have won the Dillydoun Review Flash Fiction Prize, Noir Nation Golden Fedora, and *Gemini Magazine* Short Story Award. BV's Scott Drayco novels have also been a featured *Library Journal* pick and finalists for Shamus, Silver Falchion, Daphne, and Foreword Book Reviews Awards.

*I live in the Washington, DC, area, and it's common to find street musicians performing for oblivious passersby in an often-fruitless quest for spare change. I often wonder about those musicians—their backgrounds, their stories, their hopes and dreams. The protagonist in many of my novels and stories, private eye Scott Drayco, was trained as a classical pianist but had to switch careers after injuries from a violent attack. So he knows a thing or two about music and loss. I decided to put these elements together and send Drayco off on a quest to help a down-on-his-luck street musician in hopes of maybe finding a little bit of redemption for both. Unfortunately, as Drayco (and I) have learned too well, justice is often elusive. And sometimes the fire that burns within consumes all…relationships, life, and sanity.

Andrew McAleer is the Derringer-nominated author of the London-based Private Detective Henry von Stray historical mystery series, created in 1937 by Edgar winner John McAleer during the Golden Age of Detection. His books include *A Casebook of Crime* (Level Best) and the *101 Habits of Highly Successful Novelists* (Adams Media). McAleer taught classic crime fiction at Boston College and served in Afghanistan as a US Army Historian before returning to public service in the criminal justice system. He is a member of the Private Eye Writers America. Instagram: Mcaleermysteries or Henryvonstray

*"The Singular Case of the Bandaged Bobby" was inspired by my public service in the criminal justice system. Particularly, my interest in how criminals speak, why they do what they do, how they slip up. The criminal jargon in "Bobby" is authentic and preserved in an 1859 chapbook, *The Rogue's Lexicon* by George Washington Matsell (1811–1877). Matsell served as a Special Justice and Police Chief of the New York City Police

Department. The story's confidence scheme is based on an actual scam used around the time of von Stray's exploits and even earlier prior to the telephone's invention.

Ron Miller is an illustrator and author living in South Boston, Virginia. His primary work today entails the writing and illustration of books specializing in astronomical, astronautical, and science fiction subjects. To date he has more than seventy titles to his credit, including half a dozen novels and numerous short stories. His biography of the classic illustrator Chesley Bonestell received a Hugo Award and is the basis for an award-winning documentary film. A commemorative stamp he designed for the US Postal Service is attached to the New Horizons spacecraft and is now in the *Guinness Book of World Records* as having traveled further than any stamp in history. He has been a production illustrator for motion pictures, most notably *Dune*. He has also done preproduction concepts, consultation and special effects art for David Lynch, George Miller, John Carpenter, and James Cameron. His original paintings are in numerous private and public collections, including the Smithsonian Institution and the Paul Allen Family Trust.

*While working in Mexico on *Dune* I often visited a bookstore run by the US Embassy. It consisted of thousands of vintage paperbacks from the '40s and '50s. I bought several hundred, mostly for the vintage cover art, and these turned out to be largely detective and mystery novels. Not being able to own a book without reading it, I found myself in the world of hard-boiled private eyes for the first time in my life, introduced to authors such as Mickey Spillane, Brett Halliday, Stewart Sterling, Robert Leslie Bellem, Richard Prather, and a dozen others. One thing I quickly noticed was that, with the sole exception of Modesty Blaise, there was a distinct lack of female private eyes. I decided to correct that omission with the character of Velda Bellinghausen, an ex-burlesque queen-turned-detective working in Greenwich Village in the 1950s.

Bruce W. Most, a former freelance writer, is the author of half a dozen whodunits, as well as several crime short stories and a novella. His most recent novel is *No Time for Murder*. He lives in Denver, Colorado, with his wife. You can find his books at www.brucewmost.com.

*To readers who may not be familiar with my protagonist's name, Weegee was a real-life photographer who roamed the dark streets of New York City in the 1930s and 1940s lugging a heavy 4x5 Speed Graphic photographing crime scenes, fires, accidents, and the gawkers. He made his living selling his stark black-and-white images to tabloids, though several of his photos now hang in museums. As an amateur photographer and former journalist, I've long been aware of Weegee. I thought he might make an interesting sleuth. This was my third Weegee story published in the now-defunct *Mystery Magazine*. It's based on one of Weegee's better-known photographs of a woman sitting in a lifeguard chair on Coney Island beach staring pensively out at sea in the dead of night. He took the photo with infrared film and a special flash during wartime blackouts. Pretty much everything else I made up.

Marcia Muller has written many novels, short stories, essays, and works of criticism. A *New York Times* best-selling author, she has won six Anthony Awards and a Shamus Award and is also the recipient of the Private Eye Writers of America's Lifetime Achievement Award, as well as the Mystery Writers of America Grand Master Award (their highest accolade). She lives in Sonoma County, California, with her husband and frequent collaborator, mystery writer Bill Pronzini. Her final novel in the long-running Sharon McCone series, *Circle in the Water*, was published in 2024.

*"Scamming the Scammer" was written especially for the crime-fiction anthology *Shamus & Anthony Commit Capers* and features my Private Investigator Sharon McCone. Today's all-too-prevalent cyber-scam fraud schemes helped inspire the story. This relentless, modern-day problem shows no signs of waning. The culprits perpetrating these intricate scams are extraordinarily cunning and specialize in targeting society's most vulnerable members. In most cases the perpetrators are invisible. Indeed, once these scam artists get their hands on the goods they are in the wind

and, more often than not, law enforcement is unable to track them down. No doubt about it, the deck is stacked against the unwary. Crime fiction is sometimes the great leveler—even if only for a short time while we suspend disbelief and pull a disappearing act of our own. In "Scamming the Scammer," PI McCone invites readers to disappear with her while she evens the odds for the good guys by devising a little scam of her own.

Twist Phelan is the award-winning author of eleven mystery novels. Her work has been praised by *Publishers Weekly*, *Library Journal*, *Kirkus*, and *Booklist*. She has also written several dozen short stories, most of which have appeared in *Ellery Queen's Mystery Magazine*, in addition to Mystery Writers of America and other anthologies. Accolades for her work include two Thriller Awards, the Arthur Ellis Award, and multiple nominations for the Thriller, Ellis, Shamus, Anthony, Derringer, and Lefty Awards, as well as the Crime Writers of Canada's Award of Excellence and the Irish Book Awards. An avid explorer, Twist has traveled to 93 countries, many of which serve as settings for her Finn Teller novels and stories.

*Introduced in my Corporate Spy novels and featured in several *Ellery Queen's Mystery Magazine* stories, Finn Teller is an operative for Strategic Information Associates—a private-sector CIA. She's the quintessential "stranger who comes to town," catalyzing change in the communities she encounters while remaining perpetually on the outside. Beneath her cynical exterior lies an unwavering moral compass, driving her beyond mission parameters to right the wrongs she uncovers.

The idea for "Aim" emerged from my conversations with an FSO at the US Embassy in Senegal and my travels in Romania. While the narrative follows a murder investigation with a missing suspect, the story is really about the Roma people and bad actors who believe themselves beyond accountability. I hope you enjoy it!

Neil S. Plakcy creates engaging stories that celebrate love, identity, and found family across multiple genres of mystery and romance. www.mahu-books.com

*When I moved to Miami in 1986, South Beach was a shell of its former self. Stores were boarded up, the only restaurants were hole-in-the-wall bodegas, and it was dangerous to walk around after dark. The once-proud art deco hotels were reduced to hosting Cuban refugees, and there was talk of knocking down everything south of 5th Street for a massive urban renewal project.

But tantalizing remnants remained. The names of fancy department stores, long gone, engraved in marble. The broad beach with its funky lifeguard stations. Stories told by elderly residents.

South Beach was gradually reclaimed by a coalition of artists, gay entrepreneurs, and historic preservationists. By the time I came out in the 1990s, it was full of gay bars and clubs. I couldn't help wondering, though, what it would have been like for a gay man in the sixties, before Stonewall, AIDS, and the rights we now enjoy.

George Clay is fresh out of the Navy after a stint as a Master-at-Arms, where he was charged with security and physical protection for service members. He lands in Miami Beach in 1968, attracted by the sunshine and louche atmosphere—what drew me here as well.

But George has to keep his desires in the shadows, which is a perfect place for a private eye with a sense of justice and a strong right hook. Exploring those shadows, while I am fortunate enough to live in the sunshine, makes him a hero whose stories I want to tell.

William Dylan Powell (texasmischief.com) writes crime stories, mysteries, and books about Texas. His fiction has been featured in *Ellery Queen's Mystery Magazine*, *Alfred Hitchcock's Mystery Magazine*, and *The Best American Mystery Stories 2018*. He is a former winner of the Robert L. Fish Memorial Award. Powell's thirteenth book, *Lost Treasures of Houston*, dropped in the fall of 2025.

*At the age of 12, I became obsessed with martial arts. On a sunny Saturday most of my friends in Corpus Christi, Texas, spent their time learning to throw a tight spiral or getting sunburned down at Mustang Island. Me? I was watching *Kung Fu Theater*.

While the eighties belonged to the ninja craze, martial arts films in the seventies were all about kung fu. And there was no bigger producer of Chinese martial arts films than the Shaw Brothers. For almost a century, the Shaw family ran Hong Kong's largest film studio—making hundreds of kung fu action flicks. I haven't seen them all, but I'll bet I've come close. I think *The 36th Chamber of Shaolin* is still my favorite. Bruce Lee's stardom, the general rise of globalization, and television shows like David Carradine's *Kung Fu* made "Chinese boxing" white hot in the seventies.

I found a series of schools, eventually studying styles such as Northern Praying Mantis and Wing Chun. Off and on I did martial arts for about 17 years, finally calling it quits in my early forties. These days if I'm hitting or kicking something it's probably a vending machine. But I never lost my love for the shlocky plots and masterful choreography exhibited by a classic piece of seventies Hong Kong action. So when asked to contribute to *Private Dicks and Disco Balls: Private Eyes in the Dyn-O-Mite Seventies*, I was ready to strike.

M.E. Proctor was born in Brussels and lives in Texas. The first book in her Declan Shaw PI series, *Love You Till Tuesday* (2024), came out from Shotgun Honey, with the follow up, *Catch Me on a Blue Day*, in 2025. She's the author of a short story collection, *Family and Other Ailments*, and the co-author of a retro-noir novella, "Bop City Swing." Her fiction has appeared in *Vautrin*, *Tough*, *Rock and a Hard Place*, *Bristol Noir*, *Mystery Tribune*, *Shotgun Honey*, *Reckon Review*, and *Black Cat Weekly* among others. She's a Derringer nominee.

*"Drop Dead Gorgeous" was written in response to an anthology call for crime stories inspired by the songs of Aerosmith. The title seemed ready-made for a murder mystery, but I wasn't interested in yet another variation on the beautiful, butchered woman trope. I didn't want to take the dead or the drop literally. The fascination, the gorgeous, however had possibilities. It brought up a mental image of Tex Avery's Wolf, with popping eyes and tongue dropping on the carpet, enthralled by the cute showgirl. I've written a few stories featuring private detective Harry McLean and he was

the perfect candidate for a poleaxing crush. The story grew from there: a seductive con artist tricking the wrong mark, the looming danger of bloody retribution, and the tension of a long chase that creates a strange intimacy between hunter and prey. Harry's feelings are a mixed bag of lust, desire to protect, and admiration. It was exciting to bring all these layers into play in a classic PI story.

Mark Thielman (www.markthielman.com) is a criminal magistrate working in Fort Worth, Texas. Mark's short fiction pieces have been named to the honor roll of America's best mysteries on multiple occasions. A two-time Black Orchid Award winner, Mark has published more than fifty short stories in *Alfred Hitchcock's Mystery Magazine*, *Black Cat Weekly*, and numerous anthologies. Mark serves as president of the North Dallas chapter of Sisters in Crime. Severn River Publishing released his debut novel, *The Devil's Kitchen*, and its sequel, *The Hidden River*, appeared in 2025.

*When I had the opportunity to submit to *Private Dicks and Disco Balls: Private Eyes in the Dyn-O-Mite Seventies*, I wanted to center a story on a historical event that others might overlook. I chose the chess match between Bobby Fischer and Boris Spassky. Growing up, the matches were important to my friends and me. They pitted the US against the Russians. The contest inspired me to learn to play chess, albeit poorly. As a crime fiction metaphor, the combined elements of the game's moves and countermoves coupled with Cold War politics proved irresistible.

Vicki Weisfeld is the author of more than forty-five short stories that have appeared in leading mystery magazines and anthologies, including *Ellery Queen's Mystery Magazine*, *Mystery Magazine*, *Black Cat Mystery Magazine*, *Sherlock Holmes Mystery Magazine*, and *Alfred Hitchcock's Mystery Magazine*. They've won awards from the Short Mystery Fiction Society and Public Safety Writers Association. Her first mystery-thriller, *Architect of Courage*, was published June 2022 by Black Opal Books. She blogs regularly at vweisfeld.com and is a book reviewer for the UK website, crimefictionlov er.com.

*A 2023 *Washington Post* survey on readers' pet peeves with the books they read generated "a tsunami of bile." One objection that struck a chord with me was "sexy descriptions of women in non-sexy situations." This story turns the tables on that old detective fiction trope to show how awful it is, and, with a nice sense of the ridiculous, *Yellow Mama* published it in their Valentine's Day edition.

Andrew Welsh-Huggins writes from Columbus, Ohio, where he is the Shamus-, Derringer-, and International Thriller Writers-award nominated author of *The Mailman* featuring freelance courier Mercury Carter, a starred *Library Journal* pick of the month; the stand-alone crime novel *The End of The Road*; the Andy Hayes private eye series featuring a former Ohio State and Cleveland Browns quarterback turned investigator; and editor of the short story anthology *Columbus Noir*. His stories have appeared in multiple magazines and anthologies, including *Mickey Finn: 21st Century Noir*; *Scattered, Smothered, Covered, and Chunked: Crime Fiction Inspired by Waffle House*; *Sleuths Just Wanna Have Fun: Private Eyes in the Materialistic Eighties*; and *The Best Mystery Stories of the Year* 2021 and 2024.

*I was thinking a lot about buried secrets when I wrote "Through Thick and Thin." My Columbus private eye, Andy Hayes, is used to clients leaving things out when they hire him. But even Hayes is surprised by the twists his latest case takes after a man hires him to undo a mess made by the man's infidelity. Frankly, I was surprised, too. As far as inspiration is concerned, the spark for this story came a couple of years ago when my wife and I were out bike riding and had to take shelter in a local metro park pavilion during a brief rain shower. "What if…?" I thought, and was off and running.

Sam Wiebe is an award-winning and best-selling author of Pacific Northwest crime fiction. His novels about Vancouver PI Dave Wakeland are one of the most authentic and acclaimed contemporary detective series. Wiebe's other work includes *Ocean Drive*, *Last of the Independents*, and the Ethan Brand series, set in Washington State, under the pen name Nolan

Chase. Wiebe has won the Kobo Emerging Writers Prize and two Crime Writers of Canada awards, and been nominated for the Edgar, Hammett, Shamus, and City of Vancouver book prizes. www.samwiebe.substack.com

*The detective series I write about Vancouver PI Dave Wakeland touches on social issues affecting the Pacific Northwest. The plight of international students and the invisible community they form struck me as a good if unusual backdrop for a PI story. Wakeland, if he's anything, is the kind of person who notices the hidden parts of the city.

I've written Wakeland stories for *Vancouver Noir* and *Ellery Queen's Mystery Magazine* among many others. My stories usually have some basis in the world I know. In the case of "Broken English," I focused on a world I knew firsthand.

"Broken English" takes place at a small for-profit college which caters to international students. For ten years off and on, I taught English at a college like that. Some are reputable, but others are outright scams, designed to fleece students with high fees and no chance of passing their courses.

Most students were here on work visas, working graveyard shifts at fulfillment centers or warehouses. Often, they'd not show up to class or fall asleep if they did. The system benefits the government and the school, but puts tremendous pressure on students and teachers, pitting them against each other.

"Broken English" has a bit of a traditional mystery feel, in that the victim is a teacher and the killer one of his students. In this weird world of private colleges, a failing grade can hold life or death consequences. A student could lose their visa, which means the end of their education and the loss of their chance for a better life. If the student is working to send money back home, failing can cost them a literal fortune.

The title comes from both the insult of "broken English" that allows society to write off secondary language speakers, and also the broken nature of the educational system.

Also Walking the Mean Streets

Ann Aptaker, Neon Women
  Private Dicks and Disco Balls (Down & Out Books)

John M. Floyd, Welcome to Armadillo
  Strand Magazine, Fall

James A. Hearn, For Lydia
  Alfred Hitchcock's Mystery Magazine, March/April

R.T. Lawton, Leonardo
  Black Cat Weekly, #148

Josh Pachter, Texas Kinda Attitude
  Ellery Queen's Mystery Magazine, May/June

Michele Bazan Reed, Mayhem on the Cheddar Express
  New York State of Crime: Murder New York Style, #6 (Down & Out Books)

Gary Ross, Nickel City Eavesdropper
  Alfred Hitchcock's Mystery Magazine, May/June

Jeff Soloway, The Theft of Las Meninas
  Ellery Queen's Mystery Magazine, November/December

Bev Vincent, A Tawny Brown Liveaboard
  The Amber Waves of Autumn (Kelp Books)

Dave Zeltserman, Mary & Shelly
Alfred Hitchcock's Mystery Magazine, May/June

About the Editors and Special Contributor

Editor **Matt Coyle** (www.mattcoylebooks.com) is the author of the bestselling Rick Cahill crime series. Matt knew he wanted to write crime fiction when, as a teenager, his father gave him *The Simple Art of Murder* by Raymond Chandler. His books have won the Anthony, Shamus, Lefty, and San Diego Book Awards, among others. He was named the San Diego Writers Festival 2021 Mystery Writer of the Year and received the Odin Award from the San Diego Writers and Editors Guild in 2024. Matt lives in Southern California with his yellow Lab Shamus, where he is writing a new series.

Series Editor **Michael Bracken** (www.CrimeFictionWriter.com) is an Edgar Award and Shamus Award nominee and three-time Derringer Award winner. Author of almost thirteen hundred short stories, his crime fiction has appeared in *The Best American Mystery Stories, The Best Mystery Stories of the Year,* and many other publications. Additionally, Bracken is the editor of *Black Cat Mystery Magazine* and three dozen anthologies, including a Derringer Award winner and three Anthony Award nominees. He is a recipient of the Short Mystery Fiction Society's Golden Derringer for Lifetime Achievement and, in 2024, was inducted into the Texas Institute of Letters.

SERIES EDITOR WEBSITE:

https://www.CrimeFictionWriter.com

SOCIAL MEDIA HANDLES:

Facebook: https://www.facebook.com/michael.bracken.908
Twitter: @CrimeFicWriter
Instagram: @crimefictionwriter
Bluesky: @crimefictionwriter.bsky.social
Threads: crimefictionwriter

Special Contributor **Kevin Burton Smith** (www.thrillingdetective.com/), a critic, occasional short story writer, defiant Canadian, and acquired taste, has been loitering (with intent) around the Shamus Game since he discovered Frank and Joe Hardy many years ago. His musings on the genre have popped up in *Mystery Scene*, *The Rap Sheet*, *Deadly Pleasures*, *Blue Murder*, *CrimeSpree*, assorted mystery conventions, and other dens of ill repute. He also started a little thing called the *Thrilling Detective Web Site*. He currently resides in SoCal, but please don't hold that against him. As fellow lost Canadian mystery writer Ross Macdonald once said, "There's nothing wrong with Southern California that a rise in the ocean wouldn't cure."

Books by Michael Bracken

All White Girls
Bad Girls
Deadly Campaign
Psi Cops
Tequila Sunrise
Yesterday in Blood and Bone

As Editor
The *Chop Shop* series
The Eyes of Texas
The *Fedora* series
Groovy Gumshoes
More Groovy Gumshoes
Hardbroiled
Janie's Got a Gun
The *Mickey Finn* series
Notorious in North Texas
Private Dicks and Disco Balls
Prohibition Peepers
Sleuths Just Wanna Have Fun
Small Crimes
Trouble in Texas

Edited with John Betancourt and Carla Coupe
Malice Domestic 18: Mystery Most Devious
Malice Domestic 19: Mystery Most Humorous

Edited with Barb Goffman

Murder, Neat

Edited with Gary Phillips

Jukes & Tonks

Edited with Trey R. Barker

The *Guns + Tacos* series

Edited with Stacy Woodson

Scattered, Smothered, Covered & Chunked